THE FINE ART OF UNCANNY PREDICTION

Robert Goddard

bantam

TRANSWORLD PUBLISHERS
Penguin Random House, One Embassy Gardens,
8 Viaduct Gardens, London SW11 7BW
www.penguin.co.uk

Transworld is part of the Penguin Random House group of companies
whose addresses can be found at global.penguinrandomhouse.com

First published in Great Britain in 2023 by Bantam
an imprint of Transworld Publishers

A CIP catalogue record for this book
is available from the British Library.

ISBNs 9781787635104 (cased)
9781787635111 (tpb)

Typeset in 11/15.5pt Times NR MT Std by Jouve (UK), Milton Keynes.
Printed and bound in Great Britain by Clays Ltd, Elcograf S.p.A.

The authorized representative in the EEA is Penguin Random House Ireland,
Morrison Chambers, 32 Nassau Street, Dublin D02 YH68.

Penguin Random House is committed to a sustainable future
for our business, our readers and our planet. This book is made
from Forest Stewardship Council® certified paper.

THE FINE ART OF
UNCANNY PREDICTION

www.penguin.co.uk

For my good friend Toru Sasaki with many thanks
for all his help and advice

GLOSSARY OF PRINCIPAL CHARACTERS

Anna Collins Braxton, first wife of Grant Braxton, killed in Loma Prieta earthquake, San Francisco, 1989, along with her children **Alice** and **John**

Clyde Braxton, US army officer based in Japan during US occupation, 1945–52, later founder of Braxton Winery, California, and Braxton Institute of Seismological Research and Innovation (BISRI); died 2005

Grant Braxton, son of Clyde Braxton

Lois Braxton, second wife of Grant Braxton

Norifusa Dobachi, lawyer retained by Kodaka Detective Agency

Daiju Endo, civil servant who disappeared after claiming the Kobe Sensitive had given the Prime Minister's office advance warning of 2011 earthquake and tsunami

Joji Funaki, journalist, old friend of Kazuto Kodaka

Haha, mother of Umiko and Haruto Wada

Andrew Harrington, partner at Anderson McGraw, San Francisco architectural practice that designed BISRI campus

Hosogai, inquisitive neighbour of Manjiro Nagata

Chikako Imada, assumed name of Himeko Sato

Arinobu Jinno, founder and chairman of Jinno Construction; died 1994

Hisako Jinno, adoptive daughter of Arinobu Jinno

Teruki Jinno, adoptive son of Arinobu Jinno, client of Kodaka Detective Agency, 1995

Troy Kimber, son of Lois Braxton by her first husband, stepson of Grant Braxton

Kazuto Kodaka, private detective, Kodaka Detective Agency; died 2019

Koga, successor to Rokuro Yagami as Goro Rinzaki's enforcer

Kwon Hee, assumed name of Manjiro Nagata

Connie McDermott, security officer, BISRI and Braxton Winery

Juanita Martinez, girlfriend of Manjiro Nagata

Wataru Matsuda, proprietor of Gosuringu Orphanage, Tokyo; died 1945

Mitamura, official at Tokyo Road Transport Bureau, occasional informant for Kodaka Detective Agency

Momo, Goro Rinzaki's housekeeper at Matsuda Sanso

Nagaharu Myoga, proprietor of electronic gadgets shop, Tokyo, occasionally used by Kodaka Detective Agency for analysis of sound recordings

Fumito Nagata, father of Manjiro Nagata, former husband of Hisako Jinno, client of Kodaka Detective Agency, 2022

Manjiro Nagata, son of Fumito Nagata and Hisako Jinno

Tomohiko Nakamura, husband of Umiko Wada, left in a coma after Aum Shinrikyo sarin gas attack on Tokyo Subway, 1995; died 2007

Oda, right-hand man to Koga

Yukari Otonashi, assumed name of Yuma Zaizen

Daniel Perlman, served in US Navy, 1945–52, based in Japan and worked with Clyde Braxton during US Occupation, later proprietor of Flight Deck bar, Yokosuka; died 2005

Itsuko Perlman, daughter of Daniel and Nonoka Perlman

Nonoka Perlman, wife, later widow, of Daniel Perlman

Goro Rinzaki, clerk at Gosoringu Orphanage, Tokyo, later worked for Clyde Braxton during US Occupation of Japan, 1945–52, founder and chairman of Kuraikagami Film Corporation, client of Kodaka Detective Agency, 1995

Himeko Sato, domestic servant apparently able to predict earthquakes – the so-called Kobe Sensitive

Arvad Singh, office cleaning contractor, California

Seiji Tago, disgraced former sumo wrestler, lodging with Haha

Takuto Umetsu, Bank of Japan official, regular informant for Kodaka Detective Agency

Haruto Wada, brother of Umiko Wada, based in New York

Umiko Wada, private detective, Kodaka Detective Agency, formerly secretary-cum-assistant to Kazuto Kodaka

Rokuro Yagami, chauffeur-cum-enforcer employed by Goro Rinzaki

Taro Yamato, civil servant, friend of Daiju Endo

Sonoko Zaizen, introduced to Kazuto Kodaka as former mistress of Arinobu Jinno

Yuma Zaizen, daughter of Sonoko Zaizen

1945

THE CITY IS GONE, OR SO IT SEEMS, SWEPT AWAY, BURNT OUT OF existence. The centre of imperial Japan is a scorched and hollowed wilderness, slowly revealed in its grey, smouldering vastness as the thin early morning light spreads across the sky. Smoke rises with the dawn, staining the livid sunrise indigo and purple. The full expanse of Tokyo Bay is visible as Goro Rinzaki has never known it, shimmering in the distance. And Mount Fuji too is clear to see, as he has only previously seen it depicted from here in ancient woodblock prints. This, he realizes with dismay, is how Hokusai and Hiroshige and all those other artists of the pre-Meiji world would have seen the city's surroundings. And now this is how he sees them too.

His view is perhaps less sharp than theirs would have been, thanks to the cracks in the right lens of his glasses. But it's likely to be a long time before he can call on the services of an optician again, so the blurry striations across part of his vision are merely one of the many hardships he has to endure, along with cold, hunger and an overwhelming pessimism about what the future holds. The Japan so many of his fellow countrymen have fought and died for is finished. That much is certain. It is finished, even though it is not yet done. The struggle will continue, for how long he cannot say. But eventually it will end. The Americans are coming. The drone of the bombers last night announced the fact. And the fire and destruction they unleashed confirmed it. They are coming. And when they arrive they will remake Japan in whatever image they choose.

Goro Rinzaki's thoughts are fixed on how to survive between this moment and then. He is sixteen years old, but what those sixteen years have held have hardened his soul to that of someone much older. There has been nothing carefree about his life to this point. Japan has been at war with a steadily growing number of enemies since he was eight. He is shrewd enough to have known for several years what many in Tokyo have only just begun to understand: they cannot win; they can either surrender – or die. And Goro does not want to die.

Neither does the man he is accompanying through the rubble-strewn streets. Wataru Matsuda has been his saviour in many ways, pulling strings when they needed to be pulled to ensure Goro's poor eyesight would excuse him from military service, however desperate the army became for new and ever younger recruits. Matsuda hasn't done so for altruistic reasons. He values Goro for his discretion, his energy and his reliability. As Matsuda's assistant at the Gosuringu Orphanage, and technically his ward, since he was an orphan there before he was an employee, Goro is privy to the innermost workings of the organization and therefore well placed to know that its operations stray far beyond a concern for the welfare of waifs and strays. He has seen its darker side. He has grasped the truth. And his conscience is no longer troubled by it. His conscience, indeed, is just another casualty of the war.

He stumbles as he walks, his legs heavy with fatigue, his brain fogged by the horrors of the previous night. He never seriously expected to survive once the fires began to rage, roaring and

2

moving like ravening beasts through the wooden houses and their inhabitants. Burning men and women walking in plumes of flame spring into his mind's eye. The cracking of dry timber, the unearthly noise, half wail, half roar, that the blaze and the wind united in: he can hear it still. It was a miracle most of the children remaining in the orphanage survived. Somehow he and the night staff managed to shepherd them to safety. They are huddled now, beneath a makeshift roof of bedsheets and bamboo props, down near the site of the Hama Palace, silent and immobilized by shock. When Matsuda arrived, Goro was briefly impressed by his apparent concern. He must have travelled into the city just as many were leaving it to find out what had become of them all.

But he soon realized Matsuda had more on his mind than how many of the children had been saved and how they were to be cared for in the days and weeks ahead. He wanted Goro to give him an account – a *precise* account – of the extent of the damage to the orphanage building. What was left standing? Which parts of the structure remained? Goro could not say. He had not lingered to assess the damage. He had run for his life. But the Gosuringu was built of stone. The walls would still, he reckoned, be in place. And anything fireproof within. Of which there was very little.

'We must go there,' Matsuda declared. 'We must go there now.'

'There will be nothing left, Matsuda-san,' Goro objected. But he knew what, in all likelihood, would be left. He knew what had drawn Matsuda back.

The look on the older man's face was heavy with calculation. Goro knew him to be cunning and ambitious, his occasional rages compensated for by far-sightedness and meagre hints of paternalism. He was already thinking ahead. His interests, once so wide ranging, had narrowed dramatically with Japan's retreat from its conquered lands. But still he was plotting a course ahead. And he expected Goro to join him on it. As why would

3

he not? He had got this far on Matsuda's coat-tails. He might get further yet.

But Goro was tired. His eyes were stinging. The smoke had affected his breathing. His whole body ached. 'We should wait until all the fires are out,' he meekly protested. 'We should wait until it is lighter.'

'We are not waiting,' Matsuda growled. 'Stand up. Ready yourself. It is time to go.'

And so he stood and followed, as he always had.

But now, as they pick their way forward through the debris and the carnage, Goro wonders if obedience to Matsuda is not one of the many things whose time has expired in the Japan of the present. He wonders if he should not shake himself free of this domineering man he sees striding ahead of him in his rain-coat and hat and business suit and polished black shoes – so different from the rags and tatters the few other people they see are dressed in. The few other *living* people, that is. The dead out-number them by many thousands, their mangled and blackened remains heaped and sprawled and tangled in the wreckage of the city. Matsuda pays them no heed. But Goro, glancing at them, thinks, '*I am lucky to be alive – and I must make the most of my luck.*'

Their destination looms ahead. The stone walls of the Gosu-ringu Orphanage are largely intact, though the wooden roof and floors have been reduced to ashes, along with everything the building held. The windows are charred and empty eye-sockets, staring out at them, reproachfully, it seems to Goro. The Gosu-ringu was his home, which he abandoned because he had to. But still, it was his home.

He has been carrying, since Matsuda thrust it into his hands, a collapsible bamboo ladder. He suspects he is there principally because Matsuda may need him to climb up to the first floor of

4

the building. That assumes the concrete-reinforced section of the first floor where Matsuda's office was located has survived, which will become apparent as they move round to the farther side.

Their progress slows as they do so, on account of the piles of ash and debris they have to manoeuvre round. Smoke is still rising from charred timbers, despite the early arrival on the scene of fire crews – a service Matsuda paid various officials to ensure would be made available but which, in the event, made no difference whatsoever. They would have needed to drain the bay to quench the fire that raged last night.

The extent of their efforts is nevertheless to be seen before them, as water is completely filling the basement, though much of that may have seeped in from the nearby canal, whose bank was breached in the bombing. Not that Matsuda has time to dwell on such matters. He looks up, not down, and sees, as he clearly hoped, that the concrete section of the first floor is still in place, suspended above the void of the burnt-out interior of the building.

He turns to Goro. 'You must go up there. We need to open the safe.'

The safe, an expensive and very heavy German model, was installed before Goro became Matsuda's assistant, though he well remembers the mystery surrounding its delivery, preceded as it was by the strengthening of the office floor to bear its weight. He does not ask why they need to open the safe, because he is sure he knows, although why Matsuda vests such importance in what it contains he cannot understand. It is hard to see how even the most closely guarded secrets of the Gosuringu Orphanage will be of any use to them in the hard times that lie ahead. Assuming, as Goro does not, that those contents survived the fire. 'Everything inside the safe will have been burnt as if in an oven, Matsuda-san.'

'Nonsense. The safe is fireproof. Stout German technology. Foresight, Goro. That is the essence of success. Erect the ladder and put it in place.'

Goro hesitates for a moment, then sets off. He threads a path through the cinder piles and enters the building through a doorway. From there he works his way carefully round to a position opposite the triangle of reinforced office floor in the storey above him. Matsuda follows him at a cautious distance. They are standing on a slab of the concrete foundation, with the water-filled chasm of the basement below them. Goro slots the three sections of the ladder together and braces it against the wall, then props the top against the edge of the office floor. The angle is shallower than he would like, but he suspects Matsuda isn't going to accept any excuses. He has to go up there.

'Take this.' Matsuda hands him a scrap of paper.

Goro takes the piece of paper and looks at it. It is the combination for the safe. He knows it already, but Matsuda does not know he knows it.

'The box, Goro. That is what I want. Never mind the rest. Just the box.'

It is as Goro anticipated. Matsuda wants the steel box that is stored in the safe. He wonders again how its contents can be of any value now, but he does not ask. Foresight, he supposes, is the answer. Matsuda has a plan. For the moment, Goro cannot imagine what it might be. But it exists. And its existence is in itself hopeful.

'Up you go.'

Goro nods and starts a gingerly ascent of the ladder, which slips and jolts on the jagged edges of the concrete as it bears his weight. As he can see, part of the reinforcing slabwork has been knocked off during the fire and is now protruding from the murky water filling the basement, in which he glimpses other objects floating that he has no wish to identify.

'Hurry,' Matsuda calls after him. 'I need to be gone from here.'

Goro bites his tongue and climbs on up. As ever, Matsuda has no care for the young man's safety. He simply wants him to do what he is too old and fat to do himself. But this is no easy task, no matter that Goro is neither old nor fat.

As he reaches a height where he is at eye level with the office floor, he sees piles of ash, one of which is probably what is left of Matsuda's handsome teak desk. Embers are still glowing in places. Smoke hangs acridly in the air. In the corner, untouched, it seems, by the fire, stands the safe, exposed to view where previously it was concealed beneath the desk. It is bathed in a preposterously beautiful pale pink shaft of dawn sunlight.

'Can you see the safe?' calls Matsuda, who is now at the bottom of the ladder, one foot lodged on the bottom rung.

'Yes. I see it.'

Goro reaches the top of the ladder and clambers off onto the office floor, fearing, for a second, that it will give way beneath him. But why should it? He is much lighter than the safe. The floor holds.

Avoiding the glowing embers, he steps awkwardly over the ash heaps and reaches the corner. He crouches in front of the safe. Most of its dark green paint has peeled off in the heat, but otherwise it appears undamaged. He touches the door lightly with one finger, wondering if it is still hot. But no. He is actually surprised by how cool it is.

He makes a show of looking at the piece of paper, although Matsuda cannot see him from where he is. Then he begins rotating the dial, first one way, then the other, then the first way again, then . . .

There is a click, signalling the release of the lock. Goro grasps the handle and opens the safe.

There are files and loose papers on the top shelf. They have curled at the edges, but not ignited. Stout German technology has proved its worth. On the lower shelf sits the locked steel box

Matsuda so particularly wishes to lay his hands on. Goro lifts it out and closes the safe.

'Do you have the box?' calls Matsuda.

'I have it, Matsuda-san.'

'Bring it down here. Now.'

When Goro reaches the top of the ladder, he sees Matsuda frowning up at him. He holds up the box to show him he has what he wants. Matsuda waves for him to come down. There is urgency in the wave. He wants to be away from this place.

As does Goro. But, as he turns round and climbs out onto the ladder, clutching the box under his arm, he has only one hand free to steady himself. His left foot misses the rung he is aiming for and plunges down to the next, causing him to fall to one side. The box begins to slip from his grasp.

He sees, from the corner of his eye, Matsuda flinch in alarm and jump up onto the lower rungs of the ladder. He stretches out his arms to catch the box if it falls. In that instant Goro whips his other hand round the back of the ladder and clasps the box, securing his hold on it. It does not fall.

But the ladder slips in the process, before its top comes to rest against one of the projections in the edge of the office floor. The jolt of that, combined with the sideways yaw of the ladder, throws Matsuda off balance. His eyes widen in panic as he topples off and falls into the water-filled basement.

His head strikes the lump of concrete half-submerged in the water with a sharp crack. He plunges past it into the depths and for the moment is lost to view. Goro begins scrambling down the ladder.

By the time he has reached the bottom, Matsuda has surfaced, raincoat bellied out around him, hat dislodged, head bloody. He lies face down in the water, in which plumes of something black and ugly have been stirred by his fall. He is clearly unconscious, though still alive, Goro assumes.

Goro has never learnt to swim, but with the ladder he could try to pull Matsuda closer so that he could haul him out. He sets the box down behind him and swings the ladder away from the floor above.

And then he stops. And takes a breath. And thinks.

Matsuda will die if left where he is. One man drowned among all those thousands burnt to death last night. No one would care. No one would ever even know. He would simply join the rest of them in a mass grave somewhere. Wataru Matsuda's death would excite no comment. He is not a well-liked man. Feared and intimidated by some, envied and admired by others. But not well liked. He has no wife and no children, unless all the children that have dwelt inside these walls over the years are to be counted. But they would not mourn him. No one would, amidst all the other mourning there is to be done.

Goro stares at the figure floating in the dark water. Time is slipping past. Within a few minutes, there will be nothing he can do to save him even if he wants to. Matsuda will be dead. And he, Goro Rinzaki, will be . . . free.

He thinks of all the labours he has undertaken for this man, all the indignities he has suffered in his service, all the deceptions he has been made complicit in. But he also thinks of all that he has learnt from Wataru Matsuda: all the ways he now knows by which the challenges of life can be turned into opportunities. He considers the question of what Matsuda would do in his shoes. And he has no doubt what the answer is.

He looks down at the box he has retrieved from the safe. How was Matsuda planning to use its contents to his advantage? What value did he see in them? Goro does not know. But he is confident he *will* know. When he has given the matter enough thought. When he has perfected the art of thinking as Matsuda thinks.

As he *thought*, rather. It is time to let Matsuda become part of the past. It is time to strike out into the world without him.

9

Goro lets the ladder fall into the water. The ripples from it stir Matsuda's body. Then the ripples fade. And there is no more movement.

Goro picks up the box. He does not have the key for it, of course. That is hanging on Matsuda's watch-chain. But he will find a way to open the box. When the time comes.

He hurries out of the building, gazing ahead at the sunrise . . . and his future.

2022

UMIKO WADA HAD NEVER SET OUT TO BE A PRIVATE DETECTIVE. She'd started by simply working for one. She'd answered Kazuto Kodaka's phone, managed his accounts, kept his records, talked through problems with him, greeted his visitors, fetched him bento-boxed lunches, made him tea and very occasionally been sent into the field to follow someone when only a female tail was likely to escape detection.

Since Kodaka's untimely death three years ago, however, at the outset of a case Wada had swiftly found herself caught up in, she'd taken on his role and made quite a success of it. She'd been hired by several of his clients to deal with their problems in her characteristically confidential, low-key, effective manner and had soon come to be regarded, rather to her surprise, as his professional successor.

The work kept coming. She was never idle. And that was how she liked it. Widowed young, she'd never remarried, much to her mother's disappointment. She'd discovered that she actually thrived on order and solitude, that leading her life on her own modest terms rather than anyone else's suited her perfectly. She was nearing her fiftieth birthday, but looked younger, probably because, as her mother regularly reminded her, she'd never had children to raise and worry over.

She thought of herself as Wada rather than Umiko, because that was how Kodaka had taken to addressing her. It had seemed disrespectful at first. But she'd soon become fond of it. It reinforced an image of herself she'd honed over years of being alone. Umiko was a girl she'd once been. Wada was the self-sufficient independent middle-aged woman she'd become.

Her fluency in English, which was one of the reasons Kodaka had employed her in the first place, was another facet of her apartness from many of her contemporaries. It half removed her from the Japanese world, to a place from which that world's foibles and peculiarities – amidst the intricacies of which the resolution of a case was often to be found – were clearer to her than to those who dwelt more completely within it.

The Kodaka Detective Agency, as the business was still officially called, had originally been biased towards commercial cases, hence its location near the Tokyo Stock Exchange. Since taking over, Wada had seen a gradual shift towards those other staples of the profession, divorce and missing persons. Women often hired her to enquire into their husbands' affairs. More people than she might have expected saw advantages in hiring a female private detective. She'd considered moving to less expensive premises, but the impact of the coronavirus pandemic on demand for Nihombashi office space had enabled her to strike a good deal with her landlord and so it was that the agency still occupied the same seventh-floor eyrie in the Kono Building.

Norifusa Dobachi, Kodaka's lawyer and now hers, had expressed his amazement at the favourable terms she'd negotiated, but had nevertheless gone on to offer her advice which he'd never have dreamt of offering Kodaka: that in these times of remote working and Zoom calls the need for physical office space in the commercial heart of Tokyo was questionable. Wada had begged to differ.

'Believe me, Dobachi-san, my clients prefer to discuss the sort of problems they bring to me face to face. Discretion is one of the things they pay me for. And there is nothing more discreet than a private conversation.'

It was true. Clients tended to approach her by telephone rather than email and never disclosed any of the sensitive details of what was troubling them until they were in the sanctum of her softly lit office, where, over delicately brewed tea and put at their ease as far as they could be by her stillness and readiness to listen, they little by little unburdened themselves.

Whether that would apply to Fumito Nagata, her latest client, it was too soon to say. He had originally contacted her in the hope of hiring Kazuto Kodaka and, upon learning he would have to settle for the services of Kodaka's former secretary, had not concealed his disappointment.

Not that the man who arrived exactly on time for their appointment that morning was in any way impolite. He introduced himself with no shortage of courtesy – perhaps, in fact, with too much courtesy. Wada preferred to proceed in a businesslike fashion, whereas Nagata, a lean, fussily well-tailored man whom she judged to be in his mid-seventies, seemed reluctant to come to the point, discoursing on the sad demise of a local shirtmaker whose way with collars was apparently without equal and reminiscing about the Stock Exchange in pre-computer days.

He also tendered his condolences to Wada on the death of Kodaka, which she accepted with all the politeness she could muster. 'It must be a strain for you to operate alone,' he went on. 'And particularly for a woman . . .'

Happily, he did not finish the sentence. 'It is three years since Kodaka-san died,' Wada said levelly. 'Whatever challenges there were to carrying on the business I believe I have surmounted.'

Nagata smiled awkwardly. 'Of course. You are right. The consensus is that you have surmounted them with . . . considerable skill.' So, he'd been checking up on her. Well, she couldn't blame him for that. 'And I never myself used Kodaka-san's services, so . . .'

'May I ask how you heard about the agency, then?'

'Oh, my brother-in-law mentioned that he had engaged Kodaka-san to handle a minor commercial matter some years ago and was well satisfied with . . . his performance.'

'Who is your brother-in-law, Nagata-san? I may remember the case.'

'Teruki Jinno. Chairman of Jinno Construction.'

Wada had naturally heard of the company. It featured occasionally in the business pages of *Asahi Shimbun*. She would not have been able to name its chairman, however. It was likely he'd asked Kodaka to investigate an employee thought to be on the take or leaking information to a competitor. Evidently, since her memory for such matters was excellent, the case must have dated from before her time. 'His name is not familiar to me. When was this?'

'Oh, I'm not sure. Twenty years ago. Twenty-five, maybe. Perhaps a little more. But that is by the by. I am not here to discuss . . . a commercial problem.'

'No?'

'This is altogether more . . . personal.' He sipped his tea and bent forward in his chair, as if physically pained by what he was about to disclose. Wada realized then that his earlier digressions weren't the garrulousness of an old man dwelling too much in the past but were actually the product of an extreme reluctance to talk about why he'd come to her. Though talk about it he clearly had to. 'I do not enjoy sharing . . . family matters . . . with a stranger. I do not, in truth, believe they should be shared. But . . .'

'Sometimes they have to be.'

He nodded solemnly. 'Indeed.'

14

Wada placed her hands together for emphasis. 'Nothing you tell me will go any further, Nagata-san.'

'So I hear. You are noted for your discretion.'

'I am glad to hear it.'

'And I must insist upon it. Absolute discretion.'

'That is understood.'

'Good. So . . .'

'Yes?'

'This concerns my son, Manjiro. For some years he worked at a managerial level within Jinno Construction. Then he decided to . . . strike out on his own.'

'In construction?'

'Not exactly.' Nagata lightly traced with his forefinger the arch of one eyebrow, which seemed to calm him. 'He, er . . . invested in a business developing golf resorts. The business did not prosper. The Covid restrictions finished it off and he, er . . . lost most of what he had invested. Since then, he has . . . withdrawn into himself.'

'Is he married?'

'Divorced.'

'Any children?'

'No. He lives alone, in an apartment in Musashino.'

'Do you see anything of him?'

'No. He never visits me. He never phones or emails. Nor does he reply when I phone or email. He makes no contact with me whatsoever.'

'How long has that been the case?'

'More than a year now. Quite a lot more, actually.'

'Have you called at his apartment?'

'Yes. Several times. I got no answer. Either because he was out or because he chose not to open the door to me.'

'Can I ask . . . about his mother?'

Nagata sighed heavily. 'We are estranged.'

'She is Teruki Jinno's sister?'

'Yes. Hisako. I think she is using the Jinno name now. Mine is obviously . . . an embarrassment.'

'Has she seen your son?'

'I am honestly not sure. Talking to my wife . . . is not easy. She says she is not concerned about Manjiro and I should not be either. She was evasive when I pressed her to say when she had last seen or heard from him. That may have been because . . . she does not care to answer any question I put to her. Or it may be because . . .'

'She has not seen or heard from him either?'

'Precisely. It is unsatisfactory. It is . . . worrying.'

'Yet she is not worried?'

'Apparently not. Though my ability to know my wife's state of mind has always been limited. We did not part on good terms. And consequently . . . I cannot look to her for any help in this matter.' He looked at Wada directly now, where before he'd avoided her eye. 'Manjiro and I have not enjoyed a close relationship. He has always taken his mother's side in disagreements. And now he is . . . nearly fifty years old . . . nothing is going to change between us. I accept that. I would not expect, in the normal course of things, to hear from him from one month to another. But I would expect him to respond to my efforts to contact him, if only to ensure that I left him in peace. I simply wish to know that he is . . . alive and well. I consider it my duty. He is my son, after all, for good or bad.'

'I understand, Nagata-san. It is a difficult situation.'

'Is there anything you can do for me?'

'I can take steps to confirm that he is alive and well, although I cannot guarantee that he will be willing to contact you.'

Nagata gave another heavy sigh. 'I do not ask for that. Merely confirmation that he is living . . . soundly.'

Soundly. It was a strange word to use about his own son's way

16

of life. But clearly the Nagata family had as many strangenesses as estrangements. Wada perfectly understood Fumito Nagata's problem. He had no hope of establishing cordial relations with Manjiro. But, as his father, he could not neglect him altogether. Some bonds could not be broken. Though, as to that, it was quite possible Manjiro Nagata would disagree.

'You sent me your terms of business.' Nagata took a piece of paper out of his coat pocket and laid it on the desk between them. Wada recognized the standard Kodaka Agency contract, which he'd signed. Clearly, he wanted her to act on his instructions as soon as possible. Now he'd gone so far as to consult her, he was anxious there should be no delay. 'I have with me the deposit you require. Sixty-five thousand yen. In cash.'

Cash. And the contract signed and returned by hand. It all suggested to Wada that Nagata meant what he'd said about discretion. He required it to be absolute. Which was fine by her. She liked to know where she stood with a client. 'I will make a start straight away.'

Nagata gave a slight bow. 'Thank you.'

'And I will report to you by phone. No emails. No texts.'

At that he almost smiled. 'You anticipate my requirements, Wada-san. That is good. That is very good.'

After Nagata had left, Wada scoured the Internet for information on his family. There was nothing about the Nagatas, but quite a lot concerning the Jinnos. Jinno Construction had been founded in 1933 by Arinobu Jinno (1902–94). It had profited hugely from military contracts for airstrips and barracks and, after escaping break-up under the post-war Deconcentration Law, had risen back to prominence thanks to the housing boom of the 1950s and '60s. Arinobu had retired as chairman in 1984 and been succeeded by his son Teruki (born 1944), whose son Yoichi (born 1975) was now vice-chairman. The line of succession seemed clear.

From Arinobu Jinno's various obituaries Wada learnt that both Teruki and his sister Hisako had been adopted, the timing of which suggested he'd taken this step after abandoning hope of having children with his wife Mihoko, daughter of a senior army officer, whom he'd married in 1931.

There was a photograph online of Hisako Nagata, as she was described, attending a charity event at the Imperial Hotel in 2010. She looked about sixty, cool and elegant and self-possessed enough to be smiling less broadly than others in the group. Fumito wasn't with her.

Wada was still looking for other links that might tell her something valuable when she saw her brother's name spring up on her phone as an incoming call. Haruto lived in New York and almost never called her. Nor did she call him. Neither felt the need for frequent contact. Besides, their mother passed on news of them to each other when there was any. Wada picked up, wondering why he wanted to speak to her. By her rough calculation, it was late Thursday evening in New York.

'Haruto?'

'Umiko. Are you at your office?'

'Where else would I be at this time of the morning?'

'I don't know. Out tailing some guy, I suppose.'

'I'll be doing that later.'

'You're probably wondering why I've called.'

'Is it something urgent?'

'It could be.' Wada was already beginning to regret taking the call. 'How are you?'

'I am fine, Haruto. How are you?'

'Good. But worried. About Mother.'

Why Haruto should be concerned about their mother was mystifying. She was in good health and good spirits as far as Wada knew. At any rate, she was the last time they'd spoken.

18

'I phoned her earlier to wish her a happy birthday.'

'That was good of you.'

'She mentioned receiving a text from you. But no call.'

'I plan to visit her tomorrow. We can talk then.'

'It's her eightieth, Umiko. I reckoned something more than a text was called for.'

'Well, you won't be visiting her tomorrow, will you? And I had a lot to deal with yesterday.'

'Oh yes. Mother said you are always very busy.'

Wada wondered why it was that amongst all the many irritations and frustrations of life there was nothing that tried her patience more than double-edged exchanges with close relatives. 'Why are you worried about her, Haruto?'

'Because of this . . . lodger . . . she's taken in.'

'Lodger?'

'Don't you know about him?'

'No. I do not.' Was there the faint possibility that Haha had mentioned such a development when Wada last visited her? So much of what her mother said tended to escape her attention, concerned as it was with feuds between neighbours and breaking news from the world of sumo, a sport Haha followed avidly on television but which held no appeal for Wada. 'She, er . . . has said nothing to me . . . about a lodger.'

'Well, he answered the telephone when I called with a big, booming *Moshi moshi*. Before I could ask who he was, he said, "Ah, you must be Haruto," and handed me over to Mother. She told me he was her lodger. She said it was good to have a man in the house. It made her feel less lonely.'

'She has never complained of loneliness to me.'

'Where would it get her if she did? You're not going to move back in, are you?'

Wada ignored that question. 'Who is he?'

'She said his name was Seiji Tago. I couldn't get much out of her about him. She said he was very nice. A lovely man. It was a little sickening, Umiko. I mean, I don't think she's ever spoken so warmly about you and me. Anyway, I assumed you must know and could tell me who this guy is. I mean, where's he come from? What does he do for a living? Do you think he could be some kind of . . . gold-digger?'

'If he is, he's digging in the wrong place. I will see what I make of him tomorrow. And I will let you know what I find out. Mother is not a fool, Haruto. I don't think we need to worry about her.' Wada hoped she was right about that. But this was, however she regarded it, an unwelcome development. Why had their mother done such a thing? It was, for the moment, incomprehensible.

'Couldn't you bring forward your visit?'

'No. I am busy today. I will go tomorrow, as planned.'

'It's just—'

'I do not intend to change my plans because Mother has taken in a lodger. I will go tomorrow.'

'There's obviously no point arguing with you.'

'That is true.'

'Yes.' She felt she could sense him smiling in his apartment on the other side of the world, though whether in fondness or exasperation she was not certain. 'That is always true.'

Wada consigned the minor mystery of her mother's lodger to the compartment of her mind where she stored matters to be dealt with later. She then concentrated on paperwork associated with various ongoing cases before returning to the question of Fumito Nagata's elusive son. She left the office relatively early that afternoon and took the train out to Musashino, deep in the Tokyo bedroom belt to the west of the city. She hoped to make progress by whatever means presented themselves. Nagata had paid her good money, which he was entitled to see a return on. She backed herself to learn something, even if it wasn't necessarily to his liking.

Plenty of people in Tokyo, particularly single men, had retreated into isolation, barely stirring from their homes. Lockdowns during the pandemic had only exacerbated a long-term trend. Wada's expectation was that Manjiro Nagata was merely another example of this. But she could at least establish that he was alive – and as well as the circumstances of his existence permitted.

The apartment block he lived in, ten minutes' walk from Musashi-Sakai station, was part of a complex of virtually identical apartment blocks that looked as if they dated from the 1970s. They were neither top of the range nor bottom. Altogether, though, it wasn't where most people would predict the nephew of the chairman of Jinno Construction would end up living. A damp and cloudy dusk cast an unflattering light on the grey-walled buildings and it was too cold for any of the residents to be out on their balconies. Wada's strongest impression was of anonymity and obscurity. If Manjiro Nagata had set out to lose himself in the suburban sprawl of Tokyo, he couldn't have chosen anywhere better.

She rang the phone number Fumito Nagata had given her for his son and got no answer, as had been the case when she'd rung from the office. A polite email, claiming there was a business opportunity he might wish to discuss, had likewise failed to draw him out. She entered block number five, climbed the concrete stairs to the fifth floor and reached the door of his apartment, number 514.

One reason for using the stairs rather than the lift was so that Manjiro wouldn't hear the lift stop at his floor. Wada was light-footed by nature and possessed the ability to move in virtual silence when the situation required it. She was confident no one inside apartment 514 would be aware that she was outside, although there was a spy-hole fitted in the door. She stood to one side, barely breathing as she listened for sounds within – music, running water; the rustling of paper, the rattling of pots, the shuffling of feet; maybe even the click of a computer mouse. But there was no sound of any kind.

She rang the doorbell. Nothing stirred. She rang again. Still nothing. If someone had crept to the door to look out through the spy-hole, she reckoned her hearing was acute enough to detect the movement. But there was none.

The next step, having located apartment 514, was to go back downstairs and watch the windows to see if any lights came on as darkness encroached. There was a bench she'd already scouted out from which it would be possible to keep an eye on the entrance to the block while she did that. Just inside the entrance were the apartments' mailboxes. If Manjiro returned while she was there and checked his box, she'd see him do it. It could be a long wait, though. She was going to be grateful for her stakeout parka – the deep-hooded and well-padded coat she kept at the office for such excursions.

As she reached the top of the stairs, she glimpsed a movement below her: a figure withdrawing suddenly from view. There was a rattling of keys as she hurried down to the next landing. She was met by the sight of a man laden with shopping bags who was attempting to make a swift entrance to the apartment directly below Manjiro's, but, incommoded by the bags, was still fumbling with the keys when Wada came upon him.

'*Konnichi wa*,' she said with a smile.

He didn't smile back. He was a squat, puffy-faced man of seventy or so, grey-haired and bearded, wearing oversized spectacles and a frowning expression that looked as if it was semi-permanent. '*Konnichi wa*,' he mumbled.

'Were you looking to see who was calling on Manjiro Nagata?'

22

'Who?'

'The man who lives in the apartment above you.'

'Why should I have been?'

'I thought . . . you were looking up the stairs . . . just now.'

'Maybe I was.'

'You know Manjiro Nagata?'

'I know he rents the apartment. That's all.' He succeeded in unlocking his door and pulling it open. The handle of one of the shopping bags slipped from his grasp as he did so. A packet of noodles and an onion fell out. The onion rolled across the floor towards Wada. She bent down and picked it up while the man retrieved his noodles. He murmured his thanks as she stepped forward and handed him the onion. She glimpsed some letters clutched in his hand as he took it, which he must have collected from his mailbox on his way in. From the envelopes she could see his name was Hosogai.

'Can I ask you a couple of questions about Manjiro Nagata?'

'Why?'

'I am looking for him. On behalf of his family.'

'Why don't they come and look for him themselves?'

'They have tried. But he never seems to be in.'

'That is not my concern.'

'No. But . . . they are worried about him. If you could . . . set their minds at rest . . .'

'How could I do that?'

'When did you last see him, for instance?'

Hosogai gave the question a lot of thought, then said, 'Not for a long time.'

'How long?'

'Maybe . . . a year.'

'A year?'

He nodded. 'Maybe more.'

'Have you . . . heard him moving around in the apartment?'

23

'There are noises. Sometimes there are lights.'

'So, he is up there?'

'Is he?' Hosogai seemed on the brink of smiling. But he didn't. 'His family have hired you?'

'Yes.'

'You are what, then – a private detective?'

'Yes. I am.'

'And you are your own boss, aren't you? I can tell.'

Wada was irritated by his accuracy on the point, but didn't show it. 'What can you tell me about Manjiro Nagata?'

'Something, maybe.'

'Such as?'

'The family are paying you, I suppose. Which means you must be willing to pay – for information.'

'Do you have some?'

He nodded, but didn't elaborate. 'I like whisky. Genuine Scotch, if I can afford it. Which I usually can't on my pension. Single malt. The expensive stuff, you know?'

'How expensive?'

'Oh . . .' He stroked his beard. 'Seventy-five hundred yen a bottle.'

A nosy neighbour wasn't to be underestimated as a source. Hosogai was irksome. But Wada had learnt not to be irked in such circumstances. She took some money out of her shoulder-bag, counted out ¥7500 and handed it to him. 'Buy yourself a bottle.'

'Thank you.'

'And the information?'

'It's a prediction.' He looked at his watch. 'In around twenty minutes, the lights will go on in the kitchen and the living room up there.' He gestured to the apartment above with his eyebrows. 'You'll be able to see it from outside. The blinds will close at the same time. What you won't see is anyone turning those lights on or closing the blinds. It'll just happen. Like it always does.'

24

'He does things by the clock, then.'

'And doesn't like to be seen.' Hosogai slipped his money into his pocket. 'That's right. The invisible man has fixed habits. If you can believe it.'

'But you don't believe it?'

'Hey.' There was just the suggestion of a smile under the beard now. 'You're the detective, not me. What would I know?'

Twenty minutes later, almost exactly, Wada was standing by the darkened and deserted children's play area in front of the apartment block when the lights came on in two of the windows of apartment 514. The slats of the blinds on the windows were angled so as to close off the interior from view. It was just as Hosogai had said it would be.

He stepped out onto his balcony as Wada watched, silhouetted against the lights of his own living room, and craned up to check his prediction. Then he seemed to look in her direction, though she didn't think he'd be able to see her. But it didn't matter. He knew she was there.

And he probably knew what she was thinking.

1995

KAZUTO KODAKA WAKES AND SPENDS A FEW DISORIENTATED moments pondering the question of why he feels as if someone has gouged out the back of his eyeballs before a patchwork of memories of the previous night assembles itself in his mind: the drinks with Takuto Umetsu, his Bank of Japan informant . . . so far so good; the further drinks with Joji Funaki, his journalist friend, who happened to walk into the bar where he was conferring with Umetsu. The edges of the evening began to blur around then: the karaoke session where he bellowed himself hoarse – his grating rendition of 'Born in the U.S.A.' seems still to be echoing in his ears – and the hostess club where it seemed such a good idea to go afterwards. He sincerely wishes he could forget most of what happened there.

He crawls out of his futon and stumbles into the kitchen, where he swallows half a litre of water and risks a squint at the clock above the stove. It's nearly noon and deciding not to set his alarm last night on the grounds that he had no appointments until late afternoon looks questionable in the cold, hard light of midday. He pours water into the kettle with an unsteady hand and sets it to boil, then spoons tea into the pot, spilling some as

26

he does so. He brushes the spilt leaves into his palm and adds them to the pot, then lights a cigarette, reckoning a nicotine surge might put him back in charge of his faculties.

He's beginning to feel cold in his pyjamas, so he goes back to the bedroom in search of his robe. It's not hanging where he thought it would be, so he slides open the closet, revealing a reflection of himself in the full-length mirror inside.

It's not so much his ravaged appearance that shocks him – he was expecting that. It's what – or rather who – his appearance reminds him of: his father, who is six years dead and grew to look far worse than this before his premature end. But Kodaka's earliest memories of him are disturbingly close to what he now sees. Kodaka senior drank too much and smoked too much. He also worked too hard and played too hard. Kodaka junior . . . ditto. He needs to change his ways. He needs to pull himself together. As to whether he will, his father, who no doubt often thought the same about himself, is not an encouraging example.

But there, at least, is the robe. He pulls it off the hanger and wraps it around himself as he returns to the kitchen, where the kettle is now whistling. He pours the water into the teapot and sits down to finish his cigarette.

If he hadn't met Umetsu in that particular bar, the evening might not have taken such a disastrous turn, but how was he to know that? He can't presently remember whether it was he or Umetsu who suggested meeting there. It could have been either of them.

The reason they met was the case Kodaka took on yesterday. Teruki Jinno, chairman of Jinno Construction, came to him not with the kind of commercial problem he anticipated when Jinno made the appointment several days ago but a delicate and mystifying issue arising from the financial records of his recently deceased father and the founder of the company, Arinobu Jinno.

Knowing Jinno Construction as a large and highly profitable

business, Kodaka was eager to acquire them as a client and was therefore disappointed – though also intrigued – by what, in the event, he was asked to investigate.

Arinobu Jinno was one of the last of the pre-war generation of entrepreneurs, the credit they were given for revitalizing the Japanese economy after the devastation of defeat somehow deflecting attention from their pursuit of riches in Japan's conquered territories in the 1930s. Their only acknowledgement of their earlier association with the imperialist regime was a certain reticence about their achievements, an eagerness to avoid public attention. The stock market and the average investor held high opinions of Jinno Construction, but its venerable chairman never let that go to his head.

His son Teruki followed a similar path after Arinobu's retirement from the chair. It remained to be seen whether he would pursue a more adventurous strategy now his father was dead. Kodaka read not long ago an article in the business pages of *Asahi Shimbun* speculating that the company might be planning to expand into overseas operations. Kodaka habitually scanned the business news to stay in touch with companies that might hire him, but he wouldn't have remembered the piece about Jinno Construction but for his appointment with Teruki, an appointment made personally by Teruki, not on his behalf by a secretary. In retrospect, that should have told him this wasn't going to be an orthodox commercial case.

Teruki Jinno proved to be a handsome, silver-haired man of fifty or so, smartly but unobtrusively dressed, with an air of quiet concentration that a grey-eyed gaze and lips that barely parted when he spoke only served to strengthen. He expressed his appreciation of Kodaka's condolences on the death of his father four months before and asked a few questions about Kodaka's own father that suggested he'd done a certain amount of research on the agency.

'You work alone now?' he asked.

'Yes. As you see.' Kodaka had been one of three agents working with his father, but was temperamentally a lone wolf and happy to work as one.

'Not even a secretary?'

'Not at present.' The formidable lady who'd filled that post had left with one of the other agents when Kodaka proposed a pay cut. He'd supposed for some time he could cope without an assistant, although lately he'd begun to think he really did need one and would soon have to start looking. There were disordered files lying on the floor of his office. His ashtray and his waste-paper bin both needed emptying.

'So, no one but you will have any knowledge of the work you undertake for me.' Jinno's tone suggested this was what might have particularly commended Kodaka to him.

'I can guarantee complete confidentiality.'

'Good.'

'May I ask . . .'

'This matter concerns my father, Kodaka-san. I cannot over-emphasize that nothing must be said or done to . . . tarnish his reputation.'

'I understand.'

'He lived through two catastrophes: the Kanto earthquake and the fire-bombing at the end of the war. This city was levelled not once in his lifetime but twice. And he helped rebuild it twice as well. He was a great man.'

Kodaka wasn't about to argue. 'It is a fine record.'

'And it must remain so.'

'Is there . . . any reason . . . why it shouldn't?'

Jinno looked around, as if to confirm there really wasn't anyone else there who could hear what he was about to say. 'My father's financial records – his personal records, that is, nothing to do with the company – came into my possession at his death.

From these I learnt that for many years, and for no reason that I can establish, he had been paying a substantial amount of money to . . . an unknown entity.'

'An unknown entity?'

'To a bank account, held in the name of Soroban.'

'When you say substantial . . .'

'Annual sums of . . . twenty-five million yen . . . in recent years.'

It was a lot. Yes, it *was* a lot. 'I can see why you would be concerned.'

'He could afford to lay out such sums, you understand. The money is not really the point, in and of itself.'

'But whatever . . . obligation . . . it reflects?'

'Yes. *That* is the point.'

'When was the last payment made?'

'January of last year. The records show it was always paid in January.'

'But not in January of *this* year?'

'No. Obviously.'

'Has the account-holder – Soroban – contacted you?'

'No.'

'Or . . . any other relative?'

'I have one sister. She has heard nothing. Our mother died several years ago. So, I assume Soroban has learnt of my father's death and concluded there will be no further payments.'

'Do you know when the payments began?'

'My father kept meticulous records. They show he began paying Soroban . . . in Showa twenty-two.'

Showa twenty-two: 1947. That was nearly half a century ago. 'He had been paying Soroban twenty-five million yen every year since then?'

'Not exactly. The sum increased slowly over the years. Cumulatively, though, it amounts to more than half a billion.'

Kodaka did his very best not to appear shocked. But he was. Perhaps most of all by the admission so lightly made by Jinno that his father could readily afford such an outlay. 'I must ask, Jinno-san, if either you or your sister has any idea what these payments could possibly have been for?'

'We cannot explain it.'

'The name Soroban means nothing to you?'

'As a name . . . nothing at all.'

'It could, of course, be a pseudonym.'

'I believe it must be.'

Kodaka paused to extinguish his cigarette and light another. Jinno was also smoking. A silver cigarette case had been plucked several times from an inner pocket. The cigarettes themselves smelt expensively French, whereas Kodaka favoured American. 'Where is the account held?'

'Mizunuma Bank, Nihombashi branch. Very near here, as a matter of fact.'

'Yes. I know it. You've asked the bank for information, I take it?'

'Of course. My request was politely declined. As one would expect.'

'Indeed. It is the business of bankers to be discreet about their customers. But . . . there are ways of finding out who is behind the Soroban account. I can do that for you. Establishing why your father paid him – or her – so much money could be more difficult.'

'You think Soroban could be a woman?'

'I think nothing at this stage, Jinno-san. I merely allow for the possibility. The question I need to put to you is: are you sure you want to know what the money was for?'

Jinno's cheek twitched in irritation. 'I wouldn't have come to you if I didn't want to know.'

Kodaka inclined his head apologetically. 'I understand. But still . . . Soroban has not contacted you. The payments have come to an end. If you take no action, it is likely nothing will ever be heard of this. You loved your father. You respected him. Perhaps you should . . . respect his actions in this matter.'

'No.' Jinno's stubbornness suddenly revealed itself. 'I need to know what this is about. If you are unwilling to take the case . . .'

Kodaka raised his hand, signalling he was only too eager to oblige. 'Not at all, Jinno-san. I am very happy to look into this for you.'

'Good. I want results. And I want them as soon as possible. You are to give this the very highest priority. I will pay twenty per cent above your normal rates to ensure that.'

Twenty per cent. It seemed Jinno had calculated a premium in advance. And it was a generous one. Suspiciously generous, in some ways. Perhaps Jinno really did have an inkling of what lay behind the payments and was buying Kodaka's silence in advance. It was a possibility best not dwelt on. 'I will make a start straight away.'

'Thank you. I will give instructions that you are to be put through to me at all times.' Jinno slid a business card across the desk. 'I have written my home number on the back of the card. I want to hear of anything you discover as soon as you discover it. My wife is aware of the situation. But she is not to be burdened with . . . particulars.'

'I will speak only to you, Jinno-san.'

'Good. You have my full confidence.'

'Thank you.'

And Kodaka *was* grateful. But he was also wary. Full confidence, at premium rate, carried with it high expectation.

As soon as Jinno had left, Kodaka put a call through to Takuto Umetsu, long-serving assistant to the Bank of Japan's deputy chief cashier. Umetsu passed his working days in sombre-suited dedication to financial rectitude. Unfortunately for him, but fortunately for Kodaka, his evenings were a different matter. Umetsu would certainly not want the chief cashier to learn how much money he regularly lost in the smoky upper rooms of Shinjuku mah-jongg parlours. He had resorted in the past to loan sharks to cover some of those losses and his debts had ended up in the hands of the Yakuza. Kodaka had waived his fee for negotiating an instalment repayment plan without physical retribution thrown in. His discussions with Yakuza representatives in a Yokohama hotel were more relishable in retrospect than they'd been at the time. From his point of view, however, they delivered something far more valuable than a fee. They delivered Umetsu, who was never going to kick the mah-jongg habit and would continue losing more than he won, but could now sell information to Kodaka, as and when it was required, rather than put himself in hock to the underworld.

They agreed to meet at a bar they often used in Ueno, a safe distance from Umetsu's place of work and favoured places of entertainment. Kodaka arrived deliberately early for their appointment so that he could wolf down a few of the bar's surprisingly tasty snacks to soak up the beers he was bound to end up drinking.

This also gave him the chance to catch up with that day's *Asahi Shimbun*. He planned to concentrate on the business pages, but was distracted by a feature piece on the supposed mystery of the 'Kobe Sensitive'. It was less than two months since an earthquake had devastated the city of Kobe. There'd been more than six thousand fatalities. Within days, a rumour had begun spreading that the day before the quake an unidentified woman had telephoned the Kobe police and city authorities to warn them it was going to happen. When they'd brushed her off, she'd rung the Kantei – the Prime Minister's office in Tokyo. That call, at least, had been recorded, so there was more to the story than hearsay. No one she'd spoken to had paid her any attention,

33

dismissing her as a crank. All that changed when the quake she'd predicted actually happened. She'd been specific in the recorded call to the Kantei. Kodaka had heard the leaked tape played on television. *'Kobe, tomorrow morning. A strong earthquake will lay it waste. You must evacuate people. You must save them. Listen to me. Kobe. Tomorrow morning. It will happen. Thousands will die unless you act.'*

No one had acted. And thousands *had* died. So, naturally, those who'd lost loved ones in Kobe – and others – had become obsessed with finding the woman who'd made the calls. But she hadn't called again and no one knew who she was. According to the article, there'd always been earthquake 'sensitives' who claimed to be able to detect the signs of an imminent earthquake: strange noises, odd aches and pains, weird cloud shapes, discernible changes in atmospheric pressure, indefinable vibes of one kind or another. But the Kobe Sensitive, as she'd been dubbed, was in a league of her own with a verified warning that had come horribly true. Now an anonymous party had placed an advertisement in the newspaper offering a reward of five million yen to anyone who could identify her. As yet, there'd been no takers. But the search was on.

Kodaka was still reading about the mystery of the Kobe Sensitive when Umetsu arrived, looking more than usually hangdog, which suggested he had no recent mah-jongg victories to celebrate. He accepted the offer of a beer with little sign of gratitude.

'I have a very simple job for you,' Kodaka said, grinning by way of encouragement. 'The name of the holder of this account at Mizunuma's Nihombashi branch.' He pressed into the other man's palm a piece of paper with the account number supplied by Jinno written on it.

'Simple doesn't make it legal,' Umetsu grumbled.

'But it does make it remunerative. How does a hundred thousand sound?'

'It sounds like not enough.'

'I'll make it a hundred and fifty thousand for an answer within twenty-four hours.'

'Every time I do something for you I put my whole career at risk.'

'Come on. It's one phone call. Mizunuma will give you the name. You know they will. The Bank of Japan calls. They jump.'

'But officially the Bank of Japan *isn't* calling.'

'If you think I'm not being generous enough, you could earn yourself five million by identifying the Kobe Sensitive.' Kodaka flapped the newspaper article under Umetsu's long nose.

'Funny. You're always so funny.' Umetsu signalled his reluctant acceptance of the deal with a faint nod of his head. Then he glanced past Kodaka and slid the piece of paper into his pocket. 'Someone's coming over who looks like he knows you.'

Kodaka swung round on his stool to see his old schoolfriend turned *Asahi Shimbun* journalist, Joji Funaki, bearing down on him through the ruck. Funaki was, as usual, smiling broadly. His apparent imperviousness to the ageing process – if he put on their old school uniform he could easily pass for a pupil – and his unflaggingly cheery disposition generally made his company both uplifting and exhausting.

'Dakka,' Funaki cried in greeting, using Kodaka's nickname at school. 'What are you doing here?'

'I could ask you the same.'

'I must go,' said Umetsu suddenly, draining his beer glass and making for the exit.

'Who's your unfriendly friend?' asked Funaki, watching him go.

'A client.'

'Ah. So *that's* what you're doing here. Business. The unfaithful wife kind of business?'

'I'm not going to discuss a case with you.'

'Unless I can help you with it, right?'

'Which you can't.'

'You never know.' Funaki nodded to the barman for a beer and lit a cigarette.

'What brings you to Ueno?'

Funaki smiled. 'I'm not going to discuss a scoop with you.'

'When did you last have a scoop?'

'Maybe this afternoon. You've always been fond of Hasui's woodblock prints, haven't you? What would you say if I told you some of his sketchbooks supposedly destroyed in the Kanto earthquake might *just* have survived?'

'It sounds too good to be true.'

'Yeah. And it probably is. We'll see.' Funaki took a swig of his beer. 'You'll be the first to know. You and all our other readers.'

'They're obsessed with another earthquake just now, I see.' Kodaka tapped his copy of *Asahi Shimbun* with his forefinger.

'Ah. The Kobe Sensitive. The woman of the moment. If she rang the Kantei now and told them Tokyo was going to be hit by the big one tomorrow, what do you think they'd do?'

By 'the big one' Funaki meant the kind of devastating earthquake and tsunami experts agreed was certain to strike the capital at some point, probably within fifty years. Kodaka shrugged. 'You tell me.'

'Nothing. Because by then it would already be too late to do anything. Except jump in the prime ministerial limousine and head for Nagoya, maybe calling at the palace to pick up the Emperor along the way.'

'So, for all we know, she's just made that call.'

'Right. And you and I are doomed, my friend. Which means . . . we should make sure we enjoy our last night on Earth.'

*

36

Funaki's apocalyptic hypothesis was a poor excuse for the drunken shambles they allowed last night to descend into. Now, slumped in the kitchen of his apartment, with Tokyo untouched by either earthquake or tsunami and the big one postponed until who knows when, Kodaka winces at the memory of how little self-control he displayed. He sips his tea and resolves, not for the first time, to run his life on more disciplined lines in future. He has a business to run, after all. He certainly has no intention of taking up Funaki's suggestion that he try to earn the reward himself for identifying the Kobe Sensitive: 'You're a private detective, Dakka. Just the man for the job.'

His glum review of his night of excess is interrupted by the beeping of his pager. He rises and makes his way towards the front door of the apartment, where his jacket is hanging crookedly on a hook. He fishes the pager out of one of the pockets. The display shows Umetsu's mobile number.

Kodaka has told himself several times that he should equip himself with a mobile phone, but inertia – which he's justified to himself as avoiding unnecessary expenditure – has so far got the better of him. It was actually his father who introduced pagers to the agency. He was always one to look ahead, whereas Kodaka finds living in the present more than enough to cope with.

He goes back into the kitchen, where his landline phone is, and calls Umetsu.

'Kodaka?' Umetsu responds. Traffic noise in the background suggests he's not in his office.

'Do you have something for me?'

'Yes. I'm taking my lunch break now. I can meet you outside Takashimaya in ten minutes.'

The Takashimaya department store's proximity to both the Bank of Japan and the Kono Building makes it an obvious rendezvous, but Kodaka, of course, is not in the Kono Building. He's still in his apartment in his pyjamas. 'I can't get there in that time.'

'Suggest somewhere you can get to in the next half hour, then.'

'Er . . .'

'Hibiya Park?'

'OK. Hibiya Park. By the pond at the north-east end. I'll see you there.'

It's not just for his pager that Kodaka is indebted to his father. If Kodaka senior hadn't taken a long lease on an apartment over an umbrella shop in Kobikicho soon after the end of the war, Kodaka junior wouldn't now live in an apartment in Ginza, which absorbed the area when the old canal dividing them was filled in around 1950. Kodaka's mother always believed her husband kept the apartment not for work, as he claimed, but for illicit liaisons. The truth was that it served both purposes. Now, with the umbrella shop long since replaced by a glitzy boutique, it confers on Kodaka a luxury rarer than rubies among Tokyoites – a home within walking distance of his place of work.

It's an easy walk as well to Hibiya Park, or it should be, but Kodaka finds himself racing the clock through the lunchtime crowds and arrives in a breathless state, which a cigarette on the way does nothing to improve. Umetsu is waiting for him by the pond on the eastern side of the park, as agreed, a takeaway coffee clutched in his hand. Their surroundings supply a leafy haven from the tumult of the city, but neither of them seems in a tranquil mood.

'You're late,' Umetsu instantly complains.

'It hasn't been an easy morning.'

'Are you ill?'

'Not as far as I know.'

'You look it.'

'It's great to see you too.'

'Who was that guy who came up to you last night?'

'Funaki? Staff reporter for *Asahi Shimbun*.'

'A journalist?' Umetsu sounds horrified. 'He didn't ask about me, did he?'

'Why would he? It's not as if you made yourself look suspicious by scuttling away as soon as he arrived, is it?'

Umetsu's grip on his coffee cup tightens to the point where the sides begin to crumple. Some of the coffee overflows and dribbles down over his fingers. He appears not to notice. 'No one must know I'm connected with you.'

'And no one does. Including Funaki. I protect my sources. I'd soon be out of business if I didn't.'

Umetsu finally becomes aware of the coffee spillage. He grimaces and shakes the coffee from his hand.

'What have you got for me?' Kodaka presses.

'The account is controlled by a film company based in Chofu.'

'A *film* company?'

'So I'm told. The Kuraikagami Film Corporation.'

'Never heard of them.'

Umetsu frowns. 'Really?'

'Have you, then?'

'They have quite a . . . distinctive logo. There doesn't seem to be anything on the screen, then it shatters like a sheet of glass someone's thrown a rock at and up comes the name: Kuraikagami.'

'You've seen this . . . in the cinema?'

Umetsu shrugs. 'Videos, mostly.'

'What kind of videos?'

'They make the *Mah-Jongg Mysteries* series.'

'The what?'

'They're about a top mah-jongg player who solves murders when he isn't winning big games. The murders often turn out to have a mah-jongg connection. And technically they're . . . very accurate.'

It takes a considerable effort on Kodaka's part not to laugh at this revelation concerning Umetsu's choice of entertainment.

'You just can't get enough of mah-jongg, can you?' he asks with a determinedly straight face.

Umetsu looks at him narrowly. 'Is there anything else you want to know?'

'What does the name Soroban signify?'

'Mizunuma don't have that information. All they know is that a nominated party at the Kuraikagami Corporation controls the account.'

'Who is the nominated party?'

'The company chairman. No one else.'

'That sounds unusual.'

'It does, I agree.'

'Who is the chairman?'

'His name is Goro Rinzaki.'

2022

IT WAS A STRAIGHT RUN ON THE CHUO LINE FROM OGIKUBO, WHERE Wada lived, out to Musashino. But she headed in the opposite direction, into the city, when she set off early the following morning. The next stage in her search for Manjiro Nagata required her first of all to return to her office. It was Saturday, so she was spared the commuter crush on the trains. The streets of Nihombashi were as she preferred them: quiet and orderly. Which was in fact as she preferred all things.

She rebuked herself for not taking Kodaka's set of skeleton keys with her to Musashino the previous day. It simply hadn't occurred to her that Manjiro might not really be living in his apartment, that his residence there could be part of some elaborate ruse. Now that seemed more likely than not. And there was an obvious way to find out for certain.

Kodaka had always said the keys were left to him by his father, the founder of the agency. Where he obtained them from was unknown. But the post-war world in which Kodaka senior had started up in business as a private detective was a place of corner-cutting and improvisation. The keys bore the trademark of a well-established locksmith, who, in these more legally constrained times, would probably not be happy to know a set was in Wada's possession.

The apartment building where Manjiro notionally lived was probably about fifty years old, which meant the locks were likely to be variations on a basic pattern – and therefore susceptible to the use of skeletons. With the set stowed in her shoulder-bag, Wada headed back out to the western suburbs.

There were quite a few people moving around near apartment block 5: mothers with children, people walking their dogs, ambling loners. Fortunately, Wada saw nothing of Hosogai – and could only hope he saw nothing of her as she entered the building.

To minimize the likelihood of any such encounter, she took the lift to the seventh floor, then walked down the stairs to the fifth. She stopped on the sixth when she heard the occupant of another flat on Manjiro's floor leave – a woman, accompanied by someone, to whom she addressed a stream of complaints about the speed of the lift as they waited for it to arrive. Then they were gone. Silence returned to the landing.

Wada descended, removing the bunch of skeleton keys from her bag as she went. She glanced down the stairwell and detected no movement below, then set to work.

She proceeded slowly as well as methodically, trying each key carefully. One turned further than most in the lock, but not quite far enough. That set her searching for the most similar key. Eventually, she found one that looked promising. It worked.

The door creaked slightly as she pulled it slowly open. She half-expected Manjiro to leap out of the shadowy interior, accusing her of breaking in. But he wasn't there. No one was. Something in the atmosphere that met her conveyed a certainty of human absence.

The small *genkan* area immediately inside the door contained no house shoes, which only confirmed the occupant hadn't just stepped out to the shops.

There was a linoleum-floored kitchen/diner to the left, with doors to the toilet and bathroom to the right. The kitchen had sliding doors that led onto the balcony. The blinds were up. Ahead, through half-open folding doors, were a tatami-matted lounge and bedroom. Judging by the flood of morning light, the lounge also had sliding doors onto the balcony.

Wada was instantly reminded of the apartment in Hikarigaoka where she'd spent most of her childhood, before her father moved the family to the small house in Koishikawa where her mother still lived. The layout was virtually identical, with the small kitchen and cramped dining space, although they'd boasted one more room in Hikarigaoka, subdivided by a screen into separate sleeping spaces for Wada and her brother.

The other obvious difference was how conspicuously uncluttered – indeed, un*used* – Manjiro's apartment was. There were pots and pans and other utensils in the kitchen, plus rice cooker, toaster and fridge. But the fridge was empty and there were no stains on the stove or in the sink. What there was, Wada noticed, was a thin layer of dust. It didn't look as if the tap had been run in a long time.

She checked the bathroom for toiletries and found some, sure enough, but no sign that anyone had recently made use of them. The lounge was much the same. There was a sofa, an armchair, a free-standing television and a cabinet full of books and DVDs, but everything was just too neat to believe anyone had recently read any of the books or watched any of the DVDs.

There was a timer attached to the light-switch and a similar mechanism had been fitted to the blinds, with steel rods controlling the raising and lowering of them. Those two features clinched it for Wada's purposes. Manjiro Nagata's apartment was a stage

43

set. He may once have lived there. And clearly he wanted people to believe he still did.

But he didn't. Wherever he was, it wasn't here.

Then she jumped in surprise – and fright – when she heard a gush of water from the kitchen tap.

She hurried into the kitchen . . . and saw at once that the sink was still completely dry. No water had flowed.

It took her a few minutes to track down a small loudspeaker inside one of the cupboards from which the sound must have come. Returning to the lounge, she found another loudspeaker in the cabinet. Its wires led to a box on the floor behind the television, with more wires leading from that to the TV itself: an audio system of some kind, programmed to play certain sounds at certain times, presumably – water flowing, the washing machine spinning, the toilet flushing, the kettle boiling, the TV blaring; whatever was necessary to maintain the pretence.

But a pretence was all it was.

Wada commenced a different form of search next, for any personal documentation stored in the apartment – bank account or credit card statements, passport, driving licence, tax returns. But there was no paperwork of any kind in any of the drawers or cupboards. There were clothes and towels and bedding, but it might as well have been a hotel suite for all the physical evidence there was of the existence of the supposed resident.

She sat for a few minutes on the sofa, reviewing her options. There were precious few. She could see nothing for it but to report back to Fumito Nagata that his son wasn't a recluse so much as a fugitive. And a fugitive who'd covered his tracks well. There was nothing else to be learnt from his apartment. It was time to leave.

There was a square open-weave coir mat in the *genkan*. Wada had given it no attention on her way in. Now, as she approached it with the light from the windows behind her instead of ahead, she noticed a small white object on the floor beneath the mat, visible through one of the gaps in the weave. She lifted the mat up and slid it out: a piece of paper folded in three round a card.

It was a short note, addressed to Manjiro, using the formal, respectful mode: *Nagata-sama.* It went on: *I beg you to respond to my letters. I am very worried about my friend.*

There was no name given for the sender of the note, which Wada supposed had been slid under the door when letters had gone unanswered. But it was folded round a printed card giving the telephone number and email address of one Taro Yamato. There was no date on the note either. How long it had lain there was impossible to gauge. But it was evidence that others apart from Manjiro's father were looking for him. It was a lead. And one Wada meant to follow immediately.

She left the apartment, locking the door carefully behind her, and descended the stairs cautiously, watchful for any appearance by Hosogai. But there was no sign of him. Out shopping for single malt Scotch whisky, she surmised.

In the lobby on the ground floor, she encountered the postman, making deliveries to the residents' mailboxes. She greeted him with her best effort at charm, something she would have been forced to admit wasn't her forte. She wasn't hopeful he'd divulge whether there was a mail diversion arrangement in place for Nagata, apartment 514, and, sure enough, he referred her with polite stiffness to the ward postmaster. But he didn't deny it, she noticed. On the face of it, there had to be such an arrangement, otherwise Manjiro's mail would eventually fill the box. Either that or Manjiro returned at intervals to empty it. Or he sent someone to empty it.

Perhaps it didn't matter which, though. Perhaps Taro Yamato could tell her far more than the postmaster was ever likely to.

*

45

She made her way back towards Musashi-Sakai station, stopping on a bench in the shopping centre to send an email to Yamato. The hint of desperation in his note suggested it wasn't going to be difficult to get a response, unless he'd spoken to Manjiro since delivering it, which seemed unlikely. She kept the message short and to the point: *I have information about Manjiro Nagata. I believe you are trying to contact him. I would be willing to help you. Let me know if you wish to discuss the matter.*

That was all she could do for the present, which left her with no excuse not to head for Koishikawa and call on her mother to wish her a happy birthday two days late and take the measure of the lodger who'd mysteriously entered her life.

Wada's father had been able to buy a house – albeit a small one – relatively close to the centre of Tokyo thanks to connections in the real estate business arising from his work for an auction company that sometimes handled repossessed properties. Since they would otherwise have been unable to aspire to anything more than a slightly larger and better-located apartment than the one in Hikarigaoka, her mother should have been well pleased with the move. But, for reasons beyond Wada's comprehension, she always insisted their new neighbourhood was inferior to the old. The people of Koishikawa were haughty, uncommunicative and eager to seize an advantage. They weren't to be trusted.

They seemed like people everywhere else to Wada and she for one was delighted to acquire a proper bedroom of her own. The house suited her very well in her adolescence, though not so well that she ever considered moving back there, as proposed when Wada had been widowed, Haha being a widow herself by then. Wada knew instinctively that living under the same roof as her mother again was something she could not contemplate – under any circumstances.

The house was a shortish walk from Sengoku subway station.

46

The route took Wada past the Daiei supermarket her mother had once habitually shopped at. But that was before a *combini* had opened closer to her. Wada was therefore surprised to see Haha appear ahead – her tiny, bird-like figure instantly recognizable in her long fawn raincoat and mustard-coloured hat – hurrying towards the supermarket entrance.

She'd gone in and disappeared along one of the aisles before Wada could catch up. One of her characteristics was the speed at which she walked, which showed no sign of diminishing with age. Although her stride had shortened, she'd compensated for that with ever faster steps. Wada had long expected this to end in some kind of injury, since she was so light she would come off worse in any collision, but so far she'd remained unscathed.

When Wada finally hunted her down, she already had several items in her trolley and was standing in the poultry section, examining chicken thighs.

'Mother, it's me,' Wada called.

Haha looked round in momentary dismay, then frowned at her. 'Umiko! What are you doing here?'

'I saw you come in, so I followed.'

'Ah, always the private detective.' As so often, it was hard to tell whether she was joking or not.

'You were expecting me today, weren't you?'

'Oh yes. But . . . you're not staying all day, are you? I could buy more chicken if . . .'

'No, Mother, I'm not staying all day.'

'You probably wouldn't like this dish anyway.'

'What is it?'

'Yudofu. Chicken, tofu, cabbage, mushrooms, bean sprouts, spinach, seaweed. But the key is the sauce. Great care has to be taken with the egg yolks to get it right.'

Haha wasn't noted for gourmet cuisine, rather the reverse. Wada couldn't claim any credentials in that department either,

47

but this yudofu didn't sound quite right. 'Chicken in yudofu, Haha? And egg yolks?'

'Ah, this is chanko yudofu.'

'Chanko?' Wada had maintained a studious ignorance of all matters sumo, partly because Haha was such a fan of the sport, glueing herself to the television during broadcast tournaments and happy to discourse at any prompting on who was up and who was down in wrestler rankings. But even Wada knew chanko was a dish traditionally consumed by sumo wrestlers. She was on the point of asking why her mother was planning to cook such a dish when a disturbing possibility entered her head. 'Your lodger, Mother . . .'

'Ah. You have spoken to Haruto. He telephoned me on my birthday. It was nice that one of my children did.'

Wada ignored the reproach. 'Yes. I have spoken to Haruto. He said you have a lodger. His name is Seiji Tago. Is that right?'

'It is. You've heard of him?'

'Should I have?'

'He was very successful before his knee injury.'

'Do you mean very successful . . . in sumo?'

'Yes. I'm sure he'd have become a *sanyaku* but for his injury.'

Wada drew a breath and counselled herself to remain calm. 'Why exactly have you taken in a former sumo wrestler as a lodger, Mother?'

'He had nowhere to live. After he was expelled from the sport—'

'He was expelled?'

'But he didn't take bribes. That was a terrible injustice.'

'You're telling me this man Tago was thrown out of the sport for taking bribes?'

'Yes. But he was innocent.'

'How do you know?'

'He told me, of course. He told me the whole story. Now, can

48

we get on, please? I have lots more to buy. Perhaps you could push the trolley for me.'

Wada decided to defer pursuing the matter further until Haha had completed her shopping, though many questions circulated in her head as they toured the aisles. Eventually, they emerged onto the street, Wada laden with Haha's shopping, and started walking back to the house.

Haha offered no more by way of explanation until Wada asked her directly, 'How did you meet Tago-san?' She used the respectful form in referring to him, even though she had serious doubts about whether he merited it.

'I came upon him collecting a bento box from the back of the *combini* near the post office. They put out food that's past its best-before date for the homeless. I wouldn't have recognized him but for the way he walked. He still has his . . . ring swagger. It's very distinctive.'

'He's homeless?'

'Not now.'

'But he was when you met him?'

'I'm afraid so. It's terrible, how they treated him.'

Wada was close to speechlessness. She recalled a discussion she'd had with her mother about the prefectural authority's attempts to remove homeless people from Tokyo's parks and shopping districts in advance of the Olympics so as to spare foreign visitors the sight of them (though in the event there hadn't been any foreign visitors because of coronavirus). Haha, Wada distinctly recollected, had said it was only right the city should be made to look its best for such a prestigious sporting occasion. Now, here she was, full of sympathy for one representative of those unfortunates she'd previously asserted should be ousted from view.

'Because of his injury, he slipped right down the rankings and ended up as a *tsukebito* again,' she continued.

49

'What does that mean, Mother?'

'How can you be so ignorant about our national sport, Umiko?' Haha snapped. 'A *tsukebito* is a junior wrestler who acts as a servant to a more senior wrestler, cooking his meals, carrying his bags, cleaning up after him, shopping and running errands for him. That was what happened to Tago-san. And unluckily for him the *sanyaku* he served was the infamous Igarashi. You've heard of *him*, I suppose.'

'I don't think I have.'

'It was in all the papers. About five years ago. He was bribed to throw matches. Tago-san had no idea it was going on. But he carried some messages from Igarashi to the people paying the bribes and that was enough for the Sumo Association to expel him, even though he was never charged with any criminal offence. His career was over, because another *rikishi* had betrayed the sport. Such an awful thing.'

Haha's tone made it obvious just how awful a thing she thought it was. And in principle Wada agreed. But until she could take the measure of Seiji Tago in person, a principle was all it was going to be. 'I suppose it would have been better if he'd retired after his injury,' she ventured.

'Give up, you mean?'

'Would that have been so bad?'

'How can you ask that? I've never known you give up something you believe in.'

In ordinary circumstances, that would have sounded to Wada like a compliment, but somehow she did not feel her mother meant it as one. Fortitude and persistence in a sumo wrestler were to be admired; in a childless daughter who insisted on pursuing the unwomanly profession of private detective, rather less so.

They were on the cobbled path now that led gently down to the back-street where the house stood. It was hemmed in at the front by a pottery workshop, but to the rear was a small walled

50

garden. The upper branches of the shrubs and low trees Wada's father had planted were visible ahead of them. 'How long has Tago-san been living with you, Mother?' Wada asked.

'Just over a month.'

Was it really so long since Wada had paid her mother a visit? She was going to have a lot of explaining to do to Haruto. 'He pays rent, does he?'

'He has no money for rent. They took everything from him. That is why he ended up without a roof over his head.'

'So, he's not technically your lodger, then.'

'He is my guest.'

'For how long?'

'I like having him in the house. He does all kinds of . . . practical things. He'll be cooking the yudofu, for instance.'

'But he sent you to buy the ingredients?'

'He did not send me. He was too busy with something else. As you'll shortly see.'

There was a narrow bamboo-slatted gate into the garden not far ahead of them. Wada remembered Haha complaining recently that it had dropped slightly on its hinges and could not be fully opened because it caught on the sloping cobbles of the path. She could not remember proposing any solution to the problem.

But it seemed a solution had nonetheless been forthcoming.

The gate had been removed from its hinges and was being re-hung by a tall, broad-shouldered man dressed in a white boiler suit. There was a box of tools at his feet. He looked up from his work as they approached and smiled broadly. He had a wide, deep-browed face framed by a long mop of dark, wiry hair. His hands were strikingly large. Wada would have put his age at about forty. She had no doubt he was Seiji Tago. The mountain-ous fat she associated with sumo wrestlers was lacking, but he was big and brawny enough for the role.

51

'Tago-san,' said Haha, 'this is my daughter Umiko.'

Tago bowed, rather lower than such a casual encounter required. 'It is an honour to meet you, Wada-san,' he said, his voice low and rumbling.

Wada bowed in return. 'And to meet you, Tago-san.'

He engaged her with dark, piercing eyes. 'Your mother has been my saviour. She may not have told you that. But you should know it anyway. I owe her more than I can ever repay.'

'You're exaggerating,' said Haha, who, it seemed to Wada, blushed slightly as she spoke. 'How are you getting on?'

'The gate will soon be fully functioning again.'

'That will be nice.'

'Did the shop have everything?'

'Yes.'

'Including the radish?'

'Including the radish.'

At this Tago smiled. 'Are you dining with us, Wada-san?'

'I'm afraid not. I'm . . .'

'Too busy,' said Haha. 'She is always too busy.'

Leaving Tago to his work, Wada accompanied Haha into the house. They took off their shoes and coats and Wada carried the bags to the kitchen, where they started unloading and putting away the contents. Nothing was said for several minutes. Wada did not propose to argue further with her mother, knowing from long experience that trying to shift her from a position she'd taken was entirely futile.

It was a lesson Haha herself had failed to learn about her daughter, however, as the remark she made in breaking the silence clearly demonstrated.

'You have no reason to worry about me, Umiko,' she said with a sigh. 'I have much more reason to worry about you.'

'That is not true, Mother.'

'Really? Have you forgotten what happened to Kodaka-san? I haven't.'

'It was an accident.'

'You don't believe that. Neither do I.'

Kodaka's death was officially classified as an unsolved hit-and-run car accident. Wada had never told Haha he was actually murdered. Nor had she told her that the man who'd ordered the murder was dead. But she didn't doubt that somehow Haha knew both of these things.

'I do not deserve to have a daughter who undertakes such dangerous work.'

'It is not dangerous. I don't handle the same kind of cases as Kodaka-san did. And I'm more careful than he was.'

'Your father would not have approved of you . . . spying on husbands and . . . digging up people's secrets.'

'Would he approve of Tago-san living here?'

Haha's thin lips grew thinner still. 'I don't know what to say to neighbours when they ask about you, Umiko, I truly don't. You are . . .' She shook her head in frustration. 'I just don't know.'

In a bid to lighten the mood, Wada went over to her shoulder-bag, which she'd hung behind the door, and took out the gift she'd bought for Haha's birthday. It was a fan with a scene from *The Tale of Genji* painted on it. She'd despaired of thinking of anything her mother actually wanted or needed and had settled for a fan on the grounds that at least it wouldn't take up much room.

Wada had expended a lot of care in the wrapping and ribboning of the gift and was rewarded with a shaft of pleasure on Haha's face as she received it. The tension between them eased.

And then Wada's phone rang. Looking at the caller's number, she recognized it as Taro Yamato's. 'I have to take this,' she explained apologetically.

At which her mother looked monumentally unsurprised. 'Of course you do.'

53

Wada took the phone out into the hall. 'Taro Yamato?'

'Is that Umiko Wada?' The voice sounded strained and hesitant.

'Yes. You got my email?'

'You said you have information concerning Manjiro Nagata.'

'That is correct.'

'Do you know how I can contact him?'

'I don't think we should discuss this over the phone, Yamato-san. It is a delicate matter.'

'How do you know Nagata-san?'

'As I say, it is a delicate matter.'

'Well . . .' There was a pause. Then he said, 'Perhaps . . . we could meet.'

'Later today, perhaps?'

'I'm anxious to hear what you have to tell me, Wada-san. I'd like to meet . . . as soon as possible.'

'Tell me where and when.'

'Ah . . .'

'Where are you now?'

'Here is no good.' It was a tantalizing remark. Where was *here*? 'Where are you?'

'Koishikawa.'

'Well, let me think.' He thought for a moment, then: 'There's a coffee shop near Suidobashi subway station east side. The Rose Petal. It should be pretty quiet. Can you be there one hour from now?'

'Yes.'

'OK then. One hour from now.'

Wada ended the call and went back into the kitchen. Haha cocked her head and looked enquiringly at her. 'Not staying for lunch? There's soup. Or noodles just how you like them.'

'I'm sorry. I have to go.'

'Work?'

'Yes.'

'As always.'

'I *am* sorry, Mother. Are you going to open your present before I leave?'

'If you think there's time.'

'Yes.' Wada smiled stubbornly. 'There's time.'

Wada was still annoyed with herself when she left a short while later. She shouldn't have risen to the bait Haha so often dangled in front of her during such visits. The arrival on the scene of Seiji Tago had undermined Wada's normal tactics for deflecting her mother's sundry provocations. But she'd gone there in part to celebrate Haha's eightieth birthday, so that was really no excuse. She should have managed things better. It was as simple as that.

But simplicity was often elusive in relations with her mother. Wada had been particularly wounded by the suggestion that her father would not have approved of her choice of career. It was, as no doubt it was intended to be, a frustratingly untestable proposition.

Nearly twenty years had passed since her father's death, but Wada missed him still, as, she knew, did Haha. The proof of that was in the nameplate displayed outside their front door. His name was still there, proclaimed as head of the household. He was never going to be forgotten. But he could no longer speak for himself. So now Haha had decided she would speak for him, which was calculated to annoy her daughter beyond endurance.

Wada turned up the alley beside the house and found Tago still at work on the gate. It was back on its hinges now and it looked as if he'd nearly finished. He bowed respectfully to her, his command of the courtesies undeniably impressive.

'I am sorry you are already leaving, Wada-san,' he said. 'I had hoped we would have the opportunity to talk to each other.'

'Are we not talking, Tago-san?' She flinched at the hint of rudeness in her tone.

'I meant at greater length,' he went on, undeterred.

'What would you like to talk to me about?'

'Oh, the things we have in common, I suppose.'

'What might they be?'

'Your mother, of course. And . . . our vocations.'

'Vocations?'

'Mine was sumo, which I can no longer pursue. Yours is . . . detection.'

'Perhaps it is simply a job, rather than a vocation.'

'That I doubt.'

'You hardly know me, Tago-san.'

'True.' He smiled. 'But your mother has spoken of you so much that I feel I know you quite well. And I sense your commitment to what you do is as deep as mine was to sumo. Which is as it should be.'

'I do not think my mother would agree with you.'

Still he was smiling. 'So, you see? There *is* much for us to talk about.'

'If so, it will have to be on another occasion. I must go.'

'I understand.' He bowed again.

It was only three stops on the subway to Suidobashi. But that gave Wada just enough time to scan the Internet for information about the Igarashi betting scandal that had shaken the world of sumo, whilst leaving Wada not so much unshaken as entirely unknowing, in the summer of 2016. There was a lot of detail about how matches were thrown, which ones on which occasions, which tournament results might be considered devalued by the revelations, whether there was Yakuza involvement, and what could be concluded about the state of the sport as a whole. Wada ignored most of that. Her interest was the apportionment of guilt. Igarashi himself was universally condemned, although it seemed public apologies had finally paid off in his case, since he was now running a successful gymnasium business. Other top wrestlers were tainted by associ-ation and fingers were pointed at Igarashi's stable master in particular. Seiji Tago was spoken of, when he was spoken of at all, more in sorrow than anger. Opinion was divided over whether he'd been complicit in Igarashi's activities. Some thought he'd been unfairly treated. His refusal to retire after a serious knee injury was held up by them as evidence of his commitment to sumo.

Commitment. It was the very word Tago had used himself. Not that it had done him any good. He'd been expelled from the sport he loved, along with half a dozen others. There were no reports of his current activities. He had vanished into the electronic void.

But, as Wada knew now, he had not vanished altogether.

She did her best to put the Seiji Tago problem out of her mind when the train reached Suidobashi. For the moment, the mystery of Manjiro Nagata had to take priority. Which in truth she wel-comed. She was happier delving into the secrets of strangers than analysing the behaviour of her close relations.

The Rose Petal was, as Yamato had said, close to the eastern exit from the station. It might have been busier if there'd been a play on at the nearby Noh theatre, but there was no performance, so custom was thin.

Wada was confident she'd spotted Taro Yamato as soon as she entered. A lean, spare, middle-aged man in a business suit, he was sipping coffee and glancing around nervously. He wore glasses and, with his greying hair and mournful expression, gen-erally looked like thousands of other middle-aged men who could be spotted on the subway during the rush hour.

But this was Saturday, so, if he'd come from his place of work, it was clear his duties extended beyond Monday to Friday. He certainly had a put-upon air about him and a variety of uneasy tics and twitches. He looked at Wada as she approached his table with nervous expectancy.

'Yamato-san?'

He nodded in confirmation and half-rose from his chair for an exchange of bows. They sat opposite each other, Yamato apparently lost for words, though his lips moved as if he was rehearsing what to say. He rubbed his hands together and grimaced.

'I hope we can help each other,' Wada said.

He cleared his throat. 'How did you know I was looking for Manjiro Nagata?' he asked in an undertone.

'I saw your letter to him.'

Now he looked at her in surprise. 'He showed it to you?'

'Not exactly.'

The waitress arrived at their table. Wada ordered tea. Yamato asked for another black coffee. He watched the waitress walk away, then turned back to Wada and said, 'Before we discuss anything, I need to know . . . in my own interests . . . what your connection with Manjiro Nagata is. If he didn't show you my letter, how did you come to see it?'

'Before I explain, can you tell me who the "friend" is that you mention in the letter?'

Yamato's various twitches suggested he didn't want to be the first to disclose anything. 'You put me . . . in a difficult position.'

'How so?'

'I can't say anything . . . until you tell me what your connection is with Manjiro Nagata.'

'All I've asked you for is your friend's name.'

A silence fell between them. Yamato's expression was tight with uncertainty. He didn't trust her, which was understandable. But there was more to his reticence than natural caution. It seemed to Wada that it contained an element of fear.

'One of us has to make the first move, Yamato-san,' Wada said quietly, venturing a smile of encouragement.

'You proposed this meeting.'

'I did.'

Their orders arrived. The waitress arranged the cups and left. Yamato sipped his coffee. Wada had started considering whether she would have to answer his question if she was to learn anything from him when, in a sudden mumble, he said, 'Daiju Endo.'

Wada wasn't sure she'd heard him correctly. 'Could you say that again?'

'My friend's name is Daiju Endo,' he replied with slow emphasis.

'Thank you.'

'You have heard of him?'

'No.'

'And your connection with Manjiro Nagata?'

He'd broken the ice. She couldn't hold back now. 'I am a private detective, Yamato-san, hired by Manjiro's father, who is worried about his son's . . . circumstances.'

'You are a private detective?'

'Yes.' She took one of her cards out of her shoulder-bag and slid it across the table to him.

He examined it carefully. 'Why does Nagata's father need a detective to check on his son? Why doesn't he check himself?'

'He has tried. Without success.'

'He won't even answer the door to his father?'

'There is never an answer,' Wada replied with subtle evasiveness.

'But you've seen my letter. How is that possible unless . . .'

'I have entered the apartment, Yamato-san. Manjiro is not there. He – or someone – has taken elaborate steps to create the impression that he lives there. But he does not. He is . . . absent.'

'Absent?'

'Semi-permanently, I believe.'

'You're sure?' Yamato looked as if he couldn't believe what she was saying.

She nodded. 'I am sure.'

'And my letter?'

'You slid it under the door, yes? It lodged beneath a mat, where it could easily have escaped notice. I found it there during a search of the apartment. When did you deliver it, may I ask?'

'A few months ago. It was my . . . final effort to reach Nagata . . . after calling at the apartment got me nowhere and letters to him through the post went unanswered.'

'You wanted his help regarding your friend Daiju Endo?'

'Yes.'

'What sort of help?'

'Help to find him. My friend is missing, Wada-san. Like Nagata, as you now tell me. Absent. Gone. Disappeared.'

'Why should Nagata know where he is? Are they friends also?'

'No. Not friends.'

'What, then?'

'It is difficult for me . . . to answer that question.'

'Why?'

'Do you know where Nagata is now?'

'No.'

'Have you any clues to follow?'

'So far, only your letter.'

'Then it is hopeless. And I stand to gain nothing by giving you further information.' Yamato's words were dismissive, but his tone wasn't. It seemed to Wada he was hoping she would press him further.

'What do you stand to lose?'

'More than you might suppose.'

'I am a detective, Yamato-san. I find things out. Help me and I will help you.'

'But you don't work for me. You work for Nagata's father.'

'What news have you had of your friend since you delivered your letter to Nagata's apartment?'

'None.'

'In . . . how many months?'

'Three. Maybe four. I had given up hope of hearing anything when I received your email.'

'Then I respectfully suggest . . . that cooperating with me . . . is probably your last chance of finding out what has become of Daiju Endo.'

He didn't contradict her. In fact, he didn't say anything. He looked around the other tables. As far as Wada could tell, no one was paying them the slightest attention. The waitress was playing with her phone under the cake counter. Two young women were sharing a stifled giggle at something one of them had said. Taro Yamato was exciting no interest whatsoever.

'Exactly how long do you think Endo-san has been missing?'

Yamato looked at her for several silent seconds before answering. 'Hard to say for sure. I only know how long it is since I last spoke to him.'

'And how long is that?'

It appeared to require a considerable effort on Yamato's part to supply an answer. 'It was in the first week of November.'

'What did you speak to him *about*?'

A long silence ensued. Yamato grimaced. But he said nothing.

'Without more to go on,' Wada pressed, 'I cannot help you.'

Yamato conceded the point with a nod of the head. 'I am a civil servant. My duties are . . . highly confidential. There are limits . . . to what I can disclose.'

'Did Endo-san work with you?'

'At one time.'

'But not at the time of his disappearance?'

'No. Not then.'

'Why did he leave his job?'

'Because—' Yamato broke off. He stared down at his coffee, breathing heavily, struggling, it seemed almost physically, with whatever constraints he felt he was under. 'This is not easy,' he murmured.

'Much of my work is not easy.'

'You don't understand.' Yamato sighed and flexed his shoulders. 'I should have left this alone.'

'But you didn't.'

There was the hint of a rueful smile. 'It seems I can't.'

'Just tell me . . . as much as you feel you can.'

He looked up at her. 'Endo warned me to stay out of . . . whatever he'd got himself into. He wasn't threatening me, you understand. He was trying to protect me. Or so it seemed to me. And now . . .'

'I'm listening.'

'Ah . . .'

She said nothing. She waited, patiently, expectantly.

Somewhere inside Taro Yamato, the struggle resolved itself. He leant forward, lowering his voice close to a whisper. 'Tell me, Wada-san, have you ever heard of the Kobe Sensitive?'

1995

KODAKA HAS GLEANED AS MUCH AS HE CAN ABOUT THE KURAIKAGAMI Film Corporation from publicly accessible sources. He's not much the wiser than when Umetsu first gave him the company's name, but he's confirmed Goro Rinzaki (born 1929) is the chairman of a board comprising eleven others, none of whom he's ever heard of. The company was established in 1949. Whether Rinzaki was a director then, when he'd only have been twenty years old, isn't clear. Their headquarters and studios are out at Chofu. They have a lot of films to their credit, mostly at the straight-to-video end of the market, including, of course, the *Mah-Jongg Mysteries* series. They've recently taken stakes in several of the new multi-screen cinema complexes that have sprung up in the big cities.

None of this tells Kodaka anything of real value. He needs to know what the word on the street is about Kuraikagami in general and Rinzaki in particular, if indeed there is any word. He needs to know *more* in every way.

'Called to apologize, Dakka?' Funaki asks with a chuckle when he hears Kodaka's voice on the phone.

'What do I have to apologize for?'

'Leading me astray last night.'

'It was the other way round, as I recall.'

'That's not how it looks in the photographs.'

'What photographs?'

'Just joking. Why *have* you phoned?'

'You might be able to help me with a case.'

'And what do I get out of it?'

'I'll be in your debt.'

'You already are.'

'Deeper in your debt, then. Besides . . .'

'What?'

'Aren't you curious about what I want?'

'OK. Shoot.'

'Can you tell me anything about Goro Rinzaki?'

'Rinzaki?' Funaki sounds doubtful.

'Guy in his mid-sixties. Chairman of the Kuraikagami Film Corporation.'

'Ah. That Rinzaki.'

'You know him?'

'By reputation.'

'Maybe we could meet . . . and you could tell me about his . . . reputation.'

'Mmm . . .'

'Come on. You know you want to impress me.'

'Impress *you*? OK. I give in. Make it to the Blue Fin at nine and I'll see what I can do. You're buying the beers, right?'

'Right.'

'But there'll be no karaoke. I'm on night crawl duty.'

The night crawl Funaki referred to is, as Kodaka knows from previous references, a prowl round the nightspots of Tokyo in search of politicians and other public figures getting themselves

64

into embarrassing or compromising situations (or simply becoming loose-lipped under the influence of alcohol), thus promising to fill newspaper columns with juicy material. And this is Friday, the prime night of the week for such activities.

But it's going to be past midnight before crawling serves any purpose, so Funaki has several hours to fill after leaving his newspaper's HQ and no objection to spending one or two of them with his old friend.

Kodaka has dined on ramen at a cheap Chinese restaurant before he arrives at the Blue Fin. The bar is adorned with paintings and photographs of the eponymous tuna and even a couple of stuffed specimens. This, plus subaqueous lighting and a novelty soundtrack of oceanic susurrations, creates the illusion of a submarine world for its customers to float – or drown – in.

'Has this case got anything to do with that guy I saw you with last night?' Funaki asks after a first gulp of beer.

'It might have.'

'What's his connection with Rinzaki?'

'You know I can't tell you that.'

'But you still expect me to tell you everything I know.'

'Look, if I dig up anything newsworthy about Rinzaki that doesn't damage my client, I'll let you in on it. OK?'

'I guess it'll have to be.'

'But I need to know where to dig. So, what have you got?'

Funaki takes another slug of beer and a pull on his cigarette. 'Don't get too excited. Goro Rinzaki is a bit . . . elusive. I mean, he runs Kuraikagami, as you know. Has done since it was set up in 1949.'

'When he was twenty?'

'If you say so. Young, anyway.'

'Where'd he get the money from to start a film company at that age?'

'No idea. But he's made a big success of it – without a lot of fanfare. In fact, I don't think my paper would have taken any interest in him at all but for his recent sponsorship of a new exhibition at Yushukan.'

Yushukan: the museum attached to Yasukuni-jinja, the Shinto shrine to Japan's war dead; a magnet for mourners, tourists and black-clad right-wing nostalgists for the days of empire – the latter on account of the Class A war criminals enshrined there. It's not one of Kodaka's favourite places in Tokyo. As far as the museum's concerned, he's never got further than the entrance hall, a space dominated by a preserved 1940 Zero fighter plane.

'You know it's rumoured the Prime Minister's going to make a formal apology on the fiftieth anniversary of the end of the war this summer?' Funaki continues, probably suspecting Kodaka *doesn't* know.

'That won't go down well with the right-wingers.'

'No, it won't, will it? And it could explain why Rinzaki's put his money into this new exhibition. Maybe he's decided to show his political colours.'

'What's the exhibition about?'

'The war criminals. Not just the Class A mob, but all those other Class Bs and Cs enshrined at Yasukuni. Apparently, Kurai-kagami bought up the stock of a bankrupt film company called Magunichudo years ago. Magunichudo had done a lot of film-ing for the government in Manchuria, Taiwan and Korea before the war: propaganda stuff, basically, to show how much good work was being done in our colonies. Anyway, Kuraikagami went through the reels of film they'd acquired and came up with loads of material on the Yasukuni war criminals, which is what the exhibition's centred on. Except of course it's not about their crimes. Instead, it's all school openings, road-building projects and civic improvements. There are displays on selected individ-uals, listing the crimes they were convicted of, and the visitor can select short films to watch about these people, but the films themselves tell a deceptively flattering story. At least, that's the criticism that's been levelled at the exhibition. That it's basically a whitewash.'

'Is that what you think?'

'Oh, I haven't been to see it. We sent our culture guy. A retired history professor. He called it "ethically ambiguous". But there have been quite a few letters complaining about it. Although most of those who wrote in probably only went to see the exhibition because of the incident at the opening.'

'What incident?'

'You really didn't read about this?'

'I really didn't.'

'Well, some guy started shouting that the whole thing was a travesty and threw a jar containing what a lot of people thought was blood at the wall. Actually, it turned out to be ketchup. But I suppose he made his point. He wasn't Japanese, incidentally. An American, though he did his shouting in Japanese. He was arrested, obviously, though there's been nothing since about any charges against him, so maybe the authorities reckon it's best to forget about it.'

'Was Rinzaki at the opening?'

'I don't think so. I looked back at our report on the incident – you see how much effort I go to on your behalf? – and there was no mention of him being there. But – *but* – the American evidently named Rinzaki in his tirade against the exhibition. Exactly what he said isn't clear. But if you made a living out of being ultra-suspicious about everything and everyone – like you do – you'd conclude there might be something between him and Rinzaki, wouldn't you?'

'What can you tell me about the American?'

Funaki pulls out his notebook and flips it open. He peers at his notes and reads out what he's jotted down: 'Daniel Perlman, aged sixty-eight. Runs a bar in Yokosuka, near the US naval base. The Flight Deck. That's all the information the police gave us.'

'Sixty-eight, you say?'

'Yeah.'

'Rinzaki's sixty-six. So, they're the same generation. And since Perlman speaks Japanese I'm guessing he's been here a long time. Probably came over with the occupation forces and stayed on.'

'That's a lot of guessing.'

'It comes with the job.'

'I suppose you'll be paying Perlman's bar a visit in the near future.'

'Maybe.'

'A Japanese private detective in a bar full of American sailors? Sounds like it could end badly.'

'Don't worry. I know what I'm doing.'

'Oh, I'm not worried.' Funaki grins. 'Because I won't be there with you.'

The ketchup-hurling Daniel Perlman is Kodaka's most promising lead yet. He certainly has no other obvious way of penetrating Goro Rinzaki's business activities, which surely hold the key to the large and regular payments made to Rinzaki by Arinobu Jinno. Funaki was right. A visit to the Flight Deck bar is definitely in order.

Kodaka reckons his best chance of learning anything is on a quiet night in the bar trade, which rules out Friday and Saturday. This leaves him with most of the weekend to kill before he can try his luck. Normal people, like those salarymen he pities who fill the subway during rush hour, would relax with their wife and children, or play a round of golf, maybe rent a video. But Kodaka has no wife or children, hates golf and has never mastered the art of forgetting about an ongoing case, so Saturday morning finds him running the gauntlet of the black *uyoku* vans that haunt the streets around Yasukuni-jinja, occupied by sinister men in black suits and sunglasses, the conspicuous lack of sunshine making it obvious that their glasses are being worn purely for symbolic significance.

The shrine itself is a magnificent building, and its immediate surroundings are quite beautiful. Kodaka's observance of Shinto is minimal to the point of virtual non-existence, but he has no objection to Japan's war dead being honoured at the shrine. Both his grandfathers were killed in the service of the Emperor, one in Burma, the other in the Philippines. They had no choice about fighting, but they'd have gone willingly anyway. Their world was very different from his.

Whether they'd have been happy about sharing their enshrine-ment with those convicted of – and in some cases executed for – crimes of extreme barbarity is impossible to say. Matsui, commander of Japanese forces during the Nanking massacre, is one such convicted, executed and solemnly enshrined war crim-inal. Kodaka has always been troubled by the question of what his grandfathers would have done had they been under Matsui's command. Perhaps it's just as well such a question can never be answered.

He heads for the Yushukan, the large white museum building next to the shrine. There are visitors trickling in, but it isn't obvi-ously busy. Kodaka buys his ticket while children gaze wide-eyed at the Zero, still displayed as prominently as he remembered. He checks which room houses the exhibition he's interested in and makes a beeline for it.

Images of the Condemned Dead proclaims its purpose in a leaflet handed to him as he enters the special exhibition gallery: *The presentation of restored film footage relating to various convicted war criminals enshrined at Yasukuni, donated by the Kuraikagami Film Corporation, drawing on the archives of the Magunichudo company, the restoration having been undertaken for purely historical reasons and the cost having been entirely borne by Kuraikagami.*

The disclaimer fails to convince Kodaka. He studies the large photographs on display of the subjects of the films: fuzzy ghosts of a vanished era, posing proudly in their bemedalled uniforms, gazing into an imagined and ultimately unrealized future in which the Japanese empire straddled most of east Asia and the western Pacific, brushing off all challenges to the supremacy of the Emperor.

Beneath the photographs are captions setting out in dispassionate detail the crimes for which the subjects were executed or imprisoned: variations on themes of torture, rape, murder and pillage – the predictable catalogue of wartime horrors.

Kodaka approaches one of the displays and presses a button to start the accompanying film. He dons the earphones supplied to listen to a commentary on the film. It's much as Funaki said it would be. The subject, who died during a twenty-year prison sentence for torturing prisoners in the Dutch East Indies, served as a regional commander in Korea before the war. The filmed material relates to his activities organizing relief for the victims of flooding, overseeing the construction of a railway line and inspecting troops at various locations. He emerges as some kind of general benefactor, unrecognizable as his later self.

The film ends. Kodaka removes the earphones. A small, smiling man wearing a lanyard identifying him as a museum guide stops as he's walking slowly past. 'Are you finding the exhibition . . . informative?' he asks.

'I'm finding it confusing,' Kodaka replies.

'Ah. That is actually quite a common reaction. But, you see, the filmed material is simply what we have. It is not designed with a purpose or a conclusion in mind. It is an archive showing you the kind of work the subjects were engaged in – the range of their activities – before the war came. It illustrates how the empire was run. And the sort of people who ran it.'

'War criminals, in this case.'

'That is what they became. According to those who judged them. Some would see it as victors' justice. Opinions vary.'

'Were you on duty the day the exhibition opened? I gather there was . . . an incident.'

'Ah yes. Most unfortunate. And yes, I was here.'

'An American threw . . . ketchup . . . at the wall?'

'That is correct. In a jar that smashed and . . . scattered broken glass and red gloop everywhere. A real mess.'

'According to the report I read, he shouted something . . . in Japanese.'

'He did.'

'Do you remember what it was?'

'Yes. It was a little odd, actually. I mean, you might expect an American to hold a grudge against some of the subjects. Particularly if he served in the war, which he looked old enough to have done. You know, maybe he actually fought in the same action as one of these men? But he seemed less angry with them than he was with the company that supplied the films.'

'Kuraikagami?'

'Yes. Specifically, the company's chairman.'

'Rinzaki?'

The guide looks surprised. 'That is his name, yes.'

'What did the American say about him?'

'Oh, he was very abusive. And very loud. He seemed disappointed that Rinzaki wasn't in the gallery. Maybe he was hoping to confront him. Still, there were quite a lot of people who heard what he said. He accused Rinzaki of trying to rewrite history. "But I'm not going to let him get away with it." Those were his words, as I recall. And: "We should be told about Rinzaki's crimes as well. He paid for this with blood money." Blood money. A strange phrase to use, I thought.'

'Did he explain it?'

'No. He didn't say anything more. That was when he threw the jar. There.' The guide points to an adjacent stretch of wall. 'You'd never know, would you? The painters did an excellent job.'

Kodaka is confident he's on to something significant where Daniel Perlman is concerned. His performance at Yushukan suggests he won't need much encouragement to expand on whatever he has against Goro Rinzaki. A man with a grudge is a man with information.

And information is what Kodaka needs.

The following evening, he takes the train down to Yokosuka. He was in a school party that visited the US naval base more than twenty years ago, but can recall little beyond his awe at the sheer size of the aircraft carrier they were taken aboard.

The Flight Deck is located at the naval base end of Dobuita-dori. A prominently displayed Stars and Stripes, Dolly Parton on audio and signs promising Budweiser and burgers make no appeal to a Japanese clientele. There are some Japanese customers, even so, but they're all female, a lot younger than Kodaka and in the company of large American men.

Also Japanese are the young, female sailor-suited waiting staff, one of whom greets him with a brittle politeness that seems to say 'What are you doing here?' He heads past her to the bar, enquires hopefully if there's any Japanese beer – indeed, any beer other than Budweiser – and is served a Sapporo by a bemusingly elegant Japanese woman who appears to preside over the establishment. She has dark hair, a fine-boned face on which Kodaka feels he can read weariness as well as irony and a voice like warm syrup. Many a sailor, he would guess, has poured out his sorrows to her over the years she's worked there.

Photographs displayed behind the bar suggest those years have amounted to several decades. They carry her smiling likeness from youth into late middle age, often on the arm of a man Kodaka assumes must be Daniel Perlman – squat, barrel-chested and forever check-shirted. His hair, which was always short, has thinned into a white dusting as he's aged. His face has become ever more lined, probably because of the cigarette he's usually to be seen smoking. His omnipresent grin doesn't quite disguise the volatile temper he gave way to on his visit to Yushukan.

Kodaka is happy to concede Perlman found a beautiful Japanese bride. She smiles as she enquires if he'd like a glass with his beer and he accepts the offer, also with a smile.

'How long have you run this place?' he asks disingenuously.

'I do not run it,' she replies. 'My husband does.'

'Ah. Of course. Would he be . . . Daniel Perlman?'

Her smile stiffens. 'You know his name?'

'I'm hoping to speak to him, actually.'

'What about?'

'Goro Rinzaki. I think . . . we might be able to help each other.'

She raises her chin and gives him a long, appraising look. 'I would like you to finish your beer and leave.'

'I am sorry. I didn't mean to—'

'Please just leave. There is nothing for you here.'

'Isn't that for your husband to say?'

'*I* am saying it.'

'It's just—'

There's a splash of light from a room behind the bar as a folding door opens and closes. Daniel Perlman, looking a few years older than his most recent photograph and sporting a scar on his brow that eluded the camera, hoves into view and gives Kodaka a glare. 'This guy bothering you, Nonoka?' he asks in English.

The only reply Nonoka gives is to close her eyes for a couple

of seconds. It appears she's resigned to whatever is about to follow. 'I'm not trying to bother anyone,' Kodaka says, breaking
into his serviceable but far from fluent English.

'Saw you on the CCTV,' growls Perlman, who doesn't look
convinced by Kodaka's denial. 'You'll allow me to know when
my wife's bothered by a customer.'

'He's here about Rinzaki,' says Nonoka, glancing round at her
husband. 'I told you, Dan, didn't I?'

What she told Dan and when Kodaka can only guess. Perlman
is still staring hard at him. 'Who are you and what's your interest
in Rinzaki?' he asks, resting his large, gnarled hands on the bar.

'Kodaka. Private investigator.' Prevarication is obviously not
going to get him anywhere. He proffers his card, which Perlman
makes no move to pick up. 'I'm interested . . . in Rinzaki's finances.'

'His company's share price is public information. Nothing
more I can tell you.'

'After what happened . . . at Yushukan . . . I doubt that.'

'Who are you working for?'

'I work . . . confidentially.'

'I bet you do.'

'You said he paid for the exhibition with blood money. What
did you mean?'

'I meant what I said. And I said what I meant.'

'Could we . . . talk a little?'

'What for?'

'Maybe we can . . . help each other.'

Nonoka lays her hand gently on Perlman's meaty forearm.
'Please, Dan,' she murmurs.

He looks down at Kodaka's card and fingers it. 'How do I
know you're not working for Rinzaki, Mr Kodaka? You could be
trying to find out what I have on him.'

'I *am* trying to do that. But I'm not working for him. If I
was . . . I wouldn't tell you about the secret bank account he

operates.' Kodaka gives Perlman a moment for that to sink in, then adds, 'Still sure you don't want to talk to me?'

Perlman runs a hand thoughtfully over his jaw. Then he says, 'No harm talking, I guess.' He ignores his wife's despondent sigh. She lets go of his arm. 'But that doesn't mean I trust you. Understood?'

Kodaka nods. 'Understood.'

The lack of custom means it's not difficult to find a table where privacy is assured. It's also a long way from the bar, which means Nonoka can't listen to what's said, though the withering look she gives Kodaka when she delivers whisky for her husband and another beer for him suggests she already fears the worst on that account. Kodaka has managed to draw Perlman out and she knows what that's likely to lead to.

But Perlman isn't going to give something for nothing. 'Which bank does Rinzaki hold this account at?' is his opening gambit.

'Mizunuma.'

'Under his own name?'

'No.'

'How'd you find out he operates the account, then?'

'Digging. It's what I do.'

'And who are you digging *for*?'

'I can't tell you that.'

'Give me a clue.'

'My client wants to know why a relative who died not long ago was regularly paying large sums of money into that account.'

'So, your client's dead relative was being blackmailed by Rinzaki, was he?'

'You're saying it was blackmail money?'

'I guess so. I've never come up with a better explanation for his pot of gold. He and Braxton were mining one rich seam, that's certain.'

'Braxton?'

Perlman takes a sip of whisky and lights a Marlboro cigarette. The rasp in his voice is well-seasoned. 'We'll have to cast back a ways to put Braxton in the picture. Back to the war. You remember? The one you lost?'

'I was born sixteen years *after* the war ended, Perlman-san.'

'Lucky you. I joined the Marines when I was seventeen, back end of forty-four. I was in time to see some action on Okinawa in June of forty-five. And to see a lot of good boys killed there. Truly brutal stuff. You have no idea. No one who wasn't there has. After the surrender, I wound up in Tokyo, running errands and filing memos for Captain, later Major, Clyde Braxton. He was attached to the Economic and Scientific section of SCAP – Supreme Command, Allied Powers. You're probably too young to know much about your country's post-war history, aren't you, son?'

Kodaka chooses not to challenge the observation, though he reckons he knows enough. According to his father, who was fourteen when the war ended, most of Tokyo was a cinder waste-land in 1945. The years after, the years of the American occupation, which lasted until 1952, were long and lean and above all hungry, with hundreds of the homeless sheltering in the tunnels of Ueno station and black markets springing up every-where. Kodaka senior recalled frequent visits to the biggest of them, Ameya Yokocho, in search of American sweets and choc-olate, for which he had a craving beyond endurance – or so he claimed. The Americans occupied the only parts of the centre that had survived the bombing intact and General MacArthur ruled as a second emperor (the one with the power) from his headquarters in the Daiichi Insurance Building. Japan's revival after the Americans left – its much-vaunted economic miracle, from which Kodaka himself benefited as a child of the 1960s – was a phenomenon his father never ceased to wonder at. 'So different,' he would murmur in awe. 'So different.'

'SCAP ran everything,' Perlman continues. 'We pulled your nation back together again. We gave you penicillin, for Christ's sake. Anyhow, right from the start there were Japanese who knew the best place to be was as close to us as they could get. Rinzaki was one of those. Officers lived high on the hog. Braxton got himself a requisitioned house in Azabu and servants to go with it. Rinzaki was his . . . house boy, I guess you'd call him. Later he started showing up at the office, assisting Braxton with all kinds of things he had no call to be involved in. That's when I started to smell a rat. The ESS supervised all Japanese companies. We said who could do business and who couldn't. Well, some of Braxton's decisions started to look . . . suspect.'

'You think he was taking bribes?'

'Has to have been. There was a move to break up the big conglomerates. It was official policy. They were seen as part of the imperial past. But exceptions were made. Deals were done. And I began to realize Braxton was in on most of them, using Rinzaki as some kind of go-between. There was a lot of money being made by those two. How else do you think Rinzaki could start his own company when he was barely out of his teens? Come to that, how else could Braxton buy himself so much prime vine-growing land in California when he left the army and shipped home?'

'I don't know, Perlman-san. But all this was . . . a long time ago.' And couldn't – to Kodaka's satisfaction – explain Arinobu Jinno's longstanding payments to Rinzaki.

'Because it was a long time ago doesn't mean I intend to forget it.' Perlman jabs his cigarette at Kodaka for emphasis. 'Everything goes back to that time. Where Rinzaki has his studio, out at Chofu, that was requisitioned military land. And then, hey presto, it was the property of the Kuraikagami Film Corporation. How d'you explain that?'

Kodaka shrugs. 'I don't. Like you say, deals were done. But commercial corruption – if it happened – isn't blood money, is it?'

'Oh, there was blood. Lieutenant Thwaites, CIS – the Civil Intelligence Section. He started investigating Braxton's activities. Didn't get far, though. Found at the bottom of a dry dock on the base here, with his head staved in. Now, did that happen because he fell – or before he was dropped? It was officially ruled an accidental death. Not in my book, son. Thwaites was murdered.'

'But you have no proof?'

Perlman stubs out his cigarette and takes a slug of whisky. 'Not what you'd call proof, no. Just . . . certainty. And . . . guilt, I guess. Because it was actually me who put Thwaites on to them. And that got him killed. The way Rinzaki looked at me after that told me clear as day he *knew* what I'd done and was enjoying letting me sweat on whether they'd come for me as well one day. But they never did. Maybe they knew they had me where they wanted me. I kept my head down from then on. I wanted to go home in one piece when the time came. Though ironically, thanks to Nonoka, I never did go home. She's my rock. And she always knows best. Maybe I should have listened to her about the exhibition. Maybe I should just have left well alone. But Rinzaki posing as some kind of cultural patron stuck in my craw. And what's his game with these dead war criminals anyway? Trying to rehabilitate your country's past, is he? Well, why don't we start with *his* past?'

It's not enough. It's not close to enough. Kodaka is disappointed. He hoped for more from Perlman. However underhand Rinzaki's activities may have been during the Occupation they don't – they can't – explain his arrangement with Arinobu Jinno. 'You've followed Rinzaki's career closely, Perlman-san?'

'Hard not to. Remember *Princess Quest*?'

Kodaka dimly recalls an anime film of that name – maybe a series of them – that was hugely popular with girls in their early teens ten or fifteen years ago. 'Kind of,' is as far as he'll go.

'Well, if you had a daughter who was twelve when the first

film came out, you'd remember it all right. Not to mention *Princess Quest Two, Three* and *Four.* Though thank the good Lord Itsuko had grown out of it by the time *Four* came along. They were Kuraikagami productions. You can imagine how paying for Itsuko to see them made me feel.'

'You have a daughter, Perlman-san?'

'Yeah. She's a jewel, she really is.'

'Does Rinzaki have children?'

'Not as far as I know. Been too busy making money. Or milking other people for it. He has a fancy house in landscaped grounds up near Chichibu. You know, real traditional Japanese architecture? I hiked up there once and couldn't get much more than a glimpse. My impression, though? More of a palace than a house. It dripped money.'

So, Rinzaki has a nice house in the country. It's not a crime. Perlman sounds jealous and resentful of his success. And maybe that's all there is to it. 'What about Braxton?' Kodaka asks, expecting, in truth, to learn little of value. 'Do you know what he's done with his life?'

'Made a big name for himself in the wine world. That plus lucrative investments in Californian real estate turned him into a multi-millionaire. But, since you mention children ... it hasn't been plain sailing for Clyde Braxton on the family front. I skim the *Herald Tribune* once a week or so, just to stay in touch with the old country. Well, a while back I spotted a piece about Braxton. Written up as a real public-spirited guy, as you'd expect, not the greedy schemer he truthfully is. He had a son, Grant, not long after returning to the States. Grant's expected to take over the reins of the business when Clyde retires, though why he hasn't retired already I don't know. He must be pushing eighty. Anyhow, you remember the earthquake in San Francisco in eighty-nine?'

Kodaka nods. He remembers, though what he remembers is an event much less devastating than the Kobe quake. It was in

America, though, so naturally it commanded a lot of the world's attention.

'Nothing like as bad as Kobe,' Perlman continues, echoing Kodaka's thought. 'But there were dozens killed when a double-deck flyover on the freeway collapsed. And three of the fatalities were Grant Braxton's wife, son and daughter. A real tragedy.'

'It sounds . . . terrible.'

'You bet.' Perlman stares thoughtfully into his whisky. 'Sins of the fathers, I guess.'

'Was the *Herald Tribune* article about their deaths?'

'Only in part.' Perlman stares some more, then drains his glass. 'Tell you what. I've got the clipping, so I'll run you off a copy on my Xerox.'

'There's no—' But it's useless to protest. Perlman is already on his feet and striding away towards his office behind the bar. Kodaka is going to see the article whether he wants to or not.

Nonoka seizes the opportunity of her husband's absence to hurry over to their table. 'You want another beer, Kodaka-san?'

'Ah, no. I will leave soon, I think.'

'Because Dan has given you nothing to work with. Is that how it is?'

'He has told me what he suspects. But . . .'

'He has no proof. Of any of it. Which is why . . . I would like him to drop it, to forget Goro Rinzaki and Clyde Braxton and what he thinks they did.'

'It may be too late for that.'

'You could help him to forget it, Kodaka-san.'

'Forgive me, but if he can give me any useful information then I am obliged, on behalf of my client—'

'He can't.' She bends forward, bringing her face close to his. 'But by saving Dan from himself you would place me in your debt.'

Kodaka is unsure what she means. 'I have no wish to put you in a difficult position,' he says uncertainly.

80

'I would be putting myself in it. And I see no difficulty. I am offering to give you my assistance if you need it at some time in the future, in circumstances neither of us can foresee. That may be more valuable to you than wringing further accusations against Rinzaki from my husband.'

Kodaka glances past her. 'He's coming back.'

She straightens up and takes a step away from the table. 'Think about it,' she murmurs.

And, almost involuntarily, he replies, 'I will.'

2022

WADA HAD INDEED HEARD OF THE KOBE SENSITIVE, THOUGH IT WAS
a surprise to hear Taro Yamato mention her. She had no obvious
connection with the disappearances of Daiju Endo and Manjiro
Nagata. In fact, nothing had been heard from or about her in
more than twenty-five years. It was back in 1995 that the press
and public had become briefly obsessed with the woman who'd
phoned in warnings of the Kobe earthquake that struck on January 17th, warnings that had gone unheeded, essentially because
it was believed no one could forecast an earthquake. But in this
case, someone had.

It felt strange to Wada to be reminded of events from early
1995. Everything from that period felt strange to her, because it
seemed to belong to the memory and experiences of someone
other than herself. Two months after the Kobe quake, on March
20th, her husband Tomohiko became one of the many victims of
the Aum Shinrikyo cult's sarin gas attack on the Tokyo subway.
Umiko lost Hiko that day, even though he actually spent twelve
years in a coma before dying. And she lost herself as well. The
person she became was stronger, more self-contained and self-
reliant. The person she became was Wada.

After the Tohoku earthquake and tsunami of 2011 and the near-cataclysm of meltdown at the Fukushima Daiichi nuclear power plant, there were some references in the media to the semi-legendary Kobe Sensitive. '*Where was she when we needed her?*' was the gist of them, although Wada suspected a warning would no more have been heeded in 2011 than it was in 1995. For whatever reason, the Kobe Sensitive had remained silent then, as she had since. She was a more or less forgotten figure now.

But she was not forgotten by Taro Yamato. 'I've heard of her, of course,' said Wada. 'What has she to do with this?'

Yamato kept his voice low as he replied. 'When the tsunami struck Fukushima, Endo and I were both working at the Kantei.'

'You were in the Prime Minister's office?'

'Yes. Lowly placed functionaries. But we all joined the effort to decide what to do and how to cope. Those first few days were just . . . crazy. The possibilities were worse than we ever told the public.'

Wada had always assumed that to be the case, though, as it happened, she wasn't in Tokyo when the earthquake happened on March 11th, or in the days following. Kodaka had sent her to Osaka to follow up a lead in a corruption case he was too busy to attend to himself. As it was, the lead had led nowhere, but it had taken the better part of a week to establish that to Kodaka's satisfaction. Wada had watched the explosion of one of the units at Fukushima Daiichi on NTV in her hotel room and had feared the worst at that point. But the worst hadn't come to pass. Relative calm awaited her in Tokyo on her return.

'Meltdown was a real possibility after we lost Unit Three,' Yamato went on. '*Total* meltdown, I mean. You know? China Syndrome. We could have been looking at Chernobyl times ten. Tokyo finished. March fifteenth was the day of reckoning. We got a report that radiation levels in Tokyo were a hundred times normal. There were rumours the Americans were going to start evacuating their citizens and were distributing iodine tablets in the meantime. But . . . we held it together. We came through. No China Syndrome. No Chernobyl times ten. And Tokyo . . . is still here.'

'We all remember those times, Yamato-san. But where does the Kobe Sensitive come into the story?'

'I'm coming to that. After the earthquake, the Kantei lifts were out of action, which meant getting from the crisis management centre in the basement to the Prime Minister's office and secretariat involved climbing five flights of stairs. Mobile phones couldn't be used in the basement, so there were quite a few urgent messages relayed by note or word of mouth. Endo got the job of runner for those because he was just about the fittest guy in the building. He used to run marathons. So, he saw more of the Prime Minister and his immediate team than most during that period. Anyhow, when Kan resigned the premiership later in the year and Noda came in, Endo was transferred to the Ministry of Agriculture. It was basically a demotion, even though he kept his grade. I don't know why it happened. Neither did he, as far as I could tell. We used to meet for a drink once a week, though that changed when he got married. His wife didn't like me. The marriage didn't last long, as it turned out. Endo was never the same after that. Something changed in him. I saw less of him. He became . . . I don't know exactly how to put it . . . insecure. Yes, that's it. Insecure. Like he wasn't quite anchored to his life any more. I started worrying about his . . . state of mind. And apparently I was right to.'

Yamato's voice sank lower still, so that now he was literally whispering. Wada had to strain to hear his words. 'Last year, around the time of the tenth anniversary of the tsunami, I heard he'd been fired. From the civil service? That should be impossible, barring gross misconduct. I tried to contact him, but he wouldn't return my calls. Eventually, word went round about

84

what had happened. Nothing official, you understand. In fact, very *un*official. The story was that Endo had contacted the media with a claim that the Kantei had been phoned by the Kobe Sensitive the day before the quake and warned something really bad was going to happen soon, probably within twenty-four hours, under the ocean off the coast of Tohoku, and that they should prepare for a massive tsunami.'

'She said that?' Wada was taken aback. If it was true, the Kobe Sensitive had predicted not just one major earthquake but two; and been ignored both times.

'That was the story. And when I did succeed in speaking to Endo, he didn't deny it.'

'But the media never reported it.'

'No. They didn't. Public disclosure was instantly banned under the State Secrecy Law. It was made known to the Kantei press club that Endo was mentally ill and suffering from delusions. He'd been given indefinite sick leave, apparently, rather than dismissed, though that's not what he told me. Either way, the message went out that he was deranged, no such phone call had ever been received and publicizing his claim would be deeply unpatriotic – not to mention criminal. The story was crushed.'

That didn't surprise Wada. She knew from previous experience that the provision of press club rooms at government offices, police headquarters and large corporations bred a cosy relationship between the media and their hosts, with information fed exclusively but selectively into the public domain. Or, as in this case, not fed at all.

'There was a problem with the cover story, though. According to Endo, he had a recording of the phone call, which he'd kept despite being told to destroy it by the aide who actually took the call. Well, all calls *were* recorded, so it makes sense there'd be one, *if* the call was ever made. The instruction was given to Endo in the general panic while he was acting as runner between the fifth floor and the basement of the Kantei. "Get the tapes that are in my desk drawer and burn them. Here's the key to the drawer." That's my understanding of what Endo was told to do by the aide. But he didn't do it. Suspicious about the reason for such an order, he listened to the recording – and kept it. Until his conscience couldn't allow him to keep silent about it any longer.'

'Did he give the media a copy of the recording?'

'No. He told me he was still awaiting certain . . . guarantees . . . before he did that.'

'Guarantees of what?'

'Freedom from prosecution, I suppose. Though whoever he spoke to would have needed the same.'

'Did you ask to hear it?'

'Of course. But he said he didn't have it. He'd handed it over to someone else for safekeeping, in case there was an attempt to steal it from his apartment.'

'Who did he think might make such an attempt?'

'Who do you think?'

The PSIA – the Public Security Intelligence Agency – was the obvious candidate. If they'd thought Endo was in possession of such a recording, they might well have tried to recover it. 'Who did he hand it over to?'

'A woman who'd . . . entered his life recently.'

'A lover?'

'I don't think so.' There was something – a nuance, a flicker of his expression – that made Wada suspect there was a very particular reason for Yamato's doubt on the point. It was a possibility that would explain the lengths he'd gone to on his friend's behalf, though, in the final analysis, why exactly he'd done so hardly mattered.

'Do you know her name?'

'He never said. But . . . the last time I saw him . . . he seemed to have lost faith in her. Something had happened . . . that made him suspect she wasn't on his side.'

'But you don't know what?'

'Manjiro Nagata's the only clue I have to that. Endo asked me to use my civil service clearance to trawl the intelligence records I had access to in search of information about him. He didn't explain why. He just said . . . there was a lot riding on it.'

'What did you find?'

'Merely the basics. Manjiro Nagata is the nephew of Teruki Jinno, chairman of Jinno Construction. Divorced, no children. Used to work for the company, but now . . . unemployed. But you know this, of course, since his father, Teruki Jinno's brother-in-law, is your client.'

'You found nothing else?'

'Nothing. He's a blank sheet of paper. As I would have told Endo, if I'd ever seen him again. But that was when Endo stopped answering my calls and texts. When I went to his apartment, it was in darkness. A neighbour told me he hadn't been there in weeks. One thing, though. The neighbour said Endo had been spending a lot of money in recent months. A brand new sports car, expensive clothes, that kind of thing. Well, that's . . . way out of character. Endo's no . . . hedonist. Besides, where would he get the money? He'd been on sick leave for more than six months by then, so he'd have gone down to half pay.'

'It sounds to me as if someone else was paying him.'

'That's how it sounds to me too. But . . . who? And to do what?'

'You have no idea?'

'None. That's why I tried to contact Manjiro Nagata. He seemed the only person who might be able to tell me anything. But . . . he didn't respond to calls and emails and letters. He didn't even answer his door. And now . . . you tell me he also has disappeared.'

'It seems so.'

'I stopped looking for Endo because there was nowhere else to look. And . . .'

'Something else?'

Yamato needed to wrestle with his cautious nature before he went any further. But further, in the end, he did go. 'My departmental boss called me in just before New Year and . . . advised me . . . not to involve myself in Endo's problems. He knew we'd been friends, you see. And I guessed, though he didn't say so, that Endo's apartment had been kept under surveillance and I'd been recorded as visiting him. "If your career is to continue on an upward course," he said, "I would strongly recommend that you leave the Endo matter entirely alone." Which is as explicit a warning-off as you are likely to receive in the civil service.'

'Which you have not heeded. Since you are here, talking to me about him.'

'I am not here. And I am not talking to you. That must be understood between us.' Yamato looked at her directly. 'We can have no further contact, Wada-san. This is as far as I can go to help Endo.'

'Don't you want me to tell you . . . if I find him?'

Yamato closed his eyes for a moment and nodded soulfully. 'Of course. In that event.' When he opened his eyes. Wada was surprised to notice he appeared to be on the verge of tears. 'I hope he is safe, truly I do. But I greatly fear he is not. And if that is what you find . . . if you learn the worst, I mean . . . then I think I do not want you to tell me.'

On her way home to her apartment in Ogikubo, Wada had to change train lines at Shinjuku, where the Saturday afternoon crush was formidable, even if marginally less formidable than during the weekday rush hour. She sat on a bench on the Chuo line platform, waiting patiently for a train with a level of occupancy she judged she could tolerate, while she turned over in her mind the tangled mystery which the Manjiro Nagata case had become.

A group of fashionably dressed young women, all clutching well-filled Isetan department store carrier bags, formed a giggling cordon around her, their faces blue-lit by their phones, which commanded their rapt attention. Wada was aware they hadn't registered her existence, let alone her close proximity. She was invisible to them: a small, plainly dressed, middle-aged woman with no distinguishing features. Her appearance was a guarantee of total anonymity in a city where thousands like her could be seen – and ignored – at every turn.

Oddly, however, she was evidently not invisible to an old man in a shabby anorak, baggy trousers and scuffed trainers who was sitting on the next bench along. His occasional glances in her direction could have been explained by the micro-miniskirts worn by the giggling young women, until they boarded the next train, which neither Wada nor the old man did. And the glances continued.

Some minutes and a couple more crammed trains passed. Then, at last, a train arrived on which there was at least a reasonable amount of standing room. Wada boarded and moved down the carriage for the ride to Ogikubo. The old man also boarded. He took one of the empty seats in the priority area for the elderly and disabled, allowing Wada to take the measure of him from where she was wedged between other standing passengers.

He looked to be in his seventies. He had lank grey hair and a wispy beard framing a round, sagging face. But his eyes were bright and alert. There was no slack-mouthed vagueness about him. He appeared calm . . . and watchful. And Wada was beginning to suspect it was *her* he was watching.

As the journey proceeded, the crush on the train thinned slightly. The old man began studying his phone. A moment came as passengers were entering and leaving the train at Nakano when Wada had the impression he took a picture on his phone in which she might appear. The evidence was beginning to mount towards a disturbing conclusion.

Before considering the question of who he was and why he might be following her, losing him before she arrived home was crucial and misleading him about the area she lived in would be wise. The opportunity came one stop short of Ogikubo. It would be a longer walk to her apartment, but that wasn't a problem. The train eased to a halt. Passengers disembarked and she edged towards the door at the opposite end of the carriage from the old man, but stayed on as newcomers boarded. Then, just as the station jingle sounded for the doors closing, she darted forwards and stepped adroitly out onto the platform, leaving the old man where he was.

She wondered if she'd see him looking over his shoulder at her as the train pulled out, but he didn't turn round. That could mean he wasn't really following her at all, of course. Or it could mean he was too smart to let her catch him out. Wada would have liked to believe the first of those explanations. But she knew wishful thinking was a fool's game.

If he had been following her, it seemed likely he'd picked up her trail at her rendezvous with Yamato, which suggested he'd been following him before switching to her. It was a complication, no question. But it was also evidence – if she was right – that this wasn't a case about nothing much. It was very far from that.

Back at her apartment, she looked out of the window and studied the people drifting along the footpath that ran along the bank of the Zenpukuji river below her. They were innocent Saturday afternoon wanderers. No one was loitering and gazing up at the apartment block. She'd lost the tail – at least for now. She was relieved to think her home remained the haven of order and tranquillity she so valued.

Which left her free to pursue the clues Yamato had supplied. He'd given her precious little to go on except a second missing person, but at least she could follow up his suggestion that the media had been blocked from reporting Endo's claims about the Kobe Sensitive.

She'd inherited her contact in the newspaper world from Kodaka, who'd been a friend of his since schooldays. Joji Funaki hadn't hidden his astonishment when he discovered Wada intended to carry on the business after Kodaka's death and had made some blatantly sexist suggestions about what she'd be wiser doing instead. On the last occasion they'd spoken he hadn't gone so far as to withdraw those suggestions, but at least he hadn't repeated them.

She was surprised she didn't have to leave a message when she phoned him. He answered straight away. 'Is that really you, Wada?' (He'd acquired from Kodaka the habit of addressing her simply as Wada.)

'I apologize for interrupting your weekend, Funaki-san.'

'I'm a journalist. I don't get weekends. But I do get a couple of hours on a Saturday afternoon to watch rugby on the television. Luckily for you, the match has just finished. Otherwise I'd have ignored your call.'

'Did your team win?'

'Can't you tell from my cheery manner?'

'No. It may be that you hide disappointment well.'

'Is that a joke?'

'I didn't intend it to be.'

'OK, I give in. What can I do for you?'

'I think you may be able to help me with a case. And in return . . .'

'I get a world exclusive on a story, yes?'

'Maybe.'

'What do you want to know?'

'I prefer not to discuss it on the phone. Can we meet?'

'When did you have in mind?'

'As soon as possible.'

'Can't it wait?'

'Not really.'

'Because?'

'Because it is important. Perhaps extremely important.'

'But is it extremely important to my newspaper's readers?'

'Have you ever known me to waste your time, Funaki-san?'

Funaki sighed audibly. 'Nobody would call you a time-waster. Dakka always praised your efficiency.' She sensed his reference to Kodaka was as close as he cared to come to saying he'd only answered her call because she'd once worked for his old friend.

'So, can we meet? This evening, perhaps?'

'OK. All right. I'll do anything for a scoop – or the promise of one.' Strictly speaking, she decided not to point out, she hadn't promised him anything. 'My wife escaped the rugby by going to visit our daughter in Hachioji. I'm driving out there to collect her in a couple of hours. If I left an hour early – in about an hour from now, say . . .'

'Will you take Expressway Four?'

'Probably.'

'I could wait for you at Takaido station, by the post office.'

'Takaido it is, then. I'll see you there.'

Wada threaded her way south to Takaido along quiet residential streets as evening settled in. She'd definitely thrown off the tail, which gave her only limited satisfaction. It would be back at some point, she felt certain.

She didn't have to wait long by the post office south of Takaido station. Funaki pulled up in his battered old Nissan, which appeared to be emitting illegal levels of exhaust fumes, something she refrained from mentioning as she climbed in.

Funaki turned off the main road as soon as they were past the station and parked in the deep shadow of a line of trees. He lit a cigarette and pressed a button to lower Wada's window before she could raise an objection; though, since the smoke masked the lingering smell of instant noodles, she hadn't been about to. 'How have you been, Wada?' he asked.

'I have been busy, Funaki-san.'

'Which is how you like to be, I'd guess.'

'I cannot deny it. I enjoy being busy. As do you, I suspect.'

'Less so, as I grow older. I was sixty last year. Maybe I should retire.'

'And do what?'

She sensed a shrug on his part. 'See more of my grandchildren?'

'You could have gone to Hachioji with your wife today if you had wanted to do that.'

'Ah, but there was the rugby.'

'Of course.'

'So, why don't you come to the point? What do you want from me?'

'Confirmation that the Kantei put a block on a story this time last year about the Kobe Sensitive.'

'Wow.'

'What is wrong?'

'I think I was expecting something less . . . sensational.'

'Sorry. The case I'm working on has taken me to this matter. I did not choose it.'

'What's the case?'

'Missing person.'

'Who you aren't going to name?'

93

'No. But now there is a second missing person in the case. And a third, I suppose, if you count the Kobe Sensitive.'

'Maybe you could name the second missing person. If that's not asking too much.' Funaki never stinted on irony. Wada wondered if it was a journalistic trait. She didn't know enough journalists to judge. In fact, she only really knew one. And here he was.

'Daiju Endo, civil servant. Worked in the Kantei during the tsunami.'

'Endo? That could have been the name.'

'So, you know what I'm talking about?'

'Up to a point.'

'And what is that point, Funaki-san?'

He took a long draw on his cigarette. Wada saw the smoke plume against the windscreen, tinged yellow by the gleam of a distant streetlamp. 'Delicate. That is what it is, Wada. I don't regularly attend Kantei press club briefings. I leave that to our politics team. But word went round, like you say, this time last year, when the tenth anniversary of the tsunami was coming up. I did a few stories about that, so there was some overlap. A civil servant contacted the dailies – *Yomiuri, Mainichi, Sankei*, as well as us – with a claim that the Kobe Sensitive had phoned the Kantei the day before the earthquake and warned them of a tsunami on the Tohoku coast. Just like she'd phoned them the day before the Kobe quake, sixteen years earlier. Except in 1995 we had a tape to prove the call happened, whereas this time, though the civil servant said a recording existed, it never surfaced. And we were briefed that he was basically out of his mind and on long-term sick leave. So . . .'

'The story never ran?'

'It never did. Because it wasn't a story. There was no proof. Just . . . one man's ravings.'

'The reporters who spoke to him thought he was mad, did they?'

'Ah . . . I don't know. But . . . when the government tells you he is and what he says sounds crazy to those of us who *aren't* crazy . . .'

'The normal club rules apply. Embargo the story in exchange for political gossip to fill the newspaper. Right?'

'You have a gift for making standard procedure sound sinister, Wada, you know that? You think we'd ever get to know *anything* about what's going on inside the Kantei if we printed every wild claim that came our way?'

'Did anyone check whether Endo really is mentally ill?'

'Not sure. Like I say, it wasn't my story. But there'd have been some work done before the embargo was agreed. So . . . maybe.'

'Could you ask whoever did that work how much they found out?'

'I could. But why would I? Apart from because you want me to, I mean.'

'Because Daiju Endo is missing. And perhaps because he really does have a recording of the call that was never supposed to have happened.'

Funaki half-lowered the window on his side and flicked his cigarette butt out into the darkness, then lit a second cigarette while Wada eyed a spark that had fallen from the first into the footwell in front of him. There was a brief smell of singed fibre from the carpet, but no general conflagration followed. What did follow was a period of silence, which she deemed it best not to break.

Eventually, Funaki said, 'Are you seriously suggesting the Kobe Sensitive warned the government of *both* of the two most serious earthquakes in our lifetimes?'

'I don't know, Funaki-san. But isn't the possibility worth investigating? It sounds to me like the kind of thing that sells newspapers.'

'Or the kind of thing that ends a newspaperman's career.'

Funaki sighed. 'What's the connection between Endo and missing person number one?'

'Not sure. But there *is* a connection.'

'I get to know who he is if there turns out to be something to this, right?'

'I would hope so. But obviously—'

'You'd have to clear it with your client?'

'Yes. But . . . even so, I might be able to arrange for you to meet a former colleague of Endo's . . . if it would help.'

'*Might* be able to?'

'I cannot guarantee it.'

'Seems to me you can't guarantee anything. Except taking as much information as I give you and saying thanks a lot.'

'I will be grateful, Funaki-san, for whatever you can tell me. And that is not a small thing.'

'No. Amazingly, I believe you about that. The gratitude of Umiko Wada is not easily won. Or easily lost, I hope.' Funaki took a few reflective puffs on his cigarette. 'OK, then. I'll ask a few questions. And we'll see what answers I get.'

Wada was pleased Funaki had agreed to ask questions of his colleagues, but she didn't expect instant results. Sunday loomed on the horizon, as it tended to do once a week. It was the day she caught up with shopping, washing, cleaning and other necessities. Leisure didn't feature prominently in her life.

As it happened, this Sunday started slightly differently, with a phone call to her brother. She couldn't reasonably delay telling Haruto what she'd learnt about their mother's lodger and, after giving some consideration to editing out of her account Tago's expulsion from sumo for complicity in match-throwing, decided to give Haruto the unvarnished truth as far as she knew it.

At the same time, she did her best not to sound an alarmist

96

note, especially since there was nothing Haruto could do to influence Haha any more than she could. That she knew from plentiful experience. She felt reasonably certain Tago wasn't trying to exploit their mother and had decided the situation would just have to be tolerated. He'd probably move out in due course anyway.

Perhaps predictably, Haruto was less sanguine. 'You're saying this guy is a convicted criminal?'

'No. The Sumo Association isn't a court of law.'

'But he took bribes?'

'They concluded he had. He denies it.'

'Well, he would, wouldn't he?'

'He probably would if he was guilty. He certainly would if he was innocent.'

'What's that supposed to mean?'

'It means I don't know if he took bribes or not. Mother's convinced he didn't. I . . . have an open mind.'

'Do you have an open mind about whether he might steal her savings?'

'I don't think he poses any kind of threat to her.'

'I'm not happy about this, Umiko.'

'Neither am I. But unless you have some solution to propose, I suggest we try to live with it. I'm the one who has to meet him from time to time, after all.'

Haruto couldn't dispute that and sensibly didn't try. 'You'll let me know immediately, won't you, if . . . we need to take action?'

If anybody needed to take action, it would be Wada, not Haruto, as they both knew. And as to what form of action that might be . . . 'Yes, Haruto, of course. In that event . . . I'll let you know.'

By the afternoon, Wada's chores had mostly been done. The weather was fine and unseasonably warm. She went for a walk along the riverside to Wadabori Park, striding out briskly and savouring the clarity of the air. She tried to forget about Seiji Tago altogether, though forgetting about the Nagata case wasn't even worth attempting. It was on her mind all the time.

The afternoon was waning when she got back to her apartment block. She felt pleasantly tired and was looking forward to an evening of peaceful solitude.

An unannounced visit from her mother wasn't something she regarded as remotely likely – or welcome, come to that. Yet there Haha was, waiting for her by the entrance to the block. She was seated on a low wall, eating chocolate-coated Pocky sticks from a paper bag.

'Where have you been?' she instantly demanded. 'I've been here nearly an hour.'

Wada suspected Haha was exaggerating about the length of her wait, but didn't challenge the point. 'I went for a walk.'

'I thought you'd be at home.'

'I wasn't expecting you.'

'You'd probably have made some excuse if I'd told you I was coming.'

There seemed no end to the implied rebukes. 'Shall we go up?' Wada asked.

'If it's not . . . inconvenient.'

Haha's visit, it would have been fair to say, hadn't started well.

Matters improved marginally once they were inside the apartment. Haha managed to refrain from criticizing Wada's tea-making technique, a point of contention between them in the past. Wada wondered if she'd come because of a phone call from Haruto, although it had been her understanding he wasn't planning to contact his mother after they'd spoken. In the event, though, Haha didn't mention Haruto.

Her lodger, on the other hand, cropped up almost immediately. And it was Haha who raised the subject.

'Maybe I should have made an appointment and come to your office,' she said bafflingly as she sipped her tea.

'I'm pleased to see you, Mother,' Wada said, which both of them knew wasn't completely true. 'Though I am surprised. You hardly ever come here. And we saw each other only yesterday.'

'Ah. It's about yesterday I've come.'

'Well, I'm sorry I had to leave early.'

'You left because of your work.'

'I did.'

'Which set me thinking . . . about Tago-san.'

'What about him?'

'Well, I think it would be good for him . . . to have his name cleared.'

'I'm sure it would.'

'Which is why . . . I want to hire you . . . to do that.'

'You . . . want to hire me?'

'Yes. You're a private detective, Umiko. Which is just what I need. A private detective, to investigate the case the Sumo Association brought against Tago-san and find the holes in it. I want you to prove he didn't take any bribes and didn't deserve to be banned just because he was Igarashi's *tsukebito*.'

Wada couldn't quite believe what she'd just heard. There was no doubt Haha meant what she'd said, though. Wada knew her mother's tight-lipped, frowning expression of old. She'd made her mind up. And changing her mind about anything was next to impossible.

'Then the association will have to reinstate him,' Haha went on. 'He'll have his professional pride restored to him. Maybe he'll go back into the sport, maybe not. But he'll be able to decide for himself what he wants to do.'

Wada found it hard to know where to begin listing her objections. She opted in the end for the difficulty of working for a relative. 'I really don't think having my own mother as a client . . . would be appropriate.'

'Would you rather I hired some other private detective?'

No. Emphatically she would not. In fact . . . 'I don't think you should be hiring anyone, Mother. Have you told Tago-san about this?'

'Certainly not. I don't want to raise his hopes in case you fail to exonerate him.'

'Perhaps he'd rather there was no investigation of the matter at all.'

'He might say that, of course, *if* he was asked. But that's because he's such a considerate person. He wouldn't want to put me to any expense or trouble on his account.'

'If that's how you think he'd feel, why not respect his wishes?'

'Because he's innocent. And I want to do whatever I can to prove that.'

'What if he isn't innocent?'

'You've met him, Umiko. You can recognize a pure spirit when you meet one. Don't pretend you can't. Tago-san is a pure spirit. We have to do what we can to give him back his good name.'

Argument on the merits of the idea was clearly futile. Wada fell back on professional sensitivity. 'I wouldn't be happy working for a third party in a case like this, Mother. And you are a third party.'

'That's just a quibble.' Haha was growing vexed. 'What is the point of having a private detective for a daughter if she won't work for me when I need her to?'

'It's really not as simple as that . . .'

'It is to me.'

'Apart from everything else, I know nothing about sumo. Except it's a man's world. No one in the sport would talk to me.'

100

'Nonsense. I know you, Umiko. You never take no for an answer.' If that was true, it occurred to Wada, she'd probably inherited the trait from her mother. 'Besides, most of the people you'll need to talk to aren't in the sport any more. I've made a list of them to save you some time.' Haha flourished a sheet of paper from her handbag and thrust it into Wada's hand. 'There.'

Wada ran her eye down a column of names, recorded in Haha's characteristically tiny writing. She recognized none of them. Beside the names Haha had added a description of their role in the sport: *tsukebito* – Tago's role, as manservant to a senior wrestler; referee; coach; ring announcer; hairdresser; stable mistress. She'd also added notes on where they were now and what they were doing. She'd obviously done a lot of research on the subject. It was impressive in its way – and also worrying. How exactly was Wada going to be able to deflect her from this folly?

'Shinozuka, Tago-san's stable master, was also expelled from the association and has since died,' Haha continued at something of a gallop, prodding the name Asumi Shinozuka on the list as she went. 'That leaves his widow, the stable mistress. As you can see, she runs a *ryokan* in Hakone. No one knows more about what goes on behind the scenes than the stable mistress, so I thought she'd be a good person for you to start with. The *rikishi* confide all sorts of secrets to their stable mistress.'

'Do they?'

'It's common knowledge. She's the closest the *rikishi* have to a mother. And many people confide in their mother, Umiko, hard though you may find that to believe.'

Wada took a calming breath. 'I'm very busy at the moment, Mother. I have a particularly demanding case to deal with. Work on it can't be postponed. I simply don't have time to travel out to Hakone to interview the landlady of a *ryokan*. Or to travel else-where . . . to interview these other people.'

Haha frowned. 'Are you saying I have to go to the back of the queue?'

'Well, this can't be described as urgent, can it? You said Tago-san was expelled from the sport five years ago.'

'Which is far too long for him to bear such shame.'

'Even so . . .'

'I'll pay, you know. Your standard fee. I don't expect you to do this for nothing.'

'It's not a question of money, Mother. I don't want you to pay me. Just . . . wait . . . until my caseload is . . . lighter and . . . then I can look into this for you.'

'When do you think your caseload will be lighter?'

'It's hard to say. The detective business is . . . unpredictable.'

Haha glared at her. She wasn't mollified. And she wasn't remotely convinced. 'You're trying to fob me off.'

'Of course I'm not. Just leave this with me for a while and . . . I'll see what I can do.'

Haha's eyes narrowed. 'All right,' she said grimly. 'I suppose I have to accept that you need to finish other work before moving on to this. But I'm not going to wait indefinitely. I expect to hear you can start on this list . . . within the next couple of weeks. If not . . .' Wada waited anxiously for the pay-off. And it duly came. 'If not, well, I'm sorry, but I'll have to find someone else to take the case on.'

Wada prevailed upon her mother to take a taxi back to Koishi-kawa, although her offer to pre-pay the fare was rejected. They parted on brittle terms, which Wada regretted, although she was also very annoyed at the situation Haha had put her in.

Perfect harmony had existed between Wada and her father. She missed him every day. Relations with her mother, on the other hand, had always been difficult. That, according to her

102

father, was because they were so alike, one of the very few judgements of his that Wada did not accept.

She planned to calm her jangled nerves with a bath and a few pages, chosen at random, of *The Makioka Sisters*. Tanizaki had the gift of placing all life's tribulations, particularly those relating to family relationships, in their proper context. This plan also foundered, however, when she received a late phone call from Joji Funaki, after which Tanizaki no longer suited her mood.

'I did not expect to hear from you before tomorrow, Funaki-san,' she began.

'Sundays can be good for confidential conversations with colleagues away from the office,' he explained. 'You'll want to hear what I've learnt today.'

'Please tell me.'

'Not on the phone. This is deep stuff. Deeper than you think.'

'You wish to meet?'

'I can come to your office tomorrow.'

'What time?'

'It'll have to be late. Six, six thirty.'

'I'll be there.'

'Don't do any more digging into this until we meet. OK?'

'OK.'

Wada heard a female voice in the background. Funaki's wife, she guessed. 'I have to go. See you tomorrow.' With that, he rang off.

Wada would have preferred an early appointment with Funaki. As it was, she'd have to pass most of Monday trying her best not to dwell on the meaning of his words '*Deeper than you think*'.

Still, this at least left her free to delay her journey into the office the following morning and so avoid the rush hour, which not only spared her the usual malodorous crush, but also meant anyone tailing her would be conspicuous. She was confident she'd lost her tail on Saturday. Certainly there'd been no sign of anyone hanging around her apartment block during Sunday. And no one followed her when she walked to Ogikubo station in the morning. Of that she was certain.

She performed a few double-backs in the pedestrian tunnels at Shinjuku to be doubly certain and arrived at the Kono Building satisfied that whoever the old man had been he didn't know where she lived. It seemed probable he didn't know who she was at all. And she intended to keep it that way if she could.

The day passed slowly but not unproductively. There was plenty of paperwork for Wada to catch up with. She applied herself to it diligently, never happier than when imposing order on her records. The evening came. She could sense the building gradually emptying around her.

Then, at 6.20, the call came from the porter in the lobby on the ground floor. She'd already told him she was expecting a visitor around that time. This was just to warn her he was here – and on his way up.

Funaki didn't look as relaxed as he usually did. He was unshaven, and the bags under his eyes were heavier than when they'd met on Saturday. On entering, he ran a hand through his unruly mop of steel-grey hair and glanced around the office, which he hadn't visited since Kodaka's death. 'You haven't changed much,' he said, sounding slightly surprised.

'Why would I change things?' Wada responded. 'They are as I want them to be.'

'Yes. And probably always were. It doesn't smell the same, though. Less cigarette smoke, more . . . jasmine, is it?'

'Perhaps.'

'You're not going to let me smoke, are you?'

'I would prefer you not to. This is my working space.'

'OK. How about a drink, then? Dakka used to keep a bottle of Suntory in the bottom drawer of the filing cabinet.'

'There's still one there.' Wada fetched it and poured a glass for him.

'Not having one yourself?'

'Perhaps I will.'

They sat down either side of her desk with their whiskies. The evening light, slanting through the window behind Wada, didn't flatter her visitor. He looked like a man who hadn't adjusted his lifestyle to match his advancing age. She recognized the type. Kodaka had been just the same.

'What have you found out, Funaki-san?'

He took a bracing swig of whisky. 'Well, I asked questions, as promised. And I got some answers. The embargo on the Endo story went beyond the normal press club protocol. It was made very clear any whisper about it in the press or broadcast media would result in prosecutions under the State Secrecy Law.' This was essentially what Yamato had told her. Clearly, no chances had been taken that anything would leak out. 'No journalist can ignore a threat like that. Which is why all investigation of Endo's claims stopped immediately.'

'Didn't that make your colleagues suspicious?'

'Of course it did. But they're not going to risk getting arrested and imprisoned for the sake of publicizing the claims of somebody who might not even be in his right mind, are they? I wouldn't.'

'Where does that leave Endo?'

'On his own. It's tough, I know. But he must have realized he wouldn't be allowed to say whatever he wanted. If it's true, it's just too embarrassing. It undermines public trust in the government. Besides . . .'

'What?'

'Encouraging people to believe someone like the Kobe Sensitive can actually predict earthquakes? Does that lead anywhere good?'

'I don't know. Do you?'

Funaki swallowed some more whisky. Wada topped up his glass. It looked as if she was going to need to buy another bottle tomorrow. 'You said Endo's gone missing, right?' Funaki continued.

'So I've been told.'

'Along with someone else connected to him?'

'Yes.'

'It's beginning to sound like a cover-up.'

'It is, isn't it?'

'Even so, I'm afraid there's nothing I can do about it.'

'That is . . . disappointing.' She let her gaze rest on him.

'But there may be something *you* can do about it.'

'And what would that be, Funaki-san?'

'Listen to me, Wada.' He looked her in the eye. 'Before we go into this any further, here's my advice. Close your case. Tell your client you can't find whoever it is you're looking for. Send in your bill and move on to . . . the next divorce or whatever crops up.'

'What if I'm not willing to do that?'

'You're too stubborn for your own good. You know that, don't you?'

'A private detective needs to be stubborn. Kodaka-san often said so.'

'And where did that get him?'

Dead was where it had got him. But Wada ignored the point. She wasn't ready to let this case go. As Funaki surely knew.

'Sorry. I didn't mean to . . .' Funaki flapped his hand mournfully. They both wished Kodaka was still there, presiding over the detective agency that bore his name. But he wasn't. It was all down to Wada now. 'OK. This is what I can tell you. Before the story was shut down, we put a tail on Endo: a freelancer called Sekiyama. Well, he came cheap and it meant none of our competitors would spot what we were doing. Sekiyama sent in his first report the same day as the press club meeting where the story was embargoed. So, obviously, it was never followed up. We told Sekiyama to drop it.'

'And did he?'

'Maybe, maybe not. The point is that in his report he described tailing Endo on a drive out of Tokyo a couple of days prior. Endo was easy to follow, apparently. He drove a bright yellow Toyota sports car. Anyway, he travelled to an isolated villa in the hills southeast of Chichibu. A handsome property, evidently, with lots of security. Electronic gates, high walls, CCTV, that kind of thing. He stayed an hour or so, then drove back to Tokyo. Sekiyama planned to find out who lived there, but then we called him off, so we have no idea who the property belongs to. Or why Endo went there.'

'But you know where it is? I mean, you could tell me where it is?'

Funaki nodded. 'It's marked on maps of the area as Matsuda Sanso, so Matsuda – whoever he is – might be the owner. Or he might be a former owner.'

'Have you brought one of these ... maps ... with you, Funaki-san?'

'Yes. I have.'

'Could I see it?'

'Before you do, I should tell you about Sekiyama.'

'Perhaps I ought to speak to him. In case he continued with his investigations.'

'You can't do that.'

'Why not?'

Funaki hesitated. He appeared to be struggling over his choice of words. Eventually, the words came. 'Sekiyama threw himself under a subway train three weeks after he put in his report.'

'He committed suicide?'

'So the police concluded. But the platform was crowded. Maybe he . . . lost his footing. They tell me he was a drinker.'

'There is another possibility, of course.'

'Yes. There is.' Funaki sipped his whisky uneasily. 'Still want to see that map?'

1995

Veteran wine-maker determined to turn family tragedy into legacy to protect Californians of the future

Clyde Braxton admits to making the bulk of his fortune in the real estate business, but he is better known in California for the vineyards he owns in the Sonoma valley north of San Francisco, famed for their delicate Pinot Noirs. Now, however, he is taking a bold step into a whole other area of activity – seismological research.

At 81, Braxton should by rights be enjoying his retirement, but although he leaves a lot of the day-to-day running of Braxton Winery to be overseen by his son Grant, all thoughts of a quiet life were banished five years ago when the family was hit by a terrible tragedy. Grant Braxton's wife, Anna Collins Braxton, aged 31, and their two children, John (7) and Alice (4), were killed during the Loma Prieta earthquake of October 17, 1989, when a double-deck portion of the Nimitz Freeway in Oakland collapsed and the car they were travelling in on the lower level was crushed.

'We were devastated by their loss,' says Clyde Braxton, 'but eventually I came to the conclusion that the only way to make any sense of their deaths was to do everything in my power to prevent such things happening again.' That is the guiding purpose of the seismological research institute he has built and staffed near Santa Rosa, carving land out of his wine holdings to accommodate what he aims to turn into a world centre for expertise in earthquake prediction, mitigation and understanding. The Braxton Institute of Seismological Research and Innovation (BISRI) is now up and running, funded on a level he believes will ensure that 'if there are answers to be found to the questions we have about earthquakes, they will be found here'.

Highly qualified seismologists, recruited from all over the US and from other countries with a history of seismic activity – Italy, Japan, Mexico, New Zealand and elsewhere – are now settling in to the strikingly well-appointed premises, designed to withstand the most extreme seismic shocks. The Institute's main building, set in an extensive parkland campus, has been admired for its architecture as well as its earthquake-proofing, but Braxton is adamant that the greatest strength of the centre he has established is the combined expertise of the people he has brought together there. 'We know what causes earthquakes. And we know the damage that can result, in lives lost and cities laid waste. Their greatest danger lies in their total unpredictability. My hope is that we can change that and start to gain insights into exactly when the worst shocks are likely to happen. An effective early warning system would have saved the lives of my daughter-in-law and grandchildren. At BISRI we're going to be doing our level best – we're going to be doing whatever it takes, in fact – to save the lives of others who may not even have been born yet.'

It is a noble ambition, but also a challenging one. Earthquake prediction has a chequered past littered with fraudsters and crackpots eager to capitalize on the insecurity of anyone who lives in an earthquake zone. Since its establishment in 1977 the federally-funded National Earthquake Hazard Reduction Program (NEHRP) has been striving to make progress in the science of earthquake prediction, without any measurable success. 'Earthquake lights' in the sky that might be precursory electromagnetic discharges, lunar tidal stresses, disturbances in animal behaviour and the presentiments of so-called 'earthquake sensitives' have all been investigated without reaching definitive conclusions. And memories are still raw of the hoopla and hysteria surrounding the New Madrid earthquake predicted by controversial climatologist Iben Browning for December 3, 1990 that failed to happen on cue – and hasn't happened since.

The northern section of the San Andreas fault last broke in 1906, the central section in 1857 and the southern section around the year 1690. Another break in the southern section, the fabled Big One hitting Los Angeles, is long overdue – and, as stress within the fault continues to build, is potentially getting bigger all the time. Whether it will happen next week, next year or a hundred years from now is unknown and, in the opinion of many, unknowable. But Clyde Braxton isn't having any of that. 'Science will crack this,' he reckons. And he's putting his money where his mouth is.

'I may not live to see the breakthrough,' he says, 'but I'm sure it'll happen.' His optimism is inspiring and his dedication to the task impossible not to admire. If Californians are going to get a jump on the next Big One, surely the chances are that it will happen at the institute Clyde Braxton has founded.

Only time will tell.

*

Kodaka read the *Herald Tribune* article on the train back to Tokyo, but he has to read it again at his apartment, checking various definitions in his English dictionary, before he's sure he's gleaned everything he can from it. Even then, there doesn't appear to be much that's of any use to him. It may console Dan Perlman to know Clyde Braxton and his family have been touched by tragedy, but Goro Rinzaki doesn't seem to have had anything to do with it. And Goro Rinzaki is the man Kodaka is meant to be investigating.

So far, all he has to show for his efforts are loose ends and stray hints that Rinzaki is a man with a lot of secrets. One of them, clearly, is his connection with the late Arinobu Jinno, but Kodaka is no closer to discovering what that connection is. Blackmail, according to Perlman. But without evidence – and he doesn't have a shred – that's just a theory. And theories don't close cases.

After sleeping on the problem, Kodaka decides it's time to press Teruki Jinno for information about his father that might give some substance to the blackmail notion. He calls him on his home number, but, early though it is, the chairman of Jinno Construction has already left for work. Kodaka heads for his office and calls Jinno again from there, using the other number he's been given.

Jinno's secretary puts Kodaka through without delay. She's clearly been told to treat calls from him as urgent.

'Kodaka-san?' Teruki Jinno sounds calm but expectant.

'I have made some progress, Jinno-san. But I need to speak to you . . . regarding what I have so far uncovered.'

'Very well. The sooner the better, as far as I am concerned.'

'When can you see me?'

'My diary is full all this week. But I suppose it does not actually matter where we meet.'

'Not to me.'

'And perhaps it would be best if you did not come to my office.

So . . . I am about to set off for a site visit. A big project we have underway in Nagai. Could you join me there?'

'I suppose . . . I could.'

'You will come by train?'

'Probably.'

'Well, the site is very close to the station. You will see the company name on the cranes. Let us say . . . one hour and a half from now. Yes?'

'Yes. OK. I'll be there.'

Nagai is on one of the busier lines out of Tokyo Station, so Kodaka has no difficulty getting there in time for his meeting with Jinno. In fact, he's early and, sighting the cranes blazoned with the company name as his train draws into the station, he pauses for coffee and a couple of cigarettes after disembarking. He exchanges a few sympathetic words with the cafe owner about the noise of drilling in the middle distance after noting a faint ripple in the surface of his coffee and a tinkling of his spoon against the handle of his cup. 'A new mall,' the cafe owner explains. 'Bigger than the last one. Like everything.'

Big the site certainly is, a fenced-off arena of rearing walls and unfinished floors, with machinery rumbling within and lorries manoeuvring in and out of the mud-slicked entrance. Raising his collar against the drizzle, Kodaka heads for the site office.

A phone call is made and clearance given for him to be admitted. He's fitted out with a hard hat and a high-vis jacket, then escorted to a platform lift that rises from the loading bay up through the scaffolding surrounding what the signs proclaim will one day be the Blue Sky Centre. Kodaka wonders if drizzle will be banned after it opens.

The lift stops at the sixth level, where he's met by an eager young man with a clipboard who mutters about the need to be careful, then leads him round one corner of the multi-cornered structure and points him towards a broad, open terrace that appears to be complete and which commands a panoramic view of the sprawl of Greater Tokyo.

Teruki Jinno is waiting for him there, dressed in the same uniform of hard hat and high-vis jacket, although the elegant cut of his suit trousers and the gleam of his brogues hint at his status. He is leaning against the railings, with the city stretching away behind him, talking into a mobile phone. There is no one with him. Kodaka has the immediate impression he's made sure their conversation cannot be overheard – indeed, cannot be overlooked – by anyone.

Jinno ends the call and greets Kodaka as he approaches with a cautious inclination of the head. 'I apologize for the weather, Kodaka-san,' he says with a tight little smile.

Kodaka bows. 'Occupational hazard, I imagine, Jinno-san. This is . . .' he waves a hand at the portion of the site immediately below them, where a torrent of cement is currently pouring from a massive mixer into a void within the structure, 'quite something.'

'Shopping and entertainment combined: boutiques, department stores, cafes, restaurants, a bowling alley and a six-screen multiplex cinema. It's the future. And the future has to be built, before it is rebuilt again a couple of decades down the road. Construction, you see, is a business that never stops growing.'

'I expect you're glad your father went into it.'

'I have always been grateful to my father for his choice of business. And for the example he set me. Although as to this mystery I asked you to investigate, well, I am not grateful for that.'

'Of course not.'

'But you have something to report?'

'Well, I can tell you who operates the Soroban account.'

'You have a name?'

114

'Yes. Goro Rinzaki.'

It is immediately obvious that Jinno knows the name – and the man. He flinches with shock. And then he frowns deeply. 'Rinzaki?'

'Yes. Chairman of the Kuraikagami Film Corporation.'

'I am aware of who he is and what he is, Kodaka-san. Indeed, his company is part of the consortium that has contracted us to build the Blue Sky Centre. Kuraikagami will have a substantial stake in the cinema side of the operation.'

'So, you are . . . in business with him.'

'In view of the number of projects we have on our books and the breadth of Rinzaki's own interests, that is not in itself surprising. But what you are telling me . . . *is* surprising.'

'I thought it might be.'

'You are sure of this?'

'There's no room for doubt.'

'It was Goro Rinzaki my father was paying?'

'It seems so. Which I suppose at least explains the duration of the arrangement. Rinzaki founded his company two years after the payments began.'

'And now we know how he capitalized it.' Jinno shakes his head disbelievingly. 'This is . . . monstrous. I have sat in meetings with Rinzaki. I have had dinner with him. And he has smiled at me and bowed and said nice, obliging things. But all along . . . we were subsidizing his activities.' His disbelief is beginning to give way to anger.

'Yes. The question is . . .'

'Why did my father pay him? And go on paying him . . . for nearly fifty years? What was the money *for*?'

'Blackmail is the obvious answer, Jinno-san.'

'*Blackmail?*'

'I cannot otherwise account for it. Unless there was . . . some close personal bond between your father and Rinzaki.'

115

Jinno stares at Kodaka incredulously. 'There was no bond beyond normal commercial relations.'

'In that case . . .'

'Nor am I aware of anything that could have exposed my father to blackmail. He was a man of impeccable character and strict probity. He did not gamble. He did not womanize. He barely drank. And his business ethics were irreproachable.'

'You are sure, Jinno-san, there was not something that could have given Rinzaki a hold over him?'

'I am as sure as any man's son can be. There is nothing in my father's life or career that could explain this. You have replaced one mystery with another.'

'For that I am sorry. But . . .'

'You have done what I asked of you. There is nothing to apologize for. The question I must now consider is what to do with this information.'

'The payments have ceased, Jinno-san. And no demands have been made of you. You could let the matter rest.'

'Half a billion yen is a lot to let rest.' Jinno sighs. 'What would you advise . . . if I wished to pursue this?'

'Well, let us assume only Rinzaki knows the truth now your father is no longer with us. To establish what that truth is, without alerting him, would be challenging in the extreme. It would require a lengthy effort to penetrate his personal affairs and it's my impression he is a man who guards his secrets well.'

'All of that is true.'

'Perhaps, therefore . . .' Kodaka hesitates. An idea has formed, or rather half-formed, in his mind. But he worries he might come to regret voicing it.

'Yes?'

'Well, I wonder if the best way to approach the problem . . . might be to lure Rinzaki into . . . betraying himself.'

'How would you do that?'

'Given your association with him on this project, do you think he might agree to . . . do you a favour?'

'What kind of favour?'

'Answer some questions for a researcher hired by a foreign historian who's working on a book about the post-war Japanese film industry.'

'You would be the researcher, Kodaka-san?'

'I would.'

'And the historian?'

'American. Or French, maybe. Someone Rinzaki's unlikely to check up on.'

'And how do you know me?'

'I'm the friend of a cousin of yours.'

Jinno looks as if he's taking the idea seriously, which Kodaka isn't sure is good news. But it's too late to withdraw the suggestion. 'That could work. I think he would probably agree to meet you. He would not want to refuse a request from me. But what would you be able to learn from him?'

'I don't know. But his answers to my questions might lead us towards the truth. And if not . . .'

'We would have lost nothing.'

'Exactly.'

'But to pass yourself off as a researcher you would have to display some knowledge of the Japanese film industry.'

'I am used to passing myself off as someone I am not. It's part of my job.'

Jinno nods decisively. 'Then I will approach Rinzaki and ask for the favour. If he agrees . . .'

'I will prepare myself accordingly.'

'Very well. Yes. I approve.' Jinno doesn't smile. But he does look mildly encouraged.

Though whether he should be Kodaka is far from sure.

*

On the train back to Tokyo Station, Kodaka gives further thought to his proposal, which he's beginning to regret. If he's to learn anything from Rinzaki, he'll have to give a good impression of being a student of Japanese film history. All he could currently say on the subject is that he started dreaming of following his father into the private detective business after watching various screen adaptations of the Yokomizo whodunnit novels he devoured as a teenager. Since he's not planning to volunteer the fact that he's a private detective, that sounds like a bad way to introduce himself.

There's always the chance, of course, that Rinzaki will turn Jinno down, but Kodaka suspects otherwise and reluctantly concludes he's going to have to read his way into the role. He leaves the train at Akihabara and switches to the subway, destination the bookshop district of Jimbocho, specifically the academic section of Kitazawa Shoten.

When he reaches his office several hours later, after an early lunch, he's already waded through the first few chapters of the doorstop-sized *Personalities and Practices in Japanese Cinema from the Occupation to the Video Age* and he's checked the index for references to Rinzaki. There are several, but they merely detail the titles and relative popularity of his films. He's evidently maintained a low profile in the business, despite his success and longevity.

Already, though, Kodaka has come to appreciate the many and different challenges Rinzaki has had to confront in his career, particularly at its outset, when every film produced required the approval of the Americans. And he's begun to see just how valuable the assistance of a SCAP insider like Clyde Braxton is likely to have been at that time. Where Arinobu Jinno fits in he can't imagine, but at least he'll be able to ask a few intelligent questions if and when the time comes.

*

118

Kodaka has read another few chapters between unrelated calls by the end of the day. He's preparing to head home, probably via a bar, when a call comes in. From Teruki Jinno.

'I have spoken to Rinzaki, Kodaka-san. He raised no objection to meeting you. He seemed, in fact, eager to cooperate. He was as courteous as ever, though now, of course, his courtesy leaves a sour taste in my mouth. But . . . so far so good.'

'When does he want to see me?'

'He suggested Wednesday. Which he will be spending at his country residence. He said it would be more . . . comfortable . . . if you met him there.' The country residence has to be the '*fancy house in landscaped grounds up near Chichibu*' described by Dan Perlman. It seems Kodaka is destined to get a closer look at it than Perlman managed. 'You are to phone his secretary to confirm the arrangements and be given directions.'

'I'll do that.'

'I wish you luck.'

'You should wish us both luck, Jinno-san. This is probably our best chance of learning the truth.'

'Be sure you make the most of it, then.'

'I intend to.'

Rinzaki has given them this chance, without even knowing he has done so. Kodaka cannot predict the outcome. His profession does not deal in certainties. But he has an advantage now. And he means to press it.

2022

WADA HAD DECIDED BEFORE FUNAKI LEFT HER OFFICE ON MONDAY evening – though she did not explicitly tell him so – that she would travel to Matsuda Sanso the following day. There was no certainty she would learn anything of value from the trip. But she hoped for answers to some questions. What kind of a place was it? Who owned it? And what could have drawn Daiju Endo there?

The map Funaki had given her showed a wooded landscape in hilly country south-east of Chichibu. Some hiking trails were marked, in addition to roads and railway lines. Matsuda Sanso was merely a tiny square indicating a large structure, with no details of the extent of the property. Hiking trails that ran close to it looked as if they could be reached from one of the stops on the Agano to Chichibu railway line and that was how Wada intended to approach.

Trains to Agano ran from Ikebukuro, so Wada had planned to go straight there in the morning, only to discover when she came to load her shoulder-bag that she'd left her binoculars at the office. They were likely to prove invaluable for a surveillance exercise, so there was nothing for it but to divert to Nihombashi first.

She hurried into the lobby of the Kono Building, intent on fetching the binoculars and heading for Ikebukuro as quickly as possible, but something in the posture of the woman sitting on the visitors' couch by the reception desk told her it wasn't going to be as straightforward as that.

'Umiko Wada?' the woman queried. She was quite tall, elegantly dressed, perhaps over-dressed for the weather, in a long fur coat. Her hair was immaculately styled. She had fine features weathered by age, arched eyebrows, a well-defined jawline and an unwavering gaze. She looked as if she was used to being given whatever she wanted. She also looked as if she considered Wada's highly practical outfit – complete, on this occasion, with walking boots – a serious lapse of taste.

'I am Wada, yes.'

'I am Hisako Jinno. Formerly Nagata.'

They exchanged brittle bows. The porter was watching them closely whilst trying to look as if he wasn't. Wada suspected he would be relieved when Hisako Jinno vacated the lobby.

'I would like to speak to you in private, Wada-san.'

'Please come up to my office. We can talk there.'

'Thank you.'

They entered the lift. Wada wondered whether to attempt any kind of conversation during the ride up, but this question was resolved by the late arrival, just as the doors began to slide shut, of a man who worked in the insurance brokerage one floor above Wada's office. The three ascended in silence, while Wada pondered what Hisako Jinno might want with her. Nothing good, she surmised.

They exited the lift and walked to the door with *Kodaka*

121

Detective Agency inscribed in the frosted glass panel in some-what old-fashioned calligraphy. She unlocked it and went in, switching on the lights. Jinno followed.

'You work alone?' she asked, glancing around the room, from which half-open doors led to three further rooms.

'I do.'

'What happened to Kodaka?'

'He died.'

A small expression of regret would have been appropriate. Jinno ventured none. 'Yet you continued.'

'Yes.'

'A strange choice.'

'It did not seem strange to me.'

'It would to most people.'

'Will you come into my office?' Wada pointed towards the door that led to it. 'May I offer you tea?'

'No tea.' The refusal bordered on the curt.

'Can I take your coat?'

'I will not be here long.' Jinno strode ahead into Wada's office and went straight to the window. 'You have a striking view,' she added as Wada caught up with her.

'I am glad you like it.'

'Such premises as these, in Nihombashi, for one woman . . .' Jinno shook her head in what seemed to be disapproval, though whether of what she perceived as Wada's extravagance or her effrontery was unclear. She turned and looked directly at Wada. 'I am told my estranged husband, Fumito Nagata, has engaged you to look for our son, Manjiro. You can confirm this?'

'I do not discuss my clients with third parties, Jinno-san.'

'But you do not deny it.'

'As I say, I do not—'

'Enough.' Jinno raised her hand imperiously. 'We both know

that what I have said is true. You will gain nothing by pretending otherwise.'

'What will I lose?'

Jinno nodded, as if reaching a not unexpected conclusion. 'I see you have a proud nature, Wada-san. Perhaps it is necessary for a woman undertaking the kind of work you do. You are unmarried, of course?'

'I am a widow.'

'Would your late husband . . . approve of your occupation?'

'That must be between me and my late husband.'

'Very well. Let us speak clearly. I am aware of the enquiries you have made on Fumito's behalf. He did not consult me before engaging your services. If he had, I would have advised him not to.'

'Do you know where your son is, Jinno-san?'

'Yes. I do.' There was little doubt in Wada's mind that this was true. Hisako Jinno knew exactly where her son was. She always had. 'Do you?'

'You know I don't. His apartment in Musashino is unoccupied, though elaborate methods have been employed to create the impression that he still lives there.'

'Is that so?'

'You know it is.'

'And what else do you think you have . . . established?'

'I have no intention of discussing the case further with you, Jinno-san. To do so would be unethical.'

'I will tell you now what you need to know,' said Jinno in the steadiest of tones. 'The problems Manjiro has experienced in his life have mostly been caused by the harmful influence of my estranged husband. Manjiro has recently decided, with my agreement and understanding, to cut himself off from his father, to have no contact with him and to make it impossible to be contacted *by* him. This may explain why certain . . . measures . . .

have been taken in relation to the apartment in Musashino. As Manjiro's mother, I mean to ensure that his . . . complete separation . . . from his father continues . . . for as long as it needs to.'

'I see.' In reality, Wada did not see. Fumito Nagata was no ogre. However bad a father he might have been, these tactics were extreme. Suspiciously so.

'I must ask you to cease your enquiries and to allow Manjiro to lead his life as he wishes – without interference from his father.'

'Perhaps you should explain that to his father.'

'I do not propose to have any direct communication with Fumito. Like Manjiro, I find I thrive on his absence from my life. I do not object to you telling Fumito that Manjiro is well and living as he wishes to. That should supply him with as much reassurance as he requires – or is entitled to.'

'I doubt he will find such reassurance sufficient.'

'Simply tell him to leave the matter alone, Wada-san. You understand?'

Wada bowed. 'I will tell him.'

'And you will stop looking for Manjiro?'

Wada looked Jinno in the eye. 'I will do what my client instructs me to do.'

'That is not good enough.'

'It will have to be.'

'There are legal steps I can take against you if you force me to do so.'

Were there? Wada thought not. Jinno was surely bluffing. And two could play that game. 'I suppose Manjiro could apply for an order forbidding his father from contacting or seeking to contact him, by which I would be bound. But I doubt he would succeed in such an application. And I imagine the process would be very time-consuming. I see no part for you to play in it.'

Jinno stepped away from the window and closed on Wada. 'It

would be unwise to make an enemy of me,' she said, speaking slowly to emphasize her meaning.

'I am not trying to make an enemy of you. But I cannot allow you to interfere in my dealings with a client. I will pass your message on to him. That is all I can do to meet your demands.'

'I hope for your sake it is enough – and that we do not have occasion to meet again.'

So saying, Jinno swept past Wada, who felt the soft brush of fur against her wrist as she went. She did not close the door behind her as she left the offices of the Kodaka Detective Agency. She simply left.

Wada waited until she heard the ping of the lift arriving before going out to close the door herself. Then she went back into her office and took a position by the window, from which she would be able to see her visitor leave the building.

In Wada's assessment, Hisako Jinno had made a serious tactical error. She should have presented herself as a distraught and doting mother, desperate to protect her son from the father who'd ruined his life. She should have pleaded for Wada's help. Instead, she'd haughtily demanded Wada's cooperation as if by right.

And that more or less guaranteed she wouldn't get it.

The landline phone rang on Wada's desk as she stood there, but, reluctant to leave the window, she decided to let the call go to answerphone. Below, she saw a dark limousine move slowly into position by the entrance to the Kono Building. A chauffeur slipped out of the driver's seat and hurried round to open the rear door. Wada had no doubt he was there to collect Jinno.

Then she heard Fumito Nagata's voice on the answerphone speaker. 'Wada-san, this is Nagata. It is rather important I speak to you. Could you—'

Wada darted to the desk and picked up the phone. 'Nagata-san?'

'Ah, you are there. Good.'

'There have been developments in the case, Nagata-san.' She moved back to the window, letting the flex of the phone pay out behind her. Looking down, she saw Hisako Jinno glide into view. 'I was planning to brief you tomorrow, after following up a lead today.'

'I did not call to chase you for a report, Wada-san. I wanted to warn you . . . about an . . . unfortunate development.'

'Does it concern your estranged wife?' The estranged wife slid elegantly into the back seat of the limousine as Wada watched.

'How did you know?' Nagata sounded surprised.

'She just left here.'

There was silence at the other end of the line, as Nagata absorbed the news. The chauffeur closed the passenger door and hurried round to the offside. Then Nagata said, 'I am sorry, Wada-san. Hisako has . . . an overbearing nature.'

'I noticed.' The driver climbed into the limousine.

'I only learnt this morning that, thanks to my stupidity, she has discovered I have engaged your services.'

'May I ask how she discovered that?' The limousine pulled away.

'I confided in an old friend that I was planning to hire a private detective to find Manjiro. And I named the agency I was planning to use. My friend told his wife about it. She is still in touch with Hisako. It seems she thought Hisako ought to know. Again, I am sorry.'

'Your apology is appreciated, Nagata-san. I would advise you not to confide in *anyone* about this.'

'That lesson I have now learned. What did Hisako say to you?'

'She knows where Manjiro is. Not at the apartment in Musashino, I should explain. I soon established that he no longer lives there, though he maintains a pretence of doing so. Or more likely she maintains the pretence on his behalf. She says he is well. She also says he does not wish to have any contact with you.

She demanded I stop looking for him. She also wants me to urge you to stop looking as well.'

There was another lengthy silence, broken by Nagata sighing audibly. 'This is monstrous,' he murmured dolefully.

'I am not urging you to stop, Nagata-san. And I will only stop if you instruct me to.'

'I cannot understand this. What has she made Manjiro believe about me?'

'I am not sure she has poisoned his mind against you at all.'

'You're not?'

'I do not believe his disappearance has anything to do with you. The claim that he is determined to have no contact with you is . . . a smokescreen.'

'A smokescreen for what?'

'Other people are looking for your son. I believe he has fled from them, not you. But why – or to do what – I do not yet know. I hope to learn more soon.'

'You will continue, then?'

'If you want me to.'

'Of course I do. But Hisako can be very intimidating. She always assumes people will do what she wants them to do. And that's generally how it turns out.'

'Not with me, Nagata-san.'

'I am relieved to hear it. Though I'm sure you experienced . . . the force of her personality.'

'I did.'

'I used to wonder if she really was Japanese, you know. She behaves more like a . . . Chinese empress. Technically, of course, she could be Chinese.'

'How so?'

'Well, she was adopted. Arinobu Jinno and his wife could not have children of their own. Teruki and Hisako were both adopted. But they were of Japanese birth, I'm sure. Arinobu

127

would not have taken foreign blood into the family. Still, sometimes I . . . wonder.'

'That is interesting.'

'Is it?'

'Everything is, in a case such as this.'

'If you—'

'I must end this call, Nagata-san. I have a busy day ahead of
me. I will report soon.'

'Thank you. Most especially, thank you for not giving up.'

'There is no need to thank me for that. Giving up is not in my
nature.'

Pausing only to grab the binoculars and squeeze them into her
bag, Wada headed out. She was still taking precautions against
being followed, although nothing had happened to arouse suspi-
cions of a tail since the incident on Saturday. Ikebukuro was a
straight run from Tokyo Station on the subway, but she entered
the station via the Yaezu underground arcade and spent some
time drifting between access stairs to the Shinkansen platforms
before she was satisfied no one was following her. Then she made
for the subway.

Two hours later, she found herself alone at a small station on the
Agano to Chichibu railway line, deep in wooded countryside,
loud with the absence of Tokyo's clamour. Beyond birdsong and
the fading rumble of the departing train, she could hear . . .
nothing.

Away to the east was plum blossom viewing country. She knew
this from the *umemi* party that had disembarked at Hanno, where
a coach was waiting for them. It was a cloudy day, so conditions
were hardly perfect, but still they'd come.

As it was, the grey, windless weather could hardly have suited
Wada better. She headed along a signposted path from the

128

station into the woods and started up a winding trail climbing the hill that, according to the map, lay between her and Matsuda Sanso. The name suggested a rich man's rural retreat and certainly seclusion seemed guaranteed in such surroundings. The air was sweet, tinged with sap. There wasn't another human to be seen or heard.

It might have discombobulated many Tokyoites to be in such an isolated spot, but Wada didn't feel any more alone here than when she was surrounded by thousands of her fellow citizens in the heart of the city. Solitude was for her a state of mind. And it was the one she was best suited to.

Half an hour's stiff walking took her over the crest of the hill and part of the way down into the valley beyond, which formed a bowl of less thickly wooded land. Matsuda Sanso wasn't far now, although she could see nothing of it ahead, even with the aid of the binoculars. There was a distant whine of a chainsaw, however, to prove there was at least some human activity in the area.

She pressed on along the trail until it began to lead north, away from Matsuda Sanso. There was nothing for it then but to strike out along a rough path that led deeper into the woods but which seemed to favour the right direction. The going was slower thanks to overgrowths of bramble and fallen tree limbs. She stopped and sat on one such limb to eat a rice cracker. She began to wonder if her trip was actually going to achieve anything. Maybe she was wasting her time. Or maybe not. Kodaka would have said – as he often did – that you only knew if a lead was a dead end when you reached the end. She washed the cracker down with a swig of chilled green tea and set off again.

A few minutes later, as the trees thinned ahead of her on gently falling ground, she stopped. There was something in the middle distance that didn't fit with her surroundings. She checked through the binoculars.

It was a wall – solid yellow-washed masonry, topped with a line of thick bronze tiles. Beyond it the trees had a better-tended look to them and, in the distance, there were stands of more ornamental varieties, blossoming plums among them. She adjusted the focus to maximum range and picked up a long roofline of tiles and decorative ridging. It appeared to end in a gable, above which stood the carved figure of an owl.

Nothing more of the house was visible through the greenery. But this was clearly Matsuda Sanso – the country retreat of a man of substance.

Wada swung back to focus on the wall and tracked it through the binoculars away to the south. She came to a point where its line was broken by a wide gateway, from which a paved road curved out and headed off, she assumed, towards the public road shown on the map, which was how anyone arriving by car would approach the property. There were barns and sheds inside the gate and the adjoining woodland was where the sound of chain-sawing was coming from. It looked as if this was the working entrance to the property, with the main gate further away round the perimeter.

Wada started towards the gate, moving cautiously under the cover of the trees. As yet she'd seen nothing that told her anything of value and what further exploration might reveal was an open question. But it was worth a try.

It became apparent after she'd covered about half the distance between her and the gate that it was standing open, presumably to allow estate vehicles to come and go. She stopped and trained the binoculars on the yard inside the gate, which she now had a better view of.

Facing her across the yard she could see an open-fronted wooden barn, with a tractor and some trailers stored inside. Next to this building was another barn, of much older construction, with a thatched roof and stone walls. One of its two big doors was standing open. She couldn't see any workmen moving around. The yard appeared to be deserted, although she had only a partial view of it, so there could easily be people there who were simply out of sight.

She waited to see if anyone moved into view. No one did. But shapes within the older barn revealed themselves as she did so: another couple of vehicles, stored at the back of the building under a hayloft. They were covered with a single large tarpaulin.

But the tarpaulin wasn't quite large enough. It didn't reach the floor on the right-hand side of one of the vehicles. And that revealed—

Wada caught her breath. It wasn't what she'd expected to see. Not at all.

But there it was.

1995

KODAKA APPROACHES MATSUDA SANSO, DRIVING DIFFIDENTLY IN the car he has hired. The morning is still and fitfully sunny, the air cool, the atmosphere in this hilly district of woods and fields a tranquil contrast with the city he has left behind. But in the tranquillity there is also an element of watchfulness he finds disquieting. He is not on his natural terrain, whereas the man he is going to see self-evidently is, placing Kodaka at a disadvantage even before he arrives.

There is a short stretch of curving drive from the public road to the main gate of the property. The gate itself looks to be of some antiquity, thick timber with copper reinforcements. The walls beside it are also thick, yellowish masonry topped with bronze tiles. On top of each of the gate pillars stands the carved figure of an owl.

There are twentieth-century additions in the form of a surveillance camera and a speakerphone to request entry. Kodaka presses a button and announces himself into the speakerphone. The gates swing slowly open.

He sees a small gatehouse as he drives in. A stockily built man in traditional dress of *hanten* coat and waistcoat regards him

132

impassively from the gatehouse porch. It strikes Kodaka that in a black western suit and sunglasses the man would blend in perfectly with the right-wing loiterers outside Yasukuni-jinja.

Kodaka follows the drive on through landscaped grounds of manicured trees and lawns. He sees a flash of reflected sunlight from the surface of a pond set in a glade of plum trees as he climbs the gentle slope to the terrace of land on which the house is set. He suspects he would find carp in the pond if he stopped to look.

Matsuda Sanso is low-roofed and expansive, an architecturally understated building that appears, viewed across the wide lawn that separates it from the end of the drive, as the residence of someone both discreet and affluent, content to enjoy what he does not need to exhibit. Visitors, Kodaka senses, are few, which makes him either privileged . . . or vulnerable.

He gets out of the car and follows a winding stone path round the lawn towards the villa. As he nears the steps leading up to the entrance, a man moves into view from one of the rooms opening onto the *engawa* that runs the width of the building. He is dressed, like the gatekeeper, in traditional clothes, in this case a dark kimono and striped *hakama* trousers. He is small, thin and narrow-shouldered and is wearing black-rimmed spectacles. He looks to be in his sixties, bald and smooth-skinned, his gaze both amiable and interrogatory. The spectacles give him a passing resemblance to the owls on the gatepost.

'Welcome to Matsuda Sanso, Kodaka-san,' he says, spreading his hands. 'I am Goro Rinzaki.'

'It is an honour to meet you,' says Kodaka. He slips off his shoes and moves onto the polished wooden boards of the *engawa*, feeling slightly discomposed, as perhaps he is meant to, by the contrast between Rinzaki's immaculate attire and his own rumpled western clothes. They exchange bows.

'I was intrigued by your request,' says Rinzaki, smiling warmly. 'Few come to me for insights into the past.'

'You surprise me. Kuraikagami is one of very few film production companies surviving from the Occupation in its original form.'

'We have always been too small for anyone to be interested in swallowing us up. That is the secret of our survival – if we have one.'

Rinzaki is still smiling. Kodaka can't help wondering if his reference to secrets is a tease. There's been something altogether too obliging for comfort about his agreement to this meeting.

'Please come in.' Rinzaki gestures invitingly with his hand and leads the way through half-open shoji into a large, airy reception room. The tatami mats feel yielding enough beneath Kodaka's feet to be new and certainly there is a clear, pure scent of tatami around them.

There is a low table towards one end of the room, with cushions placed on legless chairs either side of the table ready for their use. At the other end of the room is an alcove, adorned very simply with a vase holding reeds and a hanging scroll. On the scroll are two kanji, the work of a skilled calligrapher judging by their sweeping lines and perfectly judged brushwork. One of the kanji means *of long duration*, the other *to go as far as* or *to attain a desired result*. The exact meaning intended by presenting them together eludes Kodaka, though he feels sure they hold a particular significance for his host.

The two men settle at the table, bare but for a small brass bell close to where Rinzaki sits. Kodaka proffers a gift, as etiquette demands – a silk handkerchief, which Rinzaki receives courteously. His smile is still in place, but has assumed to Kodaka's eye a slightly satirical quality, matched by the twinkle in his eyes.

'May I record our conversation, Rinzaki-san?' Kodaka asks.

'I am happy for you to do so.'

'Thank you.' Kodaka places the recorder on the table between them and switches it on.

'Where shall we—' Rinzaki breaks off. 'Ah. Here is our tea.'

A maid appears in Kodaka's field of vision, surprising him somewhat, since he heard no sliding of a door or padding of footsteps to announce her entrance. She is a placid, middle-aged woman dressed in a plain kimono. She delivers the tea and pours their first cups, then withdraws as silently as she arrived.

'You look a little – how can I put this? – ill at ease, Kodaka-san,' says Rinzaki as they sip their tea.

'I think it's been too long since I left the city. There is no . . . noise here. No traffic, no hubbub.'

'It is true. You hear the whirring of the tape in your recorder?' And Kodaka can hear it, now that he listens. 'Concentrate hard enough and you will hear the beating of your heart. I could tell you I come here to be at peace. But actually I come here to be able to concentrate. In Tokyo everything is distraction and nothing is substance.'

'You put it well.'

'I am glad you think so.'

'Did you buy Matsuda Sanso from the original owner? I assume that's who it's named after.'

'No. Matsuda was already deceased . . . when I bought the property. That was in . . . Showa twenty-seven. It was very . . . run down then. I have had a lot of work done here, to produce what you see . . . and feel. But enough of domestic matters. What would your client like to learn from me about our national film industry?'

'Well, as I said a few moments ago, you're notable as a survivor in an industry where survival must often have been difficult, particularly when you started out.'

'It was a very different time from now, certainly. There were more than thirty subjects banned by the CCD – the Americans' censorship department. They were officially called "categories of deletion". I've always been rather fond of that phrase. It sounds

135

so . . . anodyne. Amongst many other things, no reference was permitted to the black market, to relationships between American service personnel and Japanese women, to the food shortages, to homelessness, to the A-bomb. So, choosing a story to film was . . . a delicate undertaking, particularly if it in any way reflected the lives real people were leading at the time. And before you suggest something set in the past – a samurai tale, perhaps – as a solution to the problem, I should mention that glorification of feudalism was also forbidden.' Rinzaki chuckles. 'Actually, as I'm sure you know, the CCD was in the process of being wound up when I started Kuraikagami. That was one of the reasons I decided to take the chance.'

Once again, Kodaka has the disquieting impression that Rinzaki is playing with him. He needs to draw his host on to the sensitive territory of his dealings with Clyde Braxton and Arinobu Jinno. But how? *Personalities and Practices in Japanese Cinema from the Occupation to the Video Age* naturally did not mention Rinzaki's work for Braxton and it's hard to see a way Kodaka can legitimately claim to know about their association. He opts for an indirect approach. 'In my researches, I've been struck by how certain directors coped with the constraints of censorship – Kurosawa, say – and others failed to.'

'Some adapt to the needs of the moment, some do not,' Rinzaki muses. 'I have always been in the former camp.'

'But to set up a working film studio you needed land . . . and finance.'

'Of course.'

'How did you . . . go about obtaining them?'

'The land was simply good fortune. The Americans were beginning to scale back and a redundant army depot . . . became available.'

'You were . . . how old then?'

'I was twenty.'

'That's very young to be engaging in such a venture.'

'We grew up fast then. We had to.'

'But you'd have needed the approval of SCAP's Economic and Scientific section to set up your studio . . . wouldn't you?'

'You are correct.'

'Did you have any contacts within ESS?'

'As it happened, I did.'

'How did that come about?'

'For a few years after the war, I worked for ESS . . . in a junior capacity.'

'Is that how you heard about the army land becoming available?'

Rinzaki permits himself a frown, though he still seems entirely untroubled by Kodaka's line of questioning. 'I can't recall how I first heard about it. But as soon as I did, I realized it was the opportunity I'd been waiting for.'

'So, you'd been planning the move for quite a while?'

'I knew the Americans would leave eventually. And I knew people would begin to crave entertainment after the initial post-war problems of hunger and homelessness had been solved. There is more to life than a bowl of noodles and a roof over your head, after all. There is cinema. There is . . . dreamland.'

'And you were going to sell tickets to take them there?'

'That is the essence of filmmaking.'

'But what about the money? To buy the land? To staff the studio? To make films? Where did a twenty-year-old junior employee of ESS get that from?'

'Investors who saw and understood the potential in what I was doing.'

'How did you . . . seek out those investors?'

'Your client is particularly interested in financial issues?'

'He is, yes.'

'Remind me of his name.'

137

'Matthieu Dupont.'

'You're sure that's it?' Rinzaki is almost smirking now.

'I am quite sure of my client's name, Rinzaki-san.'

'And so am I. Would you like to . . . reconsider your answer?'

The tranquillity prevailing within the walls of Matsuda Sanso has suddenly given way to a close and threatening expectancy. Kodaka avoided specifying to Rinzaki's secretary when he spoke to her which French university the fictitious Dr Dupont was attached to. There can have been no checking up on his credentials. Yet it is only too obvious that Rinzaki does not believe Kodaka's account of himself. And in the next few seconds Kodaka is going to have to decide what to do about that.

'Perhaps you would like to switch off the recorder before we proceed,' Rinzaki says in a tone that suggests he is merely trying to be helpful.

To switch off the recorder at this point would represent an admission of defeat. 'There's no need as far as I'm concerned,' Kodaka insists.

'Well, let me simplify the situation for you. I would like you to switch off the recorder. Because I have something to say . . . that your client will not wish to be preserved on tape.'

'My client . . . Dr Dupont?'

'Switch off the machine, please.'

Kodaka shrugs in a show of incomprehension, picks up the recorder and switches it off.

'Please take the tape out.'

'Very well.' Kodaka removes the tape and sets it down next to the now empty recorder.

'Thank you.'

'What do you want to say to me, Rinzaki-san?'

'I want to say that the time has come to drop the pretence. There is no Dr Dupont, is there? There is only your real client. Teruki Jinno.'

'Who?'

'Did you really think you could pry into my affairs without my becoming aware of it? There was always the possibility, following his father's death, that Teruki Jinno would have the Soroban account investigated. And you are the person he hired to investigate it. I am not complaining about your attempt to deceive me as to your reasons for wishing to speak to me. No doubt that is the kind of thing a private detective does all the time. The invention of a French academic with an interest in the history of Japanese filmmaking was entertaining in its way. I only hope you did not spend too long preparing for your role as his researcher, however, because, as you see, it was time wasted.'

Kodaka does his level best to keep a poker face. For the moment, he tells himself, he is merely professionally embarrassed. He does not want to make the situation worse than it is, so he deems further denials unwise. There may still be some way, after all, to obtain information valuable to his client. 'May I ask how you learnt of my enquiries, Rinzaki-san?' he asks with respectful neutrality.

'Word reached me. How or from whom I do not propose to say.'

'But you acknowledge that Arinobu Jinno paid you large sums of money through the Soroban account over a period of forty-seven years?'

'I will tell you as much as your client is entitled to know on that subject – and perhaps a little more. I met Arinobu Jinno through my work at ESS. I disclosed to him my ambition to enter the film industry. I saw the potential for cooperation where the construction of a studio and in due course cinemas was concerned. He agreed to invest in Kuraikagami when it was launched. I was grateful for that investment. I bought him out of his stake when I decided to assume independent control of the company. That was in . . . Showa fifty-two, when my media-mix strategy had really begun to pay off. It's actually a pity Dr Dupont doesn't exist, because if he did he'd find my reminiscences quite fascinating. Anyway, there was no Jinno money in my business from then on.'

'I don't understand. What about the Soroban money?'

Rinzaki sighs. 'I kept none of it.'

'What do you mean?'

'Arinobu Jinno was a valued investor. I trusted him and he trusted me. I had also discovered by chance a certain . . . arrangement . . . that he had made in his life. Learning that I knew of it, he asked for my help in . . . managing the situation. I agreed to give that help. The Soroban account did not benefit me, directly or indirectly, other than in the way that favours tend to be returned, which can be highly advantageous in the commercial world. As it was, he deposited money in the account on a regular basis and I simply . . . passed it on.'

'Passed it on . . . to whom?'

'Teruki Jinno should have let this matter rest with his father. The payments have ceased. There was no need to hire someone such as you. He should have respected his father's discretion.'

'His discretion? Or his secrecy?'

'There is often no difference. But we are past that, are we not? You must have the truth to report to him. Only then can you send in your bill.'

'I make no apology for the work I do.'

'Nor should you. *I* apologize.' This – and the faint bow that accompanies it – rather disarms Kodaka. 'So, the truth. Her name is Sonoko Zaizen.' A woman. This is the answer. A long-term mistress, maintained by Arinobu Jinno, with Rinzaki as go-between. No blackmail. Just an arrangement. Just a favour, as an advance against other favours. Kodaka is surprised by how surprised he feels. 'She worked briefly in Arinobu Jinno's office. Then she became his mistress. He was – and he remained – entirely besotted

140

with her, though he continued to be a devoted husband and father. He had no difficulty in . . . compartmentalizing his feelings. He was a disciplined man. But he wanted Zaizen to have the best of everything in the absence of the marriage he could not give her. And that is what she has had. My lawyer manages all financial and legal matters affecting her, funded by the Soroban account. And those funds are a long way from being exhausted.'

'When they are exhausted?'

'Thanks to my investment advice, I doubt they ever will be.'

'Where does she live?'

'I am not free to give you any details of her life. She is entitled to keep her own secrets.'

'Does she have any children?'

'I have said all that I intend to say about her.'

'It's not enough. How is my client to know this isn't just . . . a cover story?'

'What sordid circles you must move in, Kodaka-san. A cover story? Cover for what?'

'You tell me.'

Rinzaki leans back in his chair and cocks his head as he looks at Kodaka. 'Very well. I anticipated you would not take my word for it where this is concerned. I understand. It is the nature of your trade to be sceptical. So, I ask you: will you take *her* word for it?'

'Are you offering me the chance to speak to Sonoko Zaizen?'

'I am. Right now.'

'She's here?'

'Yes. Shall I?' Rinzaki picks up the small bell. 'She's in an adjoining room. Waiting to be called.'

Once again, Kodaka feels outmanoeuvred. Rinzaki knows what Zaizen will say. He may even have told her what to say. Everything that has happened since Kodaka arrived at Matsuda

Sanso has been planned and rehearsed. But there is no way out of it. This is an offer he cannot refuse. 'Call her in, then.'

Rinzaki rings the bell and carefully sets it back down on the table. Then he rises from his chair with surprising suppleness for a man of his age and turns towards the shoji by which they entered the room. It slides open and a woman enters.

She is dressed in a plain pink silk kimono. Her hair, black shot with grey, is pinned back. She is taller than most women of her generation – Kodaka would put her age at about the same as Rinzaki's – but delicately built. Her face is barely lined, pale and fine-boned. Her gaze is placid but direct. She seems to be looking straight through him.

Rinzaki moves past her and exits onto the *engawa*. He slides the shoji shut behind him. Kodaka springs to his feet and bows to the woman, who bows in return.

'You are Sonoko Zaizen?'

She nods. 'I am.' Her voice is soft and refined.

'I am Kazuto Kodaka.'

'Rinzaki-san has told me why you are here. Which is also why I am here.'

'Shall we sit?'

'I would . . . prefer not to.'

Kodaka rounds the table and takes a few steps towards her. Her gaze never leaves him. 'I am sorry . . . to have to ask you some difficult questions.'

'I appreciate your apology, Kodaka-san. But I have already agreed with Rinzaki-san that I need to state clearly what the nature of my relationship with Arinobu Jinno was. I would prefer not to have to do so. But . . . his son's determination to learn the truth has left me no choice in the matter.'

'You were Arinobu Jinno's . . . mistress?'

'I was.'

'When did it begin?'

142

'When I was seventeen. In Showa twenty-one.'

'And you remained so . . .'

'For the rest of his life.'

'He treated you well?'

'He was extremely generous.'

'You have led . . . a comfortable life?'

'Very.'

'Where do you live, Zaizen-san?'

'I prefer not to say. I do not want Teruki Jinno – or any other member of Arinobu's family – to be able to contact me.'

'But, wherever it is, Arinobu Jinno paid for it?'

'He did.'

'And every other advantage you have enjoyed.'

'Yes. But those advantages have not included marriage . . . or a family of my own.'

'You have no children?'

'I bore Arinobu a son. In Showa thirty. He died of Asian influenza the following year.'

'I am sorry to hear that.'

'Thank you. It was a long time ago. But in other ways . . . not so long.'

'How often did you and Arinobu . . . meet?'

'As often as his commitments allowed. Playing golf. Travelling on business. I believe they were what he claimed to be doing when he was with me. Our time together . . . was never long enough.'

That last phrase lodges itself in Kodaka's thoughts. She is effectively declaring that they loved each other. It was more than simply a pleasurable and rewarding arrangement. 'Do you think it odd that his family had no suspicion of his relationship with you?'

'Arinobu was a discreet and careful man. Even so, he told me he believed his wife realized there was another woman in his life.'

'Realized – but said nothing?'

'Wives often do . . . so I am told.'

'This will come as a shock to Teruki Jinno.'

'I am sorry for that.'

'I'm not sure he'll be able to believe it.'

'Yet he must. It is the truth.'

'How can he know that?'

'You want proof, Kodaka-san? Rinzaki-san said you would. And so . . . I have brought proof.' She slips something out of the waist-tuck of her kimono. 'Arinobu always sent me a New Year card. This is the last one I received.'

She steps forward and hands the card to Kodaka. It is a standard New Year greetings postcard, decorated with a colourful depiction of a dog – the zodiacal sign for 1994. It must have been sent in an envelope, since, turning it over, Kodaka sees there is neither address nor stamp on the back, only her handwritten name – *Sonoko*. But, as she has already said, Arinobu Jinno was a discreet and careful man.

On the front of the card, below the dog, is a message, also handwritten: *You are never out of my thoughts*. It is not signed. For Sonoko, of course, it did not need to be. She knew who the sender was. The message itself could hardly be plainer. For a man as buttoned-up as Kodaka has been told Arinobu Jinno was, this was a declaration of undying love.

'Show the card to Teruki Jinno,' Zaizen continues. 'He will recognize his father's handwriting and know then that what I have told you is true.'

Kodaka rather suspects he will. 'I will show it to him,' he says.

'I would like it back afterwards. Can you return it to Rinzaki-san please?'

Kodaka nods. 'I will do that.'

'Thank you.'

There is a momentary silence. Kodaka does not know what to

say. He believes what Zaizen has told him. It is not the conclusion he expected. But it is the conclusion Teruki Jinno will have to live with.

'I will leave now,' says Zaizen softly.

And she does, Kodaka finding no words by way of farewell. It is understood between them that they will not meet again.

After she has left the room, Kodaka gathers up the recorder and the cassette tape and slips them into his pocket. Silence has reclaimed the interior of Matsuda Sanso. He's not sure if he should stay and await Rinzaki's return. A moment passes. He decides to leave.

He slides open the shoji, which Zaizen closed behind her, and steps out onto the *engawa*. Sonoko Zaizen is nowhere to be seen. But Rinzaki is there, standing by one of the posts supporting the roof, hands folded in front of him. It is hard to tell if he is leaning against the post. Kodaka suspects not.

'Zaizen-san gave you everything you needed, I hope,' he says quietly.

'I have what she told me. And I have the New Year card.'

'So, there is nothing else to be said. The story that did not have to be told has been told. And Teruki Jinno can have the truth he might wish to have lived without.'

Kodaka shrugs. 'Yes.'

'Zaizen-san wants the card returned to her, I believe. It is a matter of . . . sentiment.'

'She said I could return it through you.'

'Make an appointment with my secretary to call at my office when you have resolved matters with Teruki Jinno.'

'I can just drop it in.' Kodaka feels deflated by the anticlimactic end of his investigation. He has no wish for a further encounter with Rinzaki.

'Please make an appointment, Kodaka-san. There will be more to discuss than a New Year card.'

'There will?'

'I want to hire you. I require the services of a private detective.'

'To do what?'

'Something entirely unconnected with the investigation you have carried out for Teruki Jinno. The fact is that I have been impressed by your professionalism.' Rinzaki smiles. 'I want you to find someone for me. It is one of your areas of expertise, I believe. Finding people . . . who do not wish to be found.'

'I'm afraid I can't work for you *and* Teruki Jinno.'

'But your work for him will cease when you show him the card and relate Zaizen-san's story.'

'Probably, yes.'

'So, then you will be free to work for me.'

'I suppose.'

'We are agreed, then? Whatever your terms are, I will accept them.'

'Who do you want me to find?'

'I will tell you when we next meet. It will be . . . something for you to look forward to.' And his smile broadens.

2022

BUT THERE IT WAS. PART OF THE BUMPER AND FRONT WING OF A bright yellow Toyota sports car was clearly visible, protruding from beneath the tarpaulin. Studying it through the binoculars, Wada didn't seriously doubt this was Daiju Endo's car, as described to her by Funaki. Two questions were instantly raised in her mind. Why was it there? And where was Endo?

It was hard to imagine she could find the answers to those questions at Matsuda Sanso. The car had been placed in the barn to keep it out of sight. But for the barn door being open and the tarpaulin not quite large enough, it would have escaped her attention. But she'd seen it now. It was no longer possible to suppose that Endo's disappearance wasn't in some way connected with whoever owned the property.

She could find that out later. There were public registers she could consult. The more pressing concern was that the car was evidence. She needed photographs of it in situ to prove it was actually there. And she was never going to get a better chance of obtaining such photographs than now.

She studied the yard again and still saw no one moving around. Swinging the binoculars round, she could see dust rising from the area of woodland where work was being carried out. It was some way from the gate into the yard. With luck, she should be able to enter, get the pictures she needed and leave without being noticed. If she *was* noticed, she could claim to be a hiker who'd lost her way and was seeking directions.

She set off along the sloping fringe of the woods. The going would have been faster on the flatter, clearer ground close to the boundary wall, but that would have made her more conspicuous. She didn't want to break cover until she had to. She paused every thirty metres or so to check the yard and gateway through the binoculars. Everything still looked reassuringly quiet. On she went.

The noise of chopping and sawing was louder by the time she reached a position close enough to the gate to warrant leaving the shelter of the trees. Still there seemed no problem. There was a Land Rover standing in the yard close to the barn, but there was no sign of its driver, or of anyone else moving around.

Wada cut down the slope onto the road where it curved round to the gate. Glancing to left and right as she went and walking at a pace just short of jogging, she headed straight in through the gate and across the yard towards the barn. So far so good.

She moved into the shadowy interior of the barn and slipped her phone out of her shoulder-bag. She took a picture from about ten metres' range of the bright yellow wing of the Toyota and the tarpaulin-covered shape of the rest of the vehicle. Then she pulled the tarpaulin back to expose the number plate and took a picture of that as well.

Those two pictures were the minimum she needed. Everything else would be a bonus. She pushed the tarpaulin back over the roof of the car, wondering if she'd be able to open the driver's door. And what she saw then was a splintered windscreen, cracks radiating from a jagged hole directly in front of the steering wheel. A blanket had been draped over the driver's seat. As to why, a horrible suspicion began to form in Wada's mind.

She tried the door handle. It yielded. The door opened.

At that moment she heard the engine of the Land Rover out in the yard rumble into life. Looking round, she saw a stockily built man in dark green overalls walking slowly towards her. He was shaven-headed, thick-necked and cold-eyed. In his right hand he held a large monkey wrench. He didn't speak.

'I'm leaving,' said Wada, hoping that would somehow appease him. She let go of the door handle and stepped away from the car. She dropped her phone into her bag as she did so and saw him register the movement. He stopped a few metres from her, judging, it seemed to her, the moment to strike. Still he didn't speak.

She took a step forward. He side-stepped to block her path to the door. He raised the wrench. His eyes narrowed. He was wearing gloves, she noticed. Why that particularly worried her she couldn't have said, but somehow it did.

He wasn't going to let her leave. And if she stayed there something bad – something very bad – was going to happen. That was clear to her. She had to get past him. He was big. He was strong. But he probably wasn't as quick on his feet as she was on hers. It was her only advantage.

She grabbed the edge of the tarpaulin with both hands and pulled. It was heavy and slid as much by its own weight as by her pulling. But it came. The man lunged towards her. She had a good hold of the tarpaulin now and was able to push it into his path. His boots caught in the heavy folds. He stumbled. She let go, darted past him and ran for the door.

She heard him curse behind her as he struggled free. Then she was in the open air, racing towards the gate.

There was another man at the wheel of the Land Rover. It took him a second or two to react to her appearance. There was a grinding noise as he put the vehicle into gear and took off in pursuit.

She made it through the gate and turned towards the belt of trees. But the Land Rover sped past her and slewed to a halt, cutting her off. The driver gave three long blasts on the horn, then jumped out. He looked as formidable as the man in the barn, who was also on her tail by now. Glancing over her shoulder, she saw him running across the yard at a musclebound gait, aiming to cut off her retreat.

Running along the road was hopeless anyway. She'd rapidly be overhauled. There were voices from the direction of the dust-plumes up in the woods. They'd heard the horn. Her options were shrinking fast. The driver of the Land Rover moved round the bonnet and advanced towards her. She heard the other man shout, 'Stop her.' The jaws of the trap were closing.

Speed and nimbleness were the only assets she had to draw on. She ran up the slope towards the woods, away from the voices of the workers above her, away from the Land Rover and the road, but away also from her route back to the railway station.

She plunged into the woods and headed uphill, diagonally across the slope of the land, running and jumping through the undergrowth, dodging brambles and branches as best she could, half-aware of sharp, slashing blows to her legs and arms.

She heard the two men coming after her, but they were too slow and blundering to overhaul her. There was a groan and a curse from one of them. He'd probably lost his footing. But they weren't going to give up. She knew that much.

She ran on, her lungs and muscles straining. The woods were thickening as she climbed. She couldn't see the ridge ahead of her. Her sense of direction wasn't holding up well. But she knew she had to keep moving – and moving fast – to shake off her pursuers.

After another few minutes of hard running she stopped,

panting for breath, aware of her heart pounding in her chest. She could still hear the two men behind her, but she'd opened up a gap. They weren't natural runners. But nor was she, come to that.

There were sounds of pursuit from higher up as well: raised voices and trampling feet. There was an engine note somewhere beyond them: a quad bike, maybe, speeding along a track through the woods. She had a lot of men on her trail now and no clear idea of how to elude them.

She ran on, keeping to roughly the same height on the slope. The next station down the railway line was a long way off, but she couldn't think of anywhere else to make for. The sound of the quad bike drew closer, then moved away. She supposed she must have got lucky with the direction of the track it was on.

They didn't know exactly where she was and if she could stay out of sight for long enough they might give up. It wasn't much of a strategy, but it was the best she could come up with. She couldn't keep running indefinitely. Her legs were already feeling heavy. She could sense her stamina beginning to ebb. She was going to have to consider stopping and hiding.

Then, through a gap in the trees to her left, she glimpsed below her a tarmac road, with white lines marking the verge. It obviously wasn't the road from the side gate into Matsuda Sanso. She must be well beyond the boundary of the property by now. This had to be the road from the front gate, which joined the main road south from Chichibu. And she knew the railway line ran parallel with that.

She weighed the possibilities in her mind for a second, then decided to descend to the road and follow it through the patchy woodland she could see on the other side as far as the junction with the main road.

She started down the slope, moving as fast as she dared on the steepening ground through thick clumps of bracken and ferns, but her next stride carried her further down than she'd anticipated and she lost her footing, slithering and sliding as the ground began to shelve rapidly.

The next thing she knew she was on a short scree slope above the road itself. She managed to stay upright, but couldn't slow down now and ended up toppling into a shallow gully at the side of the road, where she lay winded, gazing up at the grey sky and the dark overhanging crowns of the trees.

And then she heard a car brake to a halt just above her on the tarmac, skidding slightly as it did so.

She sat up. Her head was swimming. She knew she couldn't stand up just yet. She looked at the car, a grey saloon, and noticed a hire company logo next to the front number plate. Good news, she reckoned. Her pursuers wouldn't be in the habit of hiring saloon cars.

The driver's door swung open and a man climbed out. He smiled down at her. He was tall, dressed in jeans, checked shirt and a soft suede jacket. He had regular western features, with sparkling teeth and tousled blond hair, and looked to be in his mid-thirties. When he spoke, it was in English, with an American accent.

'Are you OK there?'

'I think so,' she replied in English.

He took her arm as she scrambled to her feet and didn't let go. 'You look kind of shaky.'

'Yes. I slipped. It . . . knocked the wind out of me.'

'You speak good English.'

'Thank you. You're . . . American?'

'How'd you guess? Hey, you know you're bleeding?'

'I am?'

'There's a cut on your cheek.'

She raised her hand to her face and felt blood on her fingers. 'I must have cut myself . . . on a branch. When I slipped.' There were several thorn-slashes on the back of her hand as well and, looking down, she noticed a long tear in one of her trouser legs.

'What happened? Hiking trip go sour on you?'

'Something like that, yes.'

'Where you headed?'

'Agano. Well, Tokyo . . . eventually.'

'Want a ride?'

'Ah . . .' She heard something above and behind her, up in the woods. Voices and movement. Not close, but not so very far away either.

'Were you hiking with friends?' He must have heard the sounds as well.

'No. I am . . . alone.'

'Well, don't let me stop you walking on . . . alone . . . if that's what you want to do. But on the other hand . . .'

'Thank you.' She nodded decisively. 'I will accept your kind offer of a ride.' In fact, she thought, it was a kinder offer than he could possibly imagine.

He held the passenger door open for her as she climbed in. Then he got back into the driver's seat and they set off. 'I'm Troy,' he said. 'Visiting from California.'

'I am Wada.'

'Well, pleased to meet you, Wada.'

'You are here on holiday?'

'Not entirely. But I'm cramming in as much sightseeing as I can. There's a substantial property back along the road. Matsuda Sanso, it's called, according to the map. Know it?'

'No.'

'So, you wouldn't have any idea who lives there?'

'I wouldn't.'

'Pity. What d'you do when you're not hiking, Wada?'

'Nothing interesting.'

'Sorry. I'm getting too curious, aren't I? It's a fault of mine.'

'Tell me what sights you have seen when you have not been working.' Wada glanced in the wing mirror and saw with relief the wooded hills around Matsuda Sanso receding from view. 'I would like to hear about your trip.'

This wasn't true, of course. She was simply trying to deflect Troy from further questions about her line of business. And it worked. She didn't pay close attention to his account of visits to assorted tourist attractions, many of which she'd never been to herself, concentrating instead on the wing mirror to make sure the road from Matsuda Sanso stayed empty.

It did, as far as the junction with the main road. But there a dark SUV parked on the verge just short of the junction pulled out behind them and followed at a discreet distance as they headed south.

Troy didn't appear to notice. In truth, there wasn't anything inherently suspicious about the manoeuvre. But Wada was suspicious nonetheless.

They had covered a few kilometres towards Agano, with Troy describing an early morning visit to Toyosu fish market, when he suddenly braked sharply and pulled into a lay-by. And the SUV cruised past without any sign of slowing.

'There's a first-aid kit in the glove box,' said Troy. 'I thought you might want to put some antiseptic and maybe a band-aid on that cut.'

'Thank you,' said Wada. She flicked open the glove compartment and took out the kit.

'Here.' Troy reached across her and lowered the sun visor to reveal a mirror.

'Thank you again.' Why hadn't he offered her the use of the kit when she first got in the car, Wada wondered. It was almost as if he'd known she wanted to leave without delay.

154

She dabbed antiseptic onto the wound with a ball of cotton wool and dabbed some on the cuts on her hands as well. Then she applied a plaster to her cheek, checking in the mirror that it wasn't too conspicuous.

'OK to keep going?' Troy asked. She nodded and he started away, pulling out onto the road and accelerating hard. 'What d'you make of the SUV?'

'I am sorry?'

'Think he was waiting for us?'

Wada stiffened. He wasn't a tourist, even a part-time one. He wasn't a helpful stranger. And that meant he had to be something else.

'Don't worry. I'm on your side.'

'My side?'

'The commotion in the woods. The goons jumping around at Matsuda Sanso's main gate like they'd been given electric shocks. And you, tumbling out of the trees right in front of me. Come on. You were running away from them. Lucky for you I happened along. Lucky for me too. Because I think we can help each other.'

'You have already helped me. And I am grateful. But . . . a ride to Tokyo is all I need.'

'And it's all you'll get. Unless you're willing to consider . . . collaboration.'

'Collaboration in what?'

'I'm interested in the activities of the owner of Matsuda Sanso. I get the feeling you are too.'

'I do not know who owns the property.'

'So, you weren't lying about that?'

'No. I was not.'

'But you weren't there for a day's hiking, were you? You were there for the same reason as me. To figure out what the hell's going on.' That was true, of course. But Wada wasn't ready to admit it. 'Look, I'll give you the owner's name. Call it an introductory offer. Goro Rinzaki, chairman of the Kuraikagami Film Corporation. Heard of him?'

'No.'

'But you were spying on his house.'

'What makes you think I was spying?'

'The binoculars.' Glancing down, Wada saw that the flap of her shoulder-bag had fallen open, revealing the binoculars as well as her map of the area. 'Then there was your hasty exit. And the unmistakable signs that your presence hadn't gone unnoticed. All of which suggested to me the binoculars weren't for bird-watching.'

'What is your interest in Goro Rinzaki?'

'Are you giving up on the hiking story?'

It seemed some measure of risk had to be taken. 'Perhaps.'

'Does that mean you're willing to trade what you know for what I know?'

'Not without more information about you.'

'Cautious, aren't you?' Troy reached into the pocket of his jacket, took out a card and handed it to her.

It was a business card, expensively embossed, identifying him as Troy Kimber, executive vice-chairman of Braxton Winery, Hurstdale, California. 'What does a Japanese filmmaker have to do with a Californian vineyard?' Wada asked.

'Nothing. Rinzaki's involvement is in another branch of my family's activities. Maybe you're wondering now why my name's not Braxton. Well, Grant Braxton, the chairman, is my step-father and has no living children, so the future of the business is *my* future. Right now I'm a little concerned about it.'

'And that concern has brought you here?'

'Yes it has. What about you? What's brought you here?'

'I am a private detective, working on a missing person case.'

'Who's missing?'

'His name is Manjiro Nagata.'

'Means nothing to me.'

'What about Daiju Endo?'

'Endo? Yeah. That name *does* mean something. Hold on.' Kimber nodded up at the rearview mirror. 'The SUV's back. How'd he manage that? I never saw him pulled over waiting for us.'

'What does the driver look like?'

'Can't see much of him. There's a tint on the windshield.'

'Old? Young?'

'Old, I guess. Not young, anyhow. Grey hair. A beard, maybe.'

'Any passengers?'

He squinted up at the mirror. 'I don't think so. Know this guy, do you?'

Kimber's description had put her in mind of the man on the platform at Shinjuku. But she wasn't about to tell him that. 'It is difficult to say.'

'I'll bet it is. Why is he after you, Wada? Got something he wants – or wants back?'

'Perhaps he is following you rather than me.'

'Well, we won't know that until we part ways, will we?'

It was a good point. And it was one complicated by Wada's uncertainty about Kimber. Could she trust him? In her present situation, she had little choice in the matter. She needed to change that. She needed time and space in which to weigh her options. 'Drop me at Agano station. I can catch a train into Tokyo from there. That will force the man in the SUV to choose. Leave his car at the station and follow me on the train. Or stick with you.'

'What if he chooses you?'

'I will lose him on the subway.'

'And then you'll have lost me as well as him. You know, I get the feeling you're not buying into this collaborative idea.'

'Tell me what you know about Endo and I can consider your proposal further.'

'I give and you take. Is that how you see this working?'

'I cannot force you to give me anything.'

'You're right. OK. Agano it is. When's the next train?'

Wada consulted the timetable on her phone. 'Sixteen minutes.'

'And Agano's about eight kilometres. That's doable. But listen. I really do think we can help each other. My phone number's on the card. Call me when you're ready to talk seriously.'

'I will.'

'Is that a promise?'

What Wada couldn't explain was that finding out he wasn't what he was presenting himself as in the middle of Tokyo, on ground she knew far better than he did, was one thing. Finding it out in a car he was driving, in the middle of the countryside, was quite another. 'It's a promise,' she said. And it was: a promise, in her mind, to call him, not when she was ready to talk seriously, but *if*.

They had several minutes in hand as they crossed the bridge spanning the Koma river and drove through the centre of Agano towards the railway station. The SUV was still behind them, hanging back but never out of sight for long.

As they neared the station, Wada spotted the two-car train already standing at the platform, ready for the return run to Ikebukuro. There were passengers boarding, so if the old man did follow her, she'd have the advantage of safety in numbers for the journey. She was confident she could shake him off in Tokyo.

Kimber pulled into a parking bay opposite the station. The SUV didn't round the bend behind them. It looked as if the driver wasn't going to take the train.

'Seems I'm stuck with him,' said Kimber.

'Will that be a problem?'

'I doubt it. As things stand, Rinzaki can't risk making a move against me. I'm the chairman's stepson, remember.'

'How long are you staying in Tokyo?'

'Long enough for you to call me.'

'I'll give the matter serious thought.'

'You should.'

'Thank you for bringing me here.'

'I did you a good turn back at Matsuda Sanso.'

'You did.'

'And they say one good turn deserves another.'

'They do.'

'So?'

'As I said, I'll give the matter serious thought.'

With that, Wada opened her door and climbed out of the car.

From the platform, as she walked towards the train, she could see further back along the station approach road than Kimber could from the parking bay he'd pulled into. There was no sign of the SUV. But the station was a dead end. Kimber would have to go back the way he'd come. And no doubt the SUV would be waiting.

Wada had actually expected the old man – if he was the driver, as she now felt sure he was – would follow her onto the train. But he hadn't, either because Kimber was a more important target . . . or because he already knew where Wada was going.

She tried to dismiss that possibility from her mind as she settled on the train. She'd lost him last time. There was no way he could have tracked her down since.

During the journey to Ikebukuro, Wada concentrated on learning as much as she could as quickly as she could about Goro Rinzaki and the Braxtons.

The Internet wasn't exactly awash with information about Rinzaki. He'd founded the Kuraikagami Film Corporation in 1949 and been its chairman ever since. He was now in his early nineties. The commercial media wrote him up as a low-profile veteran of the film world, who'd successfully diversified from filmmaking into cinemas and shopping malls. There were no interviews and precious few photographs. He looked like a hundred other elderly Japanese businessmen: dark-suited, sombre, wary. There was, for Wada's purposes, almost nothing to go on.

The Braxton Winery won plaudits from oenophiles for its Pinot Noirs and promoted on its website the joys of a vineyard visit. *Savour the cool breezes as well as the delightfully delicate wines our high-altitude limestone soils render so unique.* There was a photograph of Troy Kimber that confirmed the man she'd met wasn't an impostor. There was a photograph of his stepfather as well. Grant Braxton looked to be in his mid-sixties, sandy-haired and craggily good-looking in the American way. His late father, Clyde Braxton, who'd founded the business, was also pictured. The resemblance between father and son was striking.

There was no mention of a third generation, however. The reason for that became apparent when Wada followed a link to another family enterprise: the Braxton Institute of Seismological Research and Innovation (BISRI), founded by Clyde in 1994 to develop expertise in earthquake prediction. He'd been inspired to pour money into the project by the deaths of his son Grant's wife and two children in the San Francisco earthquake of 1989. Evidently, Grant had remarried since. His second wife was presumably Troy's mother.

There was little to suggest BISRI had made any significant breakthroughs in earthquake prediction in the years since its foundation, although its website was full of praise from seismologists for its efforts. And there was nothing to suggest a connection with Goro Rinzaki.

Except that earthquake prediction was what the Kobe Sensitive had engaged in. And Daiju Endo had vouched for her. He'd travelled to Matsuda Sanso – owned, according to Kimber, by

160

Rinzaki – in his yellow Toyota. And his yellow Toyota was still there. Wada had the photographs to prove it.

So, Rinzaki was at the centre of all of this. Though as to what *this* really was . . .

Wada didn't know. But she was going to find out. That much was certain in her mind. That much was already settled.

1995

ONE WEEK HAS PASSED SINCE TERUKI JINNO HIRED KODAKA TO establish why for close to half a century his late father regularly paid large sums of money into an anonymous account at Mizunuma Bank's Nihombashi branch.

Now Kodaka has delivered the answer. And the troubled man he met a week ago is even more troubled than ever. Kodaka feels sorry for him. He is not about to remind him that he suggested it might be wiser to let the matter lie. He understands why Jinno demanded the truth. He craved certainty. But certainty comes with a price. Which Jinno now has to pay.

'I am sorry, Jinno-san, to bring you this news. I know it is not what you would have wanted to hear.'

Jinno raises his head, which has fallen forward despondently on his chest, and grimaces. They are seated at Kodaka's desk in his office in the Kono Building. It is early afternoon. Outside it is raining. Kodaka can hear the swish of car tyres in the street below. Jinno's initial disbelief has given way to sullen acceptance of the truth. His father kept an expensive mistress. And the Soroban account was how he arranged to pay for all her comforts and conveniences.

Jinno slides the New Year card supplied by Sonoko Zaizen back across the desk to Kodaka. Although it is upside down, Kodaka can read the message written by Arinobu Jinno: *You are never out of my thoughts.* Teruki Jinno has acknowledged the writing as his father's, though he struggled to get the words out. Kodaka feels he should perhaps have spared him the effort. Because the expression on his face when he saw it confirmed the card's authenticity.

'No doubt it pleased Rinzaki to share this secret with my father,' he says at last.

'Possibly,' Kodaka agrees, though the point is irrelevant. The principal beneficiaries of the arrangement were Zaizen and Arinobu Jinno.

'We only have his word for it that none of the money went to him.'

'True. But the redemption of your father's stake in Kuraika-gami can presumably be verified.'

'Yes. No doubt he will have all the accounting details in place.'

'Then it is hard to see what further investigation might reveal.'

'When investigation has already revealed more than I might have wished to know.' Jinno's gaze drifts past Kodaka to the window behind him and the grey sky beyond the glass. 'I looked up to my father all my life. I admired what I thought of as his . . . probity and rectitude.' He shakes his head. 'And all the time *this* was going on.'

'I can only repeat how sorry I am, Jinno-san.'

'No apology is necessary.' Jinno looks at Kodaka directly. 'You did what I asked you to do. I have no complaint.'

'Thank you.'

'There was a child, you said?'

'According to Zaizen, yes. A boy. Born in Showa thirty.'

'But he did not survive?'

'He died in Showa thirty-one. Asian influenza.'

Jinno nods solemnly. 'At least I have no half-brother to contend with. That would be . . .' he rubs his forehead, 'too much.'

'I will return the New Year card to Zaizen.'

'Do that. I do not want any other member of my family to see the evidence of my father's . . .' He draws a deep breath, unable, it seems, to pronounce whatever word has entered his mind. Hypocrisy? Infidelity? Dishonour? Whichever it might be, Arinobu Jinno's memory is forever tainted by it.

'Do you wish me to say anything to Rinzaki on your behalf?'

'What do you suggest? My appreciation of his service to my father and his invaluable discretion over so many years?' Jinno winces and raises a hand. 'I am sorry. Your question was entirely reasonable. This revelation has . . . discomposed me.'

'I understand.'

'I do not wish you to pass any kind of message to Rinzaki. Return the card. And forget you ever heard the name Sonoko Zaizen. That is what I would like you to do, Kodaka-san.'

'Then that is what I will do.'

'Submit your bill . . . at your earliest convenience.'

'Thank you.'

'Tell me, is your own father still living?'

'No. He died six years ago.'

'Did you . . . look up to him?'

'I learnt a lot from him. But I was . . . conscious of his faults.'

'Did he have many?'

'More than a few.'

'Yet still . . . he was your father.'

'He was.'

Jinno sighs. 'I shall endeavour to start thinking of my father in such a way. Simply as my father, not as a . . . moral exemplar.' He sighs again. 'It will not be easy. But it will have to be done. Now that I know the truth.'

*

164

After Jinno has gone, Kodaka sorts the modest amount of paper-work the case has generated and deposits it in a file, which he places in the box he uses to keep material destined for the storage cage in the basement. He decides he will only submit his bill to Jinno once he has returned the New Year card. With that in mind, he puts a call through to Rinzaki's office. The great man's secretary sounds as if she has been awaiting his call.

'You wish to make an appointment, Kodaka-san?'

'Yes please. Is he free at any time tomorrow?'

'He is free this afternoon. Shall we say . . . five o'clock?'

The sooner the better, Kodaka supposes. He is undeniably curious about the case Rinzaki has tentatively offered him. 'All right. Five o'clock.'

'I will send a car to collect you from Chofu station at four forty-five.'

'I'll be there.'

And he is. He is also grateful for the car. The rain has intensified and he doesn't know Chofu. He is driven out of the centre to a semi-industrial area and through an arched entrance that to his eye has a Hollywood look about it into a maze of high-roofed studios and associated structures: the nerve centre of the Kurai-kagami Film Corporation.

It's just as the car draws to a halt in front of the administrative building that Kodaka's pager beeps. Checking it, he sees Takuto Umetsu's mobile number on the display. What does Umetsu want? Bailing out of another mah-jongg debt, maybe. Well, whatever it is, he's going to have to wait.

Rinzaki receives Kodaka in a large and airy wood-panelled office on the top floor of the building. In his three-piece suit and tie, with a pin-collared shirt, he looks the very model of west-ernized Japanese business sobriety, almost unrecognizable as the kimono-wearing traditionalist he presented himself as at Matsuda Sanso.

Framed stills from some of Kuraikagami's most successful films hang on the walls, arranged as far as Kodaka can tell in chronological order. He is surprised to discover how many films he can recall seeing turn out to have been Kuraikagami productions. It seems he was involved in the world of Goro Rinzaki long before he knew it.

'What is the first film you remember seeing in a cinema, Kodaka-san?' Rinzaki enquires as they stand looking at the pictures.

'Not sure. The one that made a really big impression on me was *The Inugami Family*. My father took me to see that. I must have been . . . fifteen.'

'Ah, of course. A detective story. You found your vocation young. Sadly, that wasn't one of mine. Kadokawa hit the jackpot there. And not just in ticket sales. Book sales and soundtrack record sales as well. Diversification is the secret of success in the film business. As in so many other businesses. Such as your own.'

Kodaka is bemused. 'I haven't . . . diversified.'

'No? But you have not limited yourself to industrial espionage and occasional divorces, have you, as your father did?'

'I didn't know you were familiar with how my father operated.'

'I never strike agreements with people whose background I am not familiar with. Naturally, I have made myself familiar with yours.'

'I see. Well, I take the cases that come my way.'

'Quite so. And now my case has come your way.'

'I am now free to work for you, Rinzaki-san, if you wish me to.'

The secretary enters with tea. She pours cups for them and leaves. They sit down at Rinzaki's large and mostly bare desk. Kodaka takes the New Year card out of his pocket and places it

166

carefully in front of Rinzaki, who makes no immediate move to pick it up.

'Teruki Jinno is satisfied?' he asks as he sips his tea.

'He accepts the money his father paid into the Soroban account was for Zaizen-san and that my investigation should proceed no further.'

'Your report must have been a blow for him.'

'As you say.'

'And for that I am sorry.'

'The truth is not always agreeable.'

'Indeed not. And, as it happens, we do have to dispose of a disagreeable subject before proceeding.'

'We do?'

'Earlier today, I received a telephone call from the manager of the Nihombashi branch of Mizunuma Bank. It seems someone has been questioning staff about an account held there and oper-ated by me, though not held under my name. He has gone so far as to offer bribes in exchange for such information.' There is a sinking feeling in Kodaka's stomach. He fears he knows what is coming. 'Unsurprisingly, he did not volunteer his name, but he is an American and the description given to me established to my satisfaction that he is Daniel Perlman, owner of the Flight Deck bar in Yokosuka.'

So, now Kodaka knows why Umetsu has paged him. He can't for the moment devise a suitable response. And the faint smile that has formed on Rinzaki's narrow lips suggests he under-stands his difficulty.

'I am acquainted with Perlman, from long ago. He bears a grudge against me, for no good reason. The issue is how he came to know of the account. I think it's obvious. You approached him because of the protest he staged at the exhibition I spon-sored at Yushukan. He claimed to have things he could tell you about me and you told him about the Soroban account – without naming it – in order to draw him out. I imagine he alleged I engaged in corrupt activities – and worse – while working for ESS. Is that essentially what happened?'

Kodaka weighs his words carefully as he replies. 'I would deny it if formally accused of that.'

'Of course, since to admit it would raise the question of how you came by what was supposed to be highly confidential information. I already knew you'd spoken to Perlman, so this news from the bank didn't altogether surprise me. It's actually quite impressive in its way. How does a private detective circumvent bank security so effectively? I'd like to know. But you're not going to tell me, are you?'

'Perhaps it would be best if you didn't engage my services after all, Rinzaki-san.' Kodaka endeavours to sound respectful, regretful . . . and as defiant as he can in the circumstances.

'I disagree. This simply . . . enhances your credentials. You're obviously someone who can obtain information that might elude others. And that's just who I need.'

'Even so . . .'

'I have received satisfactory assurances from the bank that Perlman will gain nothing from his clumsy attempts at bribery. He has lived here most of his life, but he still doesn't understand how such things work. I am not worried about him in the least. I assume I can rely on you to have no further dealings with him?'

'The Soroban case is closed.' Something beyond the embarrassment Perlman has caused him is niggling at Kodaka. He feels he is being manipulated. The unspoken implication is that the question of how Perlman found out about the Soroban account will not be pursued if Kodaka joins Rinzaki's payroll. He is being bought. And he didn't even know he was for sale. 'There is no reason for me to contact Daniel Perlman.'

'Excellent. So, with that settled, we can turn to the case I hope you will agree to take on.' There's that smile of Rinzaki's again, which Kodaka is beginning to dislike. 'Will you accept me as a client, Kodaka-san?'

There's only one answer Kodaka can give – only one answer he can *imagine* giving. 'I would be honoured, Rinzaki-san.' They exchange measured nods of understanding. 'You said you wanted me to find someone for you.'

'Yes.'

'Someone who has gone missing?'

'In a sense.'

'Could we begin with the person's name?'

'Actually, we could not, since I do not know it.'

'But you are acquainted with this person?'

'No. I am not. Let me explain. I feel sure Perlman will have told you I worked at ESS under Captain, later Major, Clyde Braxton. Braxton-san now runs a winery in California. We remain . . . in contact. Some years ago, his family suffered a great misfortune. His daughter-in-law and grandchildren were killed in the earthquake in San Francisco in October 1989.' Kodaka sees no reason to admit he already knows this. What he doesn't know is how it relates to the case Rinzaki wants him to handle. 'Braxton-san has since established a seismological research institute to investigate ways of predicting earthquakes, to spare others the kind of loss he suffered.'

'Without success?'

'As you say. Without success. So far. But imagine if earthquake prediction became possible – and reliable. Imagine how many lives would not have been lost in the Kobe earthquake, for instance. Five thousand people died there not so many weeks ago, Kodaka-san. *Five thousand.*'

'No one can predict an earthquake.'

'Are you sure? The newspapers believe there is someone who may be able to. And I would like to arrange for that person to assist the seismologists Braxton-san has engaged in this work. I

169

would like to do what I can for a man who helped me find my place in the world at a time when the world seemed to have collapsed around me. I hope you will not think that ignoble of me.'

'Of course not. But . . . am I to understand the person you wish me to find is . . . the Kobe Sensitive?'

'Yes. You are to understand that.' Rinzaki slides open the drawer of the desk and takes out a cassette tape which he places in front of Kodaka. 'This is a recording of the telephone call she made to the Kantei on January sixteenth, the day before the Kobe earthquake, warning that it would happen. You have probably heard it played on the television. But this is the *unedited* version, which you will not have heard.'

'There are two versions?'

'Yes. This one includes her exchanges with the woman on the Kantei switchboard before she was put through to an officer. And there is a little more at the end as well, after she has finished speaking but not yet rung off. There are . . . sounds on it which may offer clues to her identity.'

'May I ask how you obtained this?'

'You may ask. And I may choose not to answer. But this is all the evidence there is. It is not much. But you are a detective, an expert in taking not much and . . . extracting the truth from it.' Rinzaki leans back in his chair. 'Who is the Kobe Sensitive, Kodaka-san? Who is she and where is she? That is what I want you to discover.'

2022

WADA HAD CONCLUDED BY THE FOLLOWING MORNING THAT SHE was going to have to take up Troy Kimber's proposal of cooperation if she was to make further progress. But she meant to ensure that such cooperation proceeded on her terms, not his. And there was one substantial precaution to be taken before contacting him.

She stored the pictures she'd taken of the yellow Toyota in a file and sent it to lawyer Dobachi with instructions that he should preserve the images in case of . . . well, Dobachi didn't need to be told what it was in case of. He'd come to accept that she took as many risks as Kodaka – possibly more – in her professional life.

There was no denying, though, that she wouldn't have been able to accomplish as much as she had as a private detective without the contacts she'd inherited from Kodaka, one of whom – Mitamura – worked at the Tokyo Road Transport Bureau, where he had access to national car registration details. Mitamura had been divorced three times and Kodaka had gathered evidence against him in one of those divorces. Ultimately, however, Mitamura's ongoing need for cash had cancelled out any resentment he may have felt towards Kodaka, for whom he became an occasional source of valuable information on car ownership.

The standing arrangement with Mitamura was to leave an anodyne message on his mobile. He would then phone back on the Kodaka Agency's landline and use the same means to deliver the required information later, avoiding all use of traceable technology. He was not a garrulous man. He was, in fact, just the sort of person Wada liked to deal with: brisk and businesslike. 'I should have the name and address of the registered owner for you by the end of the day,' was how he ended their brief conversation. 'Usual terms.'

Wada made a foray to the nearest cashpoint to make sure she'd have the ¥30,000 ready to deliver to whichever pachinko parlour Mitamura nominated (where he would probably lose most of it), then turned her mind to other matters. She'd decided not to contact Kimber until she was absolutely certain that the yellow Toyota she'd seen at Matsuda Sanso belonged to Daiju Endo.

Confirmation came late in the afternoon. 'Endo, Daiju,' Mitamura reported without preamble. 'Lives in Warabi. You want the full address?'

Wada did want the full address. With that in her possession and a rendezvous agreed for eight o'clock that evening in Mitamura's choice of pachinko joint, Wada put in a call to Troy Kimber.

'Kimber-san. This is Wada.'

'I wondered if I was ever going to hear from you again.' Kimber sounded as if he was joking; though, as he was American, it was hard to be certain. 'And I thought you were going to call me Troy.'

'OK. Troy. How was your return journey to Tokyo?'

'If you mean did our SUV friend follow me, the answer is yes. But I lost him with a late turn off the expressway when we got

172

into the city. Scared the shit out of the guy in the inside lane when I swerved across him, but it worked. So, are we going to talk seriously about you know who?'

'Yes. I am willing to talk.'

'Great. How about this evening?' He clearly didn't intend to waste time.

And that suited Wada just fine. 'What time?'

'I'll be honest with you, Wada, I've had enough sushi to last me a lifetime. There's an Italian restaurant I've found in Ginza that ticks all the boxes for me. Why don't you join me there at, say, eight thirty?'

An agreement to talk had suddenly turned into a dinner invitation. But Mitamura's chosen pachinko parlour was near Yurakucho station, putting anywhere in Ginza within a half hour's range, so Wada reckoned she could keep both appointments. 'Very well. Eight thirty. What is the restaurant called?'

'Tuscania. You'll love it.'

Wada wasn't convinced on that point, but she didn't quibble. She wasn't going for the food.

She worked on as dusk fell over the city. She was as happy in the office as she was at home, if not happier, since the office was bigger and often, as now, quieter.

When her phone rang, she was inclined not to answer. But then she saw who the caller was: Taro Yamato.

'Yamato-san?'

'Yes. Yamato here.' He sounded breathless and distracted. 'There has been . . . a development.'

'What kind of development?'

'Well, it is . . . most unexpected, I must say.'

'What is?'

'Daiju. Daiju Endo.'

'Yes. Your friend. What about him?'

'He's back. He has returned.'

If this was true, 'most unexpected' was a considerable under-statement. 'You've heard from him?'

'Yes. I have just spoken to him. I am going to his apartment now to see him. Everything is all right, he told me. He is well. And quite happy, actually.'

'I don't understand . . . how that can be.'

'Speaking frankly, neither do I. He has promised to explain everything, though. Where he has been. What he has been doing. I wondered . . . if you wanted to hear what he has to say.'

'Of course.'

'So, will you come to the apartment as well? He is expecting me there . . . in an hour.'

A trip out to Warabi was going to make it difficult to meet Mitamura *and* be on time for her dinner with Kimber, but Endo's reappearance had to take priority. 'I will meet you there.'

'Good. I would like . . . you to be with me.' It sounded to Wada as if Yamato had doubts about what his friend had told him. And she didn't blame him. 'This is the address.'

Wada already had Endo's address, of course, courtesy of Mitamura. But she wasn't about to tell Yamato that. 'Go ahead.'

Still conscious of the need to take precautions against being followed, Wada used the underground arcade route to Tokyo Station. The arcade and the station were both crowded, as they were bound to be at such an hour. But that didn't bother her. Threading her way through the commuting horde was second nature. She made straight for the anticlockwise platform of the Yamanote circular line. However crammed the next train proved to be, she intended to get on it. She wanted to hear Daiju Endo 'explain everything', she really did – particularly how his car had ended up under a tarpaulin in a barn at Matsuda Sanso.

*

174

Fortunately, Endo's apartment wasn't far from Warabi station. It was in a fairly small block, raised on pillars, with parking beneath. Access was via an external staircase leading to open walkways at the rear.

Wada made her way up to the top floor and approached the door of Endo's apartment, at the far end of the walkway. She'd made it there in slightly under the hour, but thought it likely Yamato had already arrived. Whether he'd have warned Endo to expect her as well she didn't know. Maybe, maybe not.

She glanced through the window next to the door before ringing the bell, but couldn't see much of the interior through half-closed blinds. The room looked to be the kitchen. She went ahead and rang the bell.

There was no response, which was surprising. She tried again. As she waited, she noticed that the door wasn't closed. She could easily push it open and walk in.

At that point caution kicked in. Doors standing ajar were inherently suspicious in her line of business. Also suspicious was the lack of a response to the bell, since Endo was supposed to be at home even if Yamato hadn't yet joined him. She decided to go back downstairs and ring Yamato from there.

She saw the shadow of the approaching figure before she'd turned away from the door. Suddenly, he was on her, a large, broad-shouldered man in dark clothes, wearing a black woolly hat and a ski-mask obscuring his face. He grabbed her by the shoulders and barged through the door, carrying her with him as if she weighed no more than a child.

'Let go of me,' she shouted, but he took no notice. Her attempt to push him off was futile. He was far too strong for her. They passed the kitchen in a rush and turned into the room at the front of the apartment, sparsely furnished and dimly lit by one weak bulb.

He slammed her against the wall so hard most of the breath shot out of her. Another man rose slowly from a chair and moved to stand directly in front of her. She recognized him as the old man who'd tried to follow her on the subway. She could hear his wheezy breathing above her own panting breaths.

'Umiko Wada,' he rasped.

'Who . . . are you?' She did her best to sound unintimidated.

'Phone,' was his terse reply. He pulled her bag off her shoulder and upended it, the contents rustling and clunking to the floor. Her phone was among them. The old man stooped and picked it up. He tapped the blank black screen. But Wada had turned it off during the train journey. She wondered now what instinct had prompted her to do that. 'Security code,' he demanded.

'Where's Endo?' she countered.

'Who?'

'Daiju Endo. The tenant of this apartment.'

'Wouldn't know.' The old man looked weary, almost bored, as if he'd done this kind of thing far too often in his time. 'Security code.'

'I'm saying nothing until I speak to Daiju Endo or Taro Yamato.'

'Not possible.'

'Are they here?'

'What do you think?'

He nodded to his friend, a signal, apparently, for more extreme measures to be taken. The man's large hand closed round Wada's throat. 'Code,' he growled.

They wanted the pictures of Endo's car. That was obvious. And they wanted to know what she knew, some of which the phone would tell them, though not as much as they might have hoped. Yamato was either in league with them or had been forced to lure her there. As for Endo, she had no doubt his reappearance was a fiction.

176

Wada choked as the grip on her throat tightened. The old man stretched out a bony finger and traced the line of the cut on Wada's cheek. He nodded to his friend, who relaxed his grip. He looked Wada in the eye. 'Speak,' he said.

'I will tell you nothing,' she replied, holding his gaze.

'You're annoying me. I don't like being annoyed.'

'Let me go. Then I will stop annoying you.'

At that he slapped her hard across the face. She cried out involuntarily. His lip curled angrily. She felt certain he was going to slap her again.

He never did.

At that moment, a figure every bit as big and brawny as the man holding her strode into the room. He was wearing a long dark raincoat. He had a wide face framed by a mop of unruly hair. He was Seiji Tago. And Wada could never have imagined being so glad to see him.

He looped his arm under the old man's and, whirling him round, flung him across the floor. He slid as far as the opposite wall and struck it with some force. His friend released Wada and lunged towards Tago. Wada saw a flash of steel as he pulled a knife out of his belt. But Tago saw it as well. He kicked the knife out of the man's hand, then punched him hard in the throat. The man fell to his knees, gagging. Tago placed a hand on his forehead and bounced the back of his head violently against the wall behind him several times. He slumped to the floor and stayed there. And the old man, eyeing them woozily from the other side of the room, didn't move either.

It had all happened so quickly Wada could hardly register the sequence of events. Tago carefully picked up the knife and slipped it into a pocket of his raincoat. 'You want some help with your bag, Wada-san?' he asked gently. 'Only we should leave as soon as possible.'

'No. It's all right.' She gathered up her belongings, including

177

the all-important phone, which the old man had dropped, and dumped them unceremoniously back in her bag. She noticed she was trembling and clenched her fists to try to stop it. It didn't work.

'Just a reaction,' said Tago in a comforting tone. 'We go now?'

Wada nodded and led the way out of the room. Tago was close behind her as they stepped through the open front doorway. He closed the door and touched her shoulder, urging her to move. 'It's best to leave while they're still out of action,' he said in his strangely soft voice.

Wada nodded again and set off along the walkway at a swift pace, reasoning as best she could as they went. What would they have done to her if Tago hadn't intervened? And what had brought him there? For the moment, she was simply relieved something had. But she was going to have to find out.

They descended the external stairs to the street. 'The station?' asked Tago.

'Yes,' Wada replied. 'Let's get to the station.'

They set off through the quiet streets. 'Don't worry,' said Tago. 'They're not following us. And even if they were . . .' He paused by a drain grille and dropped the knife down through the bars. Then they pressed on.

'Thank you . . . for what you did back there.'

'I do not enjoy violence. Outside the rules and traditions of sumo, it is . . . distasteful to me. But I had no choice. I thought they might kill you.'

'I walked into a trap.'

'Does that happen to you often?'

'No, Tago-san, it doesn't.' She was beginning to feel exasperated with herself now.

'You are a brave woman.'

'Or a stupid one. What brought you here?'

'You did. I came to speak to you at your office. It was later than I intended. I wasn't sure visiting you was wise. I still wasn't sure when I saw you get on the train I was about to get off at Tokyo Station, so I stayed on. When you changed trains at Tabata, I started to worry about where you were going, so I followed you. I was planning to ask you not to investigate my expulsion from sumo, you see. Your mother told me she'd asked you to get me . . . reinstated. But that . . . can't happen. Anyway, one of the people on her list lives here, in Warabi. I thought you might be on your way to see him. A former stablemate of mine.'

'Well, I wasn't. You may as well know I have no plans to look into all that, despite my mother asking me to.'

'Good.'

'Don't you want to be exonerated, then?'

'I can't be exonerated, Wada-san.'

'Why not?'

'Can we make a deal?'

'What kind of deal?'

They turned a corner and there, straight ahead, was the frontage of Warabi station. Tago stopped and touched Wada's shoulder, signalling for her to stop as well. He looked down at her, his expression indecipherable in the patch of shadows they were standing in. 'If you don't ask me to say why I don't want you to investigate my expulsion from sumo, I won't ask you to say who those men were or what they wanted from you. And I won't tell your mother you could have died tonight. That's . . . the kind of deal I meant.'

He'd said he couldn't be exonerated and Wada guessed in that instant why not. Because he was guilty. Because he *had* taken bribes, or taken a cut from the bribes paid to Igarashi. Maybe he'd been forced into doing so, maybe not. It didn't matter in the end. That was probably why he'd ended up sleeping rough: shame; revulsion at what his own weakness had reduced him to;

179

the loss of his honour. 'There will be no investigation by me, Tago-san.'

'Thank you.'

'And I would be grateful if you did not worry my mother with an account of this evening's events.'

'She will not be worried.'

'Thank you.'

They headed on to the station and stood together on the platform, waiting for the next train back into the centre. Tago removed a flask from an inner pocket and took a swig from it. 'You want some?' he asked.

'What is it?'

'Shochu. It'll help with the trembling.'

Wada thought about it for a moment, then nodded. She watched Tago delicately wipe the mouth of the flask before handing it to her.

The spirit was fiery – and very strong. It was also just what she needed. She took a second swig before returning the flask. 'Will those men come after you again, Wada-san?' Tago asked.

'I doubt it.'

'Are you saying that to convince me – or yourself?'

'I am grateful for what you did for me, Tago-san. But you are not responsible for my safety.'

'Your mother would not want me to leave you unprotected.'

'I thought we agreed to leave her out of this.'

'I agreed to say nothing to her. That doesn't mean I don't know what she would expect of me – if she was aware of the circumstances.'

'I am going to Ginza to meet an American who has invited me to dine with him. You are going back to Koishikawa, where Mother will no doubt be delighted to prepare supper for you. Is that clear?'

'Do those men know where you live?'

'No.'

'Are you sure of that?'

The rails began to sing. The train was approaching. 'I'm sure,' Wada insisted.

But she wasn't sure, of course. She couldn't be. And though he didn't say so, Tago clearly knew that.

They parted at Tabata. Wada boarded the next clockwise train on the Yamanote circle, pleased to discover that the shochu had worked: her hands were completely steady. Her heart was also beating at its normal rate. Looking back at what had happened at the apartment in Warabi, she constructed an optimistic scenario in her mind whereby the old man and his sidekick would think twice about coming after her again in view of the impressively powerful bodyguard who might well intervene.

How Yamato had been persuaded to play his part in setting her up she didn't know and wasn't sure she wanted to know. She would return to that subject in the morning.

Meanwhile, she was in danger of being late for her appointment with Mitamura. It was a little after eight when the train reached Yurakucho and just gone ten past when she hurried towards the brightly lit entrance of the Razzler Dazzler pachinko parlour. She was already factoring in how long it would take her to locate Mitamura in the winking, beeping chaos within when, happily, he emerged, swaying gently, into the neon-splashed night.

'You're late,' he complained, pulling up and grinning at her in recognition. He didn't actually sound at all put out.

'I didn't think you'd be leaving so soon.'

'Oh, I'm not leaving for long. I've had a big win. I'm just popping out to cash in my pinballs.' Wada never gambled. She considered it the height of stupidity. And pachinko parlours

181

were for her a form of torture. But she was aware they weren't allowed to offer cash prizes, which meant winners had to use backstreet cashing shops, of which there were several in the area.

'Congratulations.' Wada pressed the envelope containing his ¥30,000 into Mitamura's hand. 'Enjoy the rest of your evening.'

'You look a little rough if you don't mind me saying, Wada. Is something wrong?'

Amazingly, he seemed genuinely concerned. Who knew there were so many white knights in Tokyo? 'I'm fine, thank you.'

'You shouldn't work so hard. Follow my example.'

'What example is that, Mitamura-san?'

His grin broadened. 'Keep hitting the jackpot.'

Tuscania occupied the top floor of a department store building in the heart of Ginza. Wada checked her appearance in the rest-room before going into the dining room, tidying her hair and smoothing out some of the creases in her clothes, although the collar of her top was stained with something from when she was grabbed round the throat. Still, she reckoned it wouldn't be obvious to Kimber. Generally speaking, men paid her appearance little attention and Kimber hadn't struck her as the observant type.

He was the garrulous and genial type, however, and he greeted her arrival so warmly anyone might have thought they were old friends. He was dressed casually but to Wada's eye expensively and insisted she join him in a Campari. It wasn't a drink she'd ever tried before, nor one she thought it likely she'd try again, but it had a punch she badly needed.

They were at a window table, with the lights of Ginza twinkling through the glass behind Kimber. The atmosphere around them was relaxed and sophisticated, with decanters being filled and delicacies enthusiastically savoured. It wasn't Wada's normal milieu, but Kimber appeared very much at his ease. Menus were delivered and dishes ordered. A bottle of white wine also appeared to succeed the Camparis.

'So . . .' he said, steepling his fingers to signal a shift in the conversation.

'So you are going to tell me all about Goro Rinzaki, Troy?' Wada said, summoning a brightness of tone along with a smile.

'What's your first name?' Kimber countered. 'I can't go on calling you Wada.'

'Technically, that is my first name. Name order in Japanese is the reverse of the western style. We switch it round so as not to confuse you. But I prefer Wada anyway.'

'OK. If you insist. Wada it is. Now, I do get some details of your missing person case in exchange for what I tell you about Rinzaki, don't I?'

'I will tell you as much as I can.'

'And how much is that?'

'You will have to rely on my judgement of what is compatible with the confidentiality I owe my client.'

'You're a hard nut, aren't you?'

'I think we can help each other. I think you think that too.'

'OK. We'll do this your way. What do you know about Rinzaki? I'm guessing you did some checking up on him after we spoke yesterday.'

'Chairman of the Kuraikagami Film Corporation. Born 1929. Well-preserved survivor of the post-war entrepreneurial generation. Nothing appears to connect him to your family's winery or the seismological research institute set up by Clyde Braxton in 1994.'

'But something does, Wada. You can trust me on that.'

'But what?'

'Rinzaki met my step-grandfather Clyde here in Tokyo during the Occupation. Clyde worked for some branch or other of SCAP – Supreme Command, Allied Powers. And Rinzaki worked

183

for Clyde. Office boy, filing clerk, something like that. Something lowly, anyhow. But that didn't stop him making himself indispensable and sliming his way up through the system. They stayed in touch after Clyde went home to California. I think Clyde may have invested in Rinzaki's film company. He set that up in 1949, three years before the Occupation ended. Hard to see how he could have pulled that off without a little help from his friends. And you'll agree an American officer was just about the most useful kind of friend to have back then. Point is, I don't really know the extent of their . . . financial connections. Or any other connections, for that matter. But they endured, to the end of Clyde's life.'

'You said Rinzaki wasn't involved in the winery, but in some other family enterprise. Would that be BISRI?'

'You've done your research, haven't you? Yes. BISRI. We'll get to that.'

'It was set up by Clyde after his daughter-in-law and grandchildren were killed in the San Francisco earthquake of 1989.'

'Yes. It was. I was three years old and living with my mother in Phoenix when they were killed. My father was already off the scene by then. My mother took a bookkeeping job at Braxton Winery after we moved to Santa Rosa. That's how she met Grant. They were married in 2003.'

'Making you heir to the business as Grant's stepson.'

'It's not quite as simple as that. But . . . I have expectations. Talking of which, that looks just about as delicious as it can get.'

Kimber's attention had turned to the bowl of wild boar ragout that was about to be placed in front of him, which, according to him, needed an accompanying bottle of red wine, leaving Wada to the white – and a modest fig and walnut salad.

After the briefest of digressions about how superior Braxtons' Pinot Noir was to the one on Tuscania's wine list, he reverted to the subject of Rinzaki's dealings with the family his mother had married into. 'The first time I met Rinzaki was when he came to

Clyde's funeral in 2005. I disliked him right from the start. I mean, the guy presents himself as this correct, cultured traditionalist. You'd think he was descended from Meiji nobility the way he carries on. Instead of which, well, who knows which gutter he crawled out of. My mother didn't like him either. He had this . . . attitude . . . towards Grant. It was as if he thought Grant owed him something because of his long association with Clyde. He kept on and on about BISRI – what a pity it was it hadn't made any breakthroughs in Clyde's lifetime; how he'd be happy to advise Grant on recruiting more Japanese experts to ginger it up. And there was something else – something more – between them that I wasn't let in on. Neither was my mother. Of course, I was a cocky nineteen-year-old then, so you could argue it was just a standard personality/generation clash. But other evidence suggests not.'

'What evidence would that be?'

'Oh, no.' He grinned at her over the rim of his wine glass. 'The time has come, Wada, for you to deliver on your side of the bargain. Who is Manjiro Nagata?'

She couldn't deny he'd revealed far more to her than she had to him. And she sensed he could be obdurate as well as forthcoming. She had to give him something. And something in this case was Nagata. 'He is the nephew of the chairman of Jinno Construction. He used to work for the company, but left some time ago and became increasingly reclusive. More recently, he seems . . . to have vanished completely. His father hired me to find him. And that's what I've been trying to do. So far without success.'

'What's the connection with Daiju Endo?'

'Endo asked a civil servant friend of his to trawl intelligence records for information about Nagata. He didn't find anything significant. And by the time he'd come up with nothing . . . Endo had disappeared as well.'

185

'So, you only got on to Endo because this favour from a friend came to light while you were looking for Nagata.'

'Basically, yes.'

'But you know the Endo story, don't you?' For all his self-confidence, Kimber judged it necessary to lower his voice at this point. 'That he was fired from a government job after telling the media – who buried the story – that there'd been a warning of the 2011 tsunami the day before it happened. A warning . . . from the Kobe Sensitive.'

'How do you know that?' Yes. How *did* he know that? There'd been no leak of the story that Wada was aware of.

'We haven't quite got to the point in our relationship where I feel I can trust you with that information, Wada, though I sense we're getting close. What took you to Matsuda Sanso?'

'Endo's known to have gone there shortly after the media agreed to embargo his claims about the Kobe Sensitive. I wondered if he might have . . . gone there again later. I was looking for a clue – any kind of clue – about what became of him.'

Kimber frowned at her. 'You're sure Endo went to Matsuda Sanso?'

'I am.'

'Can you prove it?'

'He was followed there by an investigator hired by one of the newspapers before the embargo was applied.'

'And you've spoken to this investigator?'

'No.'

'Don't you think you should?'

'I cannot speak to him. He is . . . deceased.'

Kimber's forkful of ragout froze halfway to his mouth. 'He's dead?'

'Subway suicide.'

'Jesus.' Kimber put down his fork. 'Are you going to eat any

186

more of that salad? Only I think we should take a cigarette break. They have a smoking balcony here.'

'I don't smoke.'

'Neither do I, generally. But it's more . . . private . . . out there. After what you've just said, I think a little privacy might be a good thing, don't you?'

Wada didn't argue. A few minutes later, they were standing on the restaurant balcony, holding their wine glasses and pretending to enjoy the vista of Ginza by night as Kimber puffed half-heartedly at a cigarillo. The only other diners out there were a man and woman at the far end who were entirely absorbed in each other.

'You don't believe the investigator killed himself, do you?' Kimber asked in an undertone as he leant against the parapet railings.

'I believe there is another possibility.'

'Another possibility? You're certainly not one to overreact, are you?'

'Would overreaction accomplish anything?'

'Where do you think Endo is now – on a balance of prob-ability?'

'I think there's a high likelihood he returned to Matsuda Sanso. Since then, he has been seen by no one.'

'Meaning?'

'Meaning I wouldn't put money on him ever being seen again. But, then, I never gamble.'

'Of course you don't.' He drew reflectively on the cigarillo. 'I'll tell you a story. Let's see what you make of it. Endo made his claims about the Kobe Sensitive in March of last year. Correct?'

'Yes. Around the tenth anniversary of the tsunami.'

'Right. Well, a couple of months after that, a Japanese

woman called Yukari Otonashi joined BISRI as some kind of . . . special consultant. You have to understand I'm not involved in BISRI. The winery's my area of responsibility. I got most of what I know about Otonashi from my mother and some people at BISRI I'm on good terms with. She was referred to Grant, my stepfather, by Rinzaki as someone who might be a genuine earthquake sensitive. Well, BISRI have studied a few supposed sensitives over the years and always concluded they were either faking it or deluded. Not so with Otonashi, however. She came highly recommended. The whisper was that she was actually the Kobe Sensitive, with two verifiably accurate predictions to her name. Kobe, obviously. Plus the tsunami, based on Endo's quashed story, which Rinzaki evidently knew all about. Nobody officially said she was the Kobe Sensitive. That was just a water-cooler rumour. Wishful thinking, if you like. But according to my mother Rinzaki arranged for Grant to meet Endo in order to verify Otonashi's claims. And Grant . . . believed what he was told. He wanted to believe it, of course. He'd always wanted to believe something like that was possible, so he could say his first wife and two young children hadn't died in vain – that his father's creation of BISRI had finally achieved what they'd both dreamt of.'

'How old is Yukari Otonashi?'

'I don't know exactly. Middle-aged. Probably a bit older than she looks. And, let me tell you, she is a beautiful woman. I mean, *very* attractive, even at fifty, or whatever she is. Which is part of the problem. If not the whole problem in some ways.'

'What does that mean?'

'Grant's in love with her.' Kimber chuckled mirthlessly. 'The old, old story. Mom can't compete with a beautiful younger woman who fascinates him with her supposed ability to do what he and his father set their hearts on achieving. She's worked him into a state of total infatuation.'

188

'And you fear she's going to persuade him to, what, divorce your mother, marry her, disinherit you?'

'You make that sound very self-centred, Wada. I do actually worry about my mother as well as myself. And about my stepfather as well. There's no fool like an old fool. And she's certainly fooling him.'

'You don't believe she might just be . . . the real thing? And that what there is between her and your stepfather is . . . genuine mutual attraction?'

'Maybe I could believe that, if she hadn't come into our lives thanks to Rinzaki. But this is really all about him. What he wants. What he's determined to have.'

'Which is?'

Kimber shook his head. 'I haven't the remotest fucking idea.'

'Has Otonashi returned to Japan at all since joining BISRI?'

'A couple of times. Grant went with her the first time. To get corroboration from Endo, so he told Mom. But she suspected another motive. When they came back it was obvious . . . their relationship was on a whole new level.'

'And Endo had corroborated her story?'

'So Grant said.'

'And Otonashi went back on another occasion?'

'There was a trip on her own as well, yeah.'

'When?'

'Late last year. Some . . . family issue. Supposedly.'

'Late last year is when Endo was last seen.' Wada was thinking hard now – about the woman who, according to Yamato, had entered Endo's life; about the money he'd apparently come by; about the triangle of connections between Endo, Otonashi and Goro Rinzaki. 'He was behaving erratically. He was spending a lot of money. But he was also worried . . . about something.' And he badly wanted information on Manjiro Nagata, though where

Nagata fitted in to all this Wada could not for the moment imagine. The mystery was too dense for her to penetrate – for now. 'I think he went to see Rinzaki at Matsuda Sanso. And I think he may never have left.'

'And that's why you went there yesterday? To look for evidence of Endo's visit?'

'Yes.'

'Find any?'

Wada did not speak. She supplied her answer with a nod.

'What did you find?'

'Leave that with me for the present. It is not enough in itself to clinch the matter. But it is . . . suggestive.'

'Oh yeah? And what does it suggest?'

'That the source of Endo's sudden wealth may have been Rinzaki. That it may have been payment for backing up Otonashi's claim that she is the Kobe Sensitive. And that Endo may have begun to regret what he had done, thereby becoming . . .'

'A liability.'

'It is possible.'

Kimber drained his wine glass. 'I want Otonashi out of our lives, Wada. I want Rinzaki out as well. I came over here to find the means to do that. I haven't made a lot of progress. Rinzaki covers his tracks well. Disappearances and convenient suicides add up to a cartload of suspicion but not so much as a thimbleful of proof. And proof is what I need to sway Grant. Think you can supply that? You're the private detective, after all. You're the professional here.'

'I am working on it.'

'Well, there's something more I can give you to work on, as it happens. Could be the vital lead you're looking for. Why don't we go back inside and I can tell you about it? They'll be wanting to serve our main courses.'

*

190

He was right about the main courses. They were served as soon as they sat down at their table: more meat for Kimber, fish for Wada. And Kimber seemed happy to be reunited with his bottle of red.

'Clyde's widow, Hetty – she died just a few years ago – complained on several occasions about Rinzaki. She never liked the way he somehow managed to stay in her husband's life. She also complained *to* Rinzaki, at Clyde's funeral, about harassment she said he'd been subjected to by some guy who'd worked under him in Japan, name of Perlman. Perlman had written letters to the State Department over a period of years alleging malpractice by Clyde while he was at SCAP – plus involvement in the death of an intelligence officer supposedly investigating said malpractice. Perlman had contacted the intelligence officer's family as well and roped them into his complaints. Not that anyone had taken him seriously. But he was a thorn in Clyde's side – and Hetty's. "Why didn't you ever do something useful for Clyde, like getting that crazy man Perlman off his back?" I remember her saying that to Rinzaki. She was really angry. Rinzaki just kept bowing and repeating his deep condolences – which only angered her more.'

Perlman sounded immediately interesting to Wada. 'Do you know whether this man is still alive?' she asked.

'I do now. I thought it was unlikely he'd still be above ground, but finding out as much as I could about his allegations against Clyde was one of my reasons for coming here. I reckoned those allegations probably implicated Rinzaki as well. I contacted various Navy veterans' groups and one of them told me Daniel Perlman had stayed in Japan after the Occupation ended and for many years had run a bar – the Flight Deck – near the US naval base at Yokosuka. They didn't have any up-to-date information on him. I went down to Yokosuka last weekend and paid a visit to the Flight Deck. Turns out Perlman's dead. No surprise, really.

His Japanese widow and daughter run the place now. I met the widow. She was polite but evasive, if you know what I mean.'

'Reticence about personal matters is a Japanese character-istic,' Wada pointed out, surprised to find herself instantly sympathizing with Perlman's widow when faced with cross-questioning by Troy Kimber.

'Well, maybe that's all it was. But here's the thing. Daniel Perl-man died in 2005, the same year as Clyde. Just a few months later, as a matter of fact. Now, I asked his widow how he died and she just said, "Accident." But what does that mean? I thought maybe you could find out.'

'Did she tell you the exact date of his death?'

'No. She didn't even tell me the year. In fact, she implied it was longer ago than it actually was. More than twenty years, she said. But I'd spotted the framed photo of old Dan on the wall behind the bar before I ever got talking to her. And I took a picture on my phone of the plaque underneath it. See for yourself.'

Kimber put his smartphone on the table and scrolled through various images, then, finding the one he wanted, turned the phone round and slid it across to Wada.

Daniel Perlman appeared in his photograph as a leathery old salt, with crew-cut white hair, a face lined like dried mud, bright blue eyes and a spirited grin. The plaque beneath read *Dan Perl-man, 6.16.1927–10.10.2005 – in command of the Flight Deck for nearly fifty years.* So, it was incontrovertibly true that he hadn't been dead for more than twenty years. And it seemed unlikely his widow would make a mistake on such a point.

'When did Clyde Braxton die?'

'July of 2005.' Kimber cocked an eyebrow at Wada as he replied. 'And three months later his old foe Dan Perlman meets with a fatal accident. Which sort of amounts to Rinzaki "doing something useful" about him, albeit too late to be of any value to Clyde.'

'With this date, I should be able to find out what kind of accident befell him.'

'And if it looks iffy – as I'd bet it will?'

'Then it is possible I may be able to learn something from his widow and daughter that you were not.'

'Yeah.' Kimber smiled. 'I'd bet on that as well.'

It was when they'd left the restaurant and started walking through Ginza towards Kimber's hotel, the Imperial, that he said, 'I admit I don't know what Rinzaki's objective really is. But I'm damn sure it doesn't bode well for me. So, I'm going to do everything I can to block him. There's something deep and dangerous at the root of all this, Wada. People have died. We need to know what it's really about.'

'I agree,' said Wada. 'I would suggest you try to charm Otonashi into letting slip something that might lead us to the answer.'

'OK. I'll do my best. Meanwhile, you'll be doing *your* best to find out as much as you can here?'

'Yes. I will report any progress I make. And you will do the same?'

'Sure. But you'll watch your back, won't you? I get the feeling this could turn ugly for you.'

'I go where the case takes me.'

'Yeah? Well, you don't want that carved on your tombstone, do you?'

'I do not need to worry about that.'

'You don't?'

'My name is already carved on the family gravestone. All that will happen when my ashes are buried there is that they will remove the red paint from my name to show I am no longer living.'

'Your name's already on the gravestone?'

'Yes. It is more economical to inscribe the names of the living

193

as well as the dead, with the living painted red – for the duration of their lives.'

'You find that . . . comforting?'

'I find it practical. And I am comfortable with practicality.'

'Right.'

They walked on in silence for a while.

Then Kimber said, 'Just be careful, though. For my sake.'

1995

RINZAKI DECLINED EITHER TO CONFIRM OR DENY THAT HE'D PUT up the five million yen reward Kodaka had seen advertised in the newspaper. But he did tell Kodaka he'd be welcome to claim the reward, in addition to his normal fee, if he found the Kobe Sensitive. 'It is an added incentive for you to succeed, Kodaka-san,' Rinzaki said with a smile. The smile had a patronizing edge to it, as if he were offering an idle schoolboy a bar of chocolate to encourage him in his studies. But five million yen is a lot of chocolate. Added to his fee, it would make this the best-rewarded case Kodaka has ever taken on. And with his efforts on behalf of Teruki Jinno at an end, there is nothing standing in his way.

He is unsure he wants to work for Goro Rinzaki, about whom he knows rather less than he'd like. But it's not the first time he's had reservations about a client. The work is the thing. As long as he abides by his own standards where that's concerned, his conscience can bear a lot of reservations.

He plays the tape of the Kobe Sensitive's phone call to the Kantei as soon as he reaches his office. Night has fallen and most people are on their way home. Kodaka could take the tape player back to his apartment and listen to the recording there. But it is easier to concentrate in his office. It is quieter and, as the Kono Building empties, more isolated. He smokes a cigarette as he listens to the tape. Then he pours himself a whisky and listens to it again through headphones, with the desk lamp turned off and his eyes closed. It sounds more real then, more intimate. And other layers of sound subtly reveal themselves.

'*Sori-Kantei desu.*'

'*I wish to give a warning of an earthquake. Can you put me through please?*'

'*A warning? Do you mean a report?*'

'*No. A warning. It has not happened yet.*'

'*I do not understand.*'

'*Put me through to someone who can order action to be taken.*'

'*No one can order action to be taken about—*'

'*PUT ME THROUGH TO SOMEONE.*'

'*Ah . . . Hold please . . . Hold . . .*'

'*Are you there?*'

'*Yes. Hold please.*'

'*This is urgent.*'

'*Hold please.*'

'*I—*'

'*Putting you through.*'

'*Thank you.*'

'*Yes? Aides' office. Shiota speaking. Who is calling?*'

'*You must listen to me. This is very urgent.*'

'*I am listening. What is your name, please?*'

'*An earthquake is going to happen. Tomorrow. Very big.*'

'*What?*'

'*Kobe, tomorrow morning. A strong earthquake will lay it waste. You must evacuate people. You must save them.*'

'*That is . . . not possible. No one can . . . predict an earthquake.*'

196

'Listen to me. Kobe. Tomorrow morning. It will happen. Thousands will die unless you act.'

'I can do nothing on the basis of an anonymous warning.'

'Would you act if I told you my name?'

'Tell me what your name is and we can talk about this.'

'WILL YOU ACT?'

'I cannot act. It is not possible. Kobe is not going to be laid waste tomorrow.'

'It is. I have told you. That is all I can do.'

'I can do nothing to help you.'

'Tomorrow, you will regret not listening to me.'

'I doubt—'

'Put me back to the operator.'

'Very well. Hold please.'

. . . 'Switchboard.'

'Put me through to someone else. That man, Shiota, is . . . an idiot.'

'There is no one else I can put you through to.'

'There must be.'

'Shiota is the appropriate officer.'

'Appropriate for what? There is going to be a big earthquake in Kobe tomorrow. Someone must listen to me.'

'There is no one else I can put you through to.'

'What is the point of repeating yourself? You are no better than the Kobe police.'

'You have spoken to the Kobe police?'

'DO SOMETHING.'

'There is nothing I can do.'

'You are all— It doesn't matter. Hush.'

'You are telling me to be quiet?'

'Not you.'

'Ochika.'

'Time is running out. Evacuate Kobe. Otherwise—'

'I want to go to So's, Ochika. Can we go now?'

'Hush. Soon we will go. PLEASE DO SOMETHING.'

'There is no one else I can put you through to.'

'That is the third time you have said that. Please, please, don't say it again.'

'I am sorry.'

'You will be. Tomorrow.'

'Ochika. Can we go now?'

'Yes. It seems there is no point in staying.'

'I am sorry. There is no one else I can put you through to. I . . . I am sorry.'

Kodaka replays the recording from the point where the caller was handed back to the operator. Whose was the small voice that interrupted the conversation? A child's? They addressed the caller as Ochika, an unusual name. It seems the child was not with its mother. A sister, maybe? And what is it Kodaka can *almost* hear in the background after the exchanges cease, but before the recording stops? Something musical? It's too faint to be sure.

He needs expert help to glean anything more from the recording. Fortunately, he knows someone who can give him that help. He flicks through his Rolodex in search of Nagaharu Myoga's phone number.

His own telephone rings at that moment and Kodaka knows instinctively who is calling so late. He has called several times today already. And Kodaka is going to have to speak to him sooner or later. His temper will not improve by being made to wait any longer. Kodaka picks up the phone.

'Umetsu?'

'How did you guess?' Umetsu doesn't sound in a jocular mood.

'I'm sorry if you've had any . . . difficulties . . . because of this . . . situation at Mizunuma Bank.'

'Difficulties? My contact at Mizunuma has accused me of leaking confidential information. Which wouldn't have happened, would it, if the person I leaked it to had kept his mouth shut?'

'I understand your frustration. But a lid's been put on this. I'm assured the account holder is happy with the undertakings he's received from Mizunuma.'

'How do you know that?'

'I just do. And it means it's all going to blow over.'

'With my reputation untarnished? I don't think so.'

'Memories are short. There'll be something else for your boss to fret over soon enough.'

'My boss's memory *isn't* short. Neither is mine. You didn't keep your side of the bargain, Kodaka. I sell you information. I *never* hear anything more about it. That's how it's supposed to work.'

'I agree there's been a . . . miscalculation . . . on my part. I am truly sorry.'

'Your apology does not help me.'

'Well, maybe a bonus on top of the original payment would be . . . appropriate. Shall we say . . . half as much again?'

There's a silence while Umetsu chokes back further reproaches in the face of a cash offer Kodaka reckons such a hapless mahjongg player won't be able to refuse. In the end, Umetsu grits out a terse acceptance. 'OK.'

'I can hand it over tomorrow.'

'OK.'

'Where and when?'

'Outside Takashimaya, one fifteen.'

'I'll see you there.'

With Umetsu mollified – or, if not mollified, at least bought off – Kodaka returns to his Rolodex. A few minutes later, he puts a call through to Myoga. He's optimistic about getting an answer, since Myoga isn't a man with an extensive social life. His entire existence seems to revolve around the tiny electronic gadgets shop he operates in Akihabara and the equally tiny apartment he occupies nearby. Kodaka has caught him at the shop.

'Ah, Gumshoe.' It is Myoga's standard greeting. 'Who do you want me to bug? A greedy executive? An adulterous husband? Or maybe an adulterous wife? They're the most fun.'

'No customers?'

'You're my first in . . . ten minutes.'

'I need your ear.'

'It is a sensitive instrument. And therefore expensive.'

'Can we haggle over the terms when I get there?'

'Who says I'll still be here when you arrive?'

'I say. This is a real puzzle. You know you love puzzles.'

'You'd better not be over-hyping this.'

'I'm not.'

'All right, then. You have an appointment. I'll see you soon.'

Myoga's shop is in a warren of similarly minuscule premises beneath the elevated tracks leading in and out of Akihabara station. Kodaka heads for Tokyo Station, knowing most northbound trains will deliver him to Akihabara in short order.

It's a straightforward journey and the train is busy, but Kodaka, always alive to such possibilities, senses he is receiving a suspicious amount of attention from one of the other passengers, a middle-aged, scruffily dressed man with lank greying hair and a wispy beard framing a round face. He clearly hasn't just emerged from an office, but there's no sign of work dust on his clothes. He's reading – or pretending to read – an evening edition of *Yomiuri Shimbun*. He may be following Kodaka, he may not: time will tell.

The man gets off at Akihabara, rising from his seat only after Kodaka has risen from his. Altogether, it looks to Kodaka as if he has a tail. He loses him swiftly enough, using a technique his father taught him. It involves getting back on the train, waiting for the tail to follow, then leaving again just before the doors close. Effective, when you're quick enough on your feet to pull it off, as Kodaka is.

Kodaka's assumption is that the man works for Rinzaki and has been instructed to keep an eye on him. He is not a serious threat, then, but certainly an annoyance. Although Kodaka has shaken him off, he is aware he will probably be back at some point.

He hurries out of the station and makes a beeline for Myoga's shop. It looks drab and unalluring compared with its gaudily lit neighbours, but to Myoga there is no such thing as passing trade, only established customers who have no interest in trappings and fripperies.

There are no customers of any kind at present, because the *CLOSED* sign is displayed on the door. Kodaka rings the bell and Myoga emerges from a back room. He is a small, thin, almost completely bald man and is clad in his customary outfit of cardigan, collarless shirt and baggy trousers. His eyes register Kodaka's presence through a pair of thick-lensed glasses. A second pair of glasses, for extra magnification, is perched on top of his dome-like head.

He opens the door and closes it behind Kodaka, then leads him through to the back room, which is really no bigger than a cupboard. There are no windows and the light is subdued. But there's a bank of audio equipment along the rear wall and a small bench which serves as the centre of Myoga's operations. 'What have you got for me?' he asks with transparent eagerness.

Kodaka takes the tape out of his pocket. 'Recording of a telephone call. I'm trying to track down the caller. I have no name and no address, just the call.'

'Made from?'

'A public phone, I'm guessing.'

'And made to?'

'You'll soon find out.'

'No clues in what the caller says to their identity?'

'None.'

'What does that leave me to work with, then?'

'I don't know. You're the audio magician.'

'Let me play it.'

Kodaka hands the tape over. Myoga slips it into a player and sits down at the bench. He puts on earphones, twiddles some buttons and listens, frowning in concentration.

Before enough time has passed for him to have heard the tape to the end, he presses the *STOP* button, takes off his earphones and gives Kodaka a leery look. 'You could have told me before I started listening.'

Yes, he could have done. But . . . . 'I didn't want to spoil your fun.'

'How did you get this?'

'I can't tell you that.'

'Only there's more here than in the version they played on the television.'

'It seems they edited it.'

'It seems they did. The chat with the operator, the name of the official. We didn't get that, did we?'

'We did not.'

'You're looking for the caller, right?'

'Right.'

'And the caller is the Kobe Sensitive.'

'Well, you heard what she said.'

'Yes. And I read the advertisement in *Asahi*. A reward of five million yen for information leading to the identification of the Kobe Sensitive. You've given up working on divorces and industrial espionage and turned into . . . a bounty hunter.'

'I'm working for a client, as usual. The reward is . . . a fringe benefit.'

'A fringe benefit? Five million yen? Well, I'll want twenty per cent if I help you find her.'

Kodaka has been expecting this. 'I'll pay you ten per cent. *If* I get the reward.'

'Fifteen.'

'Ten.'

'Twelve and a half.'

'All right. Twelve and a half.'

'That's six hundred and twenty-five thousand. Just so we're clear.'

'Impressive mental arithmetic. What would you do with that kind of money?'

'Technical upgrades are always expensive.'

'I'm sure they are.'

'And this is on top of my fee, which we haven't negotiated yet.'

'OK. On top. Now, are you going to listen through to the end of the tape?'

'I am. Sit down and don't make a noise. Above all, don't touch anything.'

Kodaka sits on a low stool at one end of the bench. Myoga puts the earphones back on and starts the machine again. He bends forward, squeezing his eyes shut as he listens, making tiny adjustments to one knob or another as he proceeds, with several stops, rewinds and replays along the way. And Kodaka does his best not to move so much as a muscle.

Eventually, after long enough has passed for Myoga to have listened to the tape at least three times over, he presses *STOP*, removes the headphones and says, 'They should have acted on the warning, shouldn't they?'

'You know what they said. They often received crank calls about earthquakes and tsunamis. How were they to know this wasn't just another one?'

'Maybe it was just another one. Maybe she's the crank who got lucky.'

'So why hasn't she come forward to cash in?'

'You can ask her when you find her. She's quite young. In her mid-twenties, I would judge.'

'Are you going to be able to help me find her?'

'Just at the end of the tape, there's a musical sound. You heard that?'

'I did. I couldn't place it.'

'Because you don't have an ear for such things. It's no more than a snatch of a couple of notes. But I think I know what it is.'

'So? What is it?'

'We need to settle the fee first.' Myoga smiles. 'I propose a hundred thousand yen.'

'A *hundred thousand*?'

'Entirely reasonable, when you consider the unique level of my expertise.'

Kodaka senses that arguing is going to get him nowhere. And ultimately Rinzaki will pay, of course. 'All right. A hundred thousand.'

'I'd like it now, please.' Myoga is still smiling, but he is clearly in earnest.

Kodaka sighs, reaches for his wallet and counts out ten ¥10,000 notes, which he places on the bench. Looking at the cash left in his wallet, he realizes he is going to have to visit the bank before meeting Umetsu tomorrow.

Myoga gathers up the money. 'Thank you.'

'Do I get to hear what the music is now?'

'Yes. Though, unfortunately, it won't help you much. It's the start of the jingle before a station announcement. You know, "Your attention please, Sendai train will soon arrive platform twelve – for your safety, please stand behind the yellow line . . ." Only there's no way of knowing where this train's going or from which platform of which station. All we get is a snatch of the jingle. Main line, though, not subway, I can tell you that. Although it doesn't . . . narrow it down a lot, I'm afraid. The only thing we can be sure of is that the call was made from inside a station . . . somewhere.'

'Is that all I'm getting for my hundred thousand yen?'

'*My* hundred thousand yen now. And, no, it's not all you're getting. What do you make of the interruptions from what sounds like a child?'

'The caller has a child with her. Not *her* child, though, because he or she addresses her by name.'

'It's he, not she.'

'You're sure?'

'I am. Aged five or six, I'd estimate.'

'OK. A boy of five or six. Who calls her Ochika.'

'No. He doesn't call her that.'

'What are you talking about? He clearly does.'

'Put on the spare headphones and listen to it with me.'

Kodaka does as he's been told. Myoga plays the tape from the point where the caller is returned to the switchboard. They hear the child's voice. Kodaka still can't detect anything in it that clinches the sex, but he's happy to accept Myoga's judgement on the point. As far as the name the boy uses is concerned, however, there's no doubt that it's Ochika.

Myoga removes his headphones and Kodaka follows suit. Myoga spreads his hands, inviting comment.

'I still hear Ochika,' says Kodaka.

'No. Not Ochika. O-chika.'

The difference is subtle and to Kodaka's mind immaterial. He shrugs.

'O is the honorific prefix O. The caller's name is actually Chika, probably short for Chikako.'

'Why the prefix?'

'My father started this business, you know.'

Kodaka does know. He recalls meeting Myoga senior, who was a conspicuously more genial man than his son, despite losing a leg in the war. His relevance to the minor mystery of the alleged prefix is not apparent to Kodaka. But he refrains from pointing that out, assuming the old man's relevance will eventually emerge.

'He bought up army surplus electronic parts that were in plentiful supply at the end of the war and started making radios. That's how it began. We were penniless when he came home, completely destitute. But he found a way to make a living. It's all the more impressive when you realize he had quite a well-to-do upbringing, so he had no experience of scraping by. He often told me about the comfortable existence he enjoyed as a child, back in the Taisho era. The family had several maids, to cook and clean and look after the children.'

'That's very interesting,' said Kodaka, his patience snapping, 'but—'

'One of the maids used to come and see him long after she left the family. I remember her visiting us quite often as an old lady. Her first name was Kikue – Kiku for short. My father didn't call her Kiku, though. He called her O-kiku, because that was how people addressed their maids before the war. It's almost unheard of now. It's very old-fashioned. But you can hear it on the tape. The boy calls the woman O-chika. She's a maid.'

'Let me hear it again.'

'Very well.'

Myoga replays the section of the tape and Kodaka listens to it very carefully. This time he hears it: the difference between Ochika and O-chika. He hears it and believes it. The caller is a maid, stopping while she's out running errands for her mistress – with the mistress's young son in tow – to make a phone call that she hopes will persuade someone at the Kantei to listen to her and to act on what she has to say.

'You are convinced now?'

Kodaka nods. 'I am convinced.'

'All you need to do is to find an old-fashioned family with a son of five or six and a maid called Chikako. They might live here in Tokyo, or Kobe, or Nagasaki, or . . .'

'Anywhere?'

'Anywhere with a main line railway station fitted with public telephones. Although, if you want me to . . . venture an opinion . . .'

'Venture one.'

'Well, I couldn't swear to this, you understand. It's more of a guess than a firm conclusion. You can't rely on it.'

'Just tell me.'

'OK. The echo in the background is . . . quite particular. All spaces create their own unique sound. It's to do with the way noises and voices bounce off their surroundings, how they mix in the air, how they . . . interact. It's in the nature of sound waves. It's how they behave. The sound on this tape . . . feels familiar to me. And I am not a well-travelled man. I have never been to Kobe. Or Nagasaki.'

'You're saying this call was made in Tokyo?'

'I'm *suggesting* it was made in Tokyo Station. It's something to do with the wooden roof they put up after the dome was wrecked by an air raid towards the end of the war. I read in *Asahi* that they're planning to restore the dome. That will alter the timbre, of course, though whether it will sound just as it did before the bombing is another matter. All my adult life, though, it's sounded' – Myoga ejects the tape from the machine and holds it up – 'rather like this.'

Kodaka takes the tape from him and stares at it. He's thinking hard now, about what he can do to track down Chikako the maid. There are agencies for domestic staff. He supposes that would be where to start. But he suspects many maids are recruited directly, or by personal recommendation. And Tokyo is a big city. In which most rail routes converge on Tokyo Station. It could be a hopeless – if not a never-ending – search.

'That's what you get for your hundred thousand yen,' says Myoga. 'You wouldn't get it anywhere else. And there's something more.'

'What?'

'On the tape, the boy says, "I want to go to So's." What is So's?'

'I don't know. Do you?'

'No.' Myoga smiles. 'But I think you should find out.'

2022

WADA WAS BEING MORE CAREFUL THAN SHE'D HAVE ADMITTED TO Troy Kimber. She didn't go home after dinner that night, but spent it at a women-only capsule hotel, where she expected to be – and was – woken early by the pre-dawn departures of other guests.

She had breakfast in a nearby coffee shop, then headed straight for the Kono Building. She had a lot to think about, principally how to go on investigating the Nagata case without further run-ins with her assailants of the previous evening. She was undecided about Yamato's role in luring her to Endo's apartment. On balance, she suspected he'd been forced into playing his part in the deception. If so, though, how had that ended for him? She decided to call the Kantei and ask to speak to him rather than trying his mobile, which might have been stolen or hacked.

It would be an hour or more before she could expect to find him at his desk. She filled the time by searching newspaper on-line archives for a report on the supposedly accidental death of Daniel Perlman in October 2005. She started with *Asahi* and had worked her way through *Yomiuri* and *Mainichi* as well, finding precisely nothing, when her landline phone rang.

She wondered if Kimber was the caller. But no. The voice on the other end of the line belonged to her saviour of last night, Seiji Tago. 'I am relieved to hear your voice, Wada-san.'

'Why?'

'I was worried that the men we . . . encountered . . . last night might have . . . come after you again.'

'I particularly asked you not to worry about me, Tago-san.'

'But what we worry about is dictated by our personality, which we are helpless to change, even if we wish to.'

'My personality requires me to be unhampered by the attentions of those who do not think I am capable of looking after myself.' She instantly regretted the harshness of her tone. What would have happened to her without his intervention, after all, wasn't pleasant to contemplate.

'In that you take after your mother. Who is currently out, which I mention in case you are concerned that she might over-hear this call.'

'Tago-san, you must let me be the judge of what risks I should run.'

'I will, of course. As we agreed. But do you object to occa-sional . . . enquiries about your situation?'

She felt she needed to make some concession to him, however much it went against the grain. 'I do not object,' she said mildly.

'Thank you, Wada-san. I wish you . . . a good day.'

She'd continued scrolling through the archived columns of the *Mainichi* as she spoke to Tago. Now, as she put the phone down, an idea suddenly leapt out at her. An accidental death in Yoko-suka wasn't necessarily going to be reported in any of the national newspapers. And there was no local newspaper for Yokosuka. Except, of course, in a sense there was. It was mentioned, in the article that had caught her eye: a small piece summarizing an interview that had appeared in *Seahawk*, the newspaper of the US naval base at Yokosuka.

Wada immediately abandoned the archives of the nationals and moved on to the *Seahawk* website, reckoning the death of a US Navy veteran and local bar owner was likely to have warranted a mention.

And she was right. In fact, it had made the paper's front page on October 14, 2005.

Veteran bar owner drowned in Green Bay

Several generations of US naval personnel who have served at Yokosuka base will be saddened to hear of the death of Dan Perlman, aged 78, who was, for nearly fifty years, proprietor of the Flight Deck bar, a short walk from the main gate of the base.

Mr Perlman's body was recovered from Green Bay Wednesday morning last. The local police have stated that the cause of death was drowning. His widow, Nonoka Perlman, who ran the bar with him and will also be widely remembered, said he had been diagnosed with dementia last year and had grown increasingly confused. He had gone missing from their apartment above the bar on several occasions recently and she had reported his latest absence to the police Sunday night.

He was seen by a passer-by wandering along the New Port wharf that evening and the police believe he must at some point have fallen or perhaps even jumped into the sea. According to his widow, he was a strong swimmer in his younger days, but, at night and in a confused condition, he was evidently unable to swim to shore, with tragic consequences.

Daniel S. Perlman was born in Providence, Rhode Island, June 16, 1927. He served in the Navy from 1944 to 1952 and saw action in the latter months of the war in the Pacific. He is survived by his wife and daughter.

There was nothing in the report to suggest Perlman's death was anything other than the accident his widow had told Kimber it was. The timing was a little suspicious, but Wada was aware that in such matters it was all too easy to multiply two by two and come up with five. Kimber had hoped there was something 'iffy' about the circumstances. In reality, though, there wasn't.

That didn't mean Wada was going to accept the *Seahawk* report at face value, however. A trip to Yokosuka might yield nothing. But it might, on the other hand, yield the breakthrough she needed.

Before setting off, she telephoned the Kantei, wondering if Yamato would be there, or if she'd be told he was absent sick, or just plain absent.

She was put through to his assistant without demur. A woman answered and Wada immediately detected something tight and distressed in her voice. 'Who . . . who is calling?'

'My name is Wada. I wish to speak to Yamato-san on an urgent personal matter.'

'I . . . I am sorry. That is not possible.'

'Is he in the office today?'

There was a lengthy silence at the other end of the line.

'Are you still there?'

'Yes. Yes, I am sorry. No. He . . . is not here.'

'When are you expecting him?'

There was a sound close to a sob, which shocked Wada. A show of emotion from a Kantei official was highly unusual. 'Are you . . . a friend of his?'

Instinctively, Wada said, 'Yes.'

'Then . . . you will wish to know . . . the news we have just had. Yamato-san is . . . deceased.'

'Deceased?'

'Yes. I am sorry. Everyone who works – worked – with him is very shocked.'

'What happened?'

'I cannot . . . give you any details. I am sorry. That is . . . all I can say.'

And with that, and another stifled sob, the woman hung up.

Another suspiciously timed accident? Wada badly needed to know what she was dealing with. The quickest way to find out how Yamato had died was to enlist the help of someone with better access to the authorities than she had. She put a call through to Funaki as she hurried out of the building, bound for Tokyo Station and a train to Yokosuka. Even as she left a message asking him to call her back she was busily checking ahead, around and over her shoulder for any signs of the old man and/ or his accomplice.

Reassuringly, there were absolutely none, though that didn't stop her taking the underground arcade route into the station. She was most of the way to the Marunouchi side, where trains to Yokohama and Yokosuka ran from, when Funaki called back.

'Is this your overdue report on your visit to Matsuda Sanso, Wada?' he asked in his normal half-grumpy half-cheery manner.

'That'll have to wait, Funaki-san. I'm . . . hard-pressed.'

'*You're* hard-pressed. What about me?'

'I will tell you as much as I can when I can. Meanwhile, I need to know how Taro Yamato, a civil servant who worked at the Kantei and was a close friend of Daiju Endo, met his death.'

'When did he meet it?'

'Last night or this morning. Circumstances unknown. But I

213

doubt it was natural causes. He appeared to be in good health when I met him.'

'Ah. You met him, did you?'

'Last weekend. I got some information from him about Endo.'

'And now he's dead. That's in addition to your two – or is it three? – missing persons.'

'Can you ask your police contact what happened to him?'

'All right. But from the sound of it this is getting serious. Do you think you might be out of your depth?'

'Definitely not.'

'I doubt it's definite, I really do. Still, at least you got back from Matsuda Sanso unscathed.'

'Exactly.'

'OK, Wada. I'll see what I can find out. Taro Yamato, you say?'

'Yes. That is the name. And thank you. Please let me know as soon as you have anything.'

'Of course. It's not as if I have any other calls on my time.'

'I am grateful, Funaki-san.'

'Good. Because sooner or later that gratitude is going to have to be translated into concrete gains for me.'

It was hard to see how anything Wada had so far learnt could be used by Funaki without breaching the media embargo on the Endo story. But maybe he was trying to make sure he was ahead of the pack when and if the embargo was lifted. She couldn't blame him. He had his job to think about just as she had hers. As for his suggestion that she might be out of her depth, she recalled something her father had said to her in her childhood when he took her for swimming lessons in the pool at Toshimaen amusement park: 'If you don't try to touch the bottom, Umiko, you won't need to worry about how deep the water is.'

*

214

There was a clean breeze blowing in off the sea when Wada walked out to the waterfront at Yokosuka. The New Port wharf was filled with cars awaiting export. The buildings of the US naval base were visible further round the bay, beyond Mikasa Park, named, as Wada knew from school history lessons, after the old Japanese battleship preserved there, a relic of the war against Russia in 1904–05. History, in fact, was all around her, though Daniel Perlman's part in it remained elusive.

She headed inland to bustling Dobuita-dori and tracked down the Flight Deck bar. It was closed, the frontage shuttered, but crates of Budweiser beer were being unloaded from a van, the driver trundling them by sack truck along a narrow alleyway to the side. Wada asked him if anyone from the management was on site and he said if she followed him along the alley she'd find 'the woman in charge' in the office at the rear.

So it proved. The 'woman in charge' must in fact have seen her coming, because she stepped out through a door next to the delivery bay just as Wada approached.

She somehow reminded Wada of herself: slightly built, about the same age, with greying black hair and an alert, businesslike expression. She was marginally taller, though, and didn't descend the short flight of steps from the door to the ground, so looked down at Wada with a considerable advantage of height.

'Can I help you?' She frowned as she posed the question. And there was the merest hint of an American accent in her voice. If she was Perlman's daughter, as Wada assumed, she might have acquired the intonation from him.

'*Konnichi wa.* My name is Wada. Are you, perhaps, Daniel Perlman's daughter?'

'I am Itsuko Perlman, yes.'

'This is the last,' the delivery man interrupted.

Itsuko nodded and hurried down the steps. She checked the

particulars on his phone and signed the screen with a digital pen. He hurried off along the alley.

'I hope this is not an inconvenient time,' said Wada.

'My father died long ago,' Itsuko replied coolly. 'What is it you want to know about him? And why do you want to know it?'

'I am a private detective.' Wada proffered one of her cards. 'Your father was mentioned to me by an American called Troy Kimber in connection with a case I am investigating.'

'Ah, Troy Kimber.' Itsuko took the card and glanced at it. 'And you are with the . . . Kodaka Detective Agency?'

'I am.' Wada did not think this was the moment to make it clear that in essence she *was* the Kodaka Detective Agency.

'Mr Kimber came here a few days ago. I did not meet him. He spoke to my mother. You know of my father's involvement with his family?'

'Yes.'

'Well, he seemed to be hoping my mother would be able to tell him my father's death was in some way suspicious. But it wasn't. Not at all.'

'He drowned, I believe.'

'He did. His mental health was poor. He was often confused. It was simply . . . a terrible accident. What is your interest in the matter?'

'I am looking for a missing person on behalf of a relative. His name is Manjiro Nagata.' Wada took out the photograph of Manjiro supplied by his father. It was a slightly overexposed snap of a man who looked much like a hundred other middle-aged men to be seen on the Tokyo subway every day: clean-shaven, gaunt, greying. No one would recognize him from it unless they had good reason to remember meeting him. 'Do you know him?'

Itsuko gave the picture her considered attention, then shook her head. 'I do not know this man.'

'You've never met him?'

216

'Not that I recall. And still I do not understand what the connection is with my father.'

'Goro Rinzaki . . . appears to be the connection.'

'Ah. Rinzaki. Well, my father fell out with him when they worked together just after the war. And it is true he sometimes – very ill-advisedly – tried to persuade others that Rinzaki wasn't to be trusted. But my father is more than sixteen years dead. And what they fell out over occurred about seventy-five years ago. Three quarters of a century. Ancient history.' Itsuko tilted her chin and looked at Wada, inviting her to justify her interest in such distant events. 'What Goro Rinzaki does now and what his dealings with Troy Kimber's family are . . .' She shrugged. 'These matters mean nothing to us.'

'By "us" you mean you and your mother?'

'Exactly so.'

'And you're sure . . . your father's death was just an accident?'

'If I were to answer that question with complete candour . . .'

Was this Wada's chance to learn something of value? 'I would be very grateful if you did.'

'Well, it has occurred to me he may have decided to prevent further deterioration in his condition by ending his life on his own terms. There is no evidence to support that conclusion. The police ruled it was an accidental drowning. But he was a sailor. Maybe he resolved to . . . end his life in his natural element.'

'I see.' The thought of Perlman drowning himself for the reason his daughter was hinting at brought with it a sudden poignancy. 'My condolences, Perlman-san.'

'Is your father living, Wada-san?'

'No.'

'Then you have my condolences also. You have not told me what the missing man's connection is with Rinzaki and I prefer you not to. I do not know his face. And I have never heard his name before. There really is nothing I can tell you about him or his whereabouts. Except that his . . . disappearance, if that is what it is . . . has nothing to do with my late father and his . . . feud . . . with Rinzaki. Nothing . . . at all.'

Wada left disappointed but also impressed. Itsuko Perlman was a woman after her own heart. She'd seemed clear-minded and utterly certain. She wasn't going to allow the Nagata case to touch her or her mother. It was, quite simply, nothing to do with them. Which was either the truth or a position she'd taken for reasons of her own and from which she wasn't going to be shifted.

A call had come in from Funaki during their conversation. Wada rang him back as she walked away from the bar along Dobuita-dori. He answered with uncharacteristic promptness. 'Where are you now, Wada?'

'Yokosuka.'

'What's taken you there?'

'I've been following a lead.'

'Are you going to share it with me?'

'What can you tell me about Yamato?'

'Nothing pleasant. It's suicide, apparently. He hanged himself with his belt from a drainpipe on the balcony of his apartment. His next-door neighbour found him when she went out onto her balcony to air her futon. It can't have been a nice start to her day.'

This was much as Wada had feared. She had no doubt Yamato's death was actually murder dressed up to look like suicide. And she also had no doubt that to continue ignoring the level of threat this meant she was under was foolhardy. But what was she to do? 'I don't believe Yamato killed himself,' she said simply.

'Any more than you believe Sekiyama threw himself in front of that subway train?'

'What do you believe, Funaki-san?'

'That you should drop this case. Too many people are dying or disappearing. I wouldn't want to hear you were next.'

'I will do my very best to ensure that does not happen.'

'By dropping the case?'

'I did not say that.'

'No. You didn't. You didn't even say you'd think about it seriously. But you should. Someone hires you to take on an investigation in return for a fee. It's not a religious calling, Wada. It's just a commercial transaction.'

'I am contracted.'

'Cancel the contract. That's my advice.'

'Thank you, Funaki-san. Your advice is appreciated.'

'When I hit a dead end,' Kodaka was fond of saying, 'I go back to the beginning.' Wada decided to follow her late employer's advice rather than Funaki's. She headed back into Tokyo, collected the skeleton keys from the office, then set off for Musashino.

It was mid-afternoon and the scene at the apartment building where Manjiro Nagata notionally lived was much as it had been on Wada's last visit. The few people moving around paid her no attention, a state of affairs she was well used to. Something about her made her easy to ignore, which she valued both personally and professionally. She had as little wish to impose herself on the world as to have it imposed on her.

She used the same tactics to reach Nagata's apartment without encountering Hosogai as she had previously: a ride in the lift to the seventh floor, then a walk down the stairs to the fifth. She'd tied a piece of string round the key that fitted the lock of apartment 514. She separated it from the bunch carefully to avoid rattling and opened the door.

She'd expected to find everything exactly as she'd left it. Her plan was to conduct a painstaking search for clues about where Nagata might have gone. She wasn't confident of finding any, but there was a chance, so the effort was worth it.

Except that there was, it transpired, no chance at all.

The apartment was empty, stripped of furniture and fittings. The coir mat in the *genkan* area under which she'd found the note from Yamato was gone. The kitchen was devoid of pots and pans. The dining table had vanished. The lounge held nothing: no TV, no cabinet, no sofa, no armchair. The loudspeakers had been removed from their various places of concealment. All the props and devices of Nagata's fictitious residence were gone.

This had to be the work of Hisako Jinno. It was her response to Wada's unwelcome intervention in the matter of her son's whereabouts. Wada regretted now revealing that she knew the arrangements at the apartment were a charade. She supposed Jinno had decided as a result that the charade had to end.

Which left Wada with nowhere to search for clues.

That wasn't quite true, though. She knew someone who might have taken a keen interest in the removal operation. It was time to pay a call on Nagata's inquisitive neighbour.

'Ah,' said Hosogai when he opened the door to her. 'The lady detective.' He was looking no better than when Wada had last spoken to him: puffy-faced and unkempt, with a musty smell drifting out past him from the interior of his apartment.

'*Konnichi wa*,' said Wada. 'I was wondering if you'd seen anything of Manjiro Nagata since I was last here.'

'You haven't found him, then?'

'No.'

'Do you generally have better results than this?'

'It is a complicated case.'

'Is it?'

'Have you . . . heard any unusual activity in his apartment?'

'The problem with drinking good whisky, you know,' said Hosogai, licking his lips meaningfully, 'is that you get the taste for it. The standard stuff loses its appeal. And the answer to your question is . . . yes, I have heard unusual activity. And seen some too.'

Wada sighed and made a show of counting out ¥7500 in notes, though she didn't hand the money over at once.

'I underestimated the cost of single malt last time,' said Hosogai. 'I'll need another fifteen hundred.'

Wada sighed again, more heavily. He was pushing his luck. But maybe he knew he could. She added ¥1500. 'Well?'

'Nagata's gone. I mean, he went a long time ago, of course. But he's *officially* gone now. Terminated the lease, according to the block supervisor. And yesterday the removal men came and stripped the apartment. They weren't very friendly. They didn't want to talk, which is strange: these guys are normally happy to chat. Not this bunch. In and out. Unmarked white van. Vroom.' Hosogai gestured with his hands. 'Bye-bye.'

'Yesterday, you say?'

'Yesterday.' Hosogai gently tugged the money loose from Wada's fingers. 'Coincidence, so soon after your visit? What do you think?'

'I couldn't say.'

'Well, if the lady detective doesn't know, what chance have I got?'

Wada walked back to Musashi-Sakai station, turning over in her mind possible next steps she could take in pursuit of the secret behind Manjiro Nagata's disappearance. None were convincing. What she needed – but could see no way of finding – was a way to cut through the layers of deception surrounding his current activities and whereabouts. His father knew nothing. His mother would reveal nothing. His known associates were either dead or had also vanished. He was a man with a sketchy recent past and an utterly opaque present. Where he was and what he was doing there she had no idea. Worse still, she had no trail to follow. He had stepped through a curtain she could not penetrate.

The late afternoon was warm, in the fickle way of early spring. She sat down on a bench in the shade of a tree outside the station entrance and ate a tub of green tea ice cream: a small treat to cheer herself up. As it did.

But not for long. Checking her phone for messages, she found an email from Fumito Nagata. She was surprised, since it had been clearly established when he hired her that they would communicate only in person or by telephone conversation. There were to be no texts or emails. Yet here one was. And the message it contained was even more surprising.

Wada-san,

Due to an unforeseen change in my circumstances, I am obliged to terminate the contract between us with immediate effect. Thank you for the work you have done to this point. I wish to make it clear that I do not want you to carry out any more work on my behalf. My lawyer will deliver to your office tomorrow a letter, which I would ask you to sign, confirming the cessation of all such work on your part. Please submit your account for your services to date, which will be settled promptly.

Kind regards,

Nagata Fumito

At first, she did not know what to think. It was unprecedented in her experience to be pulled off a case for no apparent reason by the client who'd asked her to take it on. But there was a reason, of course. By some means or other, Fumito Nagata had been forced to do this. The promised letter from his lawyer was surely proof of that. Whoever had brought pressure to bear on

222

him also required her personal guarantee that she would stop looking for his son. Someone badly wanted Manjiro Nagata to stay missing.

As far as Wada could tell, they were likely to get their way. Funaki had urged her to abandon the Nagata case. She'd been determined not to. But that didn't matter any more. Because now the Nagata case had abandoned her.

So, that was it, was it?

1995

IT IS THE FOURTH DAY OF KODAKA'S STAKEOUT OF SO & SO ICES OF Sunshine City, Ikebukuro. The bright pinks and blues of the decor are beginning to make him feel slightly sick, although that might equally be due to the two or three tubs of variously fla- voured ice cream he consumes, along with doses of black coffee intended to nullify the effect, each afternoon as he sits in the small cafe area adjoining the service counter, catching up with paperwork whilst listening carefully to the chatter of customers as they come and go.

A trawl through all the Sos in the Tokyo telephone directory turned up just one candidate as a favoured destination for a boy of five or six. So & So have been purveying their excellent ice creams to eager consumers, many of them children, since Showa 25, according to a sign by the entrance, though it must have started somewhere else, since Sunshine City has only existed since the late 1970s. Filled with shops, offices and galleries, the mall was built on the site of Sugamo prison, where Tojo and six other Class A war criminals were executed just two years before the So brothers started in the ice cream business, doubtless with a much more limited range of flavours than Kodaka has been working his way through.

Having alighted on So & So as the likely destination for the Kobe Sensitive and the child in her care after they left Tokyo Station following her desperate phone call to the Kantei, Kodaka was anxious to shake off for good the man he believes to have been trying to follow him since he was hired by Rinzaki to find the Kobe Sensitive. He can deploy the assorted tactics at his disposal to lose a tail, but the effort stales with repetition. Accordingly, after spotting the man when he went to pay off Umetsu outside Takashimaya at lunchtime on Friday – a none too amiable encounter, during which Umetsu did a good deal of grumbling whilst readily accepting the envelope containing his bonus – Kodaka lost the man easily enough before proceeding to So & So for the first time, but stopped on the way to phone Rinzaki from a call box outside Ikebukuro station.

He was put through with surprising speed, suggesting Rinzaki had instructed his secretary to give Kodaka's calls priority, perhaps in case he had good news to deliver. But it was too soon for that.

'Has there been a development, Kodaka-san?' Rinzaki asked.

'Not yet. Nor will there be if I have to continue looking over my shoulder.'

'I am not sure I understand.'

'I think you put a tail on me. Now, before you assure me otherwise, just let me say that if the tail isn't called off I will abandon the case.'

'I see.'

'So, can I take it that I won't be followed from now on? Because regularly having to shake him off is becoming tiresome.'

'Interesting. You are very . . . forthright, Kodaka-san.'

'I think we should both know where we stand.'

'I agree.'

'If I learn anything, I'll report it to you. That's how it works. There can be no monitoring of my activities. My clients have to trust me.'

'But trust has to be won before it can be conferred.'

'Do you trust me, Rinzaki-san?'

'I trust you more now. The . . . tail . . . you refer to was a way of testing your competence and integrity. You will be pleased to know that with this phone call . . . you have passed the test.'

'I am glad to hear that.' Kodaka wasn't sure he believed Rinzaki. This all too neatly solved the problem from his point of view. If he denied putting a tail on Kodaka, he could not then call it off and Kodaka would stop working for him. But, if he admitted it, then there had to be an explanation that didn't prompt Kodaka to walk away from the case. And this was just such an explanation. Rinzaki, it seems, is as calculating as he is condescending.

'You will not be followed . . . by anyone engaged by me. You have my word. Is that . . . satisfactory to you?'

'It is.'

'Good. Then . . . please carry on with your endeavours.'

'I will.'

'And I hope they soon bear fruit.'

'As do I, Rinzaki-san.'

Naturally, Kodaka did not take Rinzaki at his word and continued to take precautions against being followed. But he saw no sign of a tail after their conversation. It seemed he had succeeded in warning Rinzaki off.

And so it is that he finds himself sipping So & So's neither good nor bad coffee, with a tubful of sesame seed ice cream slowly melting in front of him, while he leafs through the latest report from his former colleague, Takatori, also now an independent operator, to whom he has sub-contracted some divorce-related inquiries so that he can concentrate on the Jinno case.

He is in the process of wondering whether Takatori will ever deliver a clinching piece of evidence when on some subconscious level he registers a word uttered by a child in the queue at the counter.

He raises his eyes from Takatori's report and takes stock of the young woman and child standing three back from the counter. The woman appears to be in her mid-twenties. She's casually dressed, with long dark hair and a broad, smiling face. The boy by her side looks to be close to the estimate of five or six ventured by Myoga, who has the annoying habit of being right about nearly everything.

'O-machi!' That was what he heard the boy say, with just the intonation Myoga identified on the tape. His voice sounded like the voice on the tape as well, though Kodaka is no expert in distinguishing one child's piping tones from another's. And even if the boy was using the honorific prefix O, he wasn't attaching it to the name Chika, short for Chikako, but instead to Machi, short for Machiko.

'What is it, pumpkin?' the young woman responds, shifting her weight from one foot to another as the queue edges forward. She doesn't sound like the woman on the tape. Her voice is higher-pitched, with what sounds to Kodaka like a Kansai accent.

'Is it today we see her?'

'No. Not today.'

'Tomorrow?'

'No. Not tomorrow. Or the day after. But the day after that.'

'That's a long time.'

'It'll go quickly.'

'And then we'll see her?'

'Yes. We will.'

'With the fishes?'

'With the fishes.'

'O-chika with the fishes,' the boy says dreamily in an under-tone. But Kodaka's straining ears catch the word *O-chika* quite clearly. There is no mistake.

'What flavour do you want today, pumpkin?'

Kodaka finishes his coffee and swallows a few spoonfuls of sesame seed ice cream while the boy agonizes over his choice of three mini-scoops before he consumes them, teetering on the edge of his chair in the children's section of the cafe. The young woman drinks tea and reads a magazine as he does so. She pats him absent-mindedly on the head from time to time and asks if 'Pumpkin' is all right. Pumpkin *is* all right. Kodaka wonders why Chikako isn't with him. Perhaps she and Machiko share responsibility for look-ing after him during the day. He's probably just been collected from his nursery school. But seeing Chikako 'with the fishes' sounds odd. There's an aquarium within the Sunshine City com-plex. Kodaka has seen signs pointing to it. Is that where they'll be meeting Chikako? The arrangement sounds slightly clandestine. Kodaka doesn't know what it signifies. But he intends to find out.

He's already paid his bill, so is ready to leave when Machiko and the boy set off. She has been completely oblivious of his presence in the cafe and remains so as he follows them out of the mall. They head north, the boy scampering at her side, cross Kasuga-dori and enter a network of quiet residential streets. Fol-lowing them is slightly more demanding now, but Kodaka requires little in the way of guile. Machiko doesn't once glance over her shoulder. Unlike many of the people Kodaka finds him-self following, she isn't even remotely furtive.

They reach a walled and iron-gated house opposite a small, neatly hedged cemetery. The house is traditionally built. Kodaka can see the decorative tilework on the roof beyond the wall. He's not going to see much more than that, though. Machiko opens a narrow pedestrian gate next to the main entrance gate and slips in with the boy. It closes automatically behind them.

Kodaka walks on slowly and glances at the nameplate on the gate pillar: Matsuzawa. The family must be quite wealthy, to afford a house this close to the centre of Tokyo that comes complete, as far as he can judge, with quite a large garden, not to mention a maid-cum-nanny, maybe even two of them.

He is not sure what to make of the reference to meeting Chikako on Thursday. The arrangement implies she is no longer – if she ever was – part of the household. He could ring the bell and try his luck at wheedling the facts of the matter out of Machiko. But he decides the risk isn't worth it. Thursday will give him his best chance where Chikako is concerned. He can wait until then.

2022

WADA TOOK AN UNORTHODOX ROUTE HOME THAT EVENING, walking up from Hamadayama to her apartment rather than travelling direct to Ogikubo. She remained alert for any signs of a tail, in the form of the old man or his sidekick or someone else altogether. She saw nothing remotely suspicious. Persuading Fumito Nagata to take her off the case was obviously considered sufficient by whoever was pulling his strings – Goro Rinzaki, presumably. With no client, she had no reason to continue and every reason not to. Perhaps it was felt matters were at risk of spiralling out of control with the supposed suicide of Yamato and the botched ambush at Endo's apartment. And so a softer but possibly more effective solution had been devised to the problem Wada posed. It was the businesslike approach. And Rinzaki was a businessman if he was nothing else.

The likelihood that she was now in much less danger did not make Wada feel any better about the situation. She knew her stubbornness could as easily be a handicap as a strength, but she was helpless to do anything about it. Her reluctance to admit defeat was simply part of her nature. It always had been and it always would be – until the day it proved her final undoing.

The lawyer's letter waiting for her at the Kono Building next morning, delivered early by special courier, did nothing to improve her mood. It was a legalistically wordy reiteration of what Nagata had already said in his email. Cease and desist from all inquiries on his behalf, submit your bill for prompt settlement and sign this undertaking to that effect. Sipping green tea as she read the document failed to stem her anger.

She decided to seek advice on the enforceability of such an undertaking from lawyer Dobachi. She emailed him a copy of the letter and asked for his opinion. To say she received good service from Dobachi would have been an understatement. She strongly suspected few of his clients benefited from such solicitous attention. This was partly due to a sense of responsibility for her welfare which he'd expressed when she insisted – against his advice – on continuing the business after Kodaka's death. 'He would want me to do my best for you, Wada-san,' he'd said. 'Of that I have no doubt.' Consequently, it was his best she always got. There was also the small matter of her sex, which brought out a courtly protectiveness in him she sometimes found annoying and sometimes . . . undeniably useful.

This was such an occasion. His secretary responded promptly with an invitation to have a brief discussion with Dobachi at his office that afternoon at five. 'Dobachi-san can see you then if convenient to you.'

Naturally, it was convenient. His office wasn't far from the Kono Building. She walked to it through a Nihombashi where relaxation in anticipation of the pending weekend could almost be felt in the air.

Dobachi's secretary seemed to be on the point of leaving when Wada arrived for her appointment. 'Forgive me, Wada-san,' she said. 'I have to be away early this afternoon.'

There was nothing for Wada to forgive. The secretary's time-keeping was a matter for her employer. But Dobachi, despite his old school manner, resolutely pin-striped suit and generally mournful expression, often exacerbated by frowning looks over the tops of his half-moon glasses, was secretly soft-hearted. As employers went, he was probably hard to beat.

The secretary did serve tea before departing, however. And Wada had the impression Dobachi actually welcomed her absence. Perhaps he already suspected Wada had strayed into dark and treacherous waters while investigating this case her client now so badly wanted her to abandon.

'The letter is an unusual and somewhat officious request, Wada-san,' he remarked as he sipped his tea. 'I've not come across anything quite like it.'

'Am I free to ignore it?' Wada asked.

'Certainly. But should you? That is the question. Can I ask if there is a connection with the file you sent me yesterday?'

'There is. The file contains sensitive evidence in the case.'

'And you sent it to me as a precaution against . . .?'

'Third party interference in my investigations.'

'You are a mistress of euphemisms, as ever. Did you fear the material might not be safe with you? Or that *you* might not be safe with *it*?'

'From time to time, my enquiries conflict with the interests of . . . powerful people. It is the nature of the job. Kodaka-san found the same.'

'Yes. He did. And, as his example shows, one miscalculation in the balance of risk can be, I regret to have to say . . . fatal.'

'I was hired by Fumito Nagata to find his son, who has gone missing. The investigation turned up other disappearances, all linked to an elderly businessman on whose property I found a car belonging to one of those who has disappeared. There have been incidents which suggest the businessman is aware of my activities and does not welcome them. That is why I sent you the file, which contains photographs of the car in its present location.'

'And now Nagata no longer wishes his son to be found?'

'He no longer wishes me to look for him.'

'You believe . . . what? Pressure has been brought to bear on him?'

Wada nodded. 'I believe it must have been. I do not think he would have acted without . . . inducement.'

'And this undertaking he seeks from you suggests he has been asked to obtain a guarantee that you will stop looking for his son.'

'So it seems to me.'

'But you wouldn't continue looking for him, would you, now Nagata has cancelled his contract with you? No client, no fee.'

'I am surely free to investigate what I choose to investigate.'

'That could be an arguable point, under the conditions set for licensing private detectives. But, essentially, yes, you are as free to seek the truth as any citizen.'

'And if there is criminal conduct involved . . .'

'Then you are obliged to report your findings to the police. But are they treating these disappearances as suspicious?'

'Not as far as I know.'

'And as a lawyer I can think of many ways this . . . elderly businessman . . . could explain the presence of a missing man's car on his property. Stored there by agreement and never collected springs to mind. So, your options are limited. The most obvious one is to cease the inquiry.'

'What about the undertaking?'

Dobachi adjusted his glasses thoughtfully and peered at the document on his computer screen. 'I would say it is excessively demanding. Your client has terminated his contract with you. That should be sufficient for his purposes. As to the purposes of some theoretical third party . . . you must decide for yourself whether you wish to . . . appease him in this way.'

That was the nub of the matter. Was Wada willing to give Rinzaki what he wanted? The answer was clearer than ever in her mind. 'I do not.'

'Well then . . .' Dobachi clicked the mouse and the screen went dark. He looked at Wada in his typically avuncular fashion, in which there was always a trace of bafflement. 'I suggest I contact Nagata's lawyers and open a dialogue with them about the reasonableness of what they are seeking. That may lead to a debate about wording. What we can accept and what we cannot. That could take some time. Lawyers never hurry. I certainly shan't. But while we talk, the issue is suspended. You have not given the undertaking, nor have you refused to give it. And while that remains so . . .'

'I can do as I please.'

Dobachi smiled. 'When have you ever done anything else, Wada-san?'

As Wada stepped out onto the street after leaving Dobachi's office, her phone bleeped. There was a text message from an unknown caller. The timing was so exact she wondered if someone was waiting for her to emerge before pressing *send.* But looking around she saw no sign of anyone keeping the building under surveillance.

The message read: *blue fin bar in half an hour you will get valuable information.* Wada could not imagine who'd sent it. Why the Blue Fin? It was down near the old Tsukiji fish market. Kodaka had been a frequent customer and had often used it to meet informants. Funaki was also a regular. But he would have identified himself. This was from someone else. A former contact of

Kodaka's, maybe? It was hard to see how that possibility made any sense.

Yet someone had sent the message. And they seemed confident of her response. It wasn't a desperate plea. It was a cool-headed offer – an offer Wada was bound to accept. Valuable information was currently just what she needed.

She hadn't signed an undertaking to stay out of the Nagata case. Because she wasn't going to stay out of it. Dobachi knew that. And it looked as if the sender of the message knew it as well.

1995

THURSDAY AFTERNOON BRINGS KODAKA TO SUNSHINE CITY ONCE more. He is confident the rendezvous with Chikako is to take place in the aquarium. Nowhere else would be 'with the fishes' – as the boy said and Machiko confirmed. So, missing out with some relief on yet another tub of So & So ice cream, he takes the lift to the top of the World Import Mart building, buys an admission ticket and guidebook for the aquarium, then takes a seat in the entrance hall and pretends to leaf through the book while monitoring those coming in after him.

Children unsurprisingly make up about half of the visitors. There are adults unaccompanied by children as well, though, usually in pairs. Loners are in a conspicuous minority. Kodaka sees a few young women who could theoretically be Chikako but he's not going to take any chances. He's waiting for Machiko and the boy to arrive.

Which, after some forty minutes that seem considerably longer, they do, the boy grinning and skipping as they emerge from the lift. He looks happy, perhaps even happier than when he was sucking ice cream off his spoon at So & So. Maybe that's because he's on his way to see Chikako.

Kodaka falls in inconspicuously behind them as they head into the aquarium and follow the signs leading to the rooftop deck where the seals are, according to the schedule displayed, about to commence a performance.

In fact, the seals are already out on a cloverleaf dais in the middle of the performing area, frolicking obligingly with their attendant. There's tiered bench-seating round the area, about a third full of expectant visitors, among whom children are the visibly most excited. The afternoon is fine and they're sheltered from the wind up here. Sunlight glints on the seals' bodies as they stand on their flippers and balance balls on their noses.

The boy doesn't seem to be very interested in them, though. He makes a beeline for a young woman of about Machiko's age sitting alone in one of the emptier stretches of benching. She stands and extends her arms to greet him. It has to be Chikako. Kodaka has little or no doubt on the point. He's found her. All he has to do now is make sure he doesn't lose her.

He sits on the other side of the arena from them and watches their interactions. Chikako is of unremarkable appearance, dark-haired, round-faced and slimly built. She's wearing circular-framed glasses and has a beaming smile. She presses the boy's nose with her finger and he jumps up and down with delight. Machiko appears happy to let them enjoy each other's company. She pays more attention to the seals.

Chikako is wearing jeans, a dark blue sweater and a mustard-coloured anorak. She also has a red and white scarf round her neck and a frayed leather satchel over one shoulder. Kodaka notes all this in detail, knowing he's going to have to follow her when she leaves and can't afford any slip-ups. Fate has delivered this opportunity to him. He doesn't intend to waste it.

Chikako has a gift for the boy: some kind of toy figurine which pleases him enormously; it's probably part of a set she's helped him collect. They play a game with another toy the boy has

237

brought and he squeals delightedly as it progresses. The two of them are happily absorbed in each other's company for the next quarter of an hour or so, until the seals come to the end of their routine, the attendant having exhausted her stock of fish with which to reward them.

The three leave their bench and wander off towards the penguin pool. Kodaka follows. Before they reach the pool, however, Chikako checks her pager and announces, as far as Kodaka can tell from the boy's reaction, that she has to leave. A fond farewell ensues, with lots of ruffling of his hair.

Machiko distracts the boy as best she can, though he gazes glumly after Chikako before agreeing to go and look at the penguins. Kodaka falls in behind Chikako as she heads towards the exit. She looks downcast. She obviously regrets the brevity of their meeting. Kodaka wonders why she gave up looking after him. Did her employers realize she was the Kobe Sensitive and dispense with her services to avoid publicity? Or did she leave in order to forestall such an outcome?

As they approach the lift, Chikako tags along behind a couple of mothers with children. Kodaka is last in before the doors slide shut.

The descent gives him long enough to study Chikako from close quarters, though this tells him nothing he doesn't already know. She still looks saddened by saying goodbye to the little boy. She takes from her shoulder-bag a pocket diary and leafs through it. She seems to be counting as she goes, but Kodaka can't see what's on the pages from where he's standing. The conversation of the two mothers reaches him as white noise between radio stations.

They reach the bottom. The lift doors open. The mothers bustle out with their children. Chikako moves past them, walking at some speed. Kodaka matches her pace, but keeps his distance.

She leaves the mall and hurries through the shopping streets of Ikebukuro. He guesses her destination is the station. She stops briefly at a pharmacy to buy something, then heads on. This is a straightforward tail as far as Kodaka is concerned. There's no sign Chikako has any fear of being followed. She moves through the crowds, unaware of the invisible string attaching her to Kodaka. She moves and he moves with her.

They reach the station, which is, if anything, more crowded than the streets. She's obviously familiar with the layout. She heads for the anticlockwise platform of the Yamanote circular line.

The train she boards is full, but not over-full. The rush hour has not yet begun. Kodaka has substituted a rumpled copy of that morning's *Asahi Shimbun* for the aquarium guidebook, which he dropped into a bin as they were leaving the mall. Chikako still seems to be giving her diary a lot of attention. She doesn't notice him. There is, in truth, nothing to notice.

She leaves the train at Shibuya and switches to another line. Once again it's obvious she's done this before. She boards the next southbound train and gets off at the second stop.

Kodaka follows her out into a quiet neighbourhood in one of Tokyo's more exclusive residential quarters. He adds an extra twenty metres to the gap between them to allow for the lack of other pedestrians. More of them start appearing, however, as Chikako approaches the gate of Oike Elementary School. Boys and girls are streaming out in their often oversized uniforms, lookalike rucksacks bouncing on their backs. Parents and others, such as Chikako, are meeting them. The girl Chikako is there for smiles brightly at the sight of her. She's clutching a painting or drawing she's made. Chikako admires it as they walk away.

There are fathers as well as mothers on hand, so Kodaka doesn't stand out as he threads a path through them and dawdles along behind Chikako and the girl, who gives a playful little skip every few steps and occasionally laughs. The sound drifts back to Kodaka through the tranquil afternoon.

They turn along a street lined with expensive modern houses, which in the context of Tokyo means very expensive indeed. According to something he's read recently, these properties are probably in the ¥10 million per square metre range. That puts them not so much out of the range of the average Tokyoite as in a different universe of ranges. The occupants may be renting, of course, but someone owns the houses. Someone sits on all that wealth.

Chikako and the girl reach their destination. It's a white-walled villa, flat-roofed and plain-lined, with an underground garage, a large garden and electronically operated gates. Chikako enters a code for them to pass through the gate. The view through its bars is of the ramp down to the garage. The approach to the front door of the villa is out of sight.

Kodaka notes the presence of CCTV cameras above the gate. He walks past slowly but without break of stride. There is no nameplate, but the address is displayed. Kodaka commits the *chome*, *banchi* and *go* numbers to memory. He knows where Chikako is to be found now.

He could, in theory, stop and ring the bell. He's going to have to confront her sooner or later. But he senses the encounter will be easier to manage if she's alone when it happens. Tomorrow, after she's dropped the girl off at school, will be the time to strike.

She's not going anywhere. He can wait. Patience is part of a private detective's armoury. But tomorrow the waiting will end.

2022

THE FISH MARKET HAD MOVED FROM CHAOTIC TSUKIJI TO SMOOTHLY efficient Toyosu a few years ago. But the Blue Fin had stayed where it was and preserved its maritime decor. This had conferred upon it an air of nostalgia for those attracted to such things: a moodily lit reminder of more rumbustious times in the city's history.

Simply entering the bar reminded Wada of her late employer and his undisciplined ways. He'd admitted that before her arrival at the Kodaka Detective Agency its administrative affairs had been in serious disorder. She'd introduced badly needed rigour to its operations. But though he was a defective record-keeper Kodaka was also a natural detective, sensing connections between events before those connections had become apparent, knowing how to prise crucial information from people who sometimes didn't know what they were revealing even as they revealed it.

The Blue Fin was often the venue for such prisings. It was somewhere Wada had seldom had occasion to go, especially since Kodaka's death. But she was there now, enveloped in its particular world. It was Friday evening and there were consequently more customers than usual for the time of day. She approached the bar and ordered a gin and tonic, glancing around and wondering who among the throng of thirsty, weekend-happy salarymen might have been the sender of the message that had brought her there.

She didn't have to wait long to find out. She saw him at the end of the bar, propped on a stool in the shadow beneath a fin-shaped wall-lantern, drinking Sapporo beer from the bottle with a glass of what looked like whisky parked by his elbow. He smiled crookedly at her and winked.

He was the old man who'd lured her to Endo's apartment, now sporting a leather jacket that she took to be his attempt to blend with the crowd. Wada was tempted for a moment simply to walk out. She couldn't imagine anything valuable emerging from a conversation with the man she suspected of murdering Yamato and very possibly Endo as well. But, then again, she couldn't have imagined him wanting to talk to her in the first place. Talking had never seemed to be his objective.

He beckoned her towards him and she took a few paces, stopping well short of the vacant bar-stool next to his. '*Konnichi wa*,' he said in his sandpapery voice. 'You came alone, then. That's good. So did I.'

'What do you want?'

'I want you to listen to me, that's all. Don't worry. I'm no threat to you. I wouldn't try anything in front of all these witnesses. My name is Yagami. Rokuro Yagami. Here's my driver's licence.' He held out the card for her to see. It bore his name and photograph, along with his date of birth, which put his age at seventy-three – long in the tooth for what she suspected his line of work was. 'OK? That really is my name.'

Wada nodded curtly in acknowledgement. 'All right. You are Yagami. You work for Goro Rinzaki?'

242

'Not any more.'

'When did you stop working for him?'

'Yesterday, since you ask.'

Wada took a step closer and placed her glass on the bar. She was determined to show Yagami she wasn't frightened of him. And she wasn't. He didn't have a heavy with him. He was seventy-three years old. He looked if anything older than that. And bone weary with it. Also, if he was to be believed, he no longer worked for Goro Rinzaki. 'Why did he fire you?'

He beckoned for her to draw closer still. 'We should keep our voices down,' he said, Wada barely catching his words. 'You'll want this to stay between us.'

She propped one hip on the vacant bar-stool and lowered her head, the better to hear him. 'Apparently,' he continued, 'I've been . . . getting sloppy. Showing my age. Which is ironic, coming from a guy twenty years older than me.'

'Did you kill Daiju Endo?' She matched the pitch of her voice to his.

'I solved the Endo problem, as instructed. And I solved the Yamato problem as well, though there . . . I improvised. As I saw it, he'd served his purpose after luring you to Endo's apartment. But the boss didn't approve. So, after nearly forty years, I'm out. On the scrap heap.'

'He did instruct you to eliminate Endo, though?'

'You're here to listen, Wada, not question me. This is how it is. On top of everything else the boss thinks I got rid of Manjiro Nagata. That plus the Yamato thing was what led him to fire me. But I never laid a hand on Nagata. I have no idea where he is. Well, I have an *idea*, but that's all it is. A theory. Which the boss wouldn't listen to.'

'Where do you think Nagata is?'

'We'll come to that. Stop interrupting. Whatever you think you can wheedle out of me by way of evidence to use against me you won't get, because no one's ever going to find Endo and no one's ever going to doubt that Yamato killed himself. When I rig things, they stay rigged. But that doesn't apply to things I *didn't* rig, like Nagata.'

'What about Daniel Perlman? Did you "rig" his suicide?'

'I told you to stop interrupting. I'm not here to talk about Perlman. I'm here to warn you. You're clever, Wada. The muscle-man who rescued you? I never saw him coming.' Wada saw no need to point out that she hadn't seen him coming either. 'And I never thought you'd work your way through from Nagata to Yamato and Endo. But cleverness isn't enough. You've got the boss's attention now. That only ends one of two ways. The quick and the slow. The quick you can guess. The slow? Well, that's why I suggested meeting here. It seemed . . . fitting. It was Kodaka's favourite watering hole, wasn't it?'

He'd known Kodaka. That wasn't something Wada had bargained for. It was disquieting, as Yagami must have intended. He had the advantage now. 'Didn't you know about Kodaka's dealings with the boss?' he asked with the faintest of smiles. 'I suppose not. It's hardly something he'd have boasted to you about. But you should know. Because it tells you how this is likely to play out. In Heisei seven Kodaka was hired by your ex-client Fumito Nagata's brother-in-law, Teruki Jinno, chairman of Jinno Construction, to find out why his father Arinobu, who'd died the previous year, had regularly paid the boss large sums of money since way back in Showa twenty-two.' That was a long time, Wada conceded, by anyone's reckoning.

'We closed the case down by giving Kodaka an explanation that would stop Jinno asking any more questions: a fictitious mistress for his strait-laced father. It was all carefully arranged to look genuine. The boss had actually taken steps to substantiate the mistress story years before, just in case he needed to use it.

He's a far-sighted man – you can't take that away from him. Anyway, Jinno backed off.

'As for Kodaka . . . the boss hired him to investigate something else altogether, which ensured he'd stop looking for the truth about the Jinno payments. That's what he'll do with you. Some time next week, I'd guess, he'll ask to meet you. And when you meet him, he'll offer you a job. If you make the mistake of accepting it, he'll have you exactly where he wants you. Working for him, not for his enemies.'

'What did he hire Kodaka to investigate?' Wada asked, eager to know what the case had been about. By Yagami's account, Kodaka had taken it on in 1995, the year Wada had joined the agency.

Yagami lowered his voice still further. 'The whereabouts of the Kobe Sensitive.'

'Really?' It was strange Kodaka had never mentioned the case.

'What did Kimber tell you about Yukari Otonashi? That Grant Braxton hired her as a consultant at BISRI last year on the boss's recommendation? That the rumour is she's the Kobe Sensitive, who gave a warning not just of the Kobe earthquake in Heisei seven but the tsunami in twenty-three? The only evidence for the second warning is Endo's claim to have a recording of her call to the Kantei the day before it happened. That claim was crucial to the boss persuading Braxton to take her on. The recording's never been heard and has since disappeared along with Endo. Which looks like a government cover-up if that's what you want to see. But it's not a government cover-up. It's a fiction, like Arinobu Jinno's mistress. It gets the boss a spy inside BISRI, better still a spy in Grant Braxton's house – in his bed, so I'm told. Kodaka never found the real Kobe Sensitive. It turned out she was already dead. So, the boss has invented her all over again. Otonashi's real name is Zaizen. Her mother is the woman who claimed to be Arinobu Jinno's mistress. In reality, she was the boss's mistress. Still is. Her daughter – Rinzaki's daughter as well, I've always assumed – is just as good as her mother at playing a part, maybe better. She's certainly convinced Grant Braxton she's what she claims to be. But what's it all for? What does the boss want her to do? That's the really big question. What has he sent her over there *for*?'

Yagami paused to finish his beer. He signalled to the barman for another bottle and waited for it to be delivered, along with a small bowl of dried squid strips, several of which he immediately munched before washing them down with a swig of beer.

'Are you going to tell me?' Wada asked when it seemed to her he'd been silent long enough.

'He's sent her there to find something. Something the boss entrusted to Clyde Braxton but never got back after Braxton's death. Something that earned both of them enough money in the post-war years to set them up for life. And it went on earning them money, in regular payments from people like Arinobu Jinno. Blackmail money, obviously. But what were they blackmailing those people *with*? The answer has to be in what the boss hopes Otonashi can recover for him. What is it? I only know how the boss referred to it once in a conversation I overheard between him and Clyde Braxton the last time Braxton visited Japan, in Heisei ten. He called it the Matsuda asset.'

'Matsuda?'

'That's right. The previous owner of the boss's villa. I don't know anything about him. I think the boss worked for him during the war. But he doesn't talk about what he did back then and trying to find out's a dangerous game. So, what is the asset and how can it be used for blackmail over so many years? I don't know. But that's what he's sent Otonashi to California to get her hands on if she can. I reckon that's where Manjiro Nagata has gone as well. He must have worked out what was going on after talking to Endo, who by then was proving himself dangerously unreliable. If I'm right, Nagata and Otonashi are there for the same reason. They're both looking for the asset, whatever it is. Something physical, though. Something you can actually *hold*. If you can find it.'

'Why are you telling me this?'

'Because the boss sacked me, without a moment's hesitation, after nearly forty years. Because he showed me no loyalty. I've been loyal to *him*, all that time, and now I know . . .' Yagami took a deep swallow of whisky. He was angry. That was clear. Angry that Rinzaki thought he could treat him like dirt and suffer no consequences. 'I was a fool to believe I was more to him than an employee to be disposed of when he decided I was no longer up to the job. He's replaced with me with that idiot Koga, who proved himself useless when your strongman friend showed up at Endo's apartment. But, apparently, that doesn't matter. He's younger. He's the future. So, I'm out . . . discarded . . . ignored . . . forgotten. Well, that means I owe him nothing now. He didn't even listen when I tried to explain my theory about Manjiro Nagata. He kept insisting I'd obviously got rid of him on my own initiative. Big mistake. That's why I'm giving you the chance to uncover the truth, Wada. Maybe you can use it to bring him down.'

'I take all the risks – and you get all the satisfaction?'

'Ignore me if you want to. Forget everything I've said. Take your fee from Fumito Nagata and file away the case in your archives. You can do that.' Yagami looked hard at her. 'Or can you? I don't read you that way. You don't like how easy it was for the boss to pressure Nagata into calling you off. You want the truth, whether someone's paying you to go after it or not. And then there's Kodaka, of course. The boss outmanoeuvred him. And now he'll outmanoeuvre you. If you let him. But I don't think you will. It's not in your nature. You want to put right what Kodaka got wrong.'

'I don't believe he got it wrong.'

'Fine. Prove he didn't if you can. I don't mind.'

'How did Manjiro Nagata find out about the asset? Rinzaki would never have told Endo about it. I assume he just bribed him to broadcast his claim about the Kobe Sensitive, then had you dispose of him once he became a liability.'

'It's unclear. But Yamato said Endo had been in contact with Nagata and I can't make any better sense of his disappearance. His father obviously doesn't know where he is, but I reckon his mother does. She probably put him up to this, though exactly what they stand to gain from the asset . . .' Yagami shrugged. 'I don't have all the answers, Wada. If I did I wouldn't need you to unearth them. Kimber trusts you, doesn't he? You can use him to get inside the Braxton household. Tell him about the asset if you like. Tell him whatever you need to. You can probably persuade him to hire you. Then you can get paid for doing what I know you badly want to do anyway.'

'Maybe I should just wait for that call from Rinzaki you seem certain is going to come – and tell him how many of his secrets you've betrayed to me.'

'If you do that, he'll come after me, for certain. Although he'll have his work cut out finding me. I'm planning a long holiday in foreign parts. But you'll be a threat to him as well. You'll be someone else who knows too much. And you don't want to be that, believe me.' Yagami shaped a grim smile. 'Telling the boss would be a seriously stupid thing to do. And you're not stupid. You only have two choices. Walk away from the whole thing. Or back yourself to get at the truth. Well, you know as well as I do which of those it's going to be.'

After leaving the Blue Fin, Wada walked slowly back towards Nihombashi through the crowded streets of Ginza. The shops were still open and the salarymen – and women – were out in

248

force. Lights danced and sparkled in the Tokyo night. She moved through it all like a wraith, her mind whirling. She'd originally been hired to find Manjiro Nagata and maybe she should have concentrated on that, instead of allowing herself to be side-tracked into the Endo mystery. They were related, of course, but Nagata, absent and unknowable, was actually the more import-ant figure, because he was still alive and in pursuit of the key to the entire conspiracy.

She should also have made more of Fumito Nagata's remark that Kodaka had once worked for his brother-in-law, Teruki Jinno. It had been all too easy to assume the cases were unrelated. But in her experience such connections were never meaningless. Why hadn't she checked Kodaka's files? He threw nothing away. His records of the Jinno case – and the subsequent case he'd taken on for Goro Rinzaki – should be in one of the boxes stored in the agency's cage in the basement of the Kono Building.

She was tempted to go straight there and begin searching for them. But for the moment something else – someone else – had to take priority.

She stopped near the ornate frontage of the Kabuki-za The-atre, where patrons were streaming in for an evening performance, and phoned Troy Kimber.

He answered almost instantly. 'Wada. Got any news?'

'You are still in Tokyo?'

'Oh yeah. I fly home tomorrow night.'

'Can we meet? Now?'

'So, you have got news.'

'Can we meet?'

'I'm at my hotel. Meet me in the bar.'

The bar of the Imperial Hotel, populated by slick-suited Japanese businessmen and wealthy tourists, featured subdued lighting, rich leather upholstery and a soundtrack of soft jazz – a considerable contrast with the Blue Fin. Kimber was at a corner table, slick-suited himself, sipping red wine and nibbling nuts. A half-empty cocktail glass was whisked away from beside him as Wada approached. She ordered a gin and tonic without really wanting another.

'Did I interrupt something?' she asked as she sat down.

'You're sharp, aren't you?' Kimber smiled. 'I'd arranged some entertainment for myself to brighten my last night in Tokyo. Then . . . you cropped up.'

'Why did you choose the Imperial to stay in?'

'Oh, the Frank Lloyd Wright associations, I guess. His building survived the 1923 earthquake, didn't it?'

'It did. But it did not survive the modernizers.' She glanced around. 'How do you like this version?'

'It's comfortable. I have no complaints. And I'm sure it's just as earthquake-proof as its predecessor.'

'Would you be happy to find out? If the Kobe Sensitive told you the big one was about to hit Tokyo, would you just . . . stay in your chair?'

'Probably not. But that's never going to happen, even if my stepfather flies over with Yukari Otonashi on his arm. Because she isn't the Kobe Sensitive, whatever he chooses to believe.'

'How can you be sure?'

'Because it's just too convenient. Rinzaki's using her to get some kind of hold over Grant. And she's got that for him all right.'

'A hold you want to dislodge?'

'For sure.'

'Well, maybe I can—'

She broke off as her gin and tonic and another glass of wine arrived. Kimber eyed Wada thoughtfully as the waiter departed. 'Maybe you can help me do that? Is that what you were about to say?'

Wada bowed her head and lowered her voice. Kimber bent forward to listen. 'The man who followed us from Matsuda Sanso has been fired by Rinzaki for . . . exceeding his authority.'

'How do you know that?'

'Because he has decided to punish his employer for getting rid of him after many years of loyal service . . . by confiding in me.'

'Has he though?'

'His name is Yagami. I have just come from meeting him. He told me that Otonashi has been sent to California to recover . . . an asset . . . held by Clyde Braxton, which Rinzaki believes to be rightfully his following Clyde's death but which Grant has retained. Or else Clyde concealed it somewhere and never left any instructions with Grant concerning what he was to do with it. Whatever the exact circumstances, recovering the asset is Otonashi's primary objective. Which, obviously, she has not yet accomplished.'

'And this asset is . . . what?'

'Yagami does not know. Rinzaki has only entrusted Otonashi with the information.'

'Why her?'

'It appears she may be his daughter.'

'Why doesn't that surprise me? She's certainly inherited his devious nature.'

'I suspect Manjiro Nagata is also looking for the asset.'

'Ah. Your missing man. So, he's on the trail as well, is he?'

'I think so.'

'What put him on to it?'

'Hard to say exactly. His grandfather, Arinobu Jinno, paid Rinzaki a lot of money over a period of many years. It may well have been blackmail money. And it may have been shared with—'

'Good old Clyde.'

'Very possibly. They worked together during the American occupation. The asset is linked to a man called Matsuda, original owner of Matsuda Sanso. Rinzaki worked for him during the war. I know nothing of Matsuda or what Rinzaki did for him.'

'But the asset is basically dirt Rinzaki and Clyde had on Jinno and maybe others as well. Clyde kept hold of it. And Rinzaki's been trying to recover it ever since Clyde's death.'

'All Yagami knows concerning the asset is that it is something tangible. A physical object of some kind.'

'And Rinzaki's prepared to go to great lengths to get hold of it.'

'Evidently.'

'So, if we could find it first . . .' Kimber frowned thoughtfully. 'We think it's hidden somewhere, right?'

'I would guess so.'

'Somewhere Clyde controlled.'

'That would follow.'

'Either his home or . . . his office.'

'You mean BISRI?'

'Yeah, I suppose. I mean, obviously he had an office there. It's Grant's office now.' Kimber's frown deepened. He fell back in his chair.

Wada sipped her gin and tonic, giving him time to turn the problem over in his mind. The time it took was two sips.

He leant forward again. 'You've got to come back with me, Wada. Together, we can crack this.'

His optimism was excessive. 'How would we crack it, Troy?' she asked coolly.

'I don't know. But the answer's there. It's obvious neither Otonashi nor Nagata has worked it out. We stand just as good a chance as they do. Maybe better.'

'Why better?'

'Because I know my way round the family's past. And you're a professional detective.'

She refrained from pointing out that working as a private

detective had not conferred on her magical powers. 'I cannot simply fly to California,' she objected.

'Why not? I could hire you. Whatever your terms, I'll meet them. Unless there's some . . . conflict of interest because of the Nagata case.'

'Actually, there is no conflict. Nagata's father has called me off.'

'He has? Why?'

'I do not know.'

'But I bet you have some idea. Pressure from Rinzaki?'

'Maybe.'

'Good.'

'I see nothing good about it.'

'I do.' He beamed at her. 'It means you're free to work for me. And you have the added incentive of sticking it to Rinzaki. Well?' He extended his hand, then withdrew it. 'Pardon me. You don't shake hands here, do you? So, how do we seal this deal?'

'I agree to work for you. Or not.'

'And you agree, right?'

'I will not fly back with you tomorrow. But I will follow if, after I reflect on the situation, I think we have a good chance of success.'

'No way of knowing without giving it a try.'

Wada couldn't deny that. 'You are correct.'

'So . . .'

'So, I will let you know.'

'Are you playing hard to get? Is this about your fee?'

'No. It is not about my fee.'

'What, then?'

'There are risks we will be running. Perhaps more serious than you suppose.'

'I'll take my chances. Will you?'

She made him wait for her answer. He held his smile until she delivered it. 'I will let you know.'

'Before I leave tomorrow?'

She nodded. 'Before you leave tomorrow.'

There was only one realistic alternative to working with Kimber and that was dropping the case altogether. This was, Wada knew, the most prudent course of action. She also knew it was a course of action she would find it impossible to follow. There was nothing to be gained by struggling with her own instincts. And she knew better than to try.

What had stopped her agreeing to Kimber's proposal right away wasn't fear of Rinzaki, it was the questions she badly wanted answers to concerning Kodaka's work for Teruki Jinno – and later Rinzaki himself. For those she had to return to the Kono Building and descend to the basement.

The night porter was watching sumo highlights on his small television behind the lobby desk when she entered. She toyed briefly with the notion of asking him if he remembered a wrestler called Seiji Tago, but decided against it.

'If only my wife worked as hard as you, Wada-san,' he said by way of greeting, pulling off the earphones on which he was listening to the commentary.

'I am sure she does.'

'No. She is a lazy woman. That is the truth.'

'Well, the truth is I need the key to the basement cage space.'

'You're going down there at this time of night?'

'I have to.'

'Because you work hard. You see?' He unlocked the key cupboard, lifted the key she needed off a hook and handed it over.

She took the lift up to her office and collected the key to the Kodaka Detective Agency's cage. Then she took the lift all the

254

way down to basement level 2 and exited into an anteroom that led through double doors that she unlocked to a large space lined with caged and padlocked enclosures containing overflow filing, equipment and in some cases furniture from the businesses that occupied the building. The air was cold and musty. There were layers of dust on the boxes, crates, cabinets and upended chairs that filled many of the cages. And some of that dust floated languidly in the sallow light cast by faintly humming fluorescent tubes.

She made her way to the agency's cage, the contents of which were neatly stacked, thanks to her tidy mind. She rather doubted Kodaka had been down here the entire time she'd worked for him.

She unlocked the padlock and stepped into the cage. The boxes were, naturally, arranged in sequential date order, which meant the one she was looking for, covering 1995, was easy to locate, although several boxes had to be lifted out of the way to access it, raising a good deal of dust. She was coughing by the time she'd reached the 1995 box and had no intention of delving into it where she was. Cradling it in her arms, she exited the cage, secured the padlock and made for the doors leading to the lift.

She went straight back up to the office, drank some water to clear her throat and opened the box. Each case was allotted a pocket file. The papers in the file were punched through and held together by a treasury tag. She found the Jinno case file, sat down at her desk and skimmed through the papers. Most of them were notes scrawled by Kodaka in his inelegant hand, though there was also a brochure for an exhibition at Yushukan and a photocopied clipping from the *International Herald Tribune* dating from the autumn of 1994.

The presence of the brochure and the photocopied clipping was explained as Wada read through the notes. Kodaka had kept them on a daily basis, as was his habit, even when there was nothing to record, which he marked with an extravagant dash next to the date. One of the pages was singed in the top corner – a smoking mishap in all likelihood. There were also several amber ring-marks where he'd carelessly placed his whisky glass, perhaps using it as a paperweight. These preserved signs of his existence had a sudden and profound effect on Wada which she would never have predicted. She wasn't supposed to be a sentimental person. She told herself the tears that filled her eyes were a reaction to the dust down in the basement. She went to the filing cabinet, took out the bottle of Suntory from the bottom drawer and drained it – nearly empty as it was following Funaki's recent visit – into a glass. There was a new bottle in the cupboard which she would transfer to the drawer before leaving. Order and neatness solved all problems, she believed, even though it wasn't actually true.

The glass she sipped from as she sat back down was the same one that had left the marks on the papers in the Jinno file. Unlike Kodaka, she placed it dead centre on a coaster before resuming her perusal.

The trail Kodaka had followed back in the early spring of 1995 was clearly set out, though not so clearly that anyone other than Wada would have been able to make full sense of it. Teruki Jinno had hired Kodaka to find out why his late father Arinobu had paid large annual sums for more than half his life into an anonymized account at Mizunuma Bank's Nihombashi branch. Kodaka had swiftly established that the account was controlled by Goro Rinzaki of the Kuraikagami Film Corporation. That information had been procured from *Source Mah-jongg*, which Wada knew meant Takuto Umetsu of the Bank of Japan, who, like Kodaka, was no longer in the land of the living, in his case because of a large mah-jongg debt owed to an unforgiving party.

Kodaka's notes revealed that Funaki (referred to, as ever, as *News Hound*) had alerted him to a protest staged at an

256

exhibition at Yushukan sponsored by Rinzaki. This had led Kodaka to the Flight Deck bar in Yokosuka, where Daniel Perlman, also since deceased, had alleged that Rinzaki – in cahoots with Clyde Braxton – had been blackmailing Arinobu Jinno and others and was implicated in the death of a US intelligence officer during the Occupation. It was Perlman who'd given Kodaka the clipping about the deaths of Braxton's daughter-in-law and grandchildren in the 1989 San Francisco earthquake and Braxton's creation of BISRI. Kodaka had subsequently concocted with Teruki Jinno a cover story to set up a meeting with Rinzaki. But at the meeting Rinzaki had revealed that he was not taken in by the ruse and offered an entirely unexpected explanation for the payments Arinobu Jinno had made to him: a secret mistress, maintained by Jinno with Rinzaki's help as go-between. Kodaka had spoken to Sonoko Zaizen and she'd convinced him it was true. Teruki Jinno had been convinced too. And there the case had come to a close.

All this was consistent with Yagami's version of events. But there was nothing in the Jinno file about Kodaka being asked by Rinzaki to search for the Kobe Sensitive. Nor was there a separate file detailing that case. The next file in the box concerned an obviously unrelated run-of-the-mill commercial inquiry. Looking at the dates on Kodaka's notes in that file, however, Wada spotted an unexplained lapse of a couple of weeks after the close of the Jinno case, during which Kodaka's activities were not accounted for. She checked every file in the box, earlier and later. The two-week gap remained. A holiday? It didn't seem likely. Kodaka's idea of a holiday was a night of heavy drinking and some karaoke followed by a visit to a sex club.

Wada took a sip of whisky and considered the possibilities. She only had Yagami's word for it that Kodaka had worked for Rinzaki. Maybe that just wasn't true. Or maybe it was. She hadn't yet exhausted all methods of finding out. She looked again at the

257

Jinno file. And that was when she noticed a few jagged scraps of paper still held by the tag behind the last page. It looked to her as if Kodaka had torn off several pages, leaving the top corners of them on the tag.

It was typical of him, in a way, to have been so careless. He should have neatly removed the page from the tag, rather than just tearing it off. Then there would have been no clue to follow.

But there was a clue. Wada got up and walked into the next room, where the lever arch files were stored that contained the Kodaka Agency's accounts. She'd disposed of no financial records. If Kodaka had worked for Rinzaki, he must surely have sent in his bill when the work was done. So, it should be there, archived away.

She opened the cupboard. The files were double-stacked on the deep shelves, with older ones behind newer ones. She had to use the library steps to reach the 1995 file, which was at the rear of the top shelf.

She pulled it out, climbed down and went back to her office. She opened the file and began leafing through it in the pool of light cast by her desk lamp – which once, of course, had been Kodaka's desk lamp.

She found the invoice quite easily. It was there, just where it should have been by date order. A fee, for what looked like two weeks' work, charged to Goro Rinzaki of the Kuraikagami Film Corporation, sent to him at the company's Chofu HQ. Laboriously typed out by Kodaka on his old Nippon typewriter, which Wada had immediately replaced after becoming his secretary with a word processor. The work was described, as ever on such invoices, as *investigative services*. No client needed or wanted the details of such matters to be spelt out.

But the invoice proved there'd been a case. And the absence of the papers proved Kodaka had wanted no record of what the case had involved to survive. According to Yagami, he'd been

258

tasked with finding the Kobe Sensitive, only to establish that she was already dead.

But if that was so, why destroy the case papers? It made no sense. Unless there was something he badly wanted to hide.

What had he actually found?

And what had he done after finding it?

1995

KODAKA IS OUT EARLY. HE HAS CONSCIOUSLY SMARTENED HIMSELF up so as not to attract attention in this district of walled houses and spotless pavements. And he's confident he doesn't attract the attention of the middle-aged man and woman in the large, gleamingly well-polished car that sweeps out of the gates of the villa he tracked Chikako to yesterday.

He watches them depart, to their places of work, where both, he suspects, either occupy very senior positions or are in complete charge of operations. They have money and status and a nanny for their child. They are the elite. They are the future.

It is not very much longer before Chikako comes out, holding the little girl by the hand. They head in the direction of Oike Elementary School. Kodaka hangs well back. He knows where they're going, so has no fear of losing them.

At the school gate they meet a friend of the little girl and a young woman of about Chikako's age who's escorting her. Another nanny, Kodaka assumes. They appear to know each other quite well, loitering and chatting after the two girls have gone in. Eventually, they leave – in opposite directions.

Chikako doesn't go straight back to the villa. She makes her way to a cluster of shops near the subway station and goes into a *combini*, emerging ten minutes or so later with her purchases in a string-net bag. Kodaka buys himself a takeaway coffee while he's waiting for her. He sips from it at intervals as he follows her away from the shops. Once again he hangs well back. It's obvious now she's heading back to the villa.

He doesn't close the gap between them until she's approaching the villa. She seems absorbed in her thoughts, walking quickly but unhurriedly without a backward glance. And Kodaka has long perfected the art of moving softly on his feet. He is fortunate with the weather. It is cloudy. If the sun were out it would cast his shadow ahead of him. If she noticed it . . .

But the sun is not out. There is no shadow. Just Kodaka, closing on his prey.

She reaches the gate and enters the code. It swings open. She steps through and moves towards the house as the gate begins to swing shut behind her. She glances back, to check it is closing. And then she sees him.

He is in. The gate clunks against the lock behind him. She starts with alarm and raises a hand to her mouth.

'Don't worry.' He smiles. 'I'm only here to talk to you.'

'What do you want?' Her voice is the voice on the tape. He's quite certain of that. It's her. And there's real fear in her eyes. Some part of her knows already what he wants. He has a terrible feeling she would actually be grateful if he revealed himself as no more than an opportunistic intruder.

'Like I said.' He spreads his hands in a pacifying gesture. 'Just to talk.'

She moves to one side, as if judging whether she could dodge past him and escape into the street. He is blocking her path. But he wouldn't stop her. He is a detective, not a hired heavy. But she doesn't know that.

'Don't run, Chikako-san,' he says, taking a cautious step

261

towards her. 'You've done enough running, haven't you? All you'll do is leave another trail to follow.'

'Did Rinzaki send you?' So, she knows Rinzaki. Kodaka has only been given half a story by his client. Which somehow doesn't surprise him.

'Can we go inside and talk? I mean you no harm. You can phone the police and have me arrested if you like. There's probably a panic button you can press as well, isn't there?' Kodaka glances at the house – white walls, tinted windows, all privacy and simplicity. 'They have state of the art security here, I imagine.'

'I would really like you to leave please,' she says, her voice heavy with pleading.

'If I did, someone else would come. You're better off talking to me. My name is Kodaka. Kazuto Kodaka. And you are Chikako . . .'

'Please leave.'

'I can't do that.'

She closes her eyes for a moment, as if to ward off the world that is closing in around her. Then she turns and walks along the curving paved path, edged with cobbles, that leads to the wide, porched front door.

She opens it with a key, enters and slips off her shoes. Kodaka follows and does the same. Then she pads ahead of him along a broad hallway, turning past an open doorway through which looms a vast lounge, with huge floor-to-ceiling sliding windows looking out onto the manicured garden.

Their destination is the kitchen, likewise enormous and lavishly equipped. There is a lot of white marble and brushed steel. And the only sound is the faint hum of the fridge-freezer. Chikako stops by the section of worktop housing a knife block. The handles of the knives are within her reach as she carefully places her shopping bag on a stool and looks at him. Only desperation

262

would lead her to grab one of the knives. But Kodaka has no clear idea of how desperate she might be.

'Does Rinzaki know you are here?' It is a different question, he notices. Not *Did Rinzaki send you?* But *Does he know you are here?* In other words, does he know where she is?

'I have not told Rinzaki I have found you,' Kodaka says quietly – calmingly, he hopes.

'But you will. Because you work for him.'

'Who do you work for – here?'

'The Sengs. The husband . . . is from Singapore. And they are both so busy they do not follow the news. Except . . . the business news.'

'That is to your advantage. Which I suppose is why you came to work for them.'

'How did you find me . . . Kodaka-san?'

'Won't you tell me your full name?'

'Won't you tell me how you found me?'

'All right. Those people you used to work for – the Matsu-zawas. They had old-fashioned ways, didn't they? That's why their son addressed you on the tape as O-chika. Antiquated usage of the honorific pronoun O for a maid. And the boy mentioned So's. The ice cream parlour in Sunshine City. You shouldn't have gone on seeing him, Chikako-san. That was a mistake.'

She looks down and sighs. 'Parting from a child – even one you are paid to care for – is not easy.'

'I don't imagine it is. Did the Matsuzawas recognize your voice on the tape?'

'Yes.'

'And . . . what? They sacked you?'

'No. We agreed it would be safer . . . for me to leave. They will tell no one. They are honourable people. I did not want to leave. *They* did not want me to leave. But it was . . . necessary.'

263

'A necessity you could have avoided. By not making that telephone call.'

'And letting thousands die?'

'They died anyway.'

'Not because I stayed silent.'

'You really knew there was going to be an earthquake in Kobe?'

She looks straight at him. 'What do you think?'

'I think there's something you're not telling me.'

'What would that be?'

'How do you know Rinzaki?'

'Hasn't he told you?'

'I'm a private detective, Chikako-san.' He takes out one of his cards and slides it along the worktop towards her. 'The people who hire me don't always tell me everything they could. Generally, though, I find out what it is they haven't disclosed. If it suggests bad faith on their part, I terminate the contract. My clients have obligations to me just as I have obligations to them. So, to answer your question, no, Rinzaki hasn't told me how you know him. Why don't you?'

'Did he give you my real name?'

'He gave me no name at all. Just the tape. And the task of finding the Kobe Sensitive. And here you are.'

'He mustn't find me.' She squeezes her eyes shut. 'I cannot be controlled by him again.'

'What is your real name?'

She opens her eyes and looks straight at him. 'Himeko Sato. I lose nothing by telling you that, since Rinzaki already knows it. But you work for him, so I cannot trust you with anything more. And I want you to leave. Please, Kodaka-san. Please leave.'

'What will you do then?'

She draws a deep breath. 'What is best.'

'Run, you mean? Run *again*. You can't keep doing that.'

264

'What choice do I have?'

'Tell me about your dealings with Rinzaki. If he really poses a threat to you, I will . . . do my best to protect you.'

'Why should I trust you?'

'There's no easy answer to that question. But you *can* trust me. That is the truth.'

She looks at him for a long motionless moment as the freezer motor lapses into standby and the ticking of the kitchen clock becomes suddenly audible. A weak shaft of sunlight appears between them – then disappears.

'How do you know Rinzaki?' he prompts gently.

And she begins to speak. 'I worked for him as a maid at Matsuda Sanso. That was how he discovered my . . . ability . . . to detect earthquakes before they happened. These were just minor tremors. The sort you feel but don't worry about. They come and they go. But I always knew when they would come. I could tell how far away they'd started and when they would reach me. It is like . . . judging how far away a storm is by how much time passes between the lightning flash and the thunderclap. When I was a child, I thought everyone could sense them. But then I realized it was just me. And my . . . sensitivity . . . increased as I got older. For larger ones I knew hours – even days – in advance. There was a change in the air. It became . . . electric. It was like a breeze from a particular direction that never stirred so much as a twig. I felt it. No one else did. I hate knowing. I don't want to know. But I do.'

'And you revealed this ability to Rinzaki?'

'He noticed. He is a man who notices everything. He encouraged me to demonstrate my ability. I predicted several moderate earthquakes to within a few hours for him. He was impressed. He rewarded me for doing it. The extra money was welcome. I didn't think about why he was rewarding me. I didn't ask myself if he had . . . plans for me. But then . . .'

'Then?'

'He'd told me his American friend Clyde Braxton had lost two grandchildren in the San Francisco earthquake and had set up a seismological research institute to investigate earthquake prediction. He asked me if I'd consider going there to help with their work. I said no. I didn't want to leave Japan. I didn't want to become . . . an object of study. I wanted to lead a normal life. I had a boyfriend by then. I thought we would be married. He worked on the estate as a carpenter. He was . . . very handsome. So, I made it clear to Rinzaki that I wouldn't be going to California.'

'But he didn't accept your decision?'

'I eavesdropped on a telephone conversation between him and Braxton. He promised to deliver me to Braxton. "It will be arranged," he said. And the way he said it . . . was so certain. It was as if my wishes made no difference. And they didn't. Suddenly, my boyfriend left. Took a job in Shikoku and was gone. Paid off by Rinzaki, I suspected. Or pressurized to leave in some other way. I was alone. I am an only child. My parents are deceased. There was no one I could turn to for help. And I knew it was only a matter of time before Rinzaki "arranged" for me to go to California. Once there, I would have become . . . a lab rat – a freak. I would have been nothing except . . . the earthquake predictor.'

'So, what did you do?'

'I asked the maids' agency to find me another place, planning to quit and leave Matsuda Sanso as soon as possible. It was stupid of me to think it would be as simple as that. Suddenly, the agency informed me there was a problem with my registration. There'd been a complaint. They wouldn't be able to offer me work. More manipulation by Rinzaki, obviously. He more or less admitted it. "I will look after you," he told me. "Leave all decisions to me." The way he looked at me . . .' She shakes her head ruefully. 'I would have become his creature if I'd remained

266

there. Sent to California and then . . . I made my decision. This is my life. I do not belong to anyone. I let Rinzaki think I was going along with his plans for me. But I had other plans.'

'You fled?'

She nods. 'Before dawn one morning. I walked over the hills to Tokigawa rather than go to the station closest to the villa. From Tokigawa I caught a train into Tokyo. I went to a woman I know who freelances as a maids' agent and she agreed to help me. I used the name of a cousin who died in infancy. And I went to work for the Matsuzawas. They are good people. I was happy with them. And Tokyo is a big city. Rinzaki could look for me, but his chances of finding me . . . were small.'

'Until you made that phone call.'

'I knew there would be thousands of deaths in Kobe if nothing was done. I had to warn them.'

'But they ignored your warning.'

She shrugs. 'Sometimes people cannot be helped. However hard you try.'

'Surely you realized Rinzaki would know it was you – and use the tape to try and find you.'

'I did not know there would be a tape. But even if I had . . . I would still have made the call.'

'Because?'

'My conscience would have forced me to.'

'But your conscience put you in danger.'

'Yes. The woman I know warned me there was a man looking for me. From the description I knew it was Yagami, Rinzaki's chauffeur, who's always been a lot more than just a chauffeur. Have you met him?'

'I don't know the name. But he may have crossed my path.' On the subway when he went to see Myoga is Kodaka's guess.

'She found me this job. And I thought I was safe here. But now . . .'

'I mean you no harm, Chikako-san.'

'But harm will come to me anyway, thanks to you.'

Her words shock Kodaka. He has been lied to and manipulated by Rinzaki. He is angry – and appalled that Chikako believes he will betray her. Yet he cannot blame her. It must seem obvious to her. He is the agent of her ruin. 'Don't run,' he says quietly.

'Why not?'

'Because you will never be able to stop.'

'If I do not run, he will come for me.'

'No.'

'Yes, Kodaka-san, he will.' She looks sorrowfully at him, almost pityingly.

'Do you have something to drink?'

'Tea?'

'Something stronger.'

'Whisky?'

He nods.

'Wait here.'

She walks past him and out of the kitchen. He wonders if she will take the chance to flee and is ashamed by the thought that it would be better for him if she did, since then there would be nothing he could do for her, whereas for the moment he is faced by the same dilemma she was: to follow his conscience is to accept all of the consequences.

She does not flee. She returns and places a glass tumbler and a bottle of whisky on the worktop beside him. It is Scotch – Glenfiddich. 'I do not know how much you want,' she says.

She looks at him and in her eyes he sees mirrored his own doubts about himself. There is a right thing to do and a wrong thing to do. Both are difficult in their different ways. And both are irrevocable.

He pours whisky into the glass and is about to pick it up when she raises her hand, signalling for him to wait. But wait for what? 'In a moment,' she murmurs. 'Watch the liquid.'

Kodaka looks down at the whisky. A moment passes. Then . . . he sees a shimmering as the shadow of the window frame falling on the surface of the whisky is disrupted by the faintest of tremors, which he senses only because he knows it is happening. He looks at Chikako and she looks back at him. The tremor ceases. The surface of the whisky is once again undisturbed.

'That is how it always is,' she says simply.

He picks up the glass and swallows most of the whisky. His mind locks on the decision he has just taken. Whatever he does from now on, none of it will be in the service of Goro Rinzaki. He feels liberated, as if a load has been lifted from his shoulders. He sets the glass carefully down and meets Chikako's gaze.

'He isn't going to find you,' he says at last.

'How can he fail to?' The question is a challenge. What is Kodaka really made of? Chikako needs to know.

'I'm going to stop him looking.'

'How?'

'I don't know yet. But I'm going to. I'm going to set you free of him. You have my word.'

'Even though you don't know how you're going to do it?'

He nods. 'Even though.'

2022

WADA DID NOT LEAVE KIMBER IN SUSPENSE. SHE TELEPHONED HIM early the following morning with her decision. 'I will follow you to California.'

'That's great to hear,' said Kimber. 'When?'

'I plan to leave on Sunday evening.'

'Why not make it *this* evening?'

'There are people I need to speak to before I go.'

'Can they help us crack this?'

'Perhaps.'

'You don't give a lot away, do you?'

'Raising false hopes would help neither of us. I will tell you what I learn – if anything – when we next meet.'

'OK. You want to stay at my place when you arrive? There's a guest room over the garage. And there'll be no one else around anyway.'

Kimber's proposal had the advantage that Wada would not have to register at a hotel, which meant one less clue to her whereabouts for anyone to follow. 'Thank you. That would be convenient.'

'Have you booked your flight?'

'Not yet.'

'When you do, let me know what time it gets in. I'll pick you up from the airport.'

'Thank you again.'

'Least I can do, Wada. We're in this together now.'

Her next call was to Joji Funaki. 'Can we meet at my office later this morning, Funaki-san?'

'It's Saturday. Don't you take the weekend off?'

'No,' she replied simply.

'What about relaxation? Meeting friends? Going for a walk? That kind of thing.'

'I am sorry. But this cannot wait.'

'Another urgent problem?'

'The same problem. More urgent.'

'Of course. Well, I'm working later myself, so if I leave early . . . I can be with you at eleven. Good enough?'

'Good enough.'

Wada could not help suspecting Funaki had been less than candid with her. He'd given Kodaka information that had led him to Dan Perlman and the first inklings of a connection between Goro Rinzaki and the Braxtons. Yet Funaki had said nothing of this when Wada had asked him to help her understand what had happened to Daiju Endo. Strictly speaking, of course, he'd had no reason to believe Endo was associated with Rinzaki, at least so long as he hadn't known Matsuda Sanso was owned by Rinzaki. On that point Wada was doubtful. And she also thought it distinctly possible Kodaka had confided in his old friend some time after – or before – closing the Jinno case. If that was so, Funaki had been holding out on her. Which wasn't something he'd have done lightly. There had to be a reason – a very good reason.

*

He arrived promptly at eleven, the smoke of his last cigarette still on his breath but generally looking sprucer than usual, as if his Friday night had been uncharacteristically restrained. She served him tea. He didn't ask for whisky. There was a seriousness to him, an awareness, perhaps, that Wada was no longer sure he was telling her everything he could.

'Learn anything useful at Matsuda Sanso?' he asked, sipping his tea.

'Several things. Including the identity of the owner. Goro Rinzaki.'

'Rinzaki? Really?' It was either good acting or the truth. Wada couldn't tell which.

'What do you know about him?'

'Rinzaki? Well, he's a veteran film producer. Been in the business since soon after the war. In his early nineties now. But his company – Kuraikagami – is up with all the latest developments. He gave an interview to *Yomiuri* a few months ago in which he talked about his recent ventures in open platforming. I mean, I'm too old to understand what that means. You probably are too. But not Rinzaki, even though he's decades older than both of us.'

'A smart operator, then?'

'Definitely. But what does he have to do with the missing civil servant – Endo?'

'I don't think Endo will ever be seen again, Funaki-san.'

'You don't?'

'Did Kodaka-san ever ask you about Rinzaki?'

'Dakka?' Funaki frowned. 'He asked me about so many things. He always reckoned journalists knew more than anyone else about what goes on behind the scenes in Tokyo. So, he may have done. I can't exactly recall.'

'This would have been in Heisei seven.'

'More than twenty-five years ago?' Funaki grimaced. 'I can barely remember twenty-five days ago.'

'You told him Rinzaki had sponsored a right-wing exhibition at Yushukan, which had been disrupted by a protest staged by an American who owned a bar in Yokosuka. His name was Daniel Perlman. Does that mean anything to you?'

Funaki did a lot of thoughtful frowning, then: 'You're right. There was an exhibition around that time. About war criminals. Paid for by Rinzaki. I think Dakka did ask me about it. I guess he was investigating something involving Rinzaki. Not so surprising when you consider the number of cases Dakka must have taken on over the years and the number of deals someone like Rinzaki must have done. I don't remember anything about a protest, though, or this . . . Perlman guy. But . . . it's a long time ago. How did this come to light?'

'Well, as you know, my missing person case turned out to have a Kobe Sensitive connection.'

'If you take Endo seriously.'

'Which I do. Anyway, I discovered Kodaka-san handled a case in Heisei seven for the construction magnate Teruki Jinno that led him to delve into Rinzaki's affairs. The missing person I was asked to find happens to be Jinno's nephew. Which has led *me* to delve into Rinzaki's affairs as well.'

Funaki's eyes widened. 'Sounds like a cat's cradle.'

'Indeed. After the Jinno case was closed, Rinzaki hired Kodaka-san to identify and find the Kobe Sensitive.'

Funaki's eyes widened again. 'Why did Rinzaki want to find her?'

'I was hoping you might be able to tell me that.'

'Me? What would I know about it?'

'You were Kodaka-san's best friend. You told him about the protest at the Yushukan exhibition. That led him to Perlman, who gave him a lot of information about Rinzaki's dealings during the Occupation with an American officer called Braxton, who went into the wine business in California after he left the army and later founded a seismological research institute.'

'Seismological research? That sounds like a reason to want to track down the Kobe Sensitive.'

'It does, doesn't it? So, did Kodaka-san ever mention any of this to you? You used to meet once a week or so at the Blue Fin. You must have asked him how the Rinzaki inquiry was going.'

'I probably did. But Dakka was always tight-lipped about his clients. It was different when it came to karaoke. But professionally he was . . . reticent to a fault. Just like you.' Funaki smiled. 'He trained you well.'

'He never told you what he found out about the Kobe Sensitive?'

'He never even told me he was looking for her. Are you sure he was?'

'Fairly certain.'

'Won't there be a file in your archives about it? Case notes? Something like that?'

'There should be, yes.'

'Should be?' Funaki frowned. And Wada detected the first hint of artifice. Was he mentioning the file only because he knew Kodaka had destroyed it?

Before she could pursue that suspicion, the telephone on her desk rang. The tone told her it was a call from the reception desk. She picked it up.

'Wada-san, there is a man on his way up to your office.' The weekend day porter sounded sheepish.

'What is his name?'

'He did not give his name.'

'You should have called me to check he had an appointment, which he doesn't.'

'I know, Wada-san. I am deeply sorry. He simply ignored me and went into the lift. It was difficult. He is . . . very elderly. And his manner is . . . haughty.'

Rinzaki. It could only be Rinzaki. 'Never mind. Thank you.'

She put the phone down and looked at Funaki. 'Goro Rinzaki is about to pay me a visit.'

'Rinzaki? He's here?'

'Apparently so.'

'What does he want?'

'I will find that out very soon. But if you're still here . . .'

Funaki needed no encouragement to leave. Wada had the distinct impression he wanted to avoid an encounter with Rinzaki at all costs. He stood up. 'I'll take the stairs down,' he said, grabbing his coat and heading for the exit.

He opened the main door and glanced apprehensively out, then looked over his shoulder at Wada, still seated at her desk. 'Be careful what you say to him.'

Then he was gone, giving her no chance to ask why he'd issued such a warning, although it had already become apparent to her that he knew a lot more than he was telling. He was covering for Kodaka in some way. And covering for a dead man was a strange thing to feel compelled to do.

Wada whisked Funaki's teacup out of sight as she waited for Rinzaki to arrive. She heard the distant thump of the door to the stairs closing and the chime of the lift as it reached her floor almost simultaneously. She reckoned Funaki had made it out unobserved. She walked out into the outer office and opened the main door.

A short, thin, straight-backed old man was walking slowly, though with a determined stride, towards her along the corridor. He was wearing an old-fashioned loose dark green overcoat and a hat. His face could have been that of a much younger man, taut-skinned and firm-jawed. His eyes studied her through black-rimmed spectacles as he approached.

'Rinzaki-san,' said Wada, opening the door wider and bowing as she stepped back to admit him. 'This is a surprise.'

'And yet you seem unsurprised,' he responded, stepping inside and returning the bow.

'I try to accept all turns of events, both the expected and the unexpected, in the same way.'

'An admirable policy.'

'May I take your hat and coat?'

He allowed her to help him off with the coat. The black suit, white shirt and narrow tie he was wearing were also from a bygone era. The removal of his hat revealed an almost completely bald head. His eyes were dark brown, she saw, with no sign of the wateriness she'd often noted in the very old.

'Would you care for tea, Rinzaki-san?'

'Thank you. That would be welcome.'

She showed him to the chair in her office Funaki had recently vacated, refreshed the tea and served him a cup, topping up her own at the same time. She did all this with studied deliberation. She was determined to give him no reason to think his unannounced visit had discomposed her – as in fact it hadn't.

She sat down at her desk opposite him. He smiled faintly and glanced out of the window. 'Nihombashi. The part of Tokyo in which I feel most at home. I envy you this eyrie above the historic heart of the city.'

'It is convenient for many of my clients.'

'Ah yes. Your clients. Such as Fumito Nagata.'

'He is actually a *former* client. As I think you know.'

'Well, in your line of business, Wada-san, I imagine they come . . . and they go.'

'That is undeniable.'

'That being so, I wish to discuss with you an opportunity you have to acquire a client who is likely to be altogether more valuable to you than a hundred Fumito Nagatas.'

'Who might that be?'

Rinzaki did not answer directly. He sipped his tea and regarded her studiously. 'I had some dealings many years ago with your former employer, Kazuto Kodaka. Did you know that?'

'The Jinno case.'

'Ah. You have obviously studied your files on the subject. It was a sensitive matter for me. What Teruki Jinno suspected was blackmail had a much more innocent explanation. Although, as regards certain aspects of his late father's . . . emotional life . . . innocent is hardly the correct description. But I am glad to say Kodaka-san resolved the matter with considerable delicacy.' Rinzaki's smile broadened. 'And I am confident he trained you in such methods. Your reputation, since you decided to continue the business after his death, is that of someone who can be relied upon to solve problems with a minimum of complication. Which is exactly what I need.'

'You are seeking to become my client, Rinzaki-san?'

'I am. Before I explain what I have in mind, though, I feel there are certain issues that need to be . . . cleared up. I was acquainted with Daiju Endo's father and acted for a while as Daiju's mentor. He came to look upon me as a . . . counsellor of sorts. This was particularly so after his father's death. I was very concerned when I heard about his bizarre conduct last year, lead-ing to his dismissal from the civil service. Quite frankly, I feared for his mental health. He came to see me several times at Mat-suda Sanso. On the last occasion, he left on foot, though I only realized that when I noticed he'd left his car behind. I've neither seen nor heard from him since. I have no way of knowing where he is or what his state of mind might be. It is hard, I confess, to be . . . optimistic.'

Rinzaki couldn't seriously expect Wada to believe this version of events. He'd spoken in a tone that suggested it was necessary to supply her with an explanation of what she'd seen at Matsuda Sanso, but it wasn't necessary for either of them to invest that explanation with the aura of truth.

'A man who until very recently worked for me, Rokuro Yagami, took various actions without my knowledge or consent to close down your investigations into Endo's whereabouts. I believe you have met Yagami?'

'I believe I have.'

'I was dismayed to discover how reckless and irresponsible he'd become. He was once a valued member of my team. Somehow, over the years, the discretion I allowed him must have . . . undermined his judgement. When his assistant alerted me to what he'd been doing of late, I immediately terminated his employment. You will have no more trouble from Yagami on my account.'

'That is good to hear.'

'But I still have need of the services he once performed for me so efficiently. The sort of person who can supply those services is hard to find. But I believe I may have found such a person . . . in you.'

'I am content to continue working for myself, Rinzaki-san.'

'And you can. I will not need you on a fixed basis. I will call you in as and when required to deal with any situations that may happen to arise. All I would require is a contractual arrangement conferring on me a degree of . . . priority . . . over your other clients. The remuneration for such an arrangement would be generous, I assure you.'

So, there it was: the offer Yagami had predicted. 'I am honoured by your offer, Rinzaki-san,' Wada responded after a measured pause. 'But still . . .'

'I do not require your answer now. Think about it. Reflect on the advantages it would confer on you.'

'I will. But I must warn you that I . . . value my independence.'

'Independence without power is a chimera.' He looked at her with sudden sombreness. 'You have no power, Wada-san. Therefore you have no independence. If you are not willing to come to an equitable understanding with me, it will become difficult to assume that you do not pose a threat to me.'

The real Rinzaki had at last shown himself. Wada frowned reproachfully at him. 'I have said nothing that is remotely threatening.'

'Of course not. You have in truth said virtually nothing at all. But I do not underestimate you. Your resourcefulness, which I would hope to benefit from, could pose a problem to me if applied in ways that conflict with my interests. And in that event . . .' He smiled again. 'You need to think of your future. And that of your mother, of course.'

'My mother?'

'You have a mother living, according to Yagami. An ageing parent can be an expensive burden. Hence the attraction of securing a steady stream of income as your career . . . enters its later phase.'

'Forgive me, Rinzaki-san, but in view of your own age . . .'

'What would your long-term prospects be? A fair question. I can tell you that Kuraikagami will continue without me, thanks to a partnership arrangement I have negotiated with certain American interests who will undoubtedly value the expertise I believe you will by then have developed. I will introduce you to them at an early stage with such a transition specifically in mind.'

The American interests had to be the Braxtons. Wada was under no illusions. The call-in contract Rinzaki had described was a straightforward move to swallow her within his organization. And the gratuitous mention of her mother was a method of making it clear to her that this was actually an offer she couldn't – or shouldn't – refuse. She hadn't threatened him. But he was certainly threatening her.

What he didn't know, of course, was that thanks to Yagami she knew a great deal more about his activities than he supposed. She suspected the deal with the Braxtons was no more than an

279

aspiration, contingent on Yukari Otonashi – his daughter by Sonoko Zaizen – securing control of the Matsuda asset. Nothing was fixed. Nothing was secure. He wasn't offering to employ her because he valued her abilities. He was trying to neutralize her, to take her off the shogi board. The truth, which she willed herself to remember, was that his position wasn't as strong as he was suggesting. While the asset eluded him, there was no certainty he could win the game.

'I will give serious thought to what you have said, Rinzaki-san.' Wada wasn't lying. She was going to think very carefully about every move she made from now on in the light of what Rinzaki had said. What she wasn't going to think carefully about was accepting his offer. That was never going to happen. And she was amazed he didn't appear to understand that. Long experience of having others do his bidding had evidently left him poorly equipped to deal with those who weren't prepared to be controlled by him. She'd told him how much she valued her independence. But he hadn't been listening.

'I will look forward to hearing your decision.' He rose from his chair with much less of a struggle than the average ninety-three-year-old might exhibit and looked once more towards the window.

Wada also rose. She followed his gaze. 'You will remember the city as it was at the end of the war. The contrast must be . . . astonishing.'

'There was no city at the end of the war,' he said softly. 'There was only rubble and ash. We made new lives. We made a new city.'

'It is hard to imagine.'

'It is not hard. All you have to do is remove from your mind's eye everything man-made you see through the window. What remains – the land, the sea – was what we had. You can think of it as destruction. Or you can think of it as purification. I believe they are in fact the same.' He turned and looked at her. 'Never resist change, Wada-san. It is a cardinal error.'

'Because change is always good?'

'No. Because change is inevitable. And you should always be on the side of inevitability. I am confident you will come to that conclusion.' He smiled. 'As you consider my offer.'

Wada gave her response to Rinzaki's offer shortly after he bade her a courtly farewell and left. She made a booking for a Sunday evening flight to San Francisco. As far as she was concerned, there was nothing inevitable about the triumph of whatever scheme he had in place. She meant to do everything in her power to defeat him. That was what he had accomplished by coming to see her. He had informed her of his perception of their relative statuses. And she had resolved to overturn them. He had revealed his arrogance. And she had made her decision.

She was not worried for herself, but she was troubled by the reference Rinzaki had made to her mother. It had undoubtedly been intended to throw her off balance, but still it had to be taken seriously. There was something she could do to protect Haha, however, though putting it into effect was not without difficulty. It began with a telephone call.

'Mother? It's me.'

'Ah, Umiko,' Haha replied, with that unspoken implication she'd perfected that the call was long overdue. 'I am well, if you are wondering.'

'I am glad to hear that. How is Tago-san?'

'He is well also. Nothing has changed. I am still determined to exonerate him. Are you phoning to say you can now accommodate his case in your packed schedule?'

'No. No, not yet.' Wada needed to speak to Tago. But she couldn't for the moment devise a way of arranging that without encouraging Haha to believe she was going to work on clearing his name. She hesitated.

Then her mother rode unwittingly to the rescue. 'I think Tago-san is already preparing for the day when he can return to sumo. He is eating healthily and taking regular exercise. He goes for an early morning run every day.'

'He does?'

'Without fail.'

'How early?'

'As soon as it's light.'

'That is . . . impressive.' It was also an opportunity. Since Tago had no phone that she knew of, meeting him without her mother in attendance was difficult. Wada had been prepared to visit the house and endure a grilling from Haha for the sake of a few words alone with Tago. But now it appeared she didn't actually have to visit the house at all.

'Will I be seeing you this weekend?'

'Ah . . . this weekend is difficult.'

'Is there one that isn't?'

'It's just that . . . I am so busy.'

'You cannot be busy all the time, Umiko.'

'Yet it seems I am.'

'As you say. It *seems* you are.'

Before it was light on Sunday morning, Wada was stationed on the cobbled path that ran down alongside her mother's house in Koishikawa. The train ride there had been eerily quiet and the streets around the house were largely empty, bar a few early dog-walkers and shift workers. The morning had dawned mistily, with a promise of sunshine later. The air was cool and still. Altogether, it was a delight to be up and about in Tokyo. But Wada had no leisure in which to savour the conditions. What she was there to do wasn't something she could afford to mismanage.

It was a relief when the gate into the small garden at the rear of the house opened and Seiji Tago stepped into view. He was wearing a baggy grey tracksuit and grubby trainers. He was rolling his shoulders and waggling his feet in some pre-exercise routine. With his mane of hair and his shambling gait, he looked like a middle-aged man trying to recapture lost fitness – which, Wada supposed, was exactly what he was.

He saw her almost immediately. He stopped and raised his chin and looked up the path at her. His eyes narrowed. Then he walked slowly towards her.

'*Ohayo gozaimasu*, Wada-san,' he said in his rumbling voice. He contrived to look wholly unsurprised by her presence.

'Can we talk, Tago-san?' she asked. 'It is important.'

'Of course we can talk. You could have come to the house later and talked to your mother as well.'

'This is not for her ears.'

'I thought not. Shall we walk?'

They moved off up the path, away from the house. 'I am sorry to interrupt your run.'

'I can run when we have talked.'

'How far do you go?'

'It varies, according to how well your mother has fed me the previous night, which is generally too well. I sometimes lumber as far as Ueno Park. My former home, if a homeless person can be said to have a home.'

Wada was aware the park was a haunt of the homeless. She'd often seen them huddled amongst the ginkgo trees on the other side of the road when taking the parkside exit from Ueno station. It occurred to her that Tago could easily have been one of those she'd glimpsed on such occasions. But like everyone else she paid them little or no attention. She was too busy. She was always too busy. 'How long did you live in the park?' she asked.

'I am not sure. Time became . . . elastic . . . during that period.

Sometimes I see people there I recognize. The strange thing is . . . they do not recognize me. I suppose I am no longer a member of their tribe.'

'My mother has been very kind to you.'

'Yes. She has.'

They turned east along the street at the top of the path, vaguely in the direction of Ueno. 'You will have to tell her eventually that you do not want me to try to clear you of the bribery charge, Tago-san. And you will have to tell her why.'

'It is true. I will have to. I often rehearse the words as I run. As yet, I have not found the right ones.'

'Those men you saved me from . . .'

'Did me a service. By allowing me to do *you* a service.'

'I was grateful. And I am sorry to have to ask another service of you . . .'

'You should not be sorry. You must know I value any chance to do an honourable thing to store up against the *dis*honourable things I have also done.'

'Those men you saved me from . . .' Wada repeated.

'Are you going to tell me who they work for?'

'Goro Rinzaki. Chairman of the Kuraikagami Film Corporation.'

'Kuraikagami?'

'You know the name?'

'They did some filming at our stable for a sumo documentary film about, oh, ten years ago. I remember there was a visit from the company's senior executives. Maybe the chairman was among them. Elderly, small, bespectacled, immaculately dressed.'

'That sounds like Rinzaki.'

'Your difficulties with him . . . are not about filmmaking?'

'No, Tago-san. They are not. He is a man with . . . many interests. Not all of them legitimate.'

'And he set those men on you because you have interfered with those interests?'

'Yes. That is exactly how it is.'

'Can you reach an accommodation with him?'

'No. I can only defeat him. Or be defeated by him.'

'If I were still a betting man, Wada-san, I would bet on you.'

'Thank you. I am willing to take my chances.'

'Can I . . . enhance those chances?'

'I have to go abroad for a while. The trip is crucial to resolving my conflict with Rinzaki. He is not yet aware of the move I propose to make against him. Once he becomes aware of it, he may . . . strike back. I fear he will calculate that the only way to suborn me is to threaten the safety of those closest to me.'

'You mean your mother?'

'He knows of her existence. He made a point of telling me so.'

'Ah. I see.'

'I want to ask you if—'

He stopped and placed a hand on her arm to stop her as well. She turned and looked at him. 'I will make sure nothing happens to her.' The pledge was simple and unqualified.

'I only ask that you do as much as you can to protect her.'

'You do not need to worry about her, Wada-san. She will be safe.'

He could not guarantee that, of course. But somehow it didn't seem to matter. The promise was enough. He would dedicate himself to ensuring Haha was safe. And that was all Wada could ask for.

1995

IT IS A QUIET AFTERNOON AT OI RACECOURSE, WITH AN UNEXCITING schedule of low-key races following one after the other in lethargic fashion. The crowd is thin, the drama thinner still. Even the horses seem to be running in slow motion. No one is cheering, or even tearing up losing betting slips and throwing them in the air. Animation is close to suspended.

This is as Kodaka hoped it would be. He came here because he needed to sit in the open air, a little apart from the tumult of the city, and think. He needs, in fact, to think a great deal. With each step he takes towards the deception he has planned, the risks he is running continue to grow. He hasn't bet on any of the races. But he is gambling nonetheless. And it isn't money he's gambling with.

He is relieved when he sees Funaki climbing the steps of the largely empty stand towards him, cigarette in mouth, glass of beer in hand, with a spare bottle held artfully in a crooked finger. He's smiling. Kodaka smiles back and raises his own glass in greeting.

'Good to see you, old friend,' he says as Funaki sits down on the bench beside him.

'How has your luck been, Dakka?' They clink glasses.

'Mixed. Decidedly mixed.'

'No good asking you for a tip, then?'

'Definitely not.'

'I told myself, "Dakka wouldn't drag me to the races without at least a dead cert winner to make me feel better about making the effort." Are you saying I was wrong?'

'You didn't tell yourself that.'

Funaki laughs. 'That is true. But only because you are the world's worst tipster. Even worse than that guy the paper pays to dupe our readers into wasting their money. I swear he's taking bribes from the bookmakers.'

'You could be right.'

Funaki pours some beer from his spare bottle into Kodaka's three-quarters empty glass. 'Why are we here? We could have met at the Blue Fin later if drinking beer was all you had in mind.'

'Ah, well . . .' Kodaka grins sheepishly. 'Actually . . . I need your help . . . with something.'

'Why do you need my help so much more often than I need yours?'

'Because being a journalist is safer and easier than being a private detective.'

'You really think so? There are stories I could tell you . . .'

'I know. You've told me most of them.' Kodaka pulls a folded sheet of paper out of his jacket pocket, flattens it and hands it to Funaki.

'What's this?'

'A photocopy of page twenty-three of your paper from a few weeks back. I've ringed the item of interest. "*Drowned woman found in Ariake timber dock.*" I don't suppose you remember it.'

Funaki peers at the report. 'It's tiny. And page twenty-three? Are you kidding? Why would I remember it?'

'No reason. But let's agree on the gist of it. The body of a young woman, estimated to be in her early to mid-twenties, was retrieved from the water beneath a wharf in the Ariake timber dock. It was assumed this was the same woman the driver of a van claimed to have seen jumping off Rainbow Bridge two days previously. No one had reported her missing and she was carrying nothing to identify her. The police said they had been unable to establish who she was or where she lived. Right?'

Funaki has been reading as Kodaka speaks. Now he nods. 'Right. But so what? Sad to say, this kind of thing isn't unusual. Thousands of people kill themselves in Japan every year. That probably equates to twenty or thirty every day. And half of those must be right here in Tokyo.'

'But how many of them go unidentified?'

'I don't know. Some. A few.'

'Well, it's this *one* I'm interested in.'

'Why?'

'Imagine a handbag was found in the same area, sodden from immersion in the water, snagged on some wharf upright or other, containing . . . a driving licence, maybe, or some other items . . . that gave the police the name of a young woman about the age of the one who drowned. What then?'

'Then they'd know who she was.'

'Exactly.'

Funaki frowns. 'Exactly *what*?'

Kodaka turns and looks at his friend. 'If I supplied the handbag and its contents and planted it on the wharf, could you supply someone to find it?'

Funaki's frown deepens. 'Why would you want to do that?'

'I need to help someone disappear. Having her thought dead . . . is a good way to do that. In fact, in this case, it's just about the only way . . . to stop people looking for her.'

'Is she a client of yours?'

'I suppose you could say she's become a client.'

'And these people who are looking for her . . .'

288

'Don't wish her well.'

'Does this have anything to do with Goro Rinzaki?'

It was only to be expected Funaki would suspect a connection with the subject of their last conversation. Kodaka could deny it. But Funaki wouldn't believe him. And Kodaka badly needs his friend to take him at his word. He nods.

'You've stirred up trouble for this woman, have you? Is that it?'

'I have, yes. Big trouble.'

'And now you want to get her out of it?'

'Very much.'

'By getting her recorded as dead? Isn't that a bit drastic?'

'Not in the circumstances.'

'Circumstances you're going to stay coy about, I assume.'

'It's best if I do.'

'What about her friends and relatives? Is she willing to let them think she's dead?'

'She has no friends. She's an only child and her parents are dead. So, yes, she's willing.'

'Still, it's a big thing.'

'She knows that.'

'Why don't you find someone to chance on the bag? Why ask me to arrange it?'

'There can't be any possibility of Rinzaki discovering I played a part in this. Besides, I'm hoping you'll make sure there's a report in the paper . . . for him to read.'

'Have you met Rinzaki . . . since we discussed him?'

'I have.'

'And?'

'He's a dangerous man, Joji. He doesn't behave as if he is. He doesn't look like he is. But dangerous he nonetheless is.'

'Are you going to tell me why he's looking for this woman?'

'No.'

'What if I make it a condition of helping you?'

289

'You won't.'

'Sure about that?'

'We have to do this.'

'Oh, it's *we* now, is it?'

'I'll explain everything . . . one day.'

Funaki shakes his head, apparently in bewilderment at his own susceptibility to Kodaka's plea for help. 'Am I going to regret doing this?'

'That's what I asked myself.'

'And did you get an answer?'

'Yes. The answer was . . . maybe. But I'd regret not doing it even more. That's a certainty.'

'Is that supposed to be good enough for me as well?'

Kodaka looks at Funaki frankly. They know each other better than either of them knows anyone else they're not related to by blood. It's a largely unspoken bond, camouflaged by reticence and sarcasm. But it is a bond neither of them could ever imagine breaking. 'Well?' says Kodaka. 'Isn't it?'

2022

WADA WAS NOT AN ENTHUSIASTIC TRAVELLER. HER KNOWLEDGE OF Japan was limited to the main island of Honshu. Only one of her two overseas trips had been voluntary: a honeymoon tour of Europe with Hiko way back in 1994. Her general view was that no good came from venturing to places where you didn't speak the language or understand the culture. As it was, her relative fluency in English meant only one of those reservations applied to visiting California. But she was still wary. Mistakes, she knew, would be easier to make there. And mistakes, in her shadow-boxing with Goro Rinzaki, could prove expensive.

The timing of her flight from Tokyo to San Francisco at least meant she could hope to avoid jet lag. An early evening departure offered the prospect of a reasonable night's sleep before a morning arrival. True, it was to be the morning of the same day she'd already passed in Japan, but two days for the price of one appealed to her thrifty nature.

San Francisco International Airport was less busy than Wada had feared, which didn't mean it wasn't busy. The time she had to spend queuing at the immigration desk seemed almost as long as the flight and gave her ample opportunity to contrast the signs proclaiming how welcome she was with the dilatory reception officialdom actually supplied.

Eventually, though, she was through, and happy to see Troy Kimber waiting for her, as promised. He looked subtly different in his native environment, more casually dressed and less wary of his surroundings. She worried for a moment he would try to hug her, but in the end he simply gave her a nod and a big smile. 'Quite a shock seeing you here, Wada, I have to admit,' he said.

'Why? I told you I was coming.'

'That's not what I meant. It's just . . . well, like coming across an antelope in Antarctica, you know?'

'No. I do not know.'

'Well, I guess it's not far from how I looked in Japan, when you think about it. You want breakfast?'

'I had some on the plane.'

'I'm going to need a serious infusion of coffee before I drive back to Santa Rosa, so take pity on me, okay?'

He piloted her to the nearest coffee shop, where bleary-eyed new arrivals were refuelling amidst trolley-loads of luggage. Her own luggage comprised one small, neat suitcase. Kimber found a table for them, then went to buy coffee.

He returned with Danish pastries in addition to the coffees, explaining he was happy to eat hers if she didn't want it. Rather to her surprise, Wada did eat hers, though partly in order to mask the burnt flavour of the coffee.

'Anything happen since I left Tokyo I should know about?' Kimber asked through a mouthful of pastry flakes.

'Nothing significant.' Wada had decided it wouldn't help Kimber to know about Rinzaki's attempt to intimidate her.

'Wish I could say the same.'

'What has occurred?'

'Well, it's kind of embarrassing. I told you no one else was staying at my house. But, in my absence, well . . . my mother moved in.'

'Your mother? Mrs Braxton?'

'The very same. It seems things came to a head between her and Grant. They had an argument about his relationship with Otonashi. An argument to end all arguments, apparently. It had been coming for a while. She just couldn't take it any more. I mean, Otonashi lives in the same house as Grant's "guest" and he hasn't exactly been subtle about what that really means. It's a big place, but even so. Long and the short? She packed and left. And my place was the obvious direction to head in. Temporary, obviously. And don't worry. She's onside with what I'm trying to do – what *we're* trying to do.'

'She knows about me?'

'She does now. Honestly, Wada, there isn't anything to worry about. Grant isn't going to come after her. He's probably glad she left. So am I, really. She stuck it out longer than most people would. Hoping for a change of heart on Grant's part, I guess. But that was never going to happen. Otonashi's got her hooks in too deep.'

'How much did you tell her?'

'I told her what I'd found out in Japan. I was never not going to do that.' He looked at Wada frankly. 'Mom and I both want Otonashi out of the way. She'll do whatever it takes to achieve that. So will I. And the way I see it is you can help us. Bring a contract for me to sign?'

'As a matter of fact, I did.'

'Hand it over, then. The sooner we formalize this arrangement the sooner I can let you in on my latest discovery.'

'What would that be, Troy?'

He glanced around before answering and lowered his voice. 'I'll tell you in the car. It's fair to say we don't want this to be overheard.'

*

Kimber's car was something large, styleless and modern. The drive to Santa Rosa took them along the western shore of San Francisco Bay and out of the city across the Golden Gate Bridge. Wada's mental picture of San Francisco, based on numerous Hollywood films, matched the reality to a degree that surprised her, although the details of her unfolding surroundings were hard to absorb as Kimber related his 'latest discovery'.

'I told Mom about the Matsuda asset and the possibility that, whatever it is, it's hidden either at BISRI or their house – Grant's house, I guess I should say now. Well, that jogged her memory. Apparently, soon after Clyde died and Grant took full control of his father's estate and affairs, he got involved in a legal tussle with the Sonoma County authorities. The winery and BISRI are both in Sonoma County. The tussle was about what seemed on the face of it an unimportant issue. The original plans for BISRI – elevations, layouts, services, all the standard structural stuff – were lodged with the public records office in Santa Rosa, so anyone with a mind to could go along there during office hours and request sight of same, plus run off copies. There's no Internet access. You have to visit in person. But it's not difficult. Anyhow, Grant wanted the plans redacted, so no one could see or copy them. The whole lot, I mean. Everything.'

'Why?'

'Why did he *say* he wanted them redacted, you mean? Oh, because the design of the building incorporated revolutionary earthquake-proofing measures that should rightfully be confidential. The argument went back and forth. Eventually, he called in some favours and the records officer was told to go along with his demands. So, the BISRI plans vanished from the public domain. You can't see them. No one can.'

'Presumably, you believe his real concern was to conceal something that close scrutiny of the plans might reveal.'

'Got a better explanation?'

294

'No. I haven't. If we're right about the asset and its importance, I think this means there's some detail in the BISRI plans that points to where the asset is held. That's why he wanted them redacted.'

'And he got his way. Which is what he's used to getting in life.'

'How can we get round the redaction?'

'Probably impossible. And butting heads with the bureaucrats would run the risk of attracting Grant's attention, which obviously we don't want to do.'

Wada detected a hint of smugness in Kimber's tone. 'But you have a solution to the problem?'

'I think I do. The architects Clyde employed for BISRI are an old-established San Francisco firm: Anderson McGraw. They buy their wine from us and I know one of the partners well. Andrew Harrington. He's something of an oenophile. The original blueprints will be in their files. All we have to do . . .'

'Is ask your friend for a favour.'

'Exactly. Which is why I called him last night and arranged to visit him at their offices tomorrow morning. How does that sound?'

'Like a promising start.'

'You see? We can do this, Wada, we truly can.'

Wada saw no point in denting Kimber's optimism. The reality, however, was that even if they could get hold of the original blueprints they wouldn't know exactly what they were looking for. And if they did succeed in discovering where the asset was concealed, gaining access to it without being detected was on a whole other scale of difficulty. A start truly was all this amounted to.

They drove north by Highway 101 through sun-bathed spring countryside. Wada started to notice vineyards on the slopes of the surrounding hills and wondered how far they were from the Braxton Winery, not to mention the Braxton Institute of Seismological

Research and Innovation. Shortly after passing a signpost indicating Santa Rosa was twelve miles ahead, Kimber turned off onto a side road that wound away west through gentle farmland.

'I reckoned you'd like to take a look at BISRI,' he explained. 'I can't take you in. Security's pretty tight. Besides, I don't think we should be seen there together, do you?'

'To be honest, Troy, I do not think we should be seen together at all.'

'I agree. Which is a major pain. I mean, ordinarily I'd take you to the winery and show you the sights of Santa Rosa, but it's probably best if you stay close to my house other than when we're hunting down a clue.'

Hunting down a clue sounded like some kind of recreational activity, but Wada knew – and hoped Kimber did too – that every move they made would have to be carefully considered.

'Still, you should see BISRI. It's basically why you're here, after all.'

'How many people work there?'

'Oh, there are about twenty full-time seismologists and assistants, plus visiting specialists and students on placement from various universities. Fifty or sixty people when you factor in the admin and technical staff, I guess. The place brings in a lot of consultancy fees. It seems like it's turned into more of a business operation than a research institute. I mean, it's been running for more than a quarter of a century without coming close to perfecting any reliable form of earthquake prediction.'

'Is your stepfather expecting Otonashi to change that?'

'Presumably. But she hasn't so far, has she? If she really was the Kobe Sensitive, she should have produced some results by now.'

'She is not the Kobe Sensitive.'

'Tell that to Grant.'

'If I meet him, I will.'

'You think meeting him would be a good idea?'

'Not yet. But the time may come.'

'And I'll be sure to be there if and when it does. Meanwhile . . .'

They turned a corner and crested a minor rise. A signpost ahead indicated a turning to BISRI. They cruised slowly past the entrance. Wada saw a curving drive leading to a complex of white-walled buildings, attractively balconied and porticoed under gently angled terracotta-tiled roofs. It looked at first glance more like a hotel or country club than a scientific establishment.

Kimber pulled in off the road a short distance ahead. From there they could look back down across the slope of the land towards BISRI. Nothing much seemed to be happening on the site. A flag hung limply on its pole and sunlight glistened on the car windshields in the parking area. Wada could make out two casually dressed figures walking towards what appeared to be the main building. In the distance, a hot-air balloon moved lazily across the skyline.

'Does Grant spend much time here?' she asked.

'I wouldn't really know. I'm not encouraged to show my face at BISRI. He likes me to concentrate on the winery side of the business.'

'But does he actively run BISRI?'

'Oh no. *Doctor* Sylvia Girdler is in charge. Anyhow, she thinks she is. But maybe Otonashi has other ideas.'

'How difficult would it be to get into the main building . . . undetected?'

'You think that's what it'll come down to? Breaking and entering?'

'Ideally, just entering.'

'Well, I don't see it being easy. Security's the responsibility of Connie McDermott. He oversees precautions at the winery as well, so we're well acquainted. Conscientious and discreet is how I'd describe him.'

297

'It would be better if he was neither.'

'No point me lying to you. Connie's old school.'

The phrase eluded Wada's generally excellent grasp of English. 'What does that mean exactly?'

'It means he could be a problem.'

'And not our only one.'

Kimber smiled. 'You'll find a way round all of them, Wada, I'm sure of it. Hell, that's what I'm paying you for.'

They skirted the centre of Santa Rosa and headed out along a country road that climbed a little way up into the hills, with Kimber discoursing on the wine-friendly microclimate of the Sonoma valley. Then he abruptly announced, 'Here we are,' and pulled off onto a short track leading to a large, sprawling house that looked far too big to be a single man's residence but evidently was.

There was a lot of gravel to one side, planted with succulents, and an unkempt garden to the other. The house itself was wide-eaved and modern, with a right-angled single-storey wing attached to a double-storey main block, a flagged terrace and a good deal of tinted glass. Beyond the house there was what appeared to be a paddock, though of a horse there was no sign.

'Home sweet home,' said Kimber with a grimace as he slewed to a halt next to a compact silver saloon car in front of the spacious garage, the double doors of which stood open to reveal a vintage red sports car. Her host was, as she'd suspected, a man of expensive tastes.

'There's your room,' he said, pointing upwards as they climbed out of the car. Wada noted the window above the garage door. 'With Mom here, you'll appreciate the privacy.'

'Thank you,' said Wada. 'That will be fine.'

'I have you down as a solitary person. Is that right?'

'It is not wrong.'

He frowned at her. 'Do you ever let your guard down, Wada?'

'Occasionally.'

'Am I likely to see it happen?'

'Unlikely, I would say.'

Then he grinned. 'See, that's what I like about you. You're just so damn honest.'

A figure appeared on the terrace ahead of them. Her facial resemblance to Kimber identified her immediately as his mother. She was almost as tall as him as well, slightly gangly, with grey-blonde bobbed hair and sun-weathered features. She looked to be in her mid- to late fifties, well toned and elegantly dressed in a casual fashion.

'Hi,' she said, advancing to meet them. 'You must be Wada. I'm Lois Braxton.'

Wada bowed. 'I am honoured to meet you.'

'Troy's told me a lot about you.' There was touch of steeliness to her tone and she didn't smile. Altogether, it was hard to be sure what she intended the remark to convey.

'I am here to help,' Wada ventured.

'Well, we need help. There's no question about that. My son has doubtless told you my husband and I have come to . . . a parting of the ways.'

'I was sorry to hear of it.'

'The cause of the rupture was the intrusion into our lives of a fellow countrywoman of yours. She said she was going to help us as well, now I come to think of it.'

'It's not the same, Mom,' Troy cut in.

'No. Of course not.'

Lois Braxton turned and headed back towards the house. Kimber sighed and went to fetch Wada's case.

'Sorry about that,' he said as he unloaded it. 'This has all been the most terrible strain for her. She doesn't always . . . weigh her words.'

'It does not matter. Dealing with mothers . . . can be difficult.'

'Speaking from experience?'

'Perhaps.'

'Any tips?'

Wada gave the question a few moments' serious thought, then said, 'Not a single one.'

Troy carried her case up to the room above the garage, which was actually a self-contained flat somewhat bigger than Wada's apartment in Ogikubo. It appeared to supply her with everything she could possibly need, which after all was not much. Then they went to the house.

Lois was in the midst of preparing lunch for them. The house was full of light and space, but homeliness, it struck Wada, it was certainly not full of. The kitchen, where Lois was slicing peppers and courgettes, was as well equipped as it looked to be little used.

'I apologize for my earlier comment,' said Lois. 'It's not your fault you and Otonashi are both Japanese.' She was aproned now and intent on cookery. 'I find myself lashing out before I know it's happening at the moment. I really am sorry.'

'I understand, Braxton-san.'

'Maybe you could call me Lois.'

'Very well.'

'And your first name is . . .'

'Umiko. But I prefer Wada.'

'Why is that?'

'It is who I am.'

'You sound very . . . self-sufficient.'

'I have become so.'

'I envy you. If I were self-sufficient, I wouldn't be . . .'

'I am here to do my professional best to help your son . . . Lois. I hope it will help you also.'

'If it gets Otonashi out of our lives, that'll be enough.'

300

'She is not the Kobe Sensitive.'

'I believe you. If only we could convince Grant of that.'

'Perhaps we can.'

'It won't be easy. Rinzaki used the Endo story to persuade Grant she really did give a warning of the tsunami as well as the Kobe quake. He used to say to me that predicting one earthquake only requires luck, but to predict two . . . requires possession of a unique gift. Discovering the key to earthquake prediction is as much his dream as it was his father's. So, he was always going to be susceptible to Otonashi. Besides, even if we could prise them apart, my relationship with him . . . will never be the same again.' Lois sighed. 'I thought we were so lucky to find one another when we did. A second chance for both of us. It all seemed perfect . . . until Rinzaki smuggled that woman into our world. And now . . . Troy tells me she is Rinzaki's daughter. Is that true?'

'It is what I have been told.'

'Well, she's inherited his devious nature. Though I assume her mother can take credit for her looks. Has Troy told you how beautiful she is?'

'He has.'

'It gives her a big advantage. Not just because Grant was obviously attracted to her from the start, but also because people find it easy to believe someone who's beautiful is also sincere and honest.'

'Do you by any chance have a picture of Otonashi?'

'Yes. There's one on my phone. Hold on.'

Lois went to fetch her phone from the lounge, while Wada wondered just *how* beautiful Otonashi could be. She didn't have to wonder for long.

'Here she is, with Grant. Taken shortly after she arrived from Japan. Before I'd realized . . . what a threat she was.'

Lois handed her phone to Wada. Grant Braxton was a burly, flush-faced man in his sixties, tall and broad-shouldered, but with the beginnings of a stoop, frailty somehow peeking out from beneath a bluff exterior. He was standing next to Otonashi on a terrace similar but not identical to the one visible through the window. Yukari Otonashi herself was, happy though Wada would have been to conclude otherwise, radiantly beautiful, with perfect features, captivatingly large eyes and smoother skin than any woman of her age had a right to possess. She was wearing elegantly cut clothes that contrived to show off her slim but subtly curvaceous figure. Altogether Wada imagined she would fulfil many an American man's dream of a Japanese woman, one who was, in effect, slightly American while also managing to be entirely Japanese.

'That is our enemy, Wada,' said Lois. 'How do we defeat her?'

'By not letting her win. By making sure we find the asset before she does.'

'Can you do that?'

Wada handed the phone back. 'We will find out, won't we?'

'No guarantees?'

'None. Except that I am not in this to lose.'

Troy tried his best to lighten the mood during lunch by talking about wine, which he seemed to be able to do ad infinitum, and asking Wada questions about the sake industry which she was able to answer . . . hardly any of. Lois said little, until, eventually, the conversation returned, as it was bound to, to their undeclared war with Rinzaki. And to Lois's bitter resentment of Otonashi's seduction of her husband.

'I feel so stupid for not realizing sooner what was going on,' she declared.

'Well, you realize now and so do I,' said Troy. 'And we're doing something about it.'

'I don't want you to take any serious risks trying to get the better of them, Troy. It's not worth it.'

'The hell it's not. We can't let them get away with this.'

'Sometimes you have to let people get away with things.'

'Maybe. But this isn't one of those times, is it, Wada?'

Wada suddenly became aware then of how tired she felt. A couple of glasses of Braxton's Sauvignon Blanc had revealed that the jet lag she thought she'd outpaced had merely been awaiting its opportunity to strike. 'I am sorry. I seem to be having difficulty concentrating.'

'You look done in, my dear,' said Lois. 'And after your long flight I'm not surprised. Perhaps you should have a lie-down.'

'I think I may need to.'

'It's OK,' said Troy. 'Grab a few hours' sleep. Remember, I'll need you on top form tomorrow.'

Wada headed off to the garage flat, acknowledging in her own mind that Troy was right. There was nothing more she could do today other than make sure she was properly rested for tomorrow.

There was a large watercolour painting hanging on the wall of the lounge-bedroom, depicting a set of low-roofed mustard-walled buildings nestling amidst a vineyard, with snow-capped mountains in the distance. The Braxton Winery, maybe. At present, this seemed to be the closest she was going to get to it.

She closed the curtains and lay down, turning her mind to the central mystery in all the intrigue Rinzaki had set in motion: the Matsuda asset. What was it? *What* could it possibly be?

Sleep, deep and irresistible, came long before any glimmer of an answer.

When she woke and pulled back the curtains, she saw the light was beginning to fail. The afternoon had become the evening. The hills to the west were enveloped in a violet haze.

Troy, she discovered, had slid a note under the door that read, *Come over whenever you're ready.*

She showered, put on clean clothes and headed for the house.

She found Troy watching golf on an enormous wall-mounted television. There was no sign of Lois. He snapped the set off as soon as he saw her and jumped up from the sofa.

'Feeling fresher?'

'Yes, thank you,' she replied. Then she noticed some twist of anxiety in his expression. 'Is everything all right?'

'Hardly. Golf normally relaxes me, but . . . there's too much going on in my head.'

'There is nothing we can do until we meet your friend tomorrow.'

'I know. But that's the problem. *I* won't be meeting him.'

'Why not?'

'While you were resting, Grant called me. He sounded really uptight. Angry, in fact, though exactly what about wasn't clear. He's decided to visit the winery tomorrow. He wants all the senior staff on hand. There are decisions to be made, he said. Again . . . what about I don't know. He insisted he couldn't go into details until tomorrow. So, I'm going to have to be there. Officially, I've just returned from a holiday in Hawaii. I can't tell him, well, no, actually, I was in Japan checking up on your girlfriend and I've got a few more leads I want to follow up on back here, so, sorry, you'll just have to get by without me. The only way to stop him smelling a rat is for me to put in an appearance. I'll probably have to be there all day. I suspect he'll want to talk to me about Mom as well – try to give me a sanitized account of her walk-out, something like that. I'm sorry, but there's no way I can go to San Francisco tomorrow.'

'We cannot delay meeting your friend.'

'I agree.'

'Then . . .'

'All I can suggest is I call Andy and explain you'll be meeting him on my behalf. I don't see any alternative.'

'I do not think there is one. But will he be as candid with me as he would have been with you?'

'I'll make sure he is.'

'It is unfortunate. But . . . I suggest you call him as soon as possible.'

'This is OK with you, Wada? You'll have to catch an early train to keep our appointment.'

'Absolutely.' In truth, she wasn't entirely displeased. Double-acts didn't suit her working methods. 'It is the best thing to do.'

'Yeah.' Troy frowned. 'But why do I get this . . . sinking feeling? Like Grant knew I was planning something . . . and arranged his visit to the winery to spike my guns.'

'It is much more likely to be simple coincidence.'

'You think so?'

Wada did think so. But only on a balance of probability. There was no way to be sure about any of this. 'I think we should work on that assumption, Troy. I will go to San Francisco tomorrow and meet Andrew Harrington. Alone.'

With her body clock still in some disarray, Wada lay awake for a long time after going to bed, speculations and stratagems whirling in her head. Even a chapter of Tanizaki didn't seem to help.

Sleep came eventually, however, though it wasn't destined to be uninterrupted.

A sound – the crunch of a foot on gravel – woke her. At least, she thought that was what it was, though, straining her ears, she could hear nothing more. She noted the time: 1.43. Then she slipped out of bed, went to the window and adjusted the blinds so she could see out.

There was enough of a moon to cast a few milky shadows. She could make out the shape of Kimber's car below her. Nothing seemed to be moving down there. There was no other sound she could discern. She watched and waited.

Just as she was about to give up and go back to bed, a figure rose into view from low down by the rear of the car. It was too dark to tell much. They were wearing dark clothes, including a hoodie, and could have been either male or female. Whatever they'd been doing, they'd finished, because now they turned and jogged silently away into the deeper darkness of the track and the trees shrouding the road.

Wada stood where she was, listening intently. Two or three minutes passed. Then she heard the distant note of a car engine starting. The car accelerated gently away into the night and the sound faded to nothing.

Wada put on her clothes and left the flat, taking her pen-torch with her. The stairs took her out beside the garage. She walked round to where Kimber's car was standing and headed for the rear wing where she'd seen the figure.

She wouldn't have found it without knowing where to look. It had been artfully placed, high up under the wheel-arch, where it wouldn't be noticeable. She had no doubt what it was, however, as soon as she saw it: a covert tracking device.

Someone was on to them.

1995

THE EVENING AGREED ON WITH FUNAKI HAS COME. KODAKA HAS prepared for it so meticulously he doesn't feel nervous, although he can't suppress all apprehensiveness. Experience tells him there is no plan that can't go awry if circumstances conspire against it. So, he is confident but not complacent. He is going to invest his every move with a great deal of care.

The handbag and its contents – Chikako Imada's identity card; a library membership card and a domestic staff agency registration card, both in her name; a purse holding coins and notes; a zipped toiletries and cosmetics bag containing tweezers, hairpins, lipstick and mascara; a plastic sachet of tissues; a month-old women's magazine filched from the waiting room of Kodaka's dentist – have spent several days in a bucket in his apartment, soaking in salted water, before being allowed to dry off in his bath. Now the bag is inside a black plastic bin-liner and he is en route to the place where it is going to be conveniently discovered by an off-duty policeman known to Funaki. He is relieved that this stage of the plan has finally been reached.

He walks down through Ginza to Shimbashi station and boards a Yurikamome subway line train. It follows the route of

Rainbow Bridge across the harbour to Odaiba. He leaves at the first station after the line emerges at ground level on the other side. The light has faded noticeably since he left his apartment. Darkness is encroaching, hastened by low cloud and drizzle.

His initial idea, dumping the bag on one of the wharves in the dock where the unidentified drowned woman was found, had to be abandoned when he realized so much loading and unloading went on there at unpredictable times that his activities might easily be noticed. His destination now is the scrubbily wooded end of a shingle beach extending along one side of a limb of land that stretches out into the harbour beneath the massive piers of the bridge. There's an apartment block not far away, but it's a chilly, dank midweek evening and, as he hoped, the beach is deserted.

All but deserted, anyway. A lone fisherman is down at the shoreline, rod in hand. Why anyone would consider eating fish caught in the oily waters of the Port of Tokyo is beyond Kodaka's understanding. But it occurs to him that the man might not in reality be fishing for his supper at all. He might be an off-duty police officer. Whatever the case, he gives a good impression of being reassuringly oblivious of Kodaka's presence.

Reaching the patchy woodland towards the end of the beach, where the lights of the bridge cast deep shadows among the trees, Kodaka stops, lifts the handbag out of the bin-liner and positions it among the line of rocks and seaweed separating the trees from the beach. He wedges the handle of the bag between two of the rocks and steps back to satisfy himself that it can be found easily enough by anyone knowing where to look. The bag and the rocks are a similar grey-brown colour, but are readily distinguishable, at least for the next half hour or so, before night falls completely. Glancing back at the fisherman, Kodaka suspects that will not be a problem.

He retraces his steps most of the way along the beach, then

stops, takes his pager out of his pocket and sends his number to Funaki. That done, he presses on.

Before he reaches the subway station, his pager beeps. The number sent to him by Funaki as an acknowledgement is an agreed sequence meaning the next phase of the operation will now swing into operation. Kodaka doesn't look back to see if the fisherman has made a move. He heads straight for the station and takes the next train back to Shimbashi.

Funaki is waiting for him in the Blue Fin.

'I'll have another beer, Dakka,' is Funaki's greeting. 'The drinks are definitely on you.'

'Everything going according to plan?' Kodaka asks, more nervous now than when he had an active part to play.

'If it wasn't, I'd have heard. And I've heard nothing. Stop fretting. My friend is going to impress his superiors by remembering the Rainbow Bridge suicide when he comes across the bag. Came across, I should say. He's probably already on the phone to HQ from the nearest *koban* by now. Just let bureaucracy take its course.'

Kodaka nods in agreement. He simply has to be patient, which he'll find easier to manage when he's had a few drinks. He orders a beer for himself, plus a second – or third – for Funaki.

'Of course, it's after the police have confirmed the identity of the deceased that you're going to have to be on your A game,' Funaki adds with a mischievous smile.

Kodaka doesn't rise to the bait. He's well aware he'll have to convince Rinzaki Chikako Imada really is dead. He'll have the facts – as they stand, according to the police – on his side. There's no reason Rinzaki shouldn't believe him. There's no reason at all.

'You can leave me to worry about that,' he says, taking a first gulp of his beer.

2022

WADA DID MORE THINKING THAN SLEEPING AS THE CALIFORNIAN night passed. She was up at first light and found Kimber had risen early as well. He was in the kitchen, wrapped in a bathrobe, drinking coffee and gazing out at the misty morning.

'Sleep well?' he asked, rubbing his eyes like someone who hadn't.

'No.'

'Me neither. Too much on my mind. What can I get you for breakfast?'

'There's something I need to tell you, Troy.'

He frowned at her. 'What?'

And so she told him.

There was a tracking device on Lois's car as well as Troy's. When they'd gone outside and he'd seen them for himself and stopped swearing, he started trying to dislodge the one on his car. Wada stopped him.

'We should leave them both where they are. Then whoever put them there will think you're unaware they're tracking you.'

'But that means I can't go anywhere without them knowing about it.'

'That is true.'

'Who did this?'

'Otonashi is the obvious suspect. But she would probably need help from a surveillance expert.'

'Shit.'

'It is not so surprising. I imagine she knows you're trying to stop her.'

Troy glared down at the wheel-arch of his car where the tracker was located. 'What do we do, Wada? And what do we tell my mother?'

'We tell her to carry on as normal.'

'She'll go crazy. She'll probably want to call Grant and have it out with him.'

'She mustn't do that.'

'How can you be so calm?'

'Because not being calm won't help. I will go to San Francisco and speak to your friend. You will go to the winery. The tracker will record only your journey.'

'And then?'

'Then . . . we will see.'

Lois was as angry as Troy had predicted when she heard what had happened. Eventually, though, she agreed with Wada that they should behave as if the trackers didn't exist. Troy's sports car, locked safely inside the garage, was there for untraceable use if they needed it, but it was conspicuous and as soon as whoever had planted the devices saw it they would realize what it meant.

So, Troy set off for the winery and, shortly afterwards, Lois drove into Santa Rosa, a natural enough trip for her to take. Wada went with her, playing safe by lying flat on the rear seat so she wouldn't be seen in transit. The plan was for her to be dropped along the road into the city centre, from where she could walk to the train station.

'What am I supposed to do after you've gone, Wada?' Lois complained as they headed away from the house down the winding road into the city, with the blue sky and a blur of passing trees all Wada could see from her position. 'Kill time in the stores of Santa Rosa while trying not to think about what my husband has done to me?'

'He may know nothing about the tracking devices.'

'That's not the point. He's responsible for letting Otonashi into our world. It didn't have to be like this. We were happy, for God's sake.'

'There is nothing I can tell you, Lois. Except that we – you – are not powerless. We are in a contest. And that contest is a long way from over.'

Lois dropped Wada off at a quiet corner a couple of blocks from the train station. The walk to the station gave her no cause for concern. She was sure no one was following her. In that sense, the tracking devices were good news. They suggested direct surveillance wasn't going to be attempted, at least not yet. With any luck, Otonashi had no idea Wada was even in California.

It was an hour's ride on the train through the Sonoma valley and on south to Larkspur, where it connected with a ferry across the bay to San Francisco. The weather was fine, with fitful sunlight gilding the countryside and sparkling on the wave crests. The ferry cruised past Alcatraz with the mist-fringed span of the Golden Gate Bridge in the distance. The tourists aboard were delighted, snapping away merrily while Wada sat in a corner of the passenger cabin. As usual in her experience, no one paid her any attention. Which was just as she liked it.

From the ferry terminal, Wada walked up through the city to the address she had for Anderson McGraw: the third floor of a handsome office block that looked older than she suspected it

312

was. The reverse appeared to be true of the staff of the practice, who were casually dressed, mostly in jeans and chinos, and conspicuously relaxed in what she took to be the Californian style.

The offices were open plan for the most part, but Wada was shown to a private room for her meeting with Andrew Harrington and regaled en route with offers of coffee, water and cookies, all of which she politely declined. She decided against asking for green tea, doubting as she did the ability of the young man escorting her to do anything other than ruin it.

She wasn't kept waiting for long. Andrew Harrington was a tall, rangy, good-looking man with grey-blond hair and an easy smile. He repeated the offers of coffee, water and cookies, which she declined all over again. Then he asked various amiably inconsequential questions about whether she'd visited San Francisco before and what she thought of the city. There was a view through the window of a spectacularly spired skyscraper: the Transamerica Pyramid, he told her, before saying something she didn't entirely follow about the earthquake protection measures incorporated in its design. She had the strange impression he was nervous, though what about she couldn't imagine.

Eventually, he settled at the table opposite her. 'Troy's spoken to me, as you know,' he said. 'He and I are good friends. He's asked me to help in any way I can.'

'I hope you will.'

'Absolutely.' His smile had acquired an awkward edge. 'So, what can I do for you?'

'I have some questions about the original designs for the Braxton Institute of Seismological Research and Innovation.'

'Yeah. I had a feeling this might be about BISRI.'

'You did?'

'Look, what *exactly* do you want from me?'

'Well, Mr Harrington—'

'Andrew, please.'

'What I want – what *we* want, Troy and I – is to . . . well, examine the original plans for the construction of BISRI. By that I mean . . . detailed floor plans. Would that be possible . . . Andrew?'

Harrington frowned and pushed his hair back from his forehead. 'I guessed it would be something like that. I'm not going to ask why you want to see them. Troy must have a good reason.'

'He does.'

'The practice was slow to adopt modern technology. This was all before my time. Everything was paper-based thirty years ago. So, we don't have computer records of the plans for BISRI or any other building of that age – or older. But we do have paper plans – blueprints and so forth – in our archives.'

'Can I see the plans for BISRI?'

'No. Sad to say, you can't.'

'I don't understand. What is the problem?'

'We don't have them.'

'But you said—'

Harrington held up his hand to stop her. 'We don't have the BISRI plans, Wada. We should have. But we don't. I know because we had a visit last Wednesday from the security officer at BISRI. Guy called McDermott. He wanted to see the plans as well.'

'Why?'

'We'll come to that. I was happy to accommodate his request, so I sent someone off to the archives to fetch the plans. They came back empty-handed. The plans simply weren't there. Which answered a puzzling question, actually. About a month ago, we had a break-in. It was a Sunday night. Very low-key. The building's security officer didn't even know it had happened until evidence of a forced entry via the loading bay was noticed on Monday morning. When all the cameras were checked, there were a few glimpses of a man making his way up here. He was wearing dark clothes, mask, baseball cap and hoodie. You couldn't make

314

out enough even to be sure it was a man rather than a woman. But he or she was in these offices that night. That much we knew. Didn't seem to have taken anything, though. Well, so we thought, anyhow. As it turns out, though . . .'

'They stole the BISRI plans.'

'Yes. They did.'

'How did Mr McDermott react to the news?'

'Like he'd half-expected it, if I'm honest. He said there'd been "an incident" at BISRI as well. Declined to say what kind of incident. But he was . . . on edge. Curt, actually. He seemed to have a lot on his mind. Peered at the camera footage of the intruder, agreed it was useless in terms of identification, asked what the police had made of it – which was nothing – and then . . . left.'

Why had McDermott come there? What had happened at BISRI? Wada turned the possibilities over in her mind. If the 'incident' was a burglary and detailed knowledge of the layout of BISRI's offices had been necessary to carry out the burglary, McDermott might have concluded that Anderson McGraw were the obvious source of such knowledge, since the public records had been redacted. But in that case . . . who was the burglar?

'Do you want to take a look at the footage, Wada?' Harrington asked, fishing a data stick out of his pocket and offering to plug it into the computer that stood on the desk.

Wada nodded. 'Thank you.'

'I doubt you'll get much out of it, but . . .' He activated the computer and inserted the stick, then opened a file. 'Here you go.'

Wada watched closely as split-screen images of a black-clad figure moving along various corridors and up and down various stairways played out slowly and fuzzily before her. Harrington was right. There was nothing to go on. Her prime suspect was Manjiro Nagata. And the figure might have been Manjiro Nagata for all she knew. Or it might have been virtually anyone else of medium height and medium build.

While she was looking at the images, a telephone on a side table rang, apparently to Harrington's surprise. He went to answer it. And Wada's attention was snatched away from the screen as soon as she heard him say, 'Troy?'

She looked across at Harrington, who said, 'Yes, she's here. I'll put her on.' Then he held out the phone for her. 'Troy,' he said, raising his eyebrows in bemusement. 'For you.'

Wada walked over and took the phone from him.

'I'll leave you to it,' said Harrington. He looked, in fact, relieved to do so, ambling out of the room and closing the door behind him.

Wada raised the phone to her ear. 'Troy?'

'Yeah. Listen to me, Wada. It's all gone slightly crazy here. Grant's behaving like something *really* bad has happened but he can't – or won't – say what. I told you about Connie McDermott, our security officer, didn't I? Well, he's been fired. Some new out-fit, Petersens, have taken over and they want to question lots of people – including me – about "possible security breaches", whatever the hell that means. The breach was at BISRI, but they seem to think winery staff need grilling as well. They're due to have a go at me later. I'm calling you on a borrowed phone because frankly I'm getting a bit paranoid about surveillance and don't really trust mine any more.'

'You may be right not to. McDermott was here last week. Before he was fired, I suppose.'

'What did he want?'

'To check if the BISRI plans had been accessed, I think.'

'And had they?'

'They were stolen. About a month ago.'

'Christ. Who could have done that?'

'Why is the more important question.'

'To figure out where . . . something . . . could be hidden at BISRI?'

316

'Exactly. So, maybe that too has been stolen, using information culled from the plans.'

'Which would explain Grant going apeshit, firing McDermott and calling in the heavy mob.'

'It would.'

'The burglar, there and at BISRI, could be—'

'Don't say any more.' Wada was clinging to an advantage she reckoned they had over Rinzaki. He thought – and therefore Otonashi thought – that Nagata was dead, eliminated by an overzealous Yagami. And there was no reason why Grant Braxton should know anything about Nagata all. 'We need to think carefully.'

'I've been trying to do that. No one apart from Mom knows you're here and I aim to keep it that way. As far as they're concerned, I was in Hawaii last week on vacation. That's my story and I'm sticking to it. It should buy us time if nothing else. Lie low in the city for the rest of today. I've an idea how we can outflank Grant and his goons. I can't spell it out on the phone. Catch the five thirty ferry to Larkspur. That'll get you on the six thirty train to Santa Rosa. But I want you to leave the train at Petaluma. I'll meet you there.'

'Petaluma. Right. You won't drive there in your car, will you, Troy?'

'What do you think? Leave me to worry about my transport arrangements. Just be on that train.'

In the final analysis, Wada had no choice but to trust Kimber's judgement. He was her only ally and she was his. They were in this together and Wada was a long way from home. She had to rely on his local knowledge, whether she liked it or not.

When she left the meeting room, Harrington was nowhere to be seen. 'Called to another meeting,' an almost horizontally relaxed assistant informed her. 'He said he thought you had everything you needed.' It sounded as if he'd decided to disengage himself from the whole process. She didn't blame him. It was a nice option to have.

A day of leisure in San Francisco should have been an attractive prospect, but Wada had far too much on her mind to indulge in tourist pursuits. She ate a noodle lunch in Japantown, which was comforting in its way, then sat on a bench in Lafayette Park and tried to calculate what could explain the sequence of events as she understood it to be.

The Matsuda asset had been concealed at BISRI. Nagata had discovered where it was kept by studying floor plans of the building stolen from Anderson McGraw. Then he'd gone to BISRI . . . and stolen the asset as well. He'd been in possession of the plans for a month. How long the asset had been missing there was no way to know. Maybe its absence hadn't been discovered for some time after its theft. But in that case what had Nagata done with it? This last was an unanswerable question so long as Wada didn't know what the asset actually was – and what it could be used for.

If she was right, though, Nagata had the upper hand over Otonashi and Rinzaki as well as her and Kimber. He was the underestimated contender who'd carried off the prize. Or should the credit really go to his mother? Hisako Jinno was every bit as formidable as Rinzaki. She'd assured Wada she knew where her son was and Wada didn't doubt the truth of that. She knew where he was – and why he was there. This was her victory as much as Manjiro Nagata's.

If it really was victory. If the burglar really was Manjiro Nagata. If the asset really had been stolen from BISRI. There remained the possibility that there was some other unsuspected explanation for everything that had occurred.

Kimber was waiting for her on the platform when she got off the train at Petaluma. He looked less suave than usual, rattled somehow, definitely a man under pressure. His smile on seeing her had a palpable element of relief. He was counting on her, just as she was counting on him.

'It's been a long day,' he said, as if acknowledging the visible toll it had taken on him.

'I think I had an easier time than you,' she admitted.

'I think you did.'

They walked out of the station and Wada immediately noticed the dark red pick-up truck parked in front of the building, with *Braxton Winery* painted on the side.

'That's my untracked transport,' Kimber said. 'And before you ask I did check it over before driving here.'

'Good. Where are we going now?'

'Oh, we can walk it from here. We're heading down to the river.'

'Why the river?'

'Because Connie McDermott lives there on a houseboat. And I thought BISRI's recently sacked and probably disgruntled security officer might be just the man we need to speak to.'

Night was falling rapidly and lights were twinkling on the various boats moored along the riverbank. McDermott's home was a small, smartly painted vessel, with colourful flower boxes hanging from the side of the cabin. It was tied up fore and aft, with a roped gangway connecting the bank to the open rear section of deck. The cabin windows were warmly lit and there was a scent of woodsmoke in the still air.

'Hello the boat,' Kimber called.

A moment later the cabin door opened and a figure looked out. He was a portly, broadly built Black man with grizzled hair and a moustache, dressed in jeans and a denim shirt. His initial glare softened when he saw who it was who'd called.

'Permission to come aboard?' Kimber laughed.

'You here to offer me my job back?'

'Decisions like that are above my pay grade.'

'Yeah? Well, at least you still have a pay grade.'

'So, can we . . .'

'Yeah, yeah.' McDermott waved them on. 'Mind your step. Who's your friend?'

Wada decided to speak for herself. 'I am Wada. I am pleased to meet you, Mr McDermott.'

They reached the deck and McDermott frowned at her. 'You're Japanese, right?'

'I am.'

'She's not on Otonashi's side, Connie,' said Kimber.

'No? Your side, then?'

'She's certainly helping me.'

'Helping you do what?'

'What do you think?'

'Come out on top would be my surmise. You always were too ambitious for your own good.'

'This isn't about ambition. This is about survival.'

'Maybe it is for me, with no money to fall back on. For you, Troy, I think ego has more to do with it. You just can't bear the thought of being outwitted by Grant's geisha girl.'

'Otonashi is not a geisha,' said Wada neutrally.

'No. And it's pretty obvious you're not one either.'

'I am a private detective, Mr McDermott. I am serious about my work. And I have no use for egos. Mine or anyone else's.'

At that McDermott laughed. 'OK. That's put me in my place. Pardon my manners. Getting fired from a job I was actually damn good at has left me kind of sore.'

'We understand that, Connie,' said Kimber.

'Why are you here, exactly?'

'We're hoping you can . . . point us in the right direction where these . . . "possible security breaches" are concerned.'

' "Possible" my ass.'

320

'You took the blame for the theft of a valuable article from BISRI,' said Wada, deciding nothing was to be gained by dancing round the issue. 'You were at Anderson McGraw last week, seeking to establish how the thief knew where to look. Correct?'

McDermott nodded. 'Correct. You're well informed, I gotta say. Next day I was fired. Grant had decided to bring in Petersens – hot shots in the corporate security business – and I was suddenly the fall guy for what had gone wrong.'

'What *had* gone wrong?'

McDermott chewed that question over for a moment, then said, 'You better come inside.'

He led the way down a short flight of steps into his living accommodation: a cosy, comfortably furnished bed-sitting cabin, heated by a wood-fired stove. He waved them towards a low sofa, Kimber banging his head on a low-hanging lantern as they sat down. It swung crazily to and fro until McDermott steadied it.

'You want a drink?'

'Better not,' said Kimber, rubbing his head.

'Nothing for me, thank you,' said Wada.

'Suit yourselves.' McDermott sat down at a fold-out table on which a glass of bourbon was already standing, with the bottle next to it. He took a sip. 'You understand, don't you, that I have no remote clue what it was that was stolen from BISRI? Perhaps you have the advantage of me there.'

'Not much of one,' said Kimber.

'It is referred to by Rinzaki as the asset,' said Wada.

'Ah, Rinzaki.' McDermott took another sip of bourbon. 'The guy who pulls Otonashi's strings. You know him, Wada?'

'We have met.'

'Your theory is that he's stolen this . . . asset. Or arranged for it to be stolen.'

'No. I believe someone else has stolen it.'

'And who would that be?'

'Manjiro Nagata. But I doubt he's using his real name.'

'You weren't in Hawaii last week, were you, Troy? You were in Japan, getting together with Wada here. Let me get this straight. She's working for you?'

'Troy hired me to investigate what it is Rinzaki has sent Otonashi here to obtain,' said Wada, cutting across Kimber. 'The answer is the asset, though, like you, we don't know what the asset is. We do know Nagata has also been looking for it. And we think he's now in possession of it.'

'I'd agree with you there. Early last week Grant went ballistic when he discovered "a valuable item" was missing from his office at BISRI. It was stored in a safe I didn't even know existed.'

'How could you not know about it, Connie?' Kimber asked. 'You were security officer there.'

'Good question.' McDermott topped up his glass. 'Sure you don't want any?'

'Maybe I will, then.'

McDermott poured Kimber a glass and one for Wada as well, without asking if she wanted it. She accepted without demur. Her priority was to encourage him to tell them as much as he knew.

'The safe, Mr McDermott?' she prompted as he slumped back down in his chair.

'We're getting to it, don't worry. Grant's office at BISRI – originally designed to his father's specifications – has a private bathroom and a closet attached. There's a safe in the office I knew about. What I didn't know until Grant told me was that there's a second safe accessible only from the closet. The shelving unit inside the closet is hinged to swing out, revealing . . . an inner closet, I guess you'd call it. The second safe is in there. Now, you'd never guess it was there. That was the whole point of the arrangement. You'd have to study the architect's original floor plans to realize there was a sealed-off area between the closet and the bathroom. So, if you were looking for somewhere where a "valuable item" could be hidden, that's where you'd head. *If* you knew where to look.'

'Which is why you went to see Anderson McGraw?'

'Yeah. When I found out the plans had been redacted from the public record, there was nowhere else to try. I can't say I was surprised when Mr Harrington told me the plans had been stolen. It all made sense. Of course, they were stolen a month ago. There's no way to know how soon after that the safe was opened and the "item" was lifted from BISRI. It could have been missing for a couple of weeks before Grant checked and discovered to his horror that someone had taken it right from under his nose.'

'But how could this person open the safe? He would have needed to know the combination.'

'You're right. I can't answer that one. But open it they did.'

'Did Grant say who he thought might have done it?'

'No. Except he said the thief was probably Japanese.'

'Why did he think that?'

'No idea. He wasn't in the mood for explaining much. I mean, Troy will tell you Grant Braxton's generally a phlegmatic sort of guy. Not last week. He was . . . going off in all directions. He reckoned one of the Japanese seismologists on the staff had to be responsible and instructed me to give them all the third degree. But it was obvious none of them was involved. They're mild-mannered scientists. They hadn't a clue what I was talking about. Technically, neither did I. I mean, it had to be an inside job, but without knowing what exactly had been taken, I was flying blind.'

'Were the police called in?' asked Kimber.

'No, they were not. They'd probably have insisted Grant tell them what had been stolen and he clearly didn't want to reveal that to anyone. So, it was down to me. Or so I thought. Actually, Grant had already decided to hand the problem over to Petersens. Big mistake. They do everything by the book. And they're slow on their feet. But some people are stupid enough to think the boys who charge the fattest fee are the best. So, I was shown the door. The Petersens guy never even had the sense to ask me if I was following up any leads. Can you believe that?'

'Were you . . . following up any leads?' Wada asked.

'You bet. Like I said, my feeling was it had to have been an inside job. But not done by any of the permanent staff. My money's on one of the people who drift in and out. Electricians and plumbers on standing contract, say. And then there are the cleaners. They're supplied by a contract cleaning company. We – BISRI, I mean – have no record of who exactly empties the waste baskets or polishes the desks after everyone's gone home for the night. I was planning to check with the company to see if anyone had left recently. It would have been a long shot. There's a lot of staff turnover in that line of work. And I didn't have a name or a description to work with. Anderson McGraw's CCTV was useless. I couldn't even tell the sex or race of the intruder.'

'Take a look at this,' said Wada, pulling out the photograph of Manjiro Nagata supplied by his father and handing it to McDermott. 'Seen him before?'

McDermott stared long and hard at Nagata's face. 'Maybe. Maybe he was . . . one of the cleaners. It's hard to be sure. I never paid them much attention. This is Nagata, right?'

'Right.'

'And you have good reason to think he's come over here looking for the asset?'

'Yes.'

McDermott ruminated some more, then slowly passed the photograph back to Wada and swallowed some bourbon. 'In-ter-est-ing,' he said, pronouncing the word with four distinct syllables.

'What would you do if you were still working for BISRI, Connie?' Kimber asked. 'Armed with this photograph.'

324

'I'd take it to the cleaning company. I know the guy who runs it. Arvad Singh. I'd sit down with him and find out if Nagata ever worked for them, under whatever name, if he was part of the crew assigned to BISRI and whether he left their employ in the past few weeks . . . kind of unexpectedly.'

'And then?'

'There probably wouldn't be a *then*. If you're right that this is your man, then he's got what he wanted . . . and is long gone.'

'Still, it's worth a try.'

'It would have been. If Grant hadn't fired me. Now it's Petersens' problem.'

'But they don't have the photograph,' said Wada quietly.

'No.' McDermott shook his head. 'They do not.'

'Which gives us a significant advantage.'

'There's no *us* in this.' McDermott looked at each of them in turn. 'I'll give you the name of the cleaning company and you can try your luck with Arvad. But it's nothing to do with me any more.'

'I understand that.' Wada also understood that extracting helpful information from Arvad Singh was likely to be an easier and quicker process if McDermott was involved. 'Though I suppose you would like to know if your theory is sound.'

McDermott smiled at her. 'Nice try.'

'Plus I'm confident of getting the better of Otonashi,' said Kimber. 'And after she's been sent packing I'll make sure we have the right guy overseeing security across all Braxton enterprises.'

Now McDermott turned his smile on Kimber. 'You offering me my job back?'

'If I can, I will.'

'And if you can't?'

'Well, what would you lose by helping us? I mean, are you busy right now?'

'I was thinking getting fired had given me the chance to catch up on some maintenance this boat needs, since you ask.'

'Is that a full-time occupation?'

'You'd be surprised.'

'Mr McDermott—' Wada began.

But he cut her off. 'OK. I surrender. I'll take you to see Arvad. Just for a chat. You can show him that photograph. And we'll see what he says. And then . . .'

Kimber grinned. 'You can get back to your maintenance programme.'

From Petaluma they headed for the winery, where Kimber proposed to switch back to his own car on the grounds that it would look suspicious if it stayed there overnight. He remained anxious about surveillance, fearing Grant might have authorized Petersens to conduct an intrusive probe of his activities. Generally, despite the casual bravado he'd projected to McDermott, he was anxious about every aspect of what they were doing.

Or, if not anxious, then despondent. 'Connie has to be right. Nagata's got what he wanted. So, why would he hang around waiting for us to track him down?'

'I don't know,' Wada admitted. 'But he stole the plans from Anderson McGraw a month ago and probably stole the asset from BISRI not long after that. So, why hasn't he returned to Japan and done whatever it was he needs the asset to do? When his mother came to see me, she didn't behave as if he'd already accomplished what she expected of him. There's something here we're missing.'

'Well, you're the expert, Wada. What are our chances of figuring out what that is?'

'It is hard to say.'

'Yeah. Hard to say. That just about covers it.'

Stars filled the night sky above the Braxton Winery. The vineyard was cloaked in darkness, but the winery buildings were still lit.

There was a car park, partly covered by an open-fronted barn, some way short of the main buildings. Wada spotted Kimber's car as they pulled in next to several pick-up trucks similar to the one they were in. Kimber wound down his window and peered out.

'No sign of any Petersen vehicles,' he said. 'Looks like they've given up and gone home. But they'll be back tomorrow. Grant's paying them to be remorseless sons of bitches.'

'What is there for them to find here?'

'Zilch. But they don't know that.'

'Which means Grant doesn't either.'

'True enough. We can console ourselves that he's as much in the dark as we are. Come on. Let's go.'

They climbed out of the truck and headed for Kimber's car.

As they neared it, a security light came on in the barn. Wada saw a slightly built figure in an anorak and hoodie standing by a car at the far end of the barn, holding a phone trained on them. Wada felt certain in that moment that they were being photo-graphed and quite distinctly heard, through the still air, the click of the phone lens opening and closing.

'Who's there?' shouted Kimber, suddenly noticing the figure as well.

Whoever they were, they did not linger to proffer explan-ations. They – or rather, Wada sensed, *she* – turned and jumped into the car, the door of which was already open. The engine started a second later and the car surged out of the barn in a scatter of gravel.

Kimber stepped into its path, but instantly retreated as it sped straight ahead. He glared after the vehicle as it barrelled away along the drive towards the main road, its lights only coming on after it had covered another thirty metres or so.

'Did you recognize the driver?' Wada asked as she moved to Kimber's side.

'Never got a look. There was too much reflection from the security light.'

'It was a woman.'

'You're sure?'

'I would say so.'

'Otonashi, then.'

'Do you know what car she drives?'

'Never thought I needed to. She must have sussed I was using one of the pick-ups to dodge the tracker and reckoned I'd have to come back here to switch vehicles.'

'Probably, yes.'

'Why take a picture of us?'

'Because it proves I'm here, working with you, not in Japan, preparing to work for Rinzaki. She will send him the picture. And he will know what it means.'

'What does it mean?'

'That we are both his enemies.'

1995

KODAKA IS DOING HIS VERY BEST TO APPEAR RELAXED AND confident. The thinness of the light in Rinzaki's wood-panelled office at the Kuraikagami film studios affords him some advantage in this regard. The skies over Chofu are filled with swirling cloud. The afternoon is dark with the threat of rain. And Rinzaki himself has no great liking for electric light, to judge by the gloom he has allowed to take hold.

He has open before him on his desk Kodaka's comprehensive report on the sad tale of Chikako Imada, the Kobe Sensitive, dead by her own hand before she could be tracked down and saved from herself. Kodaka has set out at length a detailed account of his search for her, proceeding from his identification of her occupation as a maid-cum-nanny to a fruitless series of enquiries at maids' agencies and several afternoons spent at So & So Ices of Sunshine City, Ikebukuro, in the vain hope that she might appear there. Alas, it transpired that she was never going to appear there or anywhere else, because the discovery of a handbag near the scene of a Rainbow Bridge suicide has since established that she was by then already dead.

Writing the report was a demanding exercise for Kodaka. He

did his best to follow the advice of his late father, who told him that if he had to lie to a client – *really* had to – it was wise to do so as little as possible and to wrap the fiction in layers of truth. It was what he called 'gilding the lie'. And what Rinzaki has in front of him is very much a gilded lie. There is nothing in the report about Chikako Imada's past in Rinzaki's employment, nor about his plan to send her to California to be studied and assessed by the seismologists of BISRI. There is nothing about what actually happened one afternoon at So & So, nor about Chikako's current position in the household of the Seng family. There is nothing in it at all that would enable Rinzaki to find her, were he minded to doubt Kodaka's sombre conclusion that she is in fact conclusively out of his reach.

'This is very . . . disappointing,' Rinzaki says, looking at Kodaka through his circular-framed glasses, his face bearing as ever that faintly serpentine expression Kodaka has come to loathe. It is for all the world as if, at any moment, a narrow forked tongue might protrude from his thin, compressed lips. 'Are you certain this woman was the woman I asked you to find?'

This is an ambiguous question, designed, perhaps, to lure Kodaka into betraying some knowledge of Chikako's previous existence at Matsuda Sanso. But he is not to be lured. 'I believe it is overwhelmingly likely that she was the woman who made the telephone call to the Kantei the day before the Kobe earthquake. The name by which the boy on the tape addressed her was clearly a respectful diminutive of Chikako Imada's name. And her occupation is confirmed by her possession of a domestic staff agency registration card. Neither that agency nor any other has a record of a placement for her, so establishing where she was working – if she was working – at the time of her death is impossible. Similarly, it has not been possible to identify the boy on the tape or the family for whom Chikako Imada was working when she made the call. I suspect she obtained that position through a freelance recruiter.

There are many of them throughout the city. It is possible she used one of them to make it difficult for anyone to trace her.'

Kodaka pauses. He has shifted the ground to an area Rinzaki will not wish to dwell on. It was he who arranged for Chikako's registration to be suspended, for reasons he cannot volunteer and which Kodaka must pretend he knows nothing of. Neither of them is free to speak of all they know, as Kodaka is well aware. What troubles him is the question of whether Rinzaki is aware of that as well.

'With no information to hand about her state of mind at the time of her suicide,' he continues, 'we can only speculate about why she might have chosen to end her life.'

'Then speculate for me, Kodaka-san,' said Rinzaki. 'I assume your fee extends to that?'

'I am forced to imagine, Rinzaki-san, that she found her ability to sense the onset of earthquakes . . . a great strain on her mind. It cannot have helped that the media whipped up so much interest in identifying her. If she was . . . private by nature . . . the prospect of public scrutiny may have so horrified her that . . .'

'She killed herself.'

'Yes. Exactly. A terrible end for one with such an ability. But I believe great abilities can also be great burdens. Especially when the Kantei refused to take her warning seriously – and thousands died.'

'You are still speculating now?'

'It is all I can do. Chikako Imada is dead. And with her the Kobe Sensitive.'

'Such a waste.'

'Indeed.'

'Suicide has a noble place in our culture. But I see nothing noble in such an act of self-destruction as this. There were those who thought at the end of the war that the Emperor should commit suicide. I was not among them. He had a duty to continue to

331

lead his people. Just as Imada should have felt bound by an obligation to serve the ability she was born with.'

An obligation to serve that ability in ways dictated by Rinzaki, presumably. Kodaka bridles his anger and mildly observes, 'We cannot enter the mind of another.'

'No. We cannot. Which may be as well.'

How true, Kodaka thinks. How very true.

'This is not the conclusion I had thought your inquiry would reach. I had hoped for altogether better news.'

'I am sorry, Rinzaki-san. I am sometimes obliged to tell a client something he would prefer not to hear. In the circumstances, I will not be seeking to claim the reward for identifying the Kobe Sensitive. I feel it would be . . . inappropriate.'

'That is very . . . fastidious of you.'

'I would suggest the matter be left as it is. No purpose would be served by publicizing what I have discovered.'

'You think not?'

'Well, *I* think not. But . . . it must be up to you. The information in the report . . . is yours to use as you see fit.'

'Quite so.'

They have come to the nub. Does Rinzaki really want to make public the death of the Kobe Sensitive? To do so would be to invite close scrutiny of her life. And he cannot want anyone following the trail in that life that leads back to him. Kodaka's calculation is that he won't risk that happening. He has too much to hide about too many things. But if Kodaka has *mis*calculated . . .

'As it is,' Rinzaki says slowly, 'I agree. This should remain between us. I am grateful for your understanding where the reward is concerned. And for your efforts on my behalf. Aside from payment of your fee, I believe our dealings in this matter . . . are at an end.'

Kodaka suppresses a sigh of relief. He has not miscalculated.

*

He exits through the outer office. Rinzaki's secretary is there, tapping away at a computer. Also present, sitting on a hard chair near the door, is a man Kodaka recognizes with complete certainty. He is the man who tried to tail him when he went to see Myoga. They do not exchange glances. But a frisson of hostility is somehow detectable as Kodaka passes him.

There is a buzz from the secretary's desk. She breaks off from her typing and says to the man seated by the door, 'You may go in now, Yagami-san.'

2022

THE INCIDENT AT THE WINERY HAD DASHED KIMBER'S LAST HOPE that there could be an accommodation with his stepfather. As he saw it, Grant's encouragement of Otonashi put him beyond the pale along with her. 'I'm going to make him suffer for what he's done to us, Wada, I swear it. The infatuated old fool won't be getting any concessions from me once we've dealt with Otonashi.' He prised the tracking device off his car and tossed it into a corner of the barn before driving away. It seemed he was done with caution. 'They've both gone too far to be tolerated any longer.'

That was a fine sentiment as far as it went. But how Kimber proposed to win this war he didn't say. And that wasn't surprising. They had precious little to show for their efforts so far. And Wada knew the only lead she had left to follow was all too likely a lead to nowhere.

Lois was no happier than her son. Marvin Dunst, a seismologist at BISRI who'd never made a secret of his attraction to her, had heard it rumoured she'd left Grant, guessed she'd probably gone to stay with Troy and called by unannounced earlier that evening to see if he could 'help her' in any way she cared to name. She was seriously considering going to stay with her sister in

Phoenix and at one point suggested Troy should go with her. 'I think we may need to put some distance between us and all this. I don't like people putting tracking devices on my car. And I certainly don't like having to fight off the attentions of Marvin Dunst.'

Dunst had supplied some valuable information, however. The mood at BISRI was tense. Rumours hadn't stopped at the state of Grant Braxton's marriage. They extended to speculation, fed by an outburst from Grant attested to by several members of staff, that he might consider closing BISRI down. Otonashi hadn't been seen on the premises for the better part of a week. Dunst claimed he'd never believed she was anything but a charlatan, although this was the first time Lois could recall him saying so. Still, it seemed all was not well in the world of Grant Braxton, or, come to that, Yukari Otonashi.

'Is that supposed to make me feel better about having these Petersens people breathing down my neck?' Troy complained.

'At least it cannot make you feel worse,' said Wada.

The thought did not appear to console him, however. Nor in truth did it console her.

They left early the following morning, when it was barely light. Kimber's destination was the winery. He drove Wada to a parking garage in Santa Rosa, where McDermott was waiting to collect her in a battered old brown Cadillac.

'I'm really counting on this getting us somewhere, Wada,' Kimber said as she was getting out of the car.

She paused and looked back at him. 'I know.' There seemed to be nothing else to say. She knew. He knew. This was very nearly the end of the line.

McDermott wasn't in a talkative mood. Something in his manner suggested he might have had second thoughts about agreeing to help them. But he'd committed himself and wasn't going to back out.

He drove Wada south out of Santa Rosa to the next town down the valley, Cotati, where the Arvad Singh Office Cleaning Company had its offices in an anonymous industrial building in the Laguna Verde Business Park.

McDermott's association with one of Singh's best customers – McDermott didn't mention his recent dismissal to the receptionist – secured them swift admittance to Singh's office, which featured as its only decoration a wall map of the surrounding area considerably larger than the desk behind which the proprietor sat tapping away like a pecking bird at a computer keyboard, inspecting the screen through the lower half of his glasses by tilting his neck back at an alarming angle.

He was a small, spry, pot-bellied man with thinning grey hair and the distracted air of someone perpetually trying to fit too much work into too few hours. But he recognized the need to oblige a client and greeted McDermott with a smile and an assurance that it was a pleasure to see him.

'What can I do for you, Mr McDermott – you and your . . . assistant?'

'This is Wada,' said McDermott. 'She's actually a private detective.'

'Really?' Singh eyed Wada with frank incredulity.

'I am pleased to meet you, Mr Singh,' said Wada. 'Mr McDermott is generously helping me with some enquiries into the whereabouts of a man who we think worked for you. The last report we have suggests his employment took him to BISRI as a member of one of your cleaning teams.'

'I see. And your interest in this person is . . .'

'It is a matter of child maintenance. He has commitments which my client would like him to honour.'

'Ah. Your client is . . . his ex-wife?'

'I am not in a position to confirm that. But your assistance, if you were able to give it, would be appreciated.'

'Much appreciated,' put in McDermott.

'Well, I will certainly do my best, subject to . . . the confidentiality I owe my workforce.'

'We think this man may no longer work for you,' Wada went on.

'No? Well, can you tell me his name?'

'Manjiro Nagata.'

'Ah. Japanese, like . . . yourself?'

'Yes.'

'Well, I don't think we've had any Japanese employees . . . in the recent past. And . . .' He consulted his computer. 'That name does not appear in our staff file. Nagata, you say?'

'He may have used a different name. Perhaps you recognize him?' Wada proffered Nagata's photograph.

She noticed, as Singh held the photograph and frowned at it through his glasses, how exceptionally well manicured his fingernails were. She assumed it was a very long time since he'd done any office-cleaning himself. 'Mmm,' he mused. 'Well, yes, I . . . do recognize him. And, yes, he did work for us. A diligent and reliable employee, as I recall. But he isn't Japanese. Korean, I believe. And Nagata is not his name.' He handed the photograph back and consulted his computer again. 'Yes. Kwon Hee. Korean, definitely. He left, ah . . . two weeks ago.'

'He *is* Japanese, Mr Singh,' Wada said with finely judged firmness. 'Real name Manjiro Nagata.'

'As to that . . . I could not say.'

'Do you have a date of birth recorded for him?'

'Well, yes, we do.'

'May ninth, 1973?' She was gambling Nagata wouldn't have bothered to change that.

Nor had he. 'Yes. May ninth . . . 1973. It is the same.'

'Because it is the same man.'

337

'Well, I suppose . . . you are right. It is not easy, of course, for us to distinguish between . . .' Singh abandoned that line of reasoning, which seemed to be heading towards troublesome territory. 'I can assure you everything was . . . in order . . . when we hired him.'

'We're not interested in how thoroughly you vetted his documentation, Arvad,' McDermott cut in. 'Did he work at BISRI?'

Singh looked flustered for a moment, but recovered himself whilst peering at the computer screen. 'Yes. He was a regular member of our BISRI contract team.'

'Until two weeks ago?'

Singh nodded. 'Until two weeks ago.'

'Do you have an address for him?' asked Wada.

Singh compressed his lips and hesitated. Wada thought it likely they'd entered that sensitive area of staff confidentiality he'd mentioned earlier.

McDermott clearly thought the same and decided to apply a little pressure. 'Like I said, Arvad, we're not interested in how thoroughly you vetted this guy's documentation. But the state authorities might be. If the matter ever came to their attention.'

A barely audible sigh was the only indication of Singh's reaction. He grabbed a pen, scrawled a few lines on a jotting pad, tore off the sheet and handed it to Wada. 'I have no way of knowing if he is still there, you understand,' he remarked dispassionately.

'Thank you,' said Wada.

'Yeah, thanks, Arvad,' said McDermott. 'You won't hear anything more from us about this.'

'Good.' Singh smiled. 'That would be very good. I am so pleased . . . to have been able to help.'

Wada had heard it said that Americans lacked a sense of irony. This she found hard to believe when they reached Palomino Mansions in the drought-parched western fringes of Cotati. The mansions were actually single-storey flat-roofed dwellings of exceptional plainness, mostly in sore need of refurbishment, enclosed by a stone wall on which the ghost of a prancing horse sign appeared as a pale patch on the masonry.

An inflatable paddling pool was standing in the courtyard round which the dwellings were grouped. Some children of Hispanic appearance were playing in it, enjoying themselves as children always manage to do. McDermott eyed the few adult residents who were visible – all women, also Hispanic, most of them sitting on plastic chairs in the shade facing the pool – and said to Wada, 'You want me to stay in the car? You might get more out of these people on your own.'

'This is the sort of place where Mr Singh's staff live?'

'Yeah. Quite a few of them will be undocumented. They probably already have us down as debt collectors.'

'I will try to persuade them otherwise.'

Wada got out of the car and headed for dwelling number 23, which looked much like all the others and was the last known residence of Manjiro Nagata, alias Kwon Hee. The women watched her, but said nothing.

She knocked at the door. There was no immediate response. But, after knocking again, she heard plodding footsteps.

The door was opened by a swarthy, unshaven man in a vest and tracksuit bottoms. He didn't smile. '*Qué?*' he growled in what she took for Spanish.

'Excuse me,' Wada said, treating him to her politest smile, 'I am looking for Kwon Hee.'

He frowned. '*Quién?*'

'Kwon Hee.'

'*El coreano?*'

'Yes. The Korean.'

'Gone. My place now.'

'Do you know . . .'

'I know nothing. Talk to his woman's friend – *número dieci-siete*.' He pointed to a door opposite them. 'One seven.'

Wada heard the door of number 23 close with a thump behind her as she crossed the courtyard. She glimpsed movement in the window of number 17. Before she reached the door, it opened narrowly.

A middle-aged woman in a thin dressing-gown, whose rumpled hair and bleary eyes suggested she hadn't been up long, looked out at Wada. Yelping and a pattering of paws revealed the presence of a dog close behind her.

'Who are you?' the woman asked. It was evident she'd seen her neighbour pointing Wada in her direction. She was frowning suspiciously.

Wada smiled. 'My name is Wada. I am looking for Kwon Hee.'

'Are you Korean?'

'No. Japanese. Like Kwon Hee, actually.'

The woman looked abashed at that. '*Si*. Japanese. Juanita said one time.'

'Juanita?'

'My friend. Kwon live with her.'

'His real name is Manjiro Nagata.'

'If you say.'

Wada showed her the photograph. 'It's him?'

The woman nodded. '*Si*.'

'They left together?'

'*Si*. Together. Juanita . . .' The woman rolled her eyes. 'She loves him.'

'When did they leave?'

'Couple weeks, maybe.'

'Do you know where they were going?'

'No.' The woman shook her head for emphasis.

'So, Juanita didn't . . . leave an address with you?'

Another shake of the head. 'No address.'

'Do you have her . . . phone number?'

'No phone number.' That didn't quite sound like the truth.

'Does she ever call you?'

The woman seemed to have trouble answering. 'I don't . . . know,' she said in the end.

'If she calls you – or you call her – could you ask her to call me?' Wada handed over one of her cards. 'Or Kwon could call me. It's very important.'

She took the card and studied it carefully. Wada thought she saw her lips moving as she read the details printed on it. Then she looked up and said, 'You come from Japan . . . to find him?'

'Yes.'

'Why so important?'

'I cannot explain. It is complicated.'

'This is bad . . . for Juanita?'

Wada had nowhere to turn from here. She sensed the woman was worried about her friend. Maybe she'd been worried about her even before Wada came to her door. It was a possibility that had to be tested. 'It could be,' Wada said, choosing her words carefully. 'I need to speak to her.' It seemed wise to emphasize the urgency of speaking to Juanita, even though she wasn't who Wada really wanted to speak to at all.

'If she calls . . .'

'Tell her I was here. Tell her to call me.'

The woman nodded. An agreement of sorts had been arrived at. Then she closed the door. And there were no more possibilities to cling to.

'What did you get?' asked McDermott as they drove away.

'Nothing. Nagata and his girlfriend left a couple of weeks ago. No forwarding address.'

'Didn't I see you giving your card to the neighbour?'

341

'You did. But that won't lead to anything.'

'No?'

'It is as you said, Mr McDermott. Nagata's got what he wanted. He's long gone.'

'And what has he got?'

'I don't know.'

'But something that puts him one up on Rinzaki and Grant Braxton?'

'Yes.'

'So, what's he doing with this . . . advantage he has over them?'

'He does not appear to be doing anything with it.'

'Why not?'

'I don't know that either. And it seems to me . . . I may never know.'

With no leads left to follow and nothing to do but wait and hope Juanita called her friend at Palomino Mansions and responded to her message, Wada asked McDermott to take her back to Kimber's house.

'I guess I have the consolation of knowing I was right about how the burglar knew where the asset was hidden,' McDermott said after he'd been driving for a while. 'That won't get me my job back, of course, but . . . it's something.'

'Troy will do his best for you, I am sure.'

'What's that going to amount to now? Face it, Wada, your client's on the losing team.'

'That is not yet certain.'

'No? Well, I get the feeling it soon will be.'

It was hard to argue with McDermott's pessimistic predictions. And Wada found she had ample time to consider how unpromising the situation was when they reached the house. Lois was out, leaving Wada to sit on the terrace and await her return. McDermott offered to drive her into Santa Rosa, but she said she'd prefer just to sit in the sun and wait. She watched him drive away and sought peace of mind in the silence that followed. She didn't find a lot. Failure was inevitable in her profession. Not every inquiry could be resolved to her and her client's satisfaction. But loose ends troubled her. They offended her orderly mind. Nagata's inaction since laying hands on the asset didn't fit any sequence of cause and effect she could readily understand. It meant something. Quite possibly it meant everything. But its meaning refused to reveal itself. However long and hard she thought, it stayed resolutely out of sight.

Wada's gloomy reverie was broken by the arrival of a car. Not Lois's, but Troy's. He took the track in off the road at excessive speed and skidded to a halt. He only saw Wada when he jumped out. And he obviously didn't see anything in her expression to raise his hopes. He walked across to join her on the terrace, his mouth set in a grim line.

'What did you get?' he asked straight away.

'Confirmation that Nagata worked as a cleaner at BISRI. He left the job two weeks ago. He also left the place where he was living. No one knows where he is now.' She wasn't sure Troy needed to hear about the complication concerning Juanita.

'As I feared.' Troy slumped down in the chair next to hers.

'You left the winery early?'

'Ah. Well spotted. I can't slip anything past you, can I?'

'I do not understand.'

'I've been suspended, Wada.' He gazed up into the sky for a moment and shook his head in bewilderment. 'For engaging the services of an unlicensed private investigator to enquire into the affairs of the company – Braxton Enterprises, that is, the umbrella corporation for BISRI and the winery – without board approval.'

'I am not unlicensed,' Wada objected.

'You are in California. Which means we could both be fined five thousand dollars and/or serve twelve months in the county jail. If this . . . serious misdemeanour . . . came to the attention of the authorities. Which was the alternative I was given to accepting suspension. That would be on top of any civil fines a court might impose, by the way. Grant's been taking advice. And Otonashi's been telling him all about you, I think we can safely assume. That contract I signed? It'd be in both our best interests if you tore it up.' He smiled ruefully at her. 'The smart move for you is to fly home as soon as possible. Put the Pacific Ocean between us.'

'I am not ready to give up.'

'No? Well, I feel ready. Trouble is, I can't. Grant's not going to stop at suspension, is he? He'll be gunning for me from now on. I'll probably be levered out of the company altogether. Made some pitiful offer my lawyer will advise me to accept.'

'I will help if I can. I left my number with a friend of the woman Nagata is living with. We may hear from her.'

'You really think so?'

'There is a chance.'

'Not much of one, by the sound of it. Anyhow, lucky old Nagata. He's got the asset and he's found love. I'm glad he's hit the jackpot.' Troy drew a deep breath. 'Want to come for a drive with me to the coast, Wada? I'll get the Pontiac out. Travel in style. Sea air is supposed to be calming. And I need a few lung-fuls of calm.'

Goat Rock Beach, on the other side of the Sonoma Mountains, offered a peaceful stretch of grey sand beside the softly lapping waters of the Pacific. Despite taking Wada along for the ride, Troy seemed to have little to say, though he assured her he preferred not to be alone.

344

The truth, she surmised as she watched him walk ahead of her along the shoreline, glancing at intervals out to sea, was that he was trying to accustom himself to the disquieting realization that he wasn't going to come out on top in this situation. Whatever Nagata did or didn't do with whatever he'd obtained, there was going to be no victory for Troy Kimber. And by making an unsuccessful strike at Otonashi and her puppet master he'd only weakened his position.

He was right, of course. In the circumstances, Wada should write the case off and go back to Tokyo before Rinzaki made any serious move against her – or those close to her. That was undoubtedly what she should do.

But she wasn't ready to do it. Not yet. Not quite yet.

Lois had returned to the house in their absence. She too had been taking advice. She was filing for divorce. And the news of Troy's suspension only increased her determination to remove Grant from her life. 'That woman' – she meant Otonashi – 'has turned him into a travesty of himself. I won't let him – or her – push either of us around. If he can lawyer up, so can we.'

'Maybe that's not the way to go, Mom,' said Troy despondently.

'It's the *only* way to go. We'll show him we mean to fight.'

'I am sorry there is not more I can do to find Nagata,' said Wada.

Lois looked at her as if she'd suddenly been reminded of the presence of someone she thought had already left. 'I'm sorry too, Wada. The fact is there's nothing for you to do here now. With this licensing issue being stirred up, you should leave as soon as possible. You'll understand I have to think of my son's well-being.'

'I understand.'

345

And so she did. Lois was taking charge. And Troy was letting her. Neither of them thought they had any use for Wada in the altered circumstances. She'd become a liability.

A glum mood prevailed at the house that evening. The unspoken assumption was that Wada would leave the following day. Lois fussed around Troy in a fit of maternal over-compensation. Wada did not challenge either of them. She was in no position to. And certainly she had no wish to stay where she was no longer welcome.

She retired to the garage flat as early as she reasonably could with no great expectation of a sound night's sleep.

She'd been leaving her phone on at night, which she never normally did. If there was an urgent call from Japan, which was sixteen hours ahead of California, she needed to be able to take it, not least because the only kind of call she was likely to get from Japan would be urgent.

As it was, there'd been no calls. But tonight, close to midnight, there was one.

It wasn't from anyone in Japan, though.

It was an unknown number. But since the caller evidently knew her number, she answered. 'Hello?'

'Wada?' It was a male voice, which she didn't recognize.

'Yes.'

'This is Manjiro Nagata.'

'Nagata-san.' She felt genuinely shocked to be talking to him at last. 'You got my message.'

'I know you've been looking for me. I thought you'd give up before now.'

'I don't give up easily.'

'Neither do I.'

'Where are you, Nagata-san?'

'What you should be asking is where will I be tomorrow morning.'

'You are willing to meet me?'

'Yes. Just you. No one else. You need to understand what I've done. And why. But you have to come alone. Will you do that?'

'Of course.'

'Then we can talk. You and I. Tomorrow.'

1995

JUST AS KODAKA IS LEAVING HIS APARTMENT, EN ROUTE TO THE Kono Building, he receives a message on his pager. He smiles to himself as he steps out into the street, because the number is one he has come to recognize – and to treasure. It is not, in fact, a telephone number at all, but a coded signal from Chikako Imada, to assure him all is well with her in her new life, where she goes by a different name and has become, as far as anyone who meets her is to know, a different person.

There is deep satisfaction to be derived from the deception they have practised on Goro Rinzaki. The Kobe Sensitive is safe from him now. She can live as she wishes to. She can be what she wants to be. She is free of him.

The weather that morning is also cheering. The sky is a flawless blue and though the air is chill the advent of spring is undeniable. The city is quieter than usual on a Monday. Many workers will have taken the day off to avail themselves of a long weekend, since tomorrow is a public holiday to mark the vernal equinox. It is not a day off for Kodaka, who as a jobbing detective cannot afford such indulgences. But his mood is quietly celebratory nonetheless. He cannot seem to stop smiling.

348

This state lasts until he reaches the Kono Building. He enters the reception area, beams at the porter and wishes him a cheery '*Ohayo!*'

He does not, however, receive a cheery response, or much of a response at all. The porter is frowning intently at the television set behind his desk. He looks shocked. 'Is something wrong?' Kodaka asks, walking across to the desk.

'It is very bad, Kodaka-san,' says the porter, not taking his eyes off the screen. The TV remote is clutched tightly in his hand. 'Some kind of terrorist attack on the subway. Nerve gas, they think.'

Kodaka squints at the screen. What he sees is a pavement crowded with commuters. But they're sitting or in some cases lying down, many of them pressing handkerchieves to their eyes. There are subway staff milling around them and an ambulance pulls up as Kodaka watches. The rolling news bar at the base of the screen is reporting three attacks involving a release of what's rumoured to be sarin on board trains, one on the Chiyoda line, two on the Marunouchi line, with some deaths already and multiple casualties.

'I come in on the Marunouchi line,' the porter mumbles. 'That could have been me.'

'Which station is that they're showing?' Kodaka asks.

'Kasumigaseki.'

Kodaka feels ashamed of the calculation that runs through his head then. Which hospital will they take the casualties from Kasumigaseki to? Toranomon must be closest. That is where relatives will go seeking news of loved ones caught up in this. It is impossible to imagine who could have been responsible. But doubtless that question will be answered soon enough. And then there will be a blame game over security and intelligence failures. It is the way of such things. Some of those affected may require the services of a private detective. It will be to his advantage if they have his card in their pocket, rather than a competitor's, when they think about hiring one.

He sighs. It is a sordid action to contemplate. But he knows what his father would say. *'You'll do a better job than anyone else, son. You'll be there for these people to turn to if they need to. You'll be doing them a service.'*

'First the Kobe earthquake, now this,' says the porter. 'What a year it's turning out to be.'

'We have to deal with whatever the year delivers,' says Kodaka as he turns and heads for the street door.

'Leaving again already, Kodaka-san?' the porter calls after him.

'Work to do. There's always work to do.'

2022

WADA ORDERED A TAXI FOR THE AIRPORT TO COLLECT HER FROM the turning on the road at first light, so she could leave without explaining to Kimber and his mother where she was going or why. She considered writing a note, but disliked lying unless forced to and telling them the truth at this stage was out of the question. What they didn't know couldn't harm them. And she was relieved not to have to debate the merits of her actions with anyone. She was acting at her own behest. And at her own risk.

There were no hold-ups on the freeway into San Francisco, but traffic around the city was already quite heavy and it was slow going on the final leg of the journey. Wada had allowed herself plenty of time, however. She wasn't going to be late for her appointment with Nagata. The taxi-driver naturally assumed she was catching a flight and ventured 'You have a great trip' when he dropped her off at the international terminal.

The airport was busy with the sights and sounds of busy airports: travellers pushing laden luggage trolleys, airline staff in smart uniforms, garish advertisements, public announcements, scrolling displays, children clutching toys. It was strange to be in such a place when the place itself was her destination.

She followed the signs for parking and made her way up to the top floor of the car park specified by Nagata. The drone of aircraft taking off and landing was audible above the rumble of cars and the soft squeal of tyres on tight ramped bends. As she climbed the stairs, the aircraft steadily won out over the cars. The top floor was three-quarters empty, the low-angled morning sun shafting across the deck. She had to shade her eyes to make out the vehicles.

At first, she couldn't see anything matching the description Nagata had given her. Then she spotted it: a beaten-up white van with one of the rear doors painted blue, parked facing away from her. She made straight for it.

He must have seen her coming in the wing mirror. As she approached, the passenger door swung slowly open, creaking on its hinges. She looked in.

Manjiro Nagata looked oddly younger than in the photograph his father had given Wada. His hair was longer and his clothes were more American than Japanese: polo shirt, zipped jacket, jeans, trainers, all well worn. Something in his expression had changed as well. He'd stopped conforming to one version of himself and become something else – maybe the man he really was.

He didn't say anything by way of greeting. Nor did she. He stretched across to take her suitcase from her. She climbed in beside it and closed the door. She caught the smell of cigarette smoke and noticed three butts crushed in an ashtray between the seats. There was a faint haze of cigarette smoke too, pierced by a flood of sunlight.

'My mother said your investigation had been stopped, Wada,' said Nagata. 'Why have you gone on looking for me?'

'I never worked for your mother,' Wada replied, disinclined to explain herself unnecessarily.

'Who have you been working for in California?'

'I see no reason to tell you.'

'Whoever it is – and I think I know – maybe you are willing to tell me if you are *still* working for them.'

That was a delicate question, the more so because Wada could not be certain which answer was more likely to draw Nagata out. But she had to make a choice. And she opted for the truth. 'I am no longer working for anyone except myself, Nagata-san.'

He nodded. 'As I thought.'

'You asked to meet me because you said you wanted me to understand what you'd done. So, here I am. Waiting to understand.'

'Yes. Waiting.' He plucked a cigarette out of a pack stored in the breast pocket of his shirt and lit it. Both windows were down already. 'Sorry for the smoke,' he said. 'I had almost given up smoking before this began.'

'When did it begin?'

'Last year. When my mother first devised this . . . scheme of hers.'

'To steal the Matsuda asset?'

'That is what her plan hinged on, yes.'

'And you have succeeded in stealing it, haven't you?'

He took a long draw on his cigarette. 'I have.'

'You worked out that it was kept in Grant Braxton's office – originally Clyde Braxton's office – at BISRI. You stole the plans of the building from Anderson McGraw because all copies had been redacted from publicly available records. The plans showed an inner closet in the office where a safe was located, containing, amongst other things . . . the asset.'

'It sounds easy the way you put it. Actually, it took me months to put myself in a position where I could pull it off. Getting the job with Singh's; surreptitiously scouting out the building; researching my options: none of it was quick or simple. But I did it. Once I knew there was an inner closet, I reckoned it had to

353

contain a safe additional to the one in the office. It seemed virtually certain the asset was stored there. And so it proved.'

'As one of Singh's cleaning team, you had after hours access to BISRI. During your last shift there, you entered the office, went into the inner closet, opened the safe and removed the asset. Correct?'

'Yes.'

'How were you able to open the safe?'

'I took a look at it during an earlier shift and researched the model online to learn how the lock operated. Most people remember combinations by choosing numbers that have some personal significance for them. I combed through the records for dates of births, deaths and weddings in the Braxton family and dates of other events that might have meant a lot to Clyde or Grant Braxton. Mostly Clyde. I reckoned Grant would have stuck with his father's choice. As it was, the combination was the third one I tried. The years of birth of Clyde's deceased daughter-in-law and grandchildren: fifty-eight, eighty-two, eighty-five. Simple, in the end.'

'Did you know what the asset consisted of before you stole it?'

'No. I had no idea. Neither did my mother. Except that it was . . . valuable. Extremely valuable.'

'So, what—'

The sudden ringing of her phone was about as untimely as it could be. Wada glanced at it to see who the caller was. Her brother, Haruto. If he wanted to ask yet more questions about their mother's lodger, she certainly had no wish to answer them – or try to – at this point. She let the call go to voicemail and looked back at Nagata, who was regarding her with mild curiosity.

'You want to know what the asset is, of course,' he said, stubbing out his cigarette. 'You want to know what this is actually all about.'

'I do.'

'The past, Wada. The remote past. So remote it can only be personally remembered by someone as old as Goro Rinzaki. Born Showa four. And where was he born? No one knows. Maybe not even Rinzaki. But when he was only a few months old he was placed in the Gosuringu Orphanage in Tokyo. How do I know that? Because Wataru Matsuda, owner of the orphanage and the country villa Rinzaki later bought, kept a register of admissions, which lists Rinzaki's arrival as a baby in Showa four. He also kept a ledger, detailing payments made and received by the orphanage. Those two books – the register and the ledger – were inside the steel box I removed from the safe at BISRI. They are the Matsuda asset.

'It took me a while to figure out what it all amounted to. It's not a pretty story. The orphanage was linked with some dirty business being done at that time by Japanese companies and individuals in our overseas possessions: Manchuria, Korea, Taiwan. There was a lot of money to be made from drugs, prostitution and forced labour. By a lot I mean fortunes. I mean companies still trading today who started out profiting from exploitation of coolie work forces in conditions no one would have tolerated in Japan. I read up about it, Wada. I informed myself. And now I know things I wish I didn't know. Things that make me feel sick just to think about them. But there it is: our nation's history – whether we like it or not.

'Where does the asset fit into all this? It's basically about prostitution. Chinese and Korean girls were forced into sex work by Japanese pimps and traffickers. After the war with China began, providing so-called comfort women for soldiers became an industry all on its own. The conditions they lived under were horrible. Inevitably, many of them became pregnant. The traffickers sought to make money even out of that, which is where Gosuringu came in. Those children that weren't disposed of were shipped to the orphanage to be sold to Japanese families who couldn't have children of their own or whose children had died. The adoptive parents were told they were the offspring of Japanese soldiers who'd been killed in action and whose wives had been so grief- or poverty-stricken they couldn't raise the child themselves. They were told nothing of where the children had really been born or under what circumstances. They wouldn't have wanted to have anything to do with them if they'd known the truth. There'd have been no money in that. As it was, the scheme supplied a stream of additional revenue to the people who ran the comfort stations where the women were housed. Matsuda took a big slice of the proceeds. It was good business for all of them. And as the war went on it was business that steadily grew.

'Matsuda kept meticulous records. Actually, Rinzaki kept them for him. For the last few years of the orphanage's existence, they're all stamped with his *hanko*. So, he knew as much as Matsuda knew. And that was a lot. Starting with the names and nationalities of the real mothers. And all the details of the Japanese families they were placed with. Plus the sums paid. And the sums that went on being paid. It's clear from the ledger that after the Pacific War began a number of families were . . . persuaded . . . to make regular payments to the orphanage. My guess is Matsuda started blackmailing those he thought would be willing to buy him off rather than have it made known that their adopted child had comfort woman blood – Chinese, Korean, alien blood. Can you imagine how unthinkable that must have been in those days, when the purity of the Japanese nation was drummed into everyone? The adoptive parents must have been too attached to their children to consider abandoning them but desperate to avoid being shamed by exposure of their origins. My family was one of those affected. My uncle Teruki was born to a Chinese comfort woman. My grandfather, Arinobu Jinno, paid Matsuda to cover it up.

'You might think that would all have come to an end when Japan lost the war and the Americans arrived. The Gosuringu Orphanage was destroyed in one of the bombing raids. Matsuda was found dead in the ruins. Nothing survived. Except Rinzaki . . . and the register . . . and the ledger. He must have sold the idea to Clyde Braxton that they could continue to blackmail the families, particularly those who were doing well in the postwar years. Bribery and corruption were commonplace under the Occupation. Braxton worked in the Economic and Scientific section at Supreme Command headquarters. He was well placed to award lucrative contracts in exchange for underhand payments. I think blackmail based on the Matsuda asset, as he and Rinzaki came to refer to the Gosuringu register and ledger, was just another money-making scam at first. But unlike the other scams it lived on after the Occupation. It lived on . . . and on.

'There are no entries in the ledger after Showa twenty-seven: the final year of the Occupation. Clyde Braxton must have taken the asset with him when he left Japan. But Rinzaki went on collecting the blackmail money for him and banking his share. It set them both up in business in their own right. And it subsidized their businesses as the decades passed. My grandfather went on paying until the day he died, though when my uncle hired your former boss to investigate why such payments had been made—'

'Rinzaki supplied a cover story he already had in place, involving a mistress your grandfather never actually had,' Wada cut in. 'I know. I have read the files.'

'Then you'll know the mistress in question was actually Rinzaki's mistress. Sonoko Zaizen. Mother of Yukari Otonashi, whose real name is Yuma Zaizen. My uncle still believes that story, by the way. He still has no idea he was born in a Manchurian comfort station.'

'But how do you know, Nagata-san? How did you find all this out?'

357

'From Sonoko Zaizen. She is horrified by the subterfuge Rinzaki has involved their daughter in and is determined to alienate her from him. Yuma Zaizen worships her father. She would do anything to please him. In this case that's involved luring Grant Braxton away from his wife by posing as the Kobe Sensitive. The Endo story was fabricated to convince Braxton she was genuine, using a faked recording of a second phone call she supposedly made to the Kantei – sixteen years after her first and in reality only call – warning them of the Tohoku tsunami.'

'What dealings did you have with Endo?'

'None.'

'Then why did he ask his civil service friend, Yamato, to dig out information about you?'

'Because he'd taken a bribe from Rinzaki to claim there was a recording of the Kobe Sensitive's tsunami warning call and had started getting paranoid about the consequences. Yuma Zaizen had acted as intermediary between him and Rinzaki, but at some point he stopped trusting her. I guess he feared he was going to end up as some kind of fall guy. Sonoko Zaizen discovered he'd tailed her from Matsuda Sanso to a meeting with my mother and then he'd tailed my mother to my apartment. Sonoko convinced Rinzaki Endo was becoming dangerously unreliable and the order was given to get rid of him. He'd outlived his usefulness as far as Rinzaki was concerned, because by then Yuma was in California, calling herself Otonashi, worming her way into Grant Braxton's affections and planning to steal the asset from under his nose. She has failed, thanks to Sonoko's intervention. Sonoko believes Rinzaki will never forgive his daughter or trust her again. He has no tolerance for failure.'

'So, Sonoko told your mother why Rinzaki had sent Yuma – Otonashi – to California?'

'Yes. She alerted my mother to the great opportunity the asset represents for us.'

'What opportunity? I do not understand.'

'Much of the initial capital for the creation of Jinno Construction was actually supplied by my great-grandfather. He imposed a condition in the company's articles of incorporation, that the chairmanship could only be held by a true Japanese native, which the wording of the clause defines as someone born in Japan – Japan as it was under the shogunate, that is, excluding even Hokkaido and Okinawa – to parents also born in Japan. If my mother can prove Uncle Teruki was born in Manchuria, the son of a Chinese comfort woman, she can take the chairmanship from him as the only legitimate successor and seize control of the company, because she was adopted at birth three years after the war, from authenticated Japanese parents. Then she can appoint me as chairman in his place.'

'That is her intention?'

'It is. And the asset gives her the proof she needs to do it. Rinzaki must have found out about the condition. He probably used it to screw extra money out of my grandfather. If the register is accepted as an authentic record, which clearly it is, the legal argument is irresistible. My uncle will probably agree to step down in my favour rather than have the truth exposed. And the future my mother believes I am destined for will have been secured.'

'But you have had the asset in your possession for the past two weeks. Why haven't you taken it back to Japan and initiated your uncle's removal from the company?'

'Ah yes. That is the question. Why haven't I done that?' Nagata lit another cigarette. 'Why haven't I even told my mother I have the asset?'

'And what is the answer, Nagata-san?'

'The answer . . . is that I do not want to.'

'You do not want to?'

'Consider . . .' He took a long draw on the cigarette. 'Why

359

does Grant Braxton want to hold on to the asset? Why does Rinzaki want to wrest it from him? All the people who were originally blackmailed must be dead by now. Did Rinzaki and Clyde Braxton succeed in some cases in moving on from blackmailing the parents to blackmailing the children? Or is Grant Braxton blackmailing Rinzaki with the evidence of what he and Clyde Braxton did? Or . . . is it just that Rinzaki wants to control the secret, to be sure it can stay hidden? I don't know. But I know why my mother wants the asset. That is about power. Hers, channelled through me. If I deliver the asset to her.'

'And so you're not going to?'

After another long draw on the cigarette, Nagata exhaled a plume of smoke. 'No,' he said quietly. 'I am not.'

'You're not even taking it back to Japan?'

'I am not even taking myself back to Japan. I love Juanita. She loves me. I have never been happier than I am here, with her. So, I will stay here . . . with Juanita. And the asset . . . will never reach the hands of any of those who want it.'

'What will you do with it?'

'We're renting a trailer home in Pacifica, on the coast west of here,' Nagata replied, with no obvious relevance. His voice had taken on a dreamy tone. 'On the other side of the street from us there's a vacant lot where an apartment block once stood. But the neighbours tell me it had to be demolished a few years ago when the cliff started to crumble in a succession of storms. El Niño was to blame, apparently. I sometimes stand on that lot, with the clifftop just a few metres away behind a fence, and imagine the people who used to live there. Nothing's permanent, Wada. It all has its span. Even Goro Rinzaki can't live for ever. And the asset . . . is steadily losing the value it once had. Eventually, it will have no value at all. Not that . . .' He smiled softly. 'Not that I intend to wait for that to happen.'

'What do you intend to do?'

He took something out of his pocket and handed it to her: a computer memory stick. 'I have made a—'

Wada's phone rang at that moment. She glanced down at the screen. Haruto *again.* She sighed. 'I think I will have to take this.'

She raised the phone to speak. 'Haruto?'

'Umiko.' He sounded anxious. 'Are you at the hospital?' Since it was just gone one a.m. in Tokyo, where he presumably thought she was, the question was baffling.

'Why should I be at a hospital?'

'Visiting Mother, of course. Haven't you been to see her?'

'I am sorry, Haruto. I don't know what you're talking about. Mother isn't in hospital. There's nothing wrong with her.'

'Are you crazy? Don't you know what's happened?'

'What has happened?'

'Didn't . . . didn't the lodger – Tago – tell you?'

'Tell me what?'

'You really don't know?'

'I really don't know, Haruto.' She was feeling anxious now as well. 'Just tell me.'

'I called Mother a few hours ago to see what was going on . . . with Tago. I mean, you said you'd keep me informed, but you haven't, so . . . I called her. But I only got Tago. He said Mother was in Takinogawa Hospital. She was mugged.'

'Mugged? In Koishikawa? That is not possible.'

'But it happened. On the steps at the side of the house. Some guy grabbed her bag and pushed her over. She fell down several steps and was knocked out. She also broke her wrist.'

'This is terrible.' It was in fact worse than terrible. Wada realized at once that this development didn't signal an outbreak of street crime in a previously peaceful district. It signalled a response from Rinzaki to the discovery that Wada was in California, digging into his secrets. The so-called mugger was almost certainly Koga, formerly Yagami's assistant, now his successor. 'How is she?'

'Well, she's conscious. I phoned the hospital. They wouldn't let me speak to her. They said she needed to rest. They're going to keep her in for a couple of nights at least. I think she's going to be all right, but . . . how can you not have known about this?'

'Tago didn't tell me.' No. Tago hadn't told her. And why hadn't he? Because he'd promised to protect their mother and had self-evidently failed to.

'Don't you . . . check on how she is?'

'Not constantly, no. She wouldn't like it. You know that. But you're saying . . . she's OK?'

'Sounds like it. Apart from the broken wrist. But a mugging, Umiko? What's happening over there?'

Nagata's phone rang at that point as well. Wada saw him pick it up and slide out of the van to speak to the caller. She caught the word *querida*. It sounded like an endearment and she guessed the call was from Juanita.

'It's not as if the mugger actually got away with anything,' Haruto went on. 'According to Tago, he dropped the bag as he was running off. Mother will be relieved about that, I suppose.'

She undoubtedly would be. But Wada wasn't. Discarding the bag only underlined the message. *Stop now or next time will be worse.* 'I will call the hospital tomorrow morning and see how Mother is then,' she said, reminding herself that she was supposed to be having this conversation in the middle of the night.

'And you'll go in to visit her?'

'Ah . . . that could be difficult.'

'Difficult?'

'I am . . . very busy . . . just now.'

'You can't be too busy to visit our mother in hospital.'

'Well, if she's . . . OK . . . there's no urgency to see her . . . is there?'

'She'll expect you to show up, Umiko. *I'll* expect you to show up. So you can tell me how she seems. What's the big problem?'

'I . . . have to be somewhere else . . . tomorrow.'

'Can't you postpone the trip?'

'Not really. I . . .'

Nagata climbed back slowly into the van. The phone call had ended. His expression was frozen. His whole body was stiff with shock of some kind. He stretched forward and started the engine.

'I have to go now, Haruto,' said Wada, sensing something was very wrong. 'I will contact you as soon as I can.'

'Hold on. I—'

Wada ended the call. Nagata turned and looked at her. 'That was McDermott,' he said thickly. 'He was using Juanita's phone.'

'What's happened?'

'He's at our trailer. He's holding Juanita at gunpoint. He says . . . if I don't take the asset to him . . . now . . . he'll kill her.'

'He said that?'

Nagata nodded. 'As good as.'

'How did he know where you're living?'

Nagata shook his head. 'No idea. But he's there. And he wants the asset. He said that if I handed it over . . . there'd be no problem.'

'Where is it now?'

'Behind you.'

Wada turned round. There was a package, wrapped in black plastic and fastened with string, lying on the floor of the van. The Matsuda asset was close enough to touch. She looked back at Nagata. 'What are you going to do?'

'I'm going to give it to him, of course. You think I'd put Juanita's life at risk for the sake of Rinzaki's ancient secrets?'

'No. I don't think that.'

'You can get out now. Or you can come with me. But I'm leaving.'

Wada didn't move. She didn't feel able to. She certainly couldn't simply climb from the van and watch Nagata drive away. 'I'll come with you,' she said.

'Sure?'

She nodded. 'I'm sure.'

It was a tense drive of five or six miles from the airport to Pacifica. Nagata's grip on the steering wheel was visibly tight. Wada said nothing, reckoning it didn't need her to point out how badly his plans had miscarried. Her own had miscarried pretty badly as well. She tried to bury her concern about her mother, reminding herself that Haha's strength of will was likely to carry her through any number of challenges.

It was obvious that all Nagata wanted to do now was hand the asset over to McDermott and make sure Juanita was all right. How McDermott had tracked them down Wada didn't know, though she suspected it had something to do with their visit to Palomino Mansions. McDermott, she assumed, saw this as a way of redeeming himself in Grant Braxton's eyes. He wasn't actually going to harm Juanita. That would make no sense. But Nagata wasn't about to take any risks with her safety and Wada didn't blame him for that. The asset wasn't worth anyone's life.

It was as they entered the outskirts of Pacifica that Nagata suddenly laughed bitterly and said, 'The stick contains a list of all the families who made regular payments to the orphanage. I was going to ask you to track them down and tell those still making payments that they could stop. I was going to ask you to record me burning the register and the ledger on your phone and show them the video to convince them there was nothing to fear any more. That's why I wanted to meet you this morning. So we could put an end to this. But it's not ending, is it? The asset will go straight back to Grant Braxton. And his stand-off with Rinzaki will continue. I've accomplished nothing. Absolutely nothing.'

'You said you're happy with Juanita.'

'I am.'

'Isn't that an accomplishment?'

'It's one good thing to come out of this, admittedly.' He nodded grimly. 'A new life for me. Which I don't intend to endanger.'

'You're doing the right thing, Nagata-san. Hand the asset over. Then you and Juanita can forget all about it.'

'Shouldn't you be trying to talk me out of handing it over? You came halfway round the world in search of it.'

'I came in search of the truth. I know that now.'

'We both know it, Wada. But where has it got us?'

Wada did not reply. And Nagata didn't press her to. Silence seemed the only right answer.

There was a long road hugging the coast on the seaward side of the town, lined by apartment blocks, trailer parks, warehouses, vacant lots and tumbling inclines of land leading down to shingly stretches of beach. The sky had clouded over and shrouds of mist hung over the silvery ocean.

Nagata and Juanita's trailer home was one of half a dozen or so spaced around an apron of concrete next to an apparently empty warehouse. Wada spotted McDermott's brown Cadillac parked on the road nearby. The area was quiet, with few people about and not much traffic. Nagata pulled in close to the trailer and grabbed the parcel containing the asset from behind his seat. 'I just want her to be OK,' he murmured. There was no mystery about what he meant. Wada felt the same. However disappointing it might be to watch him meekly surrender the asset, it was certain to be better than several alternatives.

He was already nearing the door of the trailer by the time Wada had climbed out of the van and set off after him. She could hear the cry of gulls in the distance and smelt the tang of ozone in the air.

Nagata pulled the door open and stepped up into the trailer. Wada followed. She could have hung back, it occurred to her. It might have been safer to do so. There was nothing she could do, after all, to alter or determine what happened next. But she wanted to be there to see it done. She wanted to be certain.

The trailer wasn't big and the quantity of possessions scattered about made it feel smaller still. Juanita was a small, plump, dark-haired woman who might ordinarily have sported an endearing smile, but was currently gripped by a grimace of fear. Her fingers were knotted round a toggle on the neck of her rumpled top. She was sitting on a chair next to a fold-out table scattered with the remains of breakfast – a plate of sliced fruit, a bowl of cornflakes, a mug and a glass half-filled with orange juice. The table was lit by a window, across which the curtain had been half-pulled, perhaps by McDermott to screen his presence, looming above and behind her as he was, grim-faced, gun in hand.

'You here too, Wada?' he said, displaying little surprise.

'She would make sure she was,' said another voice. And from directly behind McDermott Yukari Otonashi – real name Yuma Zaizen – stepped into view. In that instant it became apparent that the asset wasn't going back to Grant Braxton. It was going back to Rinzaki – her father, whose objectives she lovingly served.

She was as beautiful as Wada remembered from the picture on Lois's phone. Dressed in jeans and a black leather jacket, the plainness of her clothes only made her looks more striking. But they were flushed now with something that seemed likely to be anger. Her dark-eyed gaze raked over Wada. 'You can't stop interfering, can you?'

'She won't be able to interfere any more,' said McDermott, sounding as if he had no patience for Otonashi's recriminations. 'Is that the asset you have there, Nagata?'

'Yes,' said Nagata. He untied the string, opened the bag and pulled out two scuffed leather-bound books with marble-edged pages. They looked about as old as they were: as old as the secrets they contained.

'Take a look,' McDermott said over his shoulder to Otonashi. 'Make sure they're what you're after.'

'Do you know what the asset is, Mr McDermott?' asked Wada, curious to know just how mercenary he was.

'Don't know, don't care. I'm just doing a job.'

Otonashi moved past him and took the books from Nagata, shooting a glare at Wada as she did so.

'How did you find out Nagata was here?' Wada continued.

'I went back to Palomino Mansions and asked some questions my way. The way that gets answers.'

'And now you're working for Otonashi?'

'She agreed to my terms. So, yeah, I'm working for her. I can't afford to be choosy.'

Wada watched as Otonashi laid the books on the top of a cabinet and began turning the pages of the topmost volume. She nodded in evident satisfaction and began checking the second volume.

'They're what Rinzaki wants,' said Nagata. 'The register and the ledger. You can see that.'

Otonashi glanced round at him. 'I can see you are a frightened man.'

'Yes. I am. So, please, take the asset and go.'

'Makes sense to me,' said McDermott. 'They're the genuine article, right?'

'Right,' said Otonashi with oddly sarcastic precision. Then she turned and looked at Wada. 'You have something to say to me?'

Wada knew she shouldn't respond. But she couldn't seem to help herself. Otonashi was correct, after all. She did have something to say to her. 'I just wonder . . . why you are doing this. Is your father's approval really so important to you?'

Otonashi's gaze was unwavering. 'You are not going to stop, are you? Even without the asset and without a client, you will go on with this. You are a cat with a fishbone, looking for one more fragment of flesh.'

'You have not answered my question, Zaizen-san.'

Perhaps it was the use of Otonashi's real name that sparked the reaction. She reached inside her jacket, pulled out a derringer and prodded the snub nose of the barrel hard against Wada's breastbone. 'I will give you my answer if you really want it.'

'Whoa,' said McDermott, moving towards them, apparently no longer concerned about Juanita. 'Let's all calm down.'

'I am calm,' said Otonashi. And what worried Wada most was that she believed her. It seemed entirely possible in that moment that Otonashi might actually pull the trigger.

'We've got what you wanted,' said McDermott, reaching out warily between them. 'We should take it and leave. Stop pointing the gun at Wada. Put it back in your pocket and we can drive peaceably away, no harm done. And no repercussions. We're just recovering stolen property.' He laid his hand on her arm. 'This is—'

'I give you orders, McDermott,' snapped Otonashi. 'Not the other way round.' He started gently to pull her away from Wada. 'Let go of me.'

'I can't do that. You're—'

The crack of the gunshot shocked Wada into jumping back hard against the wall of the trailer. She believed for a second she'd been shot. But there was no pain, no sensation at all apart from the impact with the wall. Then she heard a loud clunk as McDermott's gun fell to the floor. And she saw he was clutching his midriff, gasping and gurgling as blood flooded out between his fingers.

He tried to speak, but no words came. He looked at Wada, bemused, it seemed, disbelieving almost of what had happened. But happened it had. He bent forward and staggered against the cabinet where Otonashi had laid the two books, put one arm out helplessly, then fell the other way, crumpling and toppling. The trailer rocked as he hit the floor. His head lolled sideways, eyes staring blankly.

'You . . . you have killed him,' murmured Nagata, stepping back towards the door.

'He shouldn't have tried to stop me,' snapped Otonashi, her voice fracturing. She swung towards Wada, the derringer still gripped tightly in her hand.

There was a scream. Juanita had launched herself across the trailer. She was clutching something in her hand, which she'd raised above her head. Otonashi seemed to register what was happening a fraction of a second later than Wada. She hadn't even turned to look in the direction of the scream when Juanita plunged a kitchen knife into the side of her neck, deep and hard.

Blood spurted out immediately. As Juanita pulled the knife out, the spurt became a fountain, splattering across her arms and breasts. Otonashi's mouth fell open. She blinked and gasped and raised her free hand to her neck. Her grip on the gun faltered and it slipped from her fingers. She tottered and slumped back against the cabinet, then slid slowly to the floor.

Wada heard Juanita drop the knife. She was still screaming, but more in horror now than the anger that had driven her to attack Otonashi, who sagged sideways as Wada watched. She came to rest with the side of her face against the floor, her expression frozen in surprise. Blood continued to stream from her neck, though more slowly now. It met the blood seeping from McDermott in a dark red spreading slick.

Juanita's screams subsided into sobs. She retreated to the table and sat down. Nagata rushed over and knelt in front of her, holding her hands in his and looking up at her. 'It is OK, *querida*,' he said. Patently, it wasn't. McDermott and Otonashi were both dead. The quantity of blood they'd shed was shocking. It was as if it was never going to stop spreading across the floor. Nagata had dashed through it to reach Juanita, bloody footprints tracing his path. He didn't seem to have noticed. 'You had no choice, *querida*,' he went on. 'The police will understand. You killed her to save me. We are all right, *querida*. We are alive.'

Yes. They were alive. So was Wada. Her extinction had seemed at one moment imminent and certain. But it hadn't happened. Instead two other people had died, one of them Goro Rinzaki's only child.

'We should call the police, Nagata-san,' she said, even as she reflected that they might not be quite as understanding as he'd assured Juanita they would be. 'I will make it clear Otonashi would have killed all of us if Juanita hadn't done what she did.'

'Will it really . . . be all right?' Juanita asked numbly.

'*Si, querida*,' said Nagata, standing up slowly. 'I will make sure it is.' He let out a long sigh. He was trembling, Wada noticed, in the same instant that she noticed she was trembling as well. He turned and looked at her. '*I* will call the police, Wada,' he said. 'You should leave before they arrive. There is no need for anyone to know you were ever here.'

'But . . . I can swear to what happened.'

'Otonashi fired the bullet that killed McDermott. They will establish that. And they will conclude Juanita acted in self-defence.'

'It is OK,' said Juanita breathlessly, looking at Wada and nodding. 'If Manjiro says you were not here, you were not here. I know how to . . . tell the police what is best for them to hear.'

'There will be much questioning and investigating,' said Nagata. 'But in the end we will be . . . exonerated.'

'You cannot know that for certain.'

'What I know for certain is that I want you to leave and take the asset with you. I want you to do what I intended to do. Destroy it. We will say McDermott and Otonashi broke in here demanding something we didn't have which they wrongly believed I stole from BISRI. With the asset gone – and you gone – there will be no clue for the police to follow. And no chance of either Grant Braxton or Goro Rinzaki laying hands on those books full of secrets.'

'I still think I—'

'There is no time for debate.' Nagata held up his hand, pleading with his eyes as much as his gesture for Wada's cooperation. 'Take the asset and leave. It will be better for you if Rinzaki does not know you were present at his daughter's death. And better for me if I can be sure the register and ledger no longer exist. Can you promise me you will destroy them?'

There seemed only one answer Wada could give. 'I will destroy them. You have my word.'

'Then we are agreed. As soon as you've gone, Juanita and I will walk out of here and call the police. We will wait for them in the open air. It is too . . .' He looked down at the bodies and the pool of blood surrounding them. 'It is too much to stay here.' Then he looked back at Wada. 'There can be no contact between us after this. We must go our own way and take our own risks. Yes?'

If his plan was to work, it had to be so. She nodded. 'Yes.'

Wada still wasn't convinced she was doing the right thing as she walked away from the trailer park along the road. She'd fetched her case and coat from Nagata's van and set off in the direction he'd said led to a bus stop. There were regular buses to Daly City, from where she could take a BART train into San Francisco. Exactly where and how she was going to destroy the Gosuringu register and ledger, which she was carrying wrapped back up in their black plastic bag, she had no idea. But it seemed a small matter set against the deaths of McDermott and Otonashi and the ramifications there would be from what had happened inside the trailer in the space of a very few seconds. She was worried about her mother as well, aware that the staged mugging would be nothing compared with Rinzaki's retribution for the killing of his daughter. Nagata had said there would be nothing to connect her with the event, but she doubted Rinzaki would believe she'd played no part in it, whatever the Pacifica police concluded.

For the moment, though, Wada was committed to Nagata's plan. Her heart was racing and she felt shaky on her feet. The shock of what had occurred couldn't be shrugged off, any more than the memory of how McDermott and Otonashi had died could be erased. Their deaths were going to live with her for a long time. How long she preferred not to consider. There were spots of blood on her trousers and top, but they weren't conspicuous against the dark cloth and most of them were obscured by her coat. Nothing marked her out as a witness to violent slayings fleeing the scene of the crime. She was just an easy to overlook Japanese woman making her way along a Californian sidewalk, pulling a small case on wheels and carrying a black plastic parcel under her arm.

She heard the bus behind her when she was still some way from a bus stop she could see ahead. She raised a hand, hoping the driver would stop. And he did, at the bus stop, where he waited patiently for her to catch up.

She bought a through ticket to San Francisco and headed for a rear seat. The bus moved off. She looked across at the flat silvery ocean. She was tempted to open the bag and examine the books she was carrying. But something stopped her. The other passengers weren't paying her any attention. But she didn't want to risk being noticed, or arouse suspicion in any way at all. So she sat with the bag on her lap, unopened, its contents concealed. How was she going to destroy them? It was easy to promise, but not so easy to arrange.

She looked again at the ocean. And a method began to form in her mind.

*

372

The journey into San Francisco proceeded uneventfully. From the BART line's Embarcadero station it was a short walk to the ferry docks. She was feeling less shaky now. She'd assimilated the magnitude of what had taken place and reconciled herself to its consequences. Sometimes she surprised herself with her own resilience. Maybe it went with the job. She was confident now she was acting for the best.

Passing a chandlery, she went in and bought a short length of heavy chain and a padlock. Then she carried on to the piers and bought a return ticket for the next ferry due to leave, bound for Alameda and Oakland.

Sitting on a bench close to the pier, Wada dared at last to open the bag and inspect the register. The earliest entries dated back ninety years or more. There were signs of ageing in the ink, which had bled slightly into the paper. She looked at the list of names – so many of them, stretching over the years. She knew the later entries must be in Rinzaki's hand – precise and legible, but with no stylistic elegance. He was careful even then. She also looked at the ledger and recognized his hand there as well. But she could do no more than glance at the contents. The ferry was approaching the pier. She put the books back in the bag, tied the string firmly round the parcel, then wound the chain tightly round it as well and padlocked the ends together.

The boat headed out into the bay, the sea churning in its wake. Wada stood by the stern rail, watching the city recede slowly behind her. The weather was overcast and cool. Most of the other passengers had retreated to the lounges. Wada had already taken the decision. She waited until the ferry appeared to be equidistant between San Francisco and the opposite shore, judging this was where the water would be deepest. She lifted the parcel up onto the rail. The chain and padlock made it much heavier than when it was just the register and the ledger. It would go straight to the bottom. Where it belonged.

She glanced around. There were no other passengers nearby. She tossed the parcel away from her with both hands. It didn't carry far before hitting the frothing wake with a splash, inaudible above the throb of the ferry's engine. And the sea swallowed it whole.

By the time Wada had waited at Alameda for a ferry back to San Francisco, it was too late to try for an afternoon flight to Tokyo. She booked for the following afternoon instead and reserved a room at the Bayfront Hilton, close to the airport. She would have preferred to leave sooner, but it couldn't be helped. Disposing of the asset had necessarily taken priority. She was relieved to be rid of it. And she was confident Nagata would give the police no reason to believe such a thing had ever existed. Whatever Grant Braxton or Rinzaki had intended to do with it they would now be unable to do. Any hold it gave them over people named in the register was broken. The asset was beyond their reach.

As the ferry neared San Francisco on the return journey, Wada called Haha's home number, calculating that at close to 5 a.m. in Tokyo Tago would be awake – supposing he had slept at all. She suspected his conscience would not be easy over what had happened to Haha.

The speed with which he answered suggested she was right.

'Tago-san?'

'Wada-san.' His voice sounded gravelly. 'I am glad to hear from you. Though sorry for the cause. I guess your brother has told you of the mugging.'

'He has. How is Mother?'

'She is doing well. I am going to visit her again this morning. She is complaining about her treatment. Which is a good sign, I think.'

374

'It is. Does she have her phone with her?'

'I am taking it in.'

'Then I will call her myself later.'

'You know of course that the mugging was not a mugging in any real sense.'

'I know.'

'I promised to protect her and I failed. I am deeply sorry.'

'How did it happen?'

'She became exasperated with my attentiveness. I insisted on accompanying her on shopping trips, you see, which irked her. She said I kept getting in her way.' Wada could not help smiling at that. 'Yesterday, she slipped out of the house without me noticing. Her attacker must have been waiting for his chance.'

'You couldn't monitor her every movement, Tago-san. I understand that.'

'I am ashamed I let it happen.'

'There is no reason to be. I will be back tomorrow evening. And while she is in hospital I do not think either of us need to worry about her.'

'She will probably be home by tomorrow evening. I do not think the hospital will want to keep her in any longer than strictly necessary. Your mother is not . . . a good patient.'

'I imagine not.' It required in truth little in the way of imagination. Haha in anything other than a coma would be a nurse's nightmare.

'I assume the attack on her was ordered by . . . the person you told me about.'

'I assume that too.'

'Have you defeated him yet?'

'It would be fairer to say he has *been* defeated.'

'How will he respond?'

'As any vengeful man might. And he is a vengeful man.'

'So, you are worried?'

'Apprehensive, certainly. But this is my problem, not yours. As soon as I am back I will relieve you of all responsibility.'

'You cannot do that, Wada-san. Responsibility, once assumed, abides with the bearer.'

Tago seemed to be governed by some kind of samurai ethic that had no place in the modern world. He was stubbornly and unapologetically anachronistic. It seemed to Wada that despite forfeiting his sumo status, he was still going to live by a strict code of honour. 'She is my mother, Tago-san, not yours. We can argue about whose responsibility she is when I get home.'

'I will look forward to your return, Wada-san. And the argument, of course. Meanwhile, take care. Take the greatest of care.'

Wada ate a late lunch in San Francisco for which she had little appetite, but which she reckoned she needed. Then she took a taxi to the Bayfront Hilton and booked in. It was as she was making her way up to her room that a call came in from Troy Kimber. She didn't answer. She suspected, as the message he left confirmed, that the call had been prompted by news of the two deaths in Pacifica.

'You're probably on a plane to Tokyo, Wada, in which case you won't get this till you land. But you ought to know what's happened here. The state police have been in touch about Connie McDermott. Shot dead at a trailer park in Pacifica this morning, for God's sake. By Otonashi. That's right. Otonashi shot him. She's dead as well. Stabbed in self-defence, apparently, by the woman who lives in the trailer Otonashi and McDermott broke into. According to the police, the woman's Korean boyfriend used to work as a cleaner at BISRI. Korean? I don't think so. He sounds like Nagata to me. Which means Otonashi must have been looking for you know what and McDermott . . . I don't know what he was doing. Maybe working for her. Until they fell out. I didn't say anything about any of this to the police, of course, or about you. I'm just waiting to see

what else comes out. It's all very weird. Can't say I'm sorry Oto-nashi's left this world. But it's rough about Connie. He should have known better than to get mixed up with her. Anyhow, call me when you get this. I may know more by then.'

Wada was happy to let him think she was in the air and there-fore out of reach. She wasn't ready to speak to him yet. She wasn't sure when she would be. She'd have to think carefully about what she told him. He wasn't her client any more, after all. She didn't owe him the truth.

Once she'd settled in her room, blandly but comfortably fur-nished, with a pleasant view of San Francisco Bay, she called Haha on her mobile, which she calculated Tago would have delivered to her by now.

And so he had. 'Umiko?' Haha sounded entirely unaffected by what she had been through. 'Where are you?'

'I had to . . . leave Tokyo . . . on business.'

'Business? Do you have a life that is not business, Umiko? I sometimes wonder.'

'I will be back tomorrow evening. Do you think you will be home by then?'

'Definitely. By *this* evening, I hope. I feel perfectly well.'

'No headaches? No dizziness?'

'My head is a little sore. But it's nothing.'

'And your wrist?'

'In plaster. And simply a nuisance. Fortunately, it's my left wrist. Though, of course, I will have to have some help. From my daughter, perhaps. To do a few things Tago-san certainly cannot help me with.'

There was no way out of the trap Wada had just walked into. 'I will do my best, Mother. As soon as I get back.' She began wondering how quickly and easily she could hire a nurse to attend to Haha's needs.

377

'You can also track down the man who attacked me if you really want to help. For such a thing to happen in the middle of the day . . . is . . . intolerable. And I don't intend to tolerate it.'

On one point Wada's mind was now at rest. Her mother was fine.

Wada tuned the television in her room to a local news channel. She didn't have to wait long to see a report on the deaths in Pacifica. The trailer, cordoned off by police tape, was visible in the background as the reporter spoke to camera.

'The peace of this quiet cliffside stretch of Pacifica was broken this morning by a double homicide in the trailer you can see behind me. Neighbours say they had no idea what had happened until the police arrived in answer to a call from the residents of the trailer, who've been named as Kwon Hee and Juanita Martinez. It appears two people, a Black man and an Asian woman, as yet unnamed, broke in looking for something they wrongly believed to be in Mr Hee's possession. Both were armed. They held Mr Hee and Ms Martinez captive and threatened them. During a disagreement, the Asian woman shot the Black man dead. Fearing she would turn her gun on them, Ms Martinez fatally stabbed the Asian woman in the neck with a kitchen knife. Many of the details remain unclear at this stage, but the police have said Mr Hee and Ms Martinez are lucky to be alive and are assisting the police with their inquiries.'

So far so good, it seemed. Nagata's plan was working. The police knew the identities of the deceased, of course. According to Kimber's message, they'd already contacted BISRI. They'd get little out of Grant Braxton, though. He could be relied upon to say nothing about the asset or its theft, since to do so would invite a host of difficult questions. Kimber wasn't about to give anything away either. Otonashi's death wasn't exactly an unwelcome development as far as he and his mother were concerned. It was in no one's interests to enlighten the police about what

378

Otonashi and McDermott had been looking for. There was a good chance Wada's role in events would go unmentioned.

But it wouldn't go unsuspected, at any rate by Rinzaki. Sonoko Zaizen would mourn their daughter as any mother would, whilst rueing her decision to interfere in Rinzaki's plans for her, but for which Yuma might still be alive. Rinzaki would mourn her also. But he wouldn't stop there. He would seek retribution. Wada had no doubt of it. And she would be one of those he sought it from. She had no doubt of that either.

Sooner or later – probably later, for he would try to lull her into thinking there was no danger – he would come after her. It was a certainty. It was fixed in her future. And there was nothing – absolutely nothing – she could do about it.

1995

IT IS EARLY EVENING, STICKY AND SOMNOLENT IN THE QUARTER OF
Ogikubo where Kodaka finds himself. He is approaching an
apartment block with the weary gait of a man who has done this
too many times already. He has contacted numerous victims – or
relatives of victims – of the subway gas attack in search of information that will strengthen the case against the Aum Shinrikyo
cult members who have so far been arrested and charged. His
clients, victims or relatives of victims themselves, are united in
wanting to see justice done. But many of those Kodaka has
spoken to on their behalf are more ambivalent. Some prefer to
forget the episode altogether. Others are reluctant to be dragged
into legal proceedings for fear of where it will lead. Still others,
mercifully a small minority, express contempt for what Kodaka
is doing. 'You are trying to profit out of their suffering,' he has
been told more than once.

Kodaka does not accept that that is what he is doing. He
believes he is providing a service to those who feel the police have
not adequately answered all their questions and who hope evidence against cult members who have not already been charged

will drag more of the guilty into the net. But he makes a point of never arguing with anyone who abuses him or rejects involvement. They are all victims, one way or another, and are entitled to say whatever they like to him.

Contact often goes no further than a telephone call. But where a telephone number is unobtainable and only an address is available Kodaka generally favours a personal visit, leaving his card and an explanatory note if no one is at home – or if no one answers the door, which he has learnt is not at all the same thing. The gas attack seems to have left many of those affected by it deeply suspicious of strangers.

This visit is to the wife of a man left in a coma after the attack – Tomohiko Nakamura. One of Kodaka's clients was in the same train carriage as Nakamura and believes he saw him talking to the cult member, later identified as Yozo Sasada, who released the gas. The issue is whether Nakamura said anything about their conversation before he lost consciousness. The hospital he was taken to has confirmed he was still conscious when he was admitted, though no one seemed certain about whether that was so when his wife arrived to see him. She may be in possession of valuable information. Or she may not. There is only one way to find out.

He takes the lift up to her floor and rings the doorbell of her apartment. There is a spy-hole in the door and he stands directly in front of it to reassure her that he is not trying to conceal himself. Half a minute or so passes. He is considering a second ring at the bell when the door opens. There is no security chain – or, if there is, she has not engaged it.

She is a small, slightly built young woman with short black hair, a round face and unremarkable features, plainly dressed in loose linen top and trousers. She is not smiling, but neither does she appear apprehensive. Her gaze is direct and open. There is the merest hint of a frown as she looks him in the eye. 'Can I help you?' she asks.

'*Gomen kudasai*,' says Kodaka, bowing politely. 'Are you Umiko Nakamura?'

'Yes. I am.'

'I wonder if I could speak to you . . . about your husband.'

'About Hiko?'

'I am a private detective, Nakamura-san.' He proffers his card. 'My name is Kodaka. Kazuto Kodaka. I am acting for a number of victims and relatives of victims of the subway gas attack. One of my clients was in the same train carriage as your husband. Could I ask you . . . a few questions?'

'There is nothing I will be able to tell you.'

'Forgive me, but people often say that, only to discover after we have discussed the matter that in fact . . .'

'They know something useful to you?'

Kodaka smiles. 'Exactly so.'

'But I do not, I assure you.'

'Even so, could I . . .'

'You may come in for a moment.'

She retreats into the apartment and he follows, removing his shoes as he goes. His immediate impression is that this is a standard 2DK apartment, exactly the kind of place a newly married couple would rent.

They enter the kitchen, which is immaculately clean and tidy. There is a table by the window, on which stands a home computer and an array of documents, with more documents still lodged in a large buff envelope. Kodaka glances at the name and address on the envelope. The addressee is Umiko Wada, rather than Nakamura.

The documents are in Japanese, but to one side of the computer, neatly stacked, are pages in English. 'You are a translator?' asks Kodaka. Then he apologizes. 'Excuse me. I'm afraid I can't help noticing small things. A detective's instinct.'

382

Wada gives a tight little smile. 'I am a translator, yes. Japanese to English, English to Japanese.'

'That must be a very useful ability to have.'

'It has been my only source of income since Hiko fell ill.'

'Doesn't his employer help you?'

'No. He had not been with them long. They found some clause in his contract entitling them to terminate his employment.'

'That sounds remarkably callous of them.'

'I agree.'

'Are you . . . contesting it?'

'No.'

'May I ask . . . why not?'

'Because I do not intend to allow Aum Shinrikyo or the company Hiko worked for to oppress me. I will live my life free of all of them.'

Kodaka is impressed and faintly awed. Umiko Nakamura – Umiko Wada – is clearly a remarkably strong-minded woman.

'Can I offer you tea, Kodaka-san?'

'Thank you.'

She fills the kettle and sets it to boil on the gas burner. 'What is it you want to know about Hiko?'

'My client, as I say, was travelling in the same carriage as your husband and the cult member who released the sarin, Yozo Sasada. He believes your husband spoke to Sasada, who was sitting next to him, perhaps about the plastic bag Sasada was carrying, which actually contained the sarin. It was wrapped in a newspaper, but it is possible your husband could see more of it from his position than my client could. Sasada pushed the bag under his seat and stabbed it with the point of his umbrella just as the train arrived at the next station, where he got off. My client remembers your husband peering suspiciously at the punctured bag, from which the evaporating sarin was by then already emerging, although of course neither of them at that point . . .'

'Knew how much danger they were in.'

'No. Neither of them did. I wondered if your husband said anything – to you or anyone else at the hospital – before he became . . . comatose.'

'Nothing to me. He was already unconscious when I arrived. But an orderly told me he was mumbling as they carried him in from the ambulance.'

'Did the orderly say what he was mumbling?'

'No one could understand him. He was delirious by then. So, you see, there really is nothing I can tell you that will strengthen the case against Sasada. But I think it is probably strong enough already.'

'My client wants to be sure he'll be sentenced to death.'

'Is there a possibility he won't be?'

'He is claiming to have been brainwashed.'

'Of course.' The kettle comes to the boil. Wada moves to the burner and turns off the gas. She fetches the tea caddy, then sighs and sets it down next to the sink. 'I try not to think about Sasada and the other cult members. They are all murderers and should be punished accordingly. But that will not restore Hiko to waking life. Nor will it help me find my way without him. I have to shape my own future.'

'What hope is there that he'll recover?'

'Realistically, none.'

'I see. I am very sorry, Nakamura-san.'

'I prefer Wada.'

'I'll remember that.' Since they are unlikely to meet again, this strikes Kodaka as a strange thing for him to have said. But said it he has.

'Would you rather have a beer?' Wada asks. 'The last six bottles of Asahi Hiko bought are still in the refrigerator.'

It seems clear to Kodaka that Wada would herself at this

384

moment much rather have a beer. And he certainly has no objection. 'Thank you. I'd like that.'

'Good. Let's take them into the living room. And we'll change the subject, if you don't mind.'

'I don't mind.'

'Perhaps you could tell me . . . all about the private detective business.'

2022

WADA'S FLIGHT LANDED ON SCHEDULE AT NARITA AIRPORT. WHEN she turned her phone on, she found a text message waiting for her from her mother, informing her that thanks to the 'fussing' of a 'twelve-year-old doctor' (who was probably more like thirty) she was being kept in hospital for one more night as a precaution against late-exhibiting complications of concussion.

This came as something of a relief. It meant Wada would not have to concern herself with Haha's domestic needs until the following day. She would go and see her that evening, however, after a brief visit to her apartment to drop off her bag and have a hot bath.

An email had come in from Dobachi as well, reporting on the increasing impatience of Fumito Nagata's lawyers for her signature on the letter they'd sent her the previous week. She decided a reply could wait. The matter of her enquiries into the whereabouts of Manjiro Nagata had been overtaken by events of which his father's lawyers were probably still unaware.

Nightfall encroached as she sat on the Narita Express, speeding through the twilight into Tokyo. Tired from the long flight, she couldn't seem to order her thoughts on what best to do to counter the ongoing threat Rinzaki represented. Perhaps Dobachi might be able to give her some good advice, perhaps not. It was hard to know where else to turn. But she would have to turn somewhere. That was certain.

The train split at Tokyo Station. She was in the section carrying on to Shinjuku. From there she planned to take a taxi to her apartment, rather than braving the Marunouchi subway line to Ogikubo at the height of the rush hour. Her exhaustion had deepened during the journey. She was having difficulty staying awake as the train rumbled on its way.

Shinjuku at last. She headed for the west exit, where there was the best chance of finding a taxi. As she left the station, she took her first breath of unfiltered Tokyo air since landing at Narita. The bright lights and purposeful bustle of her home city came as familiar comforts after the alien challenges of California. She stopped for a moment to let the freshness of the evening revive her.

Then she felt a sharp jab in her back. A man was standing very close behind her, pushing something against her ribs. 'Don't look round,' he rasped, placing a heavy hand on her shoulder. 'I'm holding a gun.' Even without turning round she could tell he was half a metre taller than her and powerfully built with it. Her guess was that he was Koga. He hadn't spoken during their encounter at Endo's apartment. Had he followed her from Narita? It was possible. Or perhaps an accomplice had. It hardly mattered which. She should have been more cautious, but fatigue had got the better of her. That plus her conviction that Rinzaki would bide his time. Now Koga had her where he wanted her. 'Walk straight ahead to the black van that's just pulled up.'

Wada saw the van at the side of the road. It wouldn't be able to stay there long and she tried to weigh in her mind the chances of Koga actually shooting her in front of hundreds of commuters and myriad CCTV cameras. He might think twice about it. Or he might not. She didn't know him well enough to say.

387

'Move,' he said. 'Or you'll die right here.'

She moved, Koga matching her stride. As they reached the van, the side door slid open. A man in dark clothes and a ski mask leant out and lifted her with apparent ease, suitcase and all, into the empty storage bay of the vehicle. Koga jumped in beside her, pulling the door shut behind him. 'Let's go,' he called to the driver, whose head and shoulders were visible through a wire-mesh barrier.

The van accelerated away. There were two fold-down bucket seats either side of the storage bay. The man holding Wada yanked the case from her hand and dropped it flat on the floor, then pushed her down into one of the seats. He snapped a hand-cuff onto her wrist. The other cuff had been secured to a bracket beneath the chair.

Koga sat down opposite her. He too was ski-masked, as he had been at Endo's apartment. She only had the look in his eyes to judge his mood by. On that basis she reckoned he was nervous, perhaps worried by what working for Rinzaki had turned out to involve. But he was nothing like as worried as she was.

'You're Koga, aren't you?' she said, aiming to sound confident and unintimidated.

The other man chuckled. Koga glared at him, then pointed the gun at Wada. 'Shut your mouth,' he growled.

'Where are you taking me?'

'Where do you think?'

'To Rinzaki? You shouldn't take me to him, you really shouldn't. You're letting him drag you into serious trouble.'

'You're the one in serious trouble.'

'Put the gun away,' the other man intervened. 'We have her now.'

Another glare. It didn't seem to Wada that Koga liked being told what to do. But as the van took a corner at some speed and he nearly slipped out of his seat, he appeared to concede the point, stowing the gun in a holster concealed inside his black leather jacket.

'You should stop the van and let me go,' said Wada. 'Follow Yagami's example. Quit working for Rinzaki while you still can.'

'Yagami didn't quit,' said Koga. 'He was fired.'

'Lucky him.'

'That's enough.' A length of duct tape was hanging on the wall of the van, as if placed there in readiness. Koga pulled it free, leant across the gap between them and plastered it across Wada's mouth.

'Try and relax,' the other man said. 'It's a fifty-kilometre drive.'

Fifty kilometres sounded like the distance to Matsuda Sanso. So, Rinzaki was waiting for her at his rural retreat. And Endo's example showed how easy it was to go there and never be seen again.

'Just sit back and enjoy the ride,' the man advised her sarcastically. 'I guarantee it'll be the best part of your evening.'

Wada's jet lag had vanished. Her mind was racing even as she sat still, gagged and handcuffed, with only shadows and washes of neon and the blare of horns reaching her from the city they were speeding through.

She could still scarcely believe how easily they'd trapped her. Reflecting that they'd have found a way of doing so eventually brought little consolation. What the grieving Rinzaki might have in mind for her was better by far not to imagine.

She concentrated on trying to calculate their route, based on the turns the van took and her aural impressions of the districts they were passing through. On the subway, she always knew when the train was on a straight or a curve, however gentle. She sometimes thought she could find her way through Tokyo even if she kept her eyes closed. The map of the city was imprinted on her brain.

Accordingly, there was little doubt in her mind about the direction they were taking. North on the Shuto Expressway to the west of Ikebukuro, then on to National Route 17, across the Arakawa river by Todabashi bridge and out of the city through Warabi. When the 17 started to veer west and they stayed on it, there could be no question: Matsuda Sanso was their destination.

There was nothing to be done to avert their arrival. It was only a matter of time. Rinzaki was waiting, still and silent. And they were moving towards him through the deepening night.

The process of convergence had begun. And soon enough it would end.

There were occasional outbreaks of bickering between Koga and his accomplice. As if to make sure Wada knew both their names, Koga addressed him as Oda a couple of times. They clearly neither liked nor trusted each other. But the circumstances gave Wada no obvious way of exploiting that. She was their prisoner and they were delivering her in accordance with their instructions. No doubt they were well paid. And they had long since made their moral choices about engagement in this kind of work. To them she was little more than a parcel – and one that didn't even require gentle handling.

A final decisive lurching stop marked their arrival at Matsuda Sanso. The driver growled something Wada didn't catch. 'Prepare yourself,' said Koga to her ominously before detaching the handcuff from the seat bracket and attaching it to his own wrist. A sudden bolt into the darkness wasn't going to be possible. Oda slid the side door of the van open and clambered out. When Koga followed, he all but pulled Wada off her feet as he jumped down.

The clear, still night air was a shock after long confinement in the van. Wada glanced up and saw the outline of trees against a star-spangled sky. Ahead loomed the silhouette of a large, low-roofed villa. Somewhere there was a tinkle of water – from an ornamental pond, perhaps. The scene was actually quite beautiful. It could have been the subject of a painting by Hasui, one of her favourite artists – also admired, as Wada had only discovered shortly before his death, by Kodaka. Perhaps he too had witnessed this composition of tree crown and night sky and been reminded of the great printmaker, whose abiding sense of serenity had sometimes, as in the present instance, carried with it an undertow of menace.

'Move,' said Koga, pulling Wada forward. They passed the van and followed a winding stone path, lit at intervals by small ground-level lanterns, round a lawn towards the house, where other larger lanterns were suspended from the sloping roof of the *engawa*, casting a golden-yellow light that seemed to merge with the darkness even as it haloed into it.

'Where's Momo?' asked Oda.

'It doesn't matter,' Koga replied. 'It looks like the boss is ready for us.'

One of the shoji on the *engawa* stood open. There was a glow of subdued lamplight within. Wada took it this was the room where Rinzaki was waiting to receive her. He must have heard the van. He must know she was about to appear. But he hadn't come to meet her. He was content to bide his time, to let her anxiety tighten by another degree.

They climbed a short flight of steps to the level of the *engawa* and paused to remove their shoes. Oda seemed to find Koga's clumsiness in managing this while handcuffed to Wada amusing, prompting Koga to pull her violently after him as he headed towards the open shoji.

They entered a large tatami-matted room. Lamps hung at the four corners. Wada could hear the faint hiss of the oil that fuelled them. She glimpsed a hanging scroll in the alcove at one end of the room, bearing artistically rendered kanji, which the dimness of the light made it impossible to decipher from where she was.

'What is this?' she heard Koga say.

Turning towards the other end of the room, she saw a low table, with legless chairs either side of it. A figure sat on one of the chairs, clad in a dark kimono. He had his back turned to them and his head was bent forward, as if he was asleep.

'Rinzaki-san?' called Koga. He sounded puzzled and a little worried. He led her across the room in the direction of the table. The figure sitting there didn't move. 'Rinzaki-san?'

As they reached the shoulder of the motionless figure, Wada knew for certain that it *was* Rinzaki. She recognized the taut skin of his face, both young and old at the same time. And his circular black-rimmed spectacles, lying on the table in front of him. He didn't stir. He didn't twitch a muscle. His head lolled forward at what appeared to be an impossible angle, so low on his chest it was as if . . .

She moved past Koga, who made no effort to restrain her, and stretched out her hand. Her fingers touched the collar of the kimono. She prised it away from Rinzaki's neck.

His neck was broken, snapped like a twig by some unknown force. The skin was split at the nape. A splintered section of vertebra protruded through the blood-clotted flesh.

Koga started back, gasping in horror. But Wada stood where she was, the handcuff chain stretching taut between them. She'd seen something beyond dried blood and fractured bone. She'd seen the truth of what had happened.

There was only one person who could have done this to Rinzaki. How he'd found him, how he'd gained access to the villa, she did not know. But she knew he had. And she knew why.

'Is he dead?' came the inane question from Oda.

Wada slowly peeled off the strip of duct tape from her mouth and turned to look at him and Koga. She was about to speak when Koga's phone trilled.

He fumbled it out of his pocket and raised it to his ear. 'What?' He frowned as he listened. '*What?*' He ended the call, then announced, 'The old lady's here.'

It was unclear if he thought Wada would know who that meant. Her guess was Sonoko Zaizen. As to what had brought her to Matsuda Sanso, a summons from Rinzaki was the only explanation that seemed to make sense. Perhaps he'd wanted her to be on hand when he questioned the woman he blamed for their daughter's death.

'Find Momo,' said Koga to Oda. 'Maybe she knows what happened here.'

'She could be anywhere,' Oda objected.

'Then look anywhere. Just find her.'

With a huffish shrug, Oda scuttled out of the room.

'Aren't you going to take your ski mask off, Koga-san?' Wada asked as Oda left. 'You can't greet "the old lady" wearing that, can you?'

'The guy who came to your rescue at Endo's apartment did this, didn't he?'

'I don't know who did this. But I do know Rinzaki's dead. Which means you and your friend – and your driver – are all out of work. As of right now.'

'We'll see about that.'

'Take these handcuffs off, Koga-san. No one is paying you to hold me captive any longer. Cut your losses.'

He didn't respond. His expression was unreadable beneath the ski mask. Wada sensed he genuinely didn't know what to do.

Then a woman stepped through the half-open shoji into the room, dressed in a long black overcoat. She was elderly, grey-haired and gaunt, her long hair secured in a bun with a pin, the fine bone structure of her face preserving a record of former beauty. Sonoko Zaizen was unusually tall for a woman of her and Rinzaki's generation. She held herself erect and looked at them with neither hostility nor dismay.

'Zaizen-san,' mumbled Koga, pulling off his ski mask and tidying his hair.

She did not return the greeting. She walked slowly to the table and gazed down at Rinzaki for a moment, then bent forwards and stared intently at his downturned face. She released a strange little plosive sigh, then straightened up and looked first at Koga, then at Wada.

'Who are you?' she asked, her voice low-pitched but firm.

'She's Wada,' said Koga. 'Did Rinzaki-san tell you about her?'

Zaizen gave him a hard glare. 'I asked you nothing,' she said coolly. 'But now I will ask you something. Who did this?'

'We . . . we don't know. We, er . . . found him like this.'

'You came here with Wada?'

'Yes. We brought her here as Rinzaki-san instructed us to.'

'*We?*'

That question at least answered itself as Oda reappeared in the room, breathless and now also bare-faced. He pulled up at the sight of Zaizen and gave a twitchy little bow. 'I am sorry,' he said.

'What are you sorry for?' asked Zaizen.

'Th-this . . .' He gestured helplessly towards Rinzaki.

'Where is the housekeeper?'

'In the kitchen. She was overpowered by an intruder. He gagged and blindfolded her and tied her to a chair. She never saw his face.'

'Then the intruder came here and snapped Rinzaki-san's neck. Yes?'

'Looks . . . like it,' mumbled Koga.

Zaizen inhaled deeply and breathed out slowly. 'You two men should leave now. I never wish to see you here again.'

'But there's—'

'*Leave.*'

Koga shrugged in an effort to imply he still had some control over the situation, then took a small key out of his pocket and released Wada from the handcuffs.

'I would like you to stay for a moment,' Zaizen said, looking at Wada.

'We're . . . owed money.' The congested note in Koga's voice told of the effort it had taken him to raise the subject.

But it did not appear to have earned him any favours with Zaizen. 'Rinzaki-san bequeathed this villa and the Kuraikagami Corporation to my daughter.' *My* daughter, Wada noticed, not *our* daughter. 'Since she is also dead, I suppose it all comes to me. As far as I am concerned, any dealings he had with the likes of you are null and void. And only your immediate departure is now required of you.' She let her gaze dwell on Koga.

And it did not need to dwell there for long. He gave another feebly defiant shrug, then jerked his head at Oda.

'I want my suitcase,' Wada cut in, remembering it was still in the van.

'We'll leave it behind,' said Koga, sounding as if he would be glad to. Then he and Oda made a sheepish exit.

Silence asserted itself, broken only by the hiss of the oil lamps. Then a sound reached them: the van pulling away in the distance. Zaizen turned and engaged Wada eye to eye.

'You are the Wada who once worked for Kazuto Kodaka?'

Wada nodded. 'Yes.'

'I met him once. He was not an unworthy man.'

'He was not.'

'Rinzaki said you were present when my daughter died.'

Instinctively, Wada felt certain complete honesty would serve her best. 'I was,' she said.

'Did you kill her?'

'No.'

'Who did?'

'You know as well as I do who killed her, Zaizen-san. He is here with us, in this room.'

Zaizen went on looking at her. Her expression did not alter. 'Perhaps you think I should have protected my daughter from him.'

'That is not for me to say.'

'Perhaps you think I should have foreseen that her devotion to him would eventually destroy her.'

'That is also not for me to say.'

A middle-aged woman in a yukata entered the room at that moment from another part of the villa. She was plump and flustered – Momo the housekeeper, Wada assumed.

Zaizen glanced at her. 'Leave us alone,' she said, speaking with the certainty that she would be obeyed.

Momo vanished.

Zaizen moved round to the other side of the table and looked across it at Rinzaki. 'The death of such a very old man as Goro Rinzaki should not be a surprise,' she said quietly, almost contemplatively. 'And yet it is. It seemed possible for a long time to believe that he would never die.'

'We all die, Zaizen-san,' said Wada.

Zaizen regarded her with a slight furrowing of the brow. 'Who was the intruder?'

'I cannot say.'

'Cannot – or will not?'

'I leave that for you to decide.'

'And you may take it I have decided.'

'What are you going to do, Zaizen-san?'

'That is not your concern. You and I, Wada, if we are both wise, will have no communication from this night forth. And as to this night . . . my driver will take you back to Tokyo. You were

396

never here. Nor were those two men. I will adjust the housekeeper's recollections for her. When the police come, as come they must, they will be met by a baffling mystery. Goro Rinzaki slain by a nameless and faceless intruder. He had in his life many more enemies than friends. And so there will be few who wonder at the fact of his demise and fewer still who will seek far for his slayer.'

Wada wanted to ask how Zaizen felt about the death of the man whose mistress she'd been for so many years and about the death of the daughter she'd had by him. She wanted to ask whether she regretted the life she'd led, the decisions she'd made, the pleasures she'd enjoyed that she must have known were paid for with the profits of Rinzaki's crimes. Wada wanted to ask her many things. For she'd never met Sonoko Zaizen before and felt sure she never would again.

But something in the old woman's gaze told her such questions could not be asked. 'You should go now, Wada,' Zaizen said. 'You are free of Rinzaki. And so am I. Let the evil he did die with him.'

No more words were spoken. The look they exchanged said all that remained to be said.

They had survived their very different battles with Goro Rinzaki. And he had not.

The drive back to Tokyo passed in silence. Zaizen's chauffeur was almost as old as her, stiff and formal and as sparing with his words as if they were drops of water in a desert. Wada slowly relaxed and began to appreciate the providential nature of Tago's intervention. She had no doubt – not the slightest – that he was the intruder who had ended Goro Rinzaki's life. And she had not much more doubt that but for the action he had taken she would not have left Matsuda Sanso alive.

The workings of fate were strange and ironic. Thanks to her mother's obsessive interest in sumo and the soft spot in her nature she reserved for its practitioners, a saviour had appeared just when Wada needed one. First at Endo's apartment and now at Rinzaki's villa. There would be no third appearance. There was no call for one. With the snapping of Rinzaki's neck Tago had broken the chain of cause and effect. She was free, as Zaizen had said she was.

Nor was she alone in that. It had been her intention to contact the people listed on the memory stick Nagata had given her and to tell them they no longer had to worry – if they *were* still worrying – about the Gosuringu Orphanage records. But they would all hear of Rinzaki's death and draw that conclusion for themselves now. Nagata could stop looking over his shoulder as well. He and Juanita could go wherever they wanted once the police had completed their investigation of the Pacifica fatalities. All thanks to Tago.

But where was Tago? Wada asked to be dropped at Ikebukuro station, cautious even at this stage about revealing her destination to anyone. From there she took the JR line to Sugamo and walked down through the quiet streets of Koishikawa, trailing her suitcase behind her, to her mother's house. It was too late for a hospital visit now. She would see Haha tomorrow anyway. But Tago? It was an open question in her mind whether she would ever see him again, though she wanted to – badly.

Wada realized when she entered the house that she hadn't been there in her mother's absence for many many years – probably not since she and Hiko had set up home together. The sensation was deeply disorientating. She felt as if she'd been transported back to her adolescence, a period of her life she had absolutely no wish to revisit.

It was immediately obvious to her Tago wasn't there either. He'd cleaned the house to a pitch of perfection Haha had certainly never achieved, so much so that he'd cleaned away all trace of his fleeting presence along with every particle of grime.

But he had left something behind: a note, placed on the kitchen table and held down by the weight of Haha's lucky cat charm. Since it began *Wada-san*, it could just as easily have been meant for Wada as for her mother. Perhaps, it occurred to her, it was actually meant for both of them.

Wada-san,
The time I have spent in this house has been one of healing for
    me.
I will never forget the kindness you have shown me.
I have tried in my own way to return that kindness.
There is still healing to be done, however, and penance also.
I must travel now for a while to seek the rest of what I have
    lost.
I hope one day to return.
Until then, some part of my thoughts will always dwell with
    you.
Take care,
Tago Seiji

So, he was gone, as she'd expected he would be but hoped he would not. Killing Rinzaki was a step he'd felt driven to take, for her sake and her mother's. But summoning the spirit to do it had doubtless taken its toll. That was what would require healing – and in his mind penance also.

Haha was not going to react well to his departure. And Wada would be unable to explain what had made him leave. He knew that, of course. But he could see nothing else for it. The difficulties he had left Wada to engage with were as nothing compared with what he had spared her. The debt was all on her side.

Wada tracked down the bottle of shochu Haha kept for special occasions so special they never actually arose and sat quietly in the living room, slowly drinking a glass – and then a second.

She'd already decided by then to spend the night there. In the morning she would call the hospital and establish when Haha would be discharged. Then . . .

But *then* was too much to think about tonight. She went up to what had once been her bedroom and in recent weeks had been Tago's and removed the impeccably laundered and folded futon from the closet.

As she unfolded it, a small object fell out onto the floor. Wada stared at it in astonishment. It was the Hello Kitty Petit Purse her mother had given her as a child to hold small coins: a translucent vinyl pouch with a metal clasp, adorned with the iconic kitty cat figure, sitting beneath the English word *HELLO!* There were still some coins inside. They'd jingled as the purse hit the floor.

Wada knelt down and picked up the purse. She doubted she'd actually seen or touched it since her teens. If asked, she would have surmised it had been thrown out. But evidently not. It had been here – somewhere – all the time.

She'd shown little enthusiasm for the Petit Purse when Haha had given it to her for her eighth birthday. The fact that almost all the girls she went to school with were Hello Kitty obsessives merely guaranteed, in fact, that Wada would display a disdain beyond her years for such commodified merchandise. But then Haha often lamented that her daughter had conformed to precisely none of the norms of girlhood. 'Why couldn't you have been more of a child, Umiko?' she'd complained once in her exasperation. 'I might have been a better mother if you had been.'

It occurred to Wada, kneeling there with the purse in her palm, that neither she nor her mother was tall enough to see all the way to the back of the highest shelf in the closet. They would have needed a stepladder to reach it. Not the towering Tago, though. To him it would have been at eye level.

He'd seen it, lodged at the back of the top shelf. He'd taken it out and guessed it was a relic of Wada's childhood. Haha was certain to have anatomized her daughter's perceived shortcomings for his benefit. Something had prompted him to leave it where he knew one or the other of them was bound in the end to discover it. Perhaps in his mind it didn't matter which of them it was. The meaning was the same. They were mother and daughter. No amount of bickering could change that. The bond between them could never be broken.

It would only take a few minutes' exposure to Haha's particular brand of skewed logic to drive Wada to distraction. And those few minutes were probably no more than twelve hours away. She knew that. Still, for the moment, all she could think of was how she would have felt if Haha had suffered some much more serious injury – or worse. Fortunately, that hadn't happened. But fortune could not always be relied upon.

It had cost Tago a lot to remove the threat from Haha's life – and Wada's – in the only way he knew would ultimately work. All he appeared to be asking for in return was that they start trying to behave a little more like mother and daughter. For her part Wada could see nothing for it, now she was so deeply in his debt, but to make the effort.

She sighed. It wasn't going to be easy. But it was going to have to be done.

1995

SEVERAL MONTHS HAVE PASSED SINCE KODAKA HAD ANY DEALINGS with Goro Rinzaki. The silence from that direction is welcome. He has been busily engaged in various cases during those months, not least a clutch of investigations on behalf of victims and relatives of victims of the Aum Shinrikyo subway gas attack. The latter in particular have generated a quantity of paperwork that would normally have threatened to overwhelm his ramshackle record-keeping arrangements. Fortunately, however, he now has the services of a secretary-cum-personal assistant: the formidably efficient Umiko Wada. He has never once regretted phoning her to draw her attention to the job advertisement he'd placed in the evening edition of *Asahi Shimbun*. In retrospect, placing the advertisement was a waste of money, just as interviewing the few serious candidates the advertisement attracted was a waste of effort. He should simply have offered the job to Wada straight away.

Funaki said the same after his first encounter with Wada and has gone so far since as to suggest that his old friend seems altogether less frazzled now he has her to organize his affairs.

'I reckon you've struck gold with her,' says Funaki as he slurps a beer at their favourite end of the bar of the Blue Fin this humid Friday night. 'Looks like Asahara and his crazed cultists did you a favour, doesn't it? A sackful of clients. Plus the perfect secretary. She's not even distractingly pretty.'

'Does being a journalist give you a special licence for tasteless remarks?' Kodaka retorts.

Funaki shrugs. 'Just facing facts. What are the chances of Wada's husband coming out of his coma?'

'Virtually zero, apparently.'

'There you are then. She'll stick with the job. Which is good news for you whichever way you look at it.'

'OK. I'm not going to deny it. I'm glad I found her.'

'Exactly. Although . . .' Funaki leans forward on his stool with a confidential hunch of the shoulders, 'I'm assuming you haven't told her about our . . . special arrangements for Chikako Imada?'

Kodaka lowers his voice as he replies. 'Of course not. And I destroyed all my notes relating to the period when Rinzaki had me working for him.'

'So, there's nothing in your files for her to come across that might set her thinking about the Kobe Sensitive?'

'No. Not a thing.'

'Would you let her in on what we did if the case blew up again?'

'Why should it do that?'

'I don't know. But with a guy like Rinzaki you never *do* know, do you?'

'As long as Chikako does nothing to draw attention to herself, Rinzaki will have no cause to suspect I deceived him.'

'But can you rely on her not to draw attention to herself? What if she senses the big one is about to hit? Isn't she going to feel obliged to warn people?'

'I think she'll remember where warning people about Kobe got her.'

'You *think*?'

403

'The alternative is to hope there's no "big one" for her to have to warn anyone about.'

'Well, we all hope that. But I don't reckon those tectonic plates we're sitting on have much interest in what we *hope*, do you?'

'You're turning into a real worrier. Maybe Rinzaki will do us a favour and die of old age before any of your apocalyptic scenarios come into play. Maybe we all will.'

'And maybe we won't.'

'Right. But just now I'm more bothered about dying of thirst.' Kodaka waggles his empty beer bottle in front of Funaki. 'Another round?'

2022

THREE DAYS HAD PASSED SINCE RINZAKI'S DEATH, TWO SINCE HAHA had been discharged from hospital. Wada had secured the services of a day nurse for her mother at great expense and been pleasantly surprised by the woman's ability to charm Haha, which lay beyond the ability of most mortals. Wada had nonetheless been obliged to help her mother with bathing, which she was determined to do every evening as usual. The arrangement had worked rather better than Wada had expected, although the restraint and tolerance she'd drilled herself to practise left her completely exhausted.

For her part, Haha seemed to be doing her level best not to fall out with her daughter. She hadn't even expressed the suspicion Wada felt sure she harboured that Wada was somehow responsible for Tago's abrupt departure. 'He'll be back soon,' Haha averred. 'I'm sure of it.' And Wada didn't argue. There was in fact a merciful lack of argument between them in general. Wada doubted it could last. But perhaps it could at least last long enough to see Haha restored to full independence.

Troy Kimber had made several attempts to speak to Wada on the phone, but so far she hadn't taken any of his calls. She had no intention of revealing anything significant in a phone call anyway and still wasn't sure how much she could afford to tell him. He'd wanted Otonashi and Rinzaki out of his life and out they decisively were. What kind of relationship with Grant Braxton he could salvage from recent events really was his problem to solve.

Dobachi's advice was that in view of the dramatic turn of events at Matsuda Sanso Wada should maintain a low profile. He didn't ask her to confirm Rinzaki was the 'elderly businessman' on whose property she'd found – and photographed – a car belonging to a missing person, but it was obvious he suspected as much. Wada's indication that she was now willing to sign the undertaking presented to her by Fumito Nagata's lawyers probably clinched the matter in his mind. The photographs in question would remain in his files. 'I would recommend a period of inaction, Wada-san,' he concluded. 'Indeed, I would recommend a holiday, although I am aware you will almost certainly not take one.'

He was right. And he would have been even without Wada's recently acquired filial responsibilities. She'd neglected various non-urgent investigations in her pursuit of the truth about Manjiro Nagata and was keen to return to them. Monday offered her a chance to do so, with Haha's nurse willing to work longer hours than at the weekend.

Naturally, she followed media reports of the Rinzaki killing, according to which the police were looking for a burglar who'd resorted to murder, though it was a strange kind of burglar who appeared to have stolen nothing, and the lack of any kind of description of him made it hard to imagine he'd ever be apprehended.

As long as the police had no reason to suspect Wada's involvement in the matter that was unlikely to change. But she wasn't

406

quite capable of the 'period of inaction' urged on her by Dobachi. The last time she'd spoken to Funaki, he'd been conspicuously evasive where Kodaka's attempts to find the Kobe Sensitive were concerned. According to Yagami, Kodaka had established that the Kobe Sensitive was in fact dead, though how she'd met her death he hadn't said. But something in Funaki's manner had convinced her he knew a lot more than he was telling. For her own satisfaction if nothing else, she wanted to find out what he was keeping from her. Perhaps Rinzaki's death might loosen his lips on the subject.

Of course, she couldn't simply go and ask him. But it had already occurred to her that she probably wouldn't need to. The police had no reason to connect her to Rinzaki's murder, but Funaki was unlikely to believe she knew nothing about it. Rin-zaki had been on his way up to see her, after all, causing Funaki to make a hasty exit, the last time he'd visited her. And he was a journalist, ever on the lookout for a new story. Sooner or later, *he* would come to *her*.

It turned out to be sooner.

As late afternoon was nudging into early evening, Joji Funaki came calling at the offices of the Kodaka Detective Agency. It was the time of day he favoured, when he could hope profes-sional reticence might start to fray at the edges. Although he had no reason to suppose Wada's reticence would ever fray.

He seemed genuinely relieved to find her safe and well, though. It was in fact the very first thing he said to her. 'I've been worried about you, Wada, more worried than you're likely to believe. See-ing you sitting there behind Dakka's old desk is a real tonic.'

She was flattered, though also puzzled, since he'd previously decided against trusting her with everything he knew, which would surely have been the best way of minimizing his worries about her. But his relief was almost tangible and she took pity on him, broaching the Suntory whisky without a preliminary and entirely redundant offer of tea.

'Where have you been since we last met?' he asked as he took a first and evidently much-needed gulp.

'Here and there, Funaki-san. Here and there.'

'Does *there* include Matsuda Sanso?'

'Certainly not.'

'So, there's nothing you can reveal to this intrepid newshound that might make sense of what happened at Goro Rinzaki's villa on Friday night.'

'A burglary gone tragically wrong, wasn't it?'

'Nobody's taking that idea seriously.'

'Then what are they . . . taking seriously?'

'A clutch of conspiracy theories that don't have a single shred of supporting evidence between them. Most of those theories focus on the secret wife – now widow – who's apparently assumed control of all Rinzaki's business interests. Did you know he was married?'

'No.' Somehow, having met Sonoko Zaizen, Wada wasn't altogether surprised by this revelation.

'Boards don't like having women in charge. You know how the corporate world is. Stubbornly clinging to the past whatever their press releases may say. The widow isn't going to have an easy time of it.'

Nor were the directors, Wada suspected. But all she said was, 'We must wish her well.'

'Listen, I don't expect you to let me in on whatever passed between you and Rinzaki when he came here, but—'

'Nothing I discussed with him has any bearing on what hap-pened to him.'

'No?'

'Absolutely not.'

Funaki swallowed some more whisky and smiled at her

sceptically. 'Come on. You know me. I'll never write anything that lands you in trouble. But the missing civil servant? Endo? There has to be a connection with Rinzaki's murder.'

'Does there? Rinzaki was very old. I think we can assume he accumulated many enemies in the course of his very long life. Perhaps one of those enemies decided the time had come . . . to exact retribution.'

'Yeah. Maybe.' Funaki squirmed uncomfortably in his chair and raised his glass, only to discover it was empty. Wada gently slid the bottle of Suntory across her desk towards him. He nodded gratefully and topped up his glass.

'There were three missing persons I was looking for, if you remember, Funaki-san. One who I can't name because of client confidentiality. Plus Endo. Plus . . . the Kobe Sensitive.'

'Ah. Yes. Her.'

'You said you didn't know Kodaka-san was hired by Rinzaki in Heisei seven, after the Jinno case was closed, to identify and find the Kobe Sensitive.'

'Er, yeah, that's right. I mean, I did say that, yes.'

'But was it true?'

'Was what true?'

'Did you really not know?'

Funaki rolled some whisky round his mouth before swallowing it, as if trying to relieve toothache. But whatever pain he was in had nothing to do with his teeth. He looked long and hard at Wada and said, 'I didn't know the same way you don't know what happened at Matsuda Sanso on Friday. There are things I'm not free to speak of, just as there are things you're not free to speak of. Though actually . . .'

Wada waited for him to continue. When he didn't, she tried some gentle prompting. 'Actually?'

It did the trick. 'We should trust each other with the truth. That's what I think.'

She felt mildly shocked. Funaki was suggesting complete mutual disclosure. For a journalist to make such a proposal to a private detective seemed inappropriate on every level. But it was clear he believed they needed to step beyond such distinctions. The question was: why? 'If that's what you think, Funaki-san, why don't we start with what you know about the Kobe Sensitive?'

'Because we have to start with Rinzaki, that's why. Is he really dead?'

'Of course he is. You've read the reports.'

'I have. But I didn't see him dead. And with a man like Rinzaki . . . who can be sure of anything? I need the word of an eye witness. Are you able to supply that?'

A silence hung between them. He was seeking a commitment from her. And she sensed it was a commitment she had to give. She nodded. 'I saw him dead,' she said softly.

Funaki nodded back at her. 'Thank you.'

'I'm not going to tell you who killed him.'

'I wouldn't expect you to. But perhaps you can tell me where you were last week. Before Matsuda Sanso.'

'California.'

'Somewhere near the Braxton Institute of Seismological Research and Innovation, maybe?'

'Somewhere near, yes.'

'What did you accomplish there?'

'I destroyed something Rinzaki badly wanted to lay his hands on.'

'Lucky for you he's no longer around to try and make you pay for that, then.'

'As you say.'

'OK. So, Rinzaki's dead. That's good. Because the Kobe Sensitive isn't dead. That's what I wasn't telling you – didn't feel I could risk telling you with Rinzaki still on the scene. She's alive and well.'

410

'Really?'

'Really and truly.'

'What made Rinzaki think she was dead?'

'Dakka and me. We made him think that. Dakka tracked her down, but, when he discovered Rinzaki planned to ship her off to BISRI so her predictive abilities could be analysed there – with no regard for her wishes – he decided to protect her from him. Rinzaki had known about her abilities before Kobe, you see. She'd worked for him at one time as a maid. She was already hiding from him when she took the risk of phoning in a warning. That put him back on her trail. It seemed to Dakka that the best way – the only way – to stop him continuing to pursue her was to convince him she was dead. I agreed to help. We supplied fake evidence that persuaded the police she was a previously unidentified young woman of about the right age who'd recently jumped to her death from Rainbow Bridge. Rinzaki must have found it easy to believe, however disappointing, that his pursuit of her had driven her to suicide. So, he was predisposed to accept the version of events we constructed for him. And he did.'

'You're still in touch with her?'

'I am. Rinzaki didn't care what effectively selling her to Clyde Braxton might mean for her. But Dakka cared. And he made me care too. She's been able to lead a life she's chosen to lead – not a life forced upon her. No one should be the plaything of someone like Rinzaki. We made sure she wasn't. I'm proud of what we did for her.' And it was apparent to Wada that he *was* proud. Perhaps prouder of this than of anything else he'd ever accomplished.

'Can she still . . . sense earthquakes before they happen?'

'The ability has faded with age. Rather to her relief, I think.'

'This means you must have known for certain Endo was lying when he said the Kobe Sensitive phoned the Kantei with a warning before the Tohoku earthquake and tsunami.'

'Well, it was possible someone else phoned claiming to be her. But it always seemed likelier to me to have been a put-up job.'

'You were right. It was. Rinzaki bribed Endo to make that claim in order to prepare the ground for supplying Grant Braxton with a fake Kobe Sensitive.'

'He never gave up, did he?'

'Not until he was forced to.'

'What did he want from the Braxtons? What was he really after? And where did he find his fake Kobe Sensitive?'

'I have a few questions to ask before I tell you as much as I can about that. The Kobe Sensitive? It sounds so . . . anonymous. Can you give me her name?'

'You mean the name she was born with? Or the name she was going by when Dakka found her? Or the name she gave when you met her in Yokosuka?'

Wada was generally in complete control of her expression. She never wanted people to be able to read her reactions in her face. Kodaka had often said she'd have made an excellent poker player, if only gambling hadn't been alien to her nature. At this moment, however, she had no doubt Funaki could see very clearly how shocked she was by what he'd just said.

'Itsuko Perlman – the real Itsuko Perlman – is married to a New Zealander,' Funaki went on. 'She lives in Auckland. Has done for many years. The woman you met in Yokosuka became the Perlmans' second daughter when they agreed to help us hide her from Rinzaki. Daniel Perlman was delighted to play his part in frustrating Rinzaki's plans, as I'm sure you can imagine. I think he ended his life when he became anxious that his failing memory would lead to him letting slip the true identity of the young woman he and Nonoka always let people *assume* was Itsuko.'

Wada topped up her glass with whisky, then stood up and walked slowly over to the window. She gazed out at the vast vista of the city: Tokyo on a spring evening. 'There are always more secrets in this world than you imagine, aren't there?'

'I'm a journalist.' Funaki joined her by the window. She could see his reflection in the glass. 'To me secrets are just stories waiting to be written. But this particular story can never be written.'

'No. It can't.'

'What happened in California?'

'Two people died, one of them Rinzaki's daughter. And he lost something else, which, pitifully, I think he prized even more highly.'

'What about you?'

'I got out in one piece.'

'You always do. I've noticed that.'

'I always *have*, you mean. So far.'

'Well, so far's as far as anyone can reasonably hope to see.'

'Yes.' Wada sipped her whisky. 'I suppose it is.'

2011

KODAKA HAS LONG SINCE TAKEN TO USING A MOBILE PHONE, BUT still keeps his trusty pager charged for the purposes of ultra-discreet communications. Messages from Chikako Imada fall into that category, even though sixteen years have passed since Goro Rinzaki was persuaded to believe her dead. Such messages are in fact increasingly rare. She is leading her life and Kodaka is leading his. There is no need for them to be in contact.

But this morning Chikako *has* been in contact. And Kodaka has come to their prearranged rendezvous – the Zorozoro coffee shop near the entrance to the Yaezu underground arcade at Tokyo Station – to find out what is troubling her. For surely something must be. And he only hopes it is not Goro Rinzaki.

Chikako is waiting for him when he arrives, cradling a mug of hot chocolate in her hands at a table on the thinly populated upper floor of the cafe. She smiles at him as he approaches and looks genuinely pleased to see him, but there is a fragile edge to her welcome.

'It is so good of you to come, Kodaka-san.'

'You look worried. Is there a problem . . . with Rinzaki?'

'No. Not Rinzaki. He and I live in the same city. But we may as well inhabit different universes. I never think of him.'

'I'm glad to hear it.'

'There's something else. Something I can only discuss with you . . . or Funaki-san.'

Kodaka frowns. There is really only one thing she can mean. But still he asks, 'What is it?'

'Massive pressure is building out to sea. I sense it. I have tried to suppress the sensation. But I can't.'

'I thought your . . . sensitivity . . . had faded.'

'It has. But it has not ceased. And the earthquake I can feel coming is bigger than any I've ever known. Perhaps bigger than *anyone* has ever known.'

'But out to sea, you say?'

'Somewhere to the north-east. There will be a huge tsunami.'

'Affecting Tokyo?'

'No. The Boso peninsula will shelter us. Besides, Tokyo Bay has good surge protection. Further north, though, it will be very different.'

'When do you think this will happen?'

'I'm not sure. In the next twenty-four hours or so, I think. The momentum . . . points to that. I've already felt several large fore-shocks. Out there . . .' She glanced over her shoulder. 'Under the ocean.'

'What do you plan to do about it?'

'What *can* I do? They took no notice of me before Kobe. They would take no notice of me now. It's too late anyway. I'm only telling you because . . . knowing this is going to happen feels slightly less awful if I can share the knowledge with someone else.'

'Have you told Nonoka?'

'No. She wouldn't leave Yokosuka. It would mean closing the

415

Flight Deck. I'm not leaving either. I don't want to . . . run from this. Whatever *it* is.'

'People are going to die. You know it and can do nothing to prevent it. I know that can't be easy.'

'Yes, Kodaka-san. People will die. Probably thousands of them. They are alive now. Soon . . . they won't be. It is a terrible thought.'

'Maybe it won't be as bad as you think.'

'And maybe it will be worse. I worry about the nuclear power stations on the east coast. I looked them up on the Internet: Higashidori; Onagawa; Fukushima; Tokai; Hamaoka. What happens if one or more of those is overwhelmed by a tsunami?'

'There must be precautions against that kind of thing.'

'I hope so.' She swallows some of her hot chocolate. 'I guess we'll find out soon enough.'

Kodaka glances around. No one is paying them any attention. No one is paying the possibility Chikako has just sketched out any attention either. On one level Kodaka can't believe some version of what she's predicted is going to come to pass in the next twenty-four hours. On another level he's almost completely certain it is. It's clear Chikako has been thinking about all the relevant factors: tsunamis; topography; surge defences; nuclear power stations. He hasn't. Nor have most of their fellow citizens.

'It's going to happen,' she says quietly, as if reading his mind. 'Go west. If you want to be safe.'

'I don't think I'll be doing that,' he says quietly, with a conviction that surprises him.

'Will you warn Funaki-san?'

'He has a wife and children now. His wife knows nothing about you. How could he explain it to her? No. I won't be warning him.'

She looks downcast. 'Perhaps I shouldn't have told you.'

Perhaps not. But she *has* told him. And it occurs to him that the tiny scintilla of doubt he's always harboured about her predictive abilities is going to be settled now, one way or another. And it's going to be settled very soon.

Kodaka stands on the station concourse, gazing up at the departure screens. A Shinkansen service to Sendai is leaving shortly. Among the stops listed is Fukushima, location of one of the nuclear power stations mentioned by Chikako. Perhaps it's as well she's already left. She doesn't have to stand with him, watching all the passengers hurrying towards the platform. Kodaka wonders how many of them are planning to disembark at Fukushima and how they would respond if he warned them against it. They would think him mad. He could end up being arrested for causing a public nuisance if he persisted. There truly is nothing to be done. No intervention is possible. The future is bound to have its way.

Walking back to the Kono Building through the crowded streets of Nihombashi, he acknowledges the dismal truth that prediction is a two-edged sword. If he urged Wada to leave the city, for instance, he'd have to explain to her why he believes what Chikako has foreseen. And he's not ready to do that, though the day will surely come when he is. Besides, he recognizes in Wada some of the fatalism that has formed his own character. He's going nowhere. And he suspects her reaction would be the same. She'd stay put.

And then it comes to him. The future is not omnipotent. He can change it – one small part of it at least. It may make no difference. But that doesn't mean it's not worth doing. Now that Chikako has burdened him with her prediction, he may as well make some use of it.

Back in his office, he pulls the file on the Mitsuhashi case out of the cabinet and opens it on his desk in order to create the impression he's been checking some salient facts. Then he calls Wada in.

'You'll recall the tip I had that the Mitsuhashi slush money was being channelled through their Osaka office?' he says matter-of-factly.

'Yes, Kodaka-san,' Wada replies, though she hardly needs to, since it is well known to both of them that she recalls almost everything.

'I doubted there was anything useful we could do with the information, but the tip has, as it were, sharpened this morning.'

'It has?'

'The wife of the head of the Osaka finance department *may* be acting as a conduit. I feel we need some detailed intelligence about her . . . lifestyle and activities. Who she meets. Where she goes. How much she spends. And what she spends it on. I realize it's short notice, but I wonder if I could ask you to conduct surveillance on her.'

'In Osaka?'

'Yes. And it needs to be done without delay, I'm afraid. It's been suggested to me that significant contact may occur between her and . . . the implicated party . . . very soon.'

'When would you like me to start, Kodaka-san?'

If there is anything inconvenient to Wada in Kodaka's request, there is no way to tell it from her tone or expression. She is, as ever, happy to oblige. 'I'd like you to start as soon as possible.'

'Well, I could leave for Osaka . . . later today.'

Kodaka smiles at her. 'Later today . . . would be perfect.'

ABOUT THE AUTHOR

Robert Goddard's first novel, *Past Caring*, was an instant best-seller. Since then, his books have captivated readers worldwide with their edge-of-the-seat pace and their labyrinthine plotting. He has won awards in the UK, the US and across Europe and his books have been translated into over thirty languages.

In 2019, he won the Crime Writers' Association's highest accolade, the Diamond Dagger, for a lifetime achievement in Crime Writing.